CROSS ROADS

STEELE RIDGE: THE BLACKWELLS

TRACEY DEVLYN

STEELE RIDGE

TEAM STEELE RIDGE

Edited by Kristen Weber

Copyedited by Martha Trachtenberg

Cover Design by Stuart Bache, Books Covered

Author Photo by Lisa Kaman Kenning, Mezzaluna Photography

Print Edition, March 2023, ISBN: 978-1-948075-88-6

Digital Edition, March 2023, ISBN: 978-1-948075-87-9

For more information contact: tracey@steeleridgepublishing.com

DISCOVER MORE STEELE RIDGE

STEELE RIDGE: THE BLACKWELLS

Flash Point, Book 1

Smoke Screen, Book 2

Cross Roads, Book 3

STEELE RIDGE: THE STEELES

The BEGINNING, A Novella

Going HARD, Book 1

Living FAST, Book 2

Loving DEEP, Book 3

Breaking FREE, Book 4

Roaming WILD, Book 5

Stripping BARE, Book 6

Enduring LOVE, A Novella, Book 7

Vowing LOVE, A Novella, Book 8

STEELE RIDGE: THE KINGSTONS

STEELE RIDGE CHRISTMAS CAPERS

ALSO BY TRACEY DEVLYN

CROSS ROADS

STEELE RIDGE: THE BLACKWELLS

TRACEY DEVLYN

STEELE RIDGE

To Heather Machel—
Thanks for your endless patience and for shining your light into the dark corners of this world.

1

An alarm jolted Rohan Blackwell awake. Reaching for his phone on the bedside table, he blinked moisture back into his dry eyes before squinting at the notification on his screen.

ATTEMPTED SECURITY BREACH DETECTED

"Sonofabitch."

He jumped out of bed, shoved his feet into tennis shoes, grabbed his keys and Maglite, and, wearing nothing but his boxer briefs, wrenched open the French doors that opened onto the ground floor patio. Taking the outside route allowed him to move faster, and he didn't have to worry about waking up the household.

Clicking on the flashlight, he hotfooted it around the enormous Friary, a large stone building that had originally housed Franciscan monks but was now home to the Blackwell clan, until he reached the flagstone path that led to the family's on-site office building.

Early morning emergencies like this made him appreciate living in Western North Carolina, where overnight temperatures in early October were still relatively mild. The sprint to the Annex took less than a minute, but it felt like a full revolution of the earth.

Fight, Lucy. Fight.

Disengaging the alarm, he rushed into his office and woke up his computer. Four large, wall-mounted monitors flickered to life. The company's silver logo—BARS—appeared above the login dialogue box and he typed in his ten-digit code.

He grabbed his glasses off the desk, crammed them on his nose, and set to work. His fingers flew across the keyboard, every passing second thundering through his veins.

He pulled up his multilayered cyber defense system, aka Lucy, and waited for the status reports. Each layer blinked, *ATTACK, ATTACK, ATTACK, ATTACK, ATTACK* in bold red letters.

"Come on, sweetheart. You can do this."

Rohan fought to keep his thoughts positive. He'd prepared for this moment, built Lucy to guard their network against viruses, malware, worms, denial of service, and all other manner of digital terrorism. But he, more than anyone else, knew there was no perfect defense, no absolute security.

The first level changed from a blinking bright red ATTACK to a steady green PROTECTED, and the knot sitting between his shoulders loosened a little.

One by one, the status of the levels updated.

PROTECTED

PROTECTED

PROTECTED

PROTECTED

Safe. Everything's safe.

He drew out his next exhale, slow and long, and rotated his head, left and right. Splayed his fingers wide on top of his desk. Squeezed his eyes shut.

We're safe.

This time.

2

THREE HOURS LATER AND FULLY CLOTHED, ROHAN STOOD sipping his coffee while monitoring the activity on his screens, scanning them for additional malicious attempts at finding and exploiting vulnerabilities in Lucy's defenses.

Blackwell Asset Recovery Services—BARS—had grown with lightning speed over the past few years, and it was Rohan's responsibility to ensure that his family's intellectual property and financial assets remained safe from people like him.

Hackers.

From firsthand experience, he understood the type of destruction cybercriminals could bring down on businesses and individual users who became too complacent about cybersecurity. Something as simple as a missed patch—or software update—could be enough for a patient and persistent hacker to wreak havoc.

Many in the industry separate hackers into three broad categories—white hats, or ethical hackers, operate under a code of ethics and only search for system vulnerabilities with the organization's permission. Then there are gray hats, who uncover security weaknesses and report them to the company. Often, gray hats request payment before fully disclosing what they have uncovered. The third category includes black hats or cybercriminals. Without consent, black hats find security vulnerabilities and exploit them.

How they exploit them depends on the hacker's motivation. Some seek proprietary or protected information and they'll implant a virus to get it. Those who like money will employ ransomware to tie up a company's data until they pay a specified amount, generally through Bitcoin.

However, payment doesn't guarantee they'll unlock the encrypted files. Some cybercriminals might disappear once they get the ransom and others might demand more money. Since there is no way of knowing how the hacker will respond, the FBI recommends not paying the ransom.

Which is doable for businesses who have good data backups. For those who don't, paying the ransom is far less painful than losing their files.

The overhead light flashed on, blinding Rohan for a split second.

"At it early again, I see," Zeke Blackwell said in a morning-roughened voice.

Rohan checked the small digital clock on his far left monitor.

6:32 a.m.

Unable to turn his back on the data flashing across his screens, he half-turned toward his brother. "You're not exactly rolling in at a normal start time."

Zeke shrugged, leaning a shoulder against the doorframe. "Mom wanted to meet with me before the team check-in to discuss hiring a fine arts copyist she found."

"Is this follow-up on Cruz's idea?"

The hint of an admiring grin formed at the corner of

Zeke's mouth. "Leave it to the hard-ass to come up with such a diabolical plan."

A genius plan. If they could find the right artist.

In his role as the FBI's new Art Crime Team leader for the region, their eldest brother Ash Blackwell had hired BARS to recover one of the Agency's Top Ten stolen art pieces, Caravaggio's *Nativity with San Lorenzo and San Francesco,* from an estate in North Asheville. An estate owned by Holster Energy president Ezra Payne.

The *Nativity's* storied past was both tragic and legendary. In 1969, two thieves, believed to have been associated with the Sicilian Mafia, broke into the Oratory of San Lorenzo in Palermo, Italy, and cut the *Nativity* from its frame.

What happened to it from there has remained a mystery that neither the Italian police, Interpol, nor the FBI have been able to crack. Over the years, several informants have offered unique and colorful stories about the stolen painting.

The most notable one came from a Mafia informant who said the thieves had damaged the seventeenth-century masterpiece so badly during the robbery that mob boss Salvatore Riina couldn't sell it. Deeming the canvas worth-less, Riina used the painting as a floor mat.

Two weeks ago, Ash had learned from a new confidential informant that Ezra Payne kept an "old painting" locked up in his ten-by-ten steel-reinforced safe. When the CI described it, Ash suspected it was the *Nativity.*

But did Payne harbor the original 1609 Caravaggio or a knockoff?

When Ash discussed getting a search warrant with his SSA, his supervisor denied his request, believing no local judge would authorize a search of Payne's property on the word of an untried CI.

Ezra Payne was a big deal in the Southeast.

The energy mogul contributed to dozens of political campaigns on both sides of the spectrum. His company poured millions of dollars into community projects like boat launches, solar fields, and pollinator gardens, while supporting the construction of fossil fuel power plants and installation of pipeline projects through Black and Brown neighborhoods and Indigenous lands, and tapping into his legislative buddies to ensure they voted to approve astronomical utility rate hikes.

Rather than let an international treasure languish on the wall of a corrupt mogul's safe, Ash had hired BARS.

While driving together to attend one of Zeke's soon-to-be-stepson's baseball tournaments, Cruz had come up with the idea that they swap Payne's copy with a reproduction. One good enough to fool Sotheby's specialists, researchers, and scientists. No sense in poking the bear by leaving a blank space on his wall.

If they were lucky, Payne would never discover the ruse. Or, if he did, it would be years from now and he wouldn't be able to link the heist to BARS.

Or Ash and his CI.

This recovery carried a significant risk, but everyone had agreed it would be worth it if they could successfully return the remarkable piece of art to its rightful owner in Italy.

"Who made it to the top of Mom's list?" Rohan asked.

"A local artist named Angelena Kamber. Heard of her?"

"No, have you?"

Zeke shook his head.

"Does she have a gallery in town?"

"Not that I'm aware of."

"You sure commissioning a local is the right call? There's

a lot at stake with this one. We can't afford to hire an amateur."

"I'm aware of the stakes." Zeke rubbed a hand over the back of his neck. "So is Mom. She won't recommend someone who looks like they paint by numbers."

An inexplicable unease stirred in Rohan's chest. Maybe he was still on edge after his early wake-up call or maybe his compulsive need to vet everyone they did business with was kicking in. Either way, he'd learned a long time ago to trust his instincts. Right now, they were screaming extreme caution. "What time is your meeting?"

Zeke checked the clock on his phone. "Twenty minutes."

Rohan set his coffee cup down on a warming plate, a ridiculous but effective gift from Zeke's significant other and BARS's new provenance expert, Liv Westcott. She'd noticed how many trips he made to the microwave to reheat his coffee because he'd gotten too wrapped up in his work to drink it.

Grabbing an arm of his chair, he rolled it closer to his electronic cockpit and sat down. "Let me see what I can find out about this artist before you make any decisions."

"Why are you getting involved in this? She either paints well or she doesn't. Mom's got a better eye than either of us for that sort of thing."

Rohan understood his brother's reluctance to interfere with their mom's part of the recovery. Last summer, Zeke had surprised them all by vowing to do less hovering and more delegating. So far, he'd kept his promise and was a great deal happier for it.

They all were.

"Honestly, I don't know," Rohan admitted. "But my gut is telling me to check out this artist. Whoever we work with is going to be curious about why a business like ours is commissioning a replica of a missing masterpiece. It's best to know who we're dealing with." He caught his brother's eye. "Intimately."

"Shit." Zeke tapped his thumb against his thigh. "I hope for both our sakes you don't find anything. Mom seemed excited about her top pick."

"All you need to do is stall her for an hour. Give me time to look into Kamber's creds."

"Thirty minutes. You take any more than that, and I'll send Mom down to chew on your ass."

Twenty-three minutes later, Rohan had all the information he needed. He marched down to Zeke's office, where he found his brother pointing at a colorful spreadsheet on his computer screen.

"Explain to me again your logic behind this formula," Zeke said.

Lynette Blackwell glared at her son as if he were a fresh-off-the-bus private who'd upended her tray of chow. "Did Liv keep you up late again last night? Is that why your brain hasn't engaged?"

"Jeezus, Mama," Zeke growled. "I just—"

"Do y'all have a moment?" Rohan asked before his blunt-speaking mom gave Zeke a heart attack.

"Yes—"

"Not now—"

They said in unison.

Lynette raised a brow at Zeke. "What about our meeting?" The twenty years their mom had spent in the military ensured she was never late and never unprepared. She demanded the same of her sons.

Rohan interjected. "What I have to discuss concerns your meeting."

"Does it." Lynette stood straighter and her blue eyes slid

from Rohan to Zeke, then back to Rohan in a careful-as-you-go warning both men knew too well.

Even at twenty-nine years old, Rohan wasn't immune to his mother's authoritarian presence. She could make perspiration break out on the back of his neck with nothing more than a look.

Zeke must have felt the pressure too, because he lifted a black coffee mug, displaying BARS's silver logo, to his lips while he surreptitiously swiped a hand over his jean-clad thigh. Then he indicated the two guest chairs in his office. "Make yourselves comfortable." When they did as instructed, he turned to Rohan. "What'd you got?"

Rohan looked at Lynette. "Zeke mentioned who you were considering for the Caravaggio commission."

"Angelena Kamber." She studied him a moment. "What's your concern?"

Lifting his hand, he listed them off, one finger at a time. "She's an unknown local artist. Her website is nothing more than a contact page. She doesn't have a gallery, nor does she appear to be selling anything on consignment at Triskelion." Many artisans in the region vied for an opportunity to showcase their wares at the gallery on Main Street. Not having a single piece there said a lot about the quality of her work.

"Miss Kamber has a studio in her loft apartment and most of her commissions are via word of mouth," Lynette said.

"How did you hear about her?" Rohan asked.

"During a chance meeting with Carlie Beth Steele. I mentioned that I was looking for a copyist, and she recommended Miss Kamber. Carlie Beth had an opportunity to view Miss Kamber's collection and confirmed the young artist has an extraordinary natural talent. Evidently, her reproductions are quite stunning."

Uncertainty picked at the edge of Rohan's mind. Married to their cousin, Grif Steele, Carlie Beth was an accomplished blacksmith and artist. She wouldn't have recommended someone she didn't trust or respect. Especially not to family. No matter the strained relations between the two clans.

"Have you met Miss Kamber?" Rohan asked.

"Briefly. We bumped into each other at Triple B."

"Bumped into you, how? Literally or figuratively?"

A muscle in Lynette's jaw flickered before she answered. "We were both waiting for our orders at the bar. She complimented me on my bracelet, and I told her I'd purchased it at Triskelion, then she asked me if I knew Carlie Beth. We continued to chat until my order arrived, at which time, she handed me a business card." Lynette cocked her head to the side. "Clear enough?"

Rohan worked to keep his features impassive, but his heart was clattering inside his chest like a five-alarm fire bell. Hackers used social engineering to get to know their targets, earn their trust until they could manipulate the person into giving them confidential information that would help them access their network.

Besides sending phishing emails to their target, hackers might also impersonate someone from the target's contacts, pull passwords and logins out of a target's curbside trash, or harvest information from "fun" polls conducted on social media. Bolder hackers, those who liked to observe their manipulation tactics in action, might make direct contact.

Like bumping into a target's mom at a local restaurant and chatting her up.

The attack on their network and this forger's sudden appearance when BARS needed a lookalike painting for an important recovery was beyond coincidental.

Rohan gritted his teeth. Was the Collective behind this morning's attempted breach? Had they already found him?

What the hell did they want? Make him pay for leaving? Force him back?

"What's bothering you, Rohan?" Zeke asked.

He couldn't tell his family his fears. It would require him admitting to a series of bad decisions that he had no interest in sharing. Best to keep things simple. Focus on what he'd found. Not what he suspected. "I did a background check."

"You did *what*?" Lynette snapped, turning her ire on Zeke. "Did you authorize this?"

Zeke set his jaw. "I did."

"This isn't on Zeke," Rohan said. "I bullied him into letting me dig deeper."

"No one bullies your brother into doing what he doesn't want to do." Her voice lowered, and she pinned Rohan with a hard look. "What makes you think I haven't dug deep enough?"

"You don't have the same capability to burrow beneath a person's veneer as I do."

When an ugly red splotch appeared on her neck, he clarified, "Mama, searching for vulnerabilities is my specialty. I use state-of-the-art technology to keep us safe, to protect everything that you, Dad, Ash, and Zeke have built. It's my purpose, and I'm damn good at it."

The tension in her shoulders and around her eyes loosened and the steel in her spine melted enough for her to ease back in her chair. Her chest lifted on a deep inhalation. "I take it you uncovered something disturbing in Miss Kamber's past?"

The giant hand squeezing Rohan's chest let go. He shook his head. "That's just it. I didn't find anything."

Zeke closed his eyes, and Lynette raised WTF eyebrows.

"I mean, nothing prior to ten years ago," Rohan elaborated. "No social media, no family, no school records, no birth certificate. It's as if she didn't exist before the age of fifteen."

Lynette's nails tapped against the metal arm of her chair. "WITSEC?"

Witness Security Program, also known as the witness protection program, a collaborative effort by the Department of Justice and Marshals Service, protected federal witnesses before, during, and after a high-profile trial. If eligible and they agreed to the program's rules, witnesses, and their immediate family, were given new identities and relocated, with the condition that they must break off contact with their old life. Completely.

"WITSEC participants are given all new identities, complete with documentation. I would have found something on Angelena Kamber."

Lynette said, "I scheduled an interview with her this morning at Blues, Brews, and Books."

"What time?" Rohan asked.

"Nine."

Rohan looked at Zeke, who nodded. "I'll go in your place and probe deeper."

Lynette rose. "I'll call Miss Kamber and update her on the change." She eyed both of them before her gaze settled on Rohan. "For the record, I had intended to have you or Cruz do a background check on her if I liked what she had to say today."

Guilt lashed through Rohan. The last thing he wanted was for Lynette to think he didn't trust her judgment. Sometimes his need for information caused unintended collateral damage. "Sorry, Mama. I acted on instinct—"

She bent to kiss Rohan's forehead. "Never apologize for

protecting our family." She straightened and turned to Zeke. The two stared at each other for a long moment. Out of her five sons, Zeke was most like Lynette, with his brute force determination. Sometimes, like this morning, that wasn't a good thing.

Lynette pressed a hand against Zeke's cheek, and he smiled in return.

Harsh words forgiven.

She left without another comment.

"What was all of that about?" Rohan asked in a low voice.

"I don't know." Zeke stared after her for a moment before shaking himself and turning to Rohan. "You okay with this recon? If not, I can call in Phin."

Rohan shook his head. "Phin's down in Charlotte, terrorizing some politician for Kayla Krowne."

This summer, Phin had accepted a part-time position in Kayla's highly successful lobbying firm. Why his little brother wanted to navigate the cutthroat world of politics was beyond Rohan, but someone had to make sure politicians made decisions that served the people of North Carolina and not themselves.

Rohan removed his glasses and cleaned the lenses with the tail of his T-shirt. "I got it."

"Let me know if you change your mind. I can put Cruz's smoldering eyes to work."

Rohan grinned and shoved his glasses back on his nose. "We need the copyist to answer our questions, not spend the hour trying to entice our brother into her bed."

"Since you've evidently sworn off women forever, I guess you're the best man to send."

"Got that right. The last thing I need is a woman distracting me right now."

3

A HORN BLASTED, AND ANGELENA KAMBER'S EYES SCRAPED open to discover the sun piercing the panes of the floor-to-ceiling windows. She blinked several times and tried to sit up. Cramped muscles screamed and her neck felt like she'd slept on a log.

Groaning, she pushed herself upright. She loved her studio chair, but it was a bitch to sleep in.

Lena stretched her arms above her head and twisted her torso left, then right, prompting a satisfying crackle to rip down her spine. Her gaze fell on her latest obsession—a painting titled *Woman Walking* by Cherokee artist Na-lih Catawnee—then her attention shifted to the copy in-progress propped against an easel next to it.

Or more specifically, on the blank space where the eyes should have been.

Why couldn't she get them right?

Three times she'd attempted to get the piercing quality of the woman's brown eyes correct and three times she'd failed.

Eyes could make or break a painting. Get them right and

the artist is lauded as an exceptional talent. Get them wrong and the artist is labeled a hack.

The eyes connected one soul to another. It didn't matter if the souls were real or imaginary. Would the *Mona Lisa, Girl with the Pearl Earring,* or *Lady Agnew of Lochnaw* have captured the hearts of millions of admirers if their masters had painted them with downcast eyes or looking off into the distance?

The subject's eyes drew the viewer's attention, held them in thrall, and triggered their imagination. She couldn't screw up the eyes.

Lena felt the pressure of her looming deadline all the way to her toes. She glanced down at the sketches in her lap.

You got this. Knock it off.

The fear receded before it could take root. With each commission, the dark shadow of doubt always crept in. It might appear before she even put paint to canvas or show up toward the end, like it was attempting to do with *Woman Walking.*

Over the years, she had learned to expect the doubts—and how to fight them off. Lena had yet to miss a client's deadline and she wasn't about to start with a commission that had the potential of taking her career to the coveted next level.

Lena would breathe a sigh of relief when she delivered both the copy and original back to the owner at the end of the week. Although her apartment building was secure, she still felt uneasy about having a piece of art worth a million dollars sitting in her studio.

So, rather than find her bed in the wee hours of the morning, she'd exchanged her paintbrush for pencil and drawing paper and curled up in her favorite red velvet chair to sketch and stare and grumble to herself. Sometimes, when she got stuck like this, going back to the basics tapped into a part of her creativity that no amount of brush strokes could awaken.

Turning her thoughts toward the day ahead, she recalled her meeting with Lynette Blackwell.

Crap, what time was it?

Unable to find her phone, she spun around to check the giant clock on the living room wall.

8:15 a.m.

She blew out a relieved breath. The meeting wasn't until nine, which gave her plenty of time to wash her hair and shower. Her hair wouldn't be completely dry, but she could fix that with a hair band.

Her building's proximity to downtown Steele Ridge was one of the many things she loved about it. She could walk pretty much anywhere in ten minutes, yet the location still offered her the privacy she craved. Especially since her loft apartment stretched across the entire second floor of the former manufacturing building.

Pushing out of her chair, she dropped her sketch pad and pencil in the seat. The loft's open concept allowed her to move effortlessly from one area to the next. She strode from studio to living room to bathroom, stripping off her clothes as she went and not caring about the disarray she left behind.

One of the many perks of living alone.

"Hey, Alexa." She stepped out of her panties and tossed her bra. "Play *The Very Best of Pat Benatar*." Lena had a thing for classic eighties tunes.

The first strains of "Love Is a Battlefield" sifted through her smart speaker. "Alexa, increase the volume thirty percent." As the uptempo beat filled the loft, Lena's body responded, and she danced her way into the shower.

Hot water cascaded over her body, taking with it her aches and pains and the last dregs of her artistic fears. She envisioned herself finishing the painting, feeling the joy and excitement of the moment.

She held that image in her mind as she sang along with Pat and finished showering.

Turning off the water, she opened the glass door to pull a thick towel from the rack and patted the water from her body. The blood-thrumming bass of "Heartbreaker" penetrated the bathroom door.

Lena considered her upcoming meeting. The interruption to her routine chafed, and her fingers itched to reach for a paintbrush. But she had a business to run, and the business fed off getting new commissions.

Although Fine Art Fakes by Lena was a successful enterprise by anyone's standards, Lena knew how quickly it could all go up in smoke. She'd suck it up and continue doing one of her least favorite things—meeting with potential clients.

Having moved to Steele Ridge only six months ago, she didn't know many of the locals. But she'd heard one name whispered around her more than once.

Blackwell.

People spoke of the family in fearful, yet reverent, tones. Though no one seemed to know much about the family tucked away in a place called the Friary. Sounded like a location right out of *Robin Hood: Prince of Thieves*.

Despite all the whispers and secrecy, Carlie Beth Steele, with whom she'd developed a friendly acquaintance, had encouraged her to accept Lynette Blackwell's invitation to breakfast.

Intrigued by the older woman's request, the blacksmith-turned-artist had had no qualms about throwing Lena into the lioness's den to satisfy her own curiosity.

Lena might have to rethink the "friendly" part of their acquaintance.

Lena couldn't help but be curious about the elusive Blackwells. Why did the townsfolk know so little about a family that had such deep roots here? What did Lynette want her to copy?

Wrapping the towel around her body, she stepped out of the shower and opened the bathroom door to clear the steam just as "Heartbreaker" ended.

In the brief silence, she heard what sounded like chair legs scraping across the floor.

Heart roaring in her chest, she inched the door open wider and searched for the intruder. When no one came barreling at her with a knife, she slipped out just as "You Better Run" kicked off.

Someone above had an inappropriate sense of humor.

Thankful for her penchant for blasting her music, Lena tiptoed to an old fisherman's basket standing in a nook near the entryway. Several walking sticks of various shapes, sizes, and mediums stood haphazardly in the basket. She lifted a sturdy one from its depths.

A quick glance at the alarm panel confirmed it was still armed, yet no alarm had sounded.

Some of the tension eased from her shoulders. The only way in and out of her apartment was through the door. The noise must have been walls settling or air running through the pipes or some equally creepy thing old buildings did.

Then she recalled that the café next door had an outdoor seating area. The noise had probably come from one of their customers pulling a metal chair across the concrete patio.

Lena took her first full breath since opening the bathroom door, but she kept a grip on her makeshift weapon.

Even though her mind told her there was no need to skulk about, her instincts hadn't quite bought into the notion.

She would just take a quick look around to set her mind at ease before getting ready for her meeting. Water dripped from her wet hair onto her bare shoulders and down her back. She tried not to think about her vulnerable state as she drifted through her loft.

A furtive movement to her right caught her eye. There, in her studio, she spotted a hooded figure. He'd already removed the original *Woman Walking* from its wooden easel and was now draping a black cloth over the painting.

All the air *whooshed* from her lungs, and she experienced a sudden lightheadedness.

He wasn't there to kill her, but to steal the painting. Lena couldn't let that happen. The loss would ruin her, professionally and financially. No way would she allow everything she'd built in the past ten years to be sucked away in ten minutes.

Raising the walking stick, she charged the intruder. Prepared to clobber him unconscious.

He must have heard her pounding feet above the music because he whirled away at the last moment, but not fast enough to avoid the totality of her downward strike. Her weapon connected with the right side of his head, raking down his ear.

He let out a grunt-scream and pressed a hand against the side of his head, as he stumbled away. A black mask covered everything but his eyes.

"Who are you? How did you get in here?" she demanded, advancing on him.

Taking in her cavewoman appearance, he stared at her wide-eyed for several heartbeats until his self-preservation chip fired up.

He kicked out, slamming his foot into her solar plexus and sending her sprawling across her wooden floor. The thick towel wrapped around her body flipped open, revealing an embarrassing view of her lady parts.

The burglar lifted the gilt frame from where he'd propped it against her red chair and bolted out of her loft.

"Stop!"

She rolled to her hands and knees and fought to catch her breath. Grabbing her stick, she pushed to her feet and took off after him.

4

Angelena Kamber had been a no-show.

Rohan had waited thirty minutes for her to appear at Triple B. Twenty minutes longer than he would have for anyone else. Mostly because he feared his mama's beetle eye, but also due to him not wanting to miss an opportunity to meet the mysterious forger.

Steering his Verge TS70 down Broad Street, he slowed until her apartment building came into view. He lowered his prescription Aviators to confirm the address. Maybe, just maybe, her car broke down, or she had a family emergency or she lost track of time.

Maybe she got spooked when she found out she'd be meeting with him instead of Lynette.

He'd soon find out.

After parking along the curb, he strode toward the newly renovated two-story brick residence. The former Bamff Furniture store now housed oversized loft apartments—two on the first floor and an enormous one on the second, occupied by the forger—copyist.

The only picture he could dig up on Angelena Kamber

was her driver's license. Most DL photos had the air of a prison mug shot. Not Miss Kamber's. Even though she didn't smile and a strange sort of tension pulled at the corners of her luminous gray eyes, she captivated the viewer's imagination.

Thick, black hair framed a golden-brown, heart-shaped face. A dark mole perched on her left cheekbone, and Rohan had had the strangest urge to brush his thumb over the area.

To the left of the door, he spotted a call panel with three buttons—1a, 1b, 2. He stared at the silver button beneath number two, wondering if he was being an idiot by coming here. Would she find his appearance creepy? Surprising? Or dare he hope, appreciated?

He lifted a hand, then dropped it. The right thing to do was go back to the office, call her, and reschedule. Tomorrow, he could grill the forger until he was satisfied she posed no threat to BARS. Then go back to his cocoon and leave the beauty to his mother.

But suspicion gnawed at him. The forger crossing paths with his mother within days of a severe attack on BARS's network smacked of a social engineering attempt.

Getting their targets to divulge something personal that could be used against them was one of the most effective tools in a hacker's arsenal. What better way to learn about BARS's operation than meeting with the company's office manager and bookkeeper?

No, it was best to catch her off-guard, observe her in her natural habitat. Resolve bolstered, he lifted his hand to press the button for apartment number two, when movement through the archer's window in the sturdy steel door caught his eye.

A resident hurried toward the door, carrying something

large and rectangular, like a mirror, draped in black material. The bulky item slanted across the carrier's upper body, obscuring his features. The person's height, large hands, and well-worn boots leaned toward male, though.

A size eleven, maybe twelve, steel-toe boot slammed against the door's crash bar. Rohan grabbed the handle from the other side before it took out his nose and swung it open wide.

"Need some help with that?" Rohan asked.

"Nah, I got it, man," the guy said, breathless, as he rushed by.

Unable to believe his good luck, Rohan entered the building's foyer—and stopped dead in his tracks.

The forger, dressed in nothing but a Scooby-Doo bath towel, was racing down the concrete and steel baluster staircase, carrying one of those sticks people used for trekking in the mountains. She leaped down the final three stairs, her bare feet slapping against the tile floor, and leveled him with a glare that could have incinerated an entire town—no, county.

"You just helped him get away with a million-dollar painting!" she yelled as she ran after the thief.

5

Lena's bruised sternum hurt with each heaving breath as she ran after the thief and Senator Palmer's very expensive painting.

The good-looking idiot who helped the intruder escape sprinted past her, toward the roar of an engine to the west. A mud-stained black truck ripped away from the curb and fishtailed its way down the street.

She looked at the license plate, but the mud extended to the rear of the truck, veiling the number, and the tinted back window prevented her from identifying the driver.

"Dammit!" She pressed a hand to her throbbing chest as panic welled inside, blinding her to her surroundings.

Ruined.

She was fucking ruined.

Would her insurance cover the loss? She didn't know. Probably, but her premium would go through the roof. She'd never worried about it before, because her bank account was healthy enough to cover it.

But this . . . This was in a different league.

She didn't even want to think about the owner's reaction.

Senator Blaise Palmer, an influential, seasoned politician many considered to be his party's forerunner in next year's presidential election.

A man used to getting what he wanted. And he'd wanted the copy of *Walking Woman* to be completed for his upcoming campaign fundraiser masked as an engagement party, so he could show her off to his rich friends.

Not that any of them would know she was a copy. The idea of his guests cooing over a fake seemed to titillate the senator.

Politicians.

Lena set Palmer's strange form of amusement aside and focused on how she was going to explain this to him. After she'd accepted the commission, he'd paid half her fee, but had almost canceled when he learned she worked from the original and not a photograph.

Evidently, his chief of staff Craig Muller had failed to pass on that vital piece of information after his initial interview with Lena. Or Palmer had thought he could change her mind.

With painstaking patience, she'd explained to the senator that in order to replicate the original with the level of detail her work was known for—and the reason he'd hired her—she avoided working from photographs.

A photograph altered hues, shielded telling brush strokes. Flattened the life out of the scene.

In the end, it hadn't been Lena's patient words that had swayed Palmer into entrusting her with his painting, but the man's fiancée. Or so Craig had informed her when he'd supervised the painting's delivery to her studio.

Didn't a senator's chief of staff have more pressing things to do than interview copyists and supervise deliveries?

And why would someone she'd never met champion her

cause? But she hoped for an opportunity to thank the woman one day. Now, she didn't know whether to shake her guardian angel's hand or scream, "What the hell were you thinking?"

"Are you all right?" a masculine voice asked.

Through her rising dread, she focused on the stranger fast-walking toward her. The same guy who'd aided the thief's escape—and failed to run him down.

Something fluttered inside her chest that had nothing to do with the kick she'd sustained. His wide shoulders tested the seams of a navy blue polo that sported a company logo on an incredibly broad chest. Tailored chinos covered powerful thighs and Birkenstock boots completed his casual, yet professional ensemble.

He tore off his Aviators, revealing a pair of hazel eyes. Not blue, not green, not brown. But a striking blend of the three. Black-rimmed, no nonsense glasses replaced his Aviators. An intriguing contrast to the two-day scruff blanketing his lower face and the wavy, dark brown hair that reminded Lena of a young Eric Bana when he played Prince Hector in the movie *Troy*.

Those penetrating eyes roamed over her as if checking for injuries. She refrained from rubbing the sore spot between her breasts.

The reminder of her run-in with the thief dissolved her tingling of awareness into a mass of fury. On one level, she knew her emotion was irrational, but she couldn't shut down her feral words. "Way to go, Stud."

A dark eyebrow rose above the rim of his glasses. "Was the painting yours or a commissioned work?"

Lena froze, his question making her feel more vulnerable in that moment than standing outside in a towel. "Who are you?"

"Your nine o'clock appointment."

Lena frowned. Had Lynette sent someone in her place?

"Blackwell?"

"In the flesh." His gaze flicked down her body. Not in a creepy way, but still assessing. "Though not as much as you."

Lena folded her arms across her chest. A protective gesture, though she was keenly aware it did nothing to enhance her cleavage. "My meeting was with Lynette."

"*Was,* until this morning. She sent you a text."

She reached for her phone in her back pocket, then remembered . . . towel. "Well, I didn't get it."

"Did you get the time?"

"Yes, I would have made it there at nine if my home hadn't been burglarized." She punctuated the last five words.

Lynette's replacement fingered his phone out of his front pocket and tapped the screen to show her the time.

9:44 a.m.

She stilled. No way had she spent that much time in the shower. "You sure that's on the correct time zone?"

"Positive."

"Either way, we were supposed to meet at Triple B."

He cocked an eyebrow. "Randi Shepherd is pretty laid back, but I think a towel, even one with Scooby-Doo on it, might have tested her relaxed dress code."

A flush crept up her throat. "What are you doing here?"

The amused smile he wore dissipated. "Hunting you down, of course."

She could see it then. His distrust. His suspicion.

But of what? Why would he consider hiring her if he distrusted her right out of the gate?

"Who are you?"

"Rohan Blackwell."

The syllables flowed over his tongue like a fine wine, and Lena imagined herself sipping them straight from the source. She blinked away the vivid image of her taking his mouth with hers.

"How are you related to Lynette?"

"Fourth son and business partner."

"Is she okay?"

"As ornery as ever."

"Why did she send you to meet with me?"

Lynette hadn't mentioned needing a copy for business purposes. Now that she thought about it, Lena had shared little about her business. Just shoved a business card into the woman's hand as she was walking out Triple B's door.

Lena glanced down at the logo on his polo. The company acronym matched the one on Lynette's card.

"A conflict came up," Rohan said, by way of an answer.

A light breeze swept over her damp shoulders, reminding Lena of her near-naked state. "I need to get dressed." She unfolded her arms and marched back to her building's front entrance, and stopped.

"Oops," Rohan said behind her, amusement once again tinting words. "I don't suppose you have a key hidden beneath a rock or planter or Scooby's collar."

For most residences, there were few good places to hide a spare key. Which made finding them child's play for would-be thieves. But she explained none of this to the man behind her. Something told her she didn't have to.

"Quite the pickle." More amusement.

Lena closed her eyes a moment, pushing back the violent urge to dropkick Rohan Blackwell. Once she was in control again, she turned to him and held out her hand. "May I borrow your phone?"

He hesitated. Lena could almost smell his mental gears churning through potential scenarios. A heartbeat later, he unlocked the phone and handed it over.

The phone's unique color ignited her curiosity. "Is this the new model they just announced yesterday?"

"Good eye."

"Color is my thing. I never forget a hue."

"Must be invaluable in your line of work."

"It is." She windmilled the phone between her thumb and fingers. "How did you get your hands on this so quickly? It's not even on sale yet."

"I'm on the beta team." When Lena's eyes widened, he said, "You're good at hues, I'm good at tech."

She started tapping the keyboard on his phone. "The building's alarm service can remotely unbolt the locking mechanism."

"Or—" He leaned past her to grasp the door handle, and Lena inhaled, catching his subtle oat and honey scent. At such close quarters, she couldn't help but notice the perfect line of his nose or the defined angle of his jaw.

Or how the door opened without obstruction.

"What the—?"

He nodded toward the ground, where a fine white linen business card was lying at her bare feet.

She bent to pick it up.

Rohan Blackwell

BLACKWELL ASSET RECOVERY SERVICES

We never fail.

HE MUST HAVE SLID THE CARD OVER THE LOCKING MECHANISM, effectively disabling it, before running after the burglar.

She stared at his card for a long time. A thought niggled. Transformed into an idea. The more she considered it, the more convinced she became that it was her best way forward.

Tucking his card into the top of her towel, she motioned for him to follow. "Come upstairs. I have a proposition for you."

6

ROHAN STOOD IN THE CENTER OF MISS KAMBER'S ENORMOUS loft, taking in elements from the building's past like the aged brick accent wall, large metal-framed windows, and industrial shelving.

The space could have felt cold and utilitarian, but artfully placed rugs, vintage furniture, and bold, eye-catching wall art created a gathering space, both warm and inviting.

The most incredible feature was the ceiling—or roof, in this case. The entire expanse was an interplay of metal and glass. It gave one the impression of standing inside a conservatory, without all the accompanying heat and humidity.

The bedroom and enclosed bathroom, where his host was currently getting dressed, occupied one side of the loft. Above the bedroom was a partial second floor, which housed the kitchen and dining area. A circular wrought iron staircase connected the two floors. With the greenhouse windows overhead, diners must enjoy a three-hundred-and-sixty-degree view of Steele Ridge.

Incredible.

Although he couldn't deny an unwise interest in exploring the forger's bedroom, he made his way to her studio on the opposite side of the loft. As he passed through the living room, an enormous clock on the wall caught his attention. The hands were locked in at eight-fifteen.

He shook his head. No wonder she'd missed their meeting.

In her studio, he found rows of different sized canvases stacked inside a nine-foot-tall teal-colored cabinet that reminded him of a nineteenth-century armoire without its doors. Beside it, in a more modern-looking cabinet, were what appeared to be the raw materials for making custom-sized canvases and frames.

Three wooden easels stood before an enormous bank of windows. One held a blank canvas, another sat empty, and the third housed a work in progress. He focused on the latter.

An indigenous woman walked barefoot on a desert floor. Sunlight glistened against her brown skin and wind fanned her dark hair out to one side like an eagle's wing. Her dress seemed to be a mixture of modern and traditional materials, with wisps of white gossamer whipping to the side as well.

The artist's strategic placement of light made the scene come alive. It glinted in the woman's hair, sparkled in the sand, and shimmered on the buttes in the distance.

What stopped him from having a truly transportive moment was the woman's missing eyes. Without them, he couldn't truly connect with the painting on an emotional or even philosophical level. Right now, it was simply a nice, unfinished painting.

Eyes were tricky to get right. Not just for painters, but

also for computer animators. Hollywood and the gaming world have spent millions of dollars trying to get their CGI eyes to look photorealistic.

A red velvet cushioned chair with a peach ottoman faced all three easels. Crumpled sheets of drawing paper littered the floor around the chair like bark from a dead tree.

He picked up several and smoothed them out on a nearby drafting table. The first few had dozens of pairs of feminine eyes. Each one slightly different from the last. Each one penetrating in its own way.

The other drawings appeared to be a representation of random thoughts. He could detect no theme, no link from one to the other. They seemed to be remnants of a brainstorming session.

He glanced at the blank canvas and wondered if she was attempting to come up with an original concept.

"What are you doing with those?" Miss Kamber asked, annoyance dripping from every word.

Rohan jerked as if Grams had caught him reading James Rollins's *Sandstorm* late at night in the garage again. Before he could respond, she snatched up the sketches and dropped them into a recycling bin by her desk.

"Now that I'm decent, let's get down to business."

He recalled her mentioning something about a proposition. "Maybe you should call the police and report the theft first."

Ignoring his suggestion, she said, "We'll be more comfortable over here." She led him to where a cream sofa and two brown leather chairs from another era created a U-formation around a faux fireplace.

He nodded at the dead clock above the mantel. "Use batteries much?"

She followed his gaze, then turned narrowed eyes on him. "It was working last night."

"Are you sure? Battery-operated clocks typically die a slow death."

"Expert on clocks, are you?" She plopped down in one of the chairs and rested her long, slender feet on the edge of the coffee table.

The sight of her unpainted toenails cranked his insides.

"Have a seat," she said when he continued to stare at her damn feet like a sick fuck.

He sat in the opposite chair, so he'd be facing her and wouldn't be tempted to look anywhere but at her face, which was distracting enough.

The luminosity of her gray eyes made him want to explore them like a new galaxy and alternately want to put up his shields and prepare the photon torpedoes.

"The way I see it, we need each other," she said, drawing him out of *Star Trek*-induced haze and back to reality.

"How so?"

"You need a reproduction and I need a recovery."

"Why not hand over the theft to the insurance company? They'll send an investigator to locate the painting."

"I have my reasons."

"Would they have anything to do with keeping the owner in the dark about the theft?"

"Are you always this antagonistic?"

"My brothers would say yes."

"And what would you say?"

"I tend not to let people step over their own bullshit."

"So, yes."

Rohan's attention dipped down to the smile teasing the corner of her mouth. It softened her features and made her even more beautiful.

No distractions, Blackwell.

He sat forward and braced his arms on his knees. "How did you come to know Carlie Beth Steele?"

"Carlie Beth?" she echoed, confused by the change of topic. "I don't know her. Not really."

"How did you become *acquainted* with her? According to my mother, Carlie Beth was the one who recommended your services."

"It appears we've switched to interview mode."

"The reason for our meeting."

"Why did Lynette send you instead?" she asked again.

"I think it had something to do with my dazzling good looks." Rohan lifted a brow. "Are you done with your merry-go-round of redirection?"   •

She held his gaze for several seconds before she said, "We met at Triskelion Gallery, where she has her artwork on consignment."

"Friends at first sight?"

She ignored his jab. "I admire artists who can build something from nothing."

Rohan scanned her loft for original paintings, but found only perfect replicas of well-known artists' work.

"I told Carlie Beth as much," she said. "One comment led to another, and before long, we were having dinner at Triple B."

Nothing about her story triggered any red flags, but Rohan couldn't shake the uneasy feeling he had about her sudden appearance at a time when someone was banging on BARS's network doors.

If her background check hadn't turned up one big sink-hole, he would've been satisfied with her answer. But her lack of personal history was a problem for him. A problem he intended to sort out, though not by partnering with her. For all he knew, the robbery and her subsequent need for their recovery services was an elaborate scheme by the Collective to get inside the lion's den, so to speak.

He stood, ready to leave before he did something insane, like say yes. "It was good speaking with you, Miss Kamber, but I'm afraid BARS must go in another direction."

"Another direction?" She rose in one fluid motion. "You have no more questions for me?"

He could ask her about her past, but she would no doubt share an elaborate tale, one she'd perfected for a decade. Best to save them both the time and aggravation.

"I have all I need in order to make my recommendation."

"Which will be, what?"

"That we choose another copyist."

"On what basis? You didn't even ask to see my work."

"I don't need to." He swirled a finger in the air. "Your artistry is all around us, and," he nodded toward the easels, "I've observed your work in progress."

An emotion he couldn't interpret flashed across her features as she looked at the artworks displayed around her loft.

Hurt? Fear?

Her reaction confused him—like everything else about her. One more reason to not get tangled up with this woman.

A pang of regret arrowed through his midsection, surprising him.

Definitely time to go.

He spoke over his shoulder as he turned to leave. "Call the police and report the theft before your painting sinks too far into the black market's underbelly."

"I'm the best, Mr. Blackwell. You won't find a better replacement."

Rohan strode away, the truth of her words haunting him all the way back to the Friary.

7

Desperation propelled Lena to do the one thing she despised above all else—ask for help.

After her failed meeting with Rohan, she set out to find Carlie Beth, hoping the whip-smart blacksmith would have some insight into the Blackwell clan.

Lena didn't have the time or resources to find a stolen painting and she couldn't get the police involved. Not yet, anyway.

She considered trying the old phone number she had for Xander and asking him for a list of potential buyers. He was immersed in the side business side of the art world like no one else she knew. But the thought quickly came and went. Alexander Douglas was one of the many doors to her past that she had no wish to reopen.

Which left her with one option—persuading the super-hot recovery agent, who seemed not to trust her, to take on her case.

What had set him against her? After her initial conversation with Lynette, she had expected a commission at the conclusion of this morning's meeting. But she was fairly certain Rohan had showed up on her doorstep with his mind made up.

Striding down Main Street, Lena headed toward a familiar blue awning in her so far fruitless search for Carlie Beth. As she neared the restaurant-bar-café, Lena's stomach picked up the scent of coffee, bacon, and other deliciousness and let out an angry growl, reminding her of its empty state.

A bell tinkled above the door as she pushed inside.

She wove her way through a tapestry of diners, from solitary businesswomen to reels-scrolling young adults to laptop-engrossed whatevers until she reached the bar.

"What will it be?" Randi Shepherd, owner of Blues, Brews, and Books or, as the locals liked to call it, Triple B, asked a few minutes later as she poured a healthy chug of milk into a metal cup.

Lena closed the menu. "I'll try the Southwestern omelet with a side of fruit."

"Jalapeños or no jalapeños?"

"Today calls for spicy."

Randi wiped her hands on a white bar towel. "One of those, huh?" She tapped Lena's order into her tablet register.

"Unfortunately." Lena clasped her hands together in a tight grip. "I'm looking for Carlie Beth Steele. Do you know where I could find her? She wasn't at her smithy or Triskelion."

"I expect her any moment. She's filling in for one of my servers." Randi studied her for a moment. "Anything I can do?"

Lena shook her head. "Not unless you have an owner's manual on the male mind."

Randi laughed. "Boyfriend trouble?"

"Lord no. Blackwell trouble."

"Blackwell?"

"Shit. Forget I said that."

"No can do, honey. Which one?"

If Lena could have bitten off her tongue, she would have done it in a heartbeat. It wasn't like her to make that kind of mistake.

She didn't know Randi well, but she and Carlie Beth seemed to be tight. They were both involved with Steele men, which sounded only slightly less frustrating than being mixed up with a Blackwell.

"Rohan."

"Brainiac, quiet, gorgeous." She turned on the expresso machine and raised her voice over the steam wand working its magic. "I've only seen him in the bar a handful of times. Never comes with a woman, never leaves with a woman."

"Maybe he leans another way."

Randi shook her head, grinning. "I didn't say he doesn't look."

Lena recalled how he'd stared at her feet for a long while. If it had been anyone else, she would've felt uncomfortable about the attention. But sensing his admiration had left her slightly breathless.

"My interest lies more in how to change his mind than who he is or isn't sleeping with."

Randi poured the frothy contents of the metal cup into a paper one, covered it with a lid, and called out a name before turning back to Lena. "I might not know much about how Rohan Blackwell's mind works, but I have intimate knowledge of Britt Steele's. If I can crack my mountain man's logic, I can surely help you with one of the elusive Blackwells."

At the word "help," Lena's muscles contracted. That small, four-lettered word had jumpstarted every pivotal moment in her life. Every new beginning, every new adventure, every deep dive into hell.

New beginnings sounded great on the surface. Who wouldn't want to reset their lives? Start over. A clean plate.

But no matter how much you licked, your plate would never truly be clean. Twenty billion bacteria lived on a person's tongue. One of those bacteria was bound to be bad news. Bound to fester unseen until a new host happened by.

Lena smiled at Randi. "Thanks for the offer, but I'd best wait for Carlie Beth."

The door to the coffee shop opened, and four laughing women crowded inside.

"Ask, and she shall appear," Randi said, humor lacing her words. "This ought to be fun."

A young blue-eyed woman led the pack inside, followed by a curvy brunette wearing a killer dress, then a bespectacled Amazon, and finally Carlie Beth.

The latter made eye contact with Lena and her smile broadened. "Hey, Lena," Carlie Beth said, her cowgirl boots tapping across the floor. "What brings you to the B?"

Please don't hug me, please don't hug me.

Lena gripped her utensils tighter when the blacksmith gave her a one-arm hug and cheek press. She produced her most cordial smile. "You, actually."

"Lena's having man trouble," Randi added, grinning.

"Join the crowd," the youngest said, sticking out her hand. "I'm Evie Steele. Soon to be Conrad. My guy is a U.S. Fish and Wildlife Special Agent masquerading as a newsletter editor." She made a face and air hissed between her teeth. Her hand waved in the air as if erasing her words off a dry erase board. "Dangnabbit, forget that last bit, would you?"

"What bit?"

Evie smiled, relieved. "I like her already."

"I'm Brynne Steele," the curvy brunette said. "Owner of La Belle Style and married to Grif's brother, Reid, who's a former Green Beret."

The tall woman with glasses peered around Brynne. "Riley Kingston. I'm engaged to Coen, a Delta Force operator, and I'm Evie's cousin."

Lena's head spun, wondering how she'd remember the women's names, let alone their significant others' names and occupations.

"Now you can see why we're all uniquely qualified to help you figure out how to change Rohan's mind," Randi said, completely letting the whole feline litter out of the bag.

"Rohan?" Evie's eyes lit up. "Blackwell?"

Lena swallowed hard, then nodded.

Riley pushed her blue-framed glasses higher on her nose. "I do love the smart ones."

Carlie Beth tied a black apron around her narrow waist. "What do we need to change?"

Five pairs of eyes settled on Lena. How in the hell had she gotten herself into this situation? If Lynette or Rohan or any of the other Blackwells found out she was airing their business agreement—or lack thereof—at the local coffee shop, they would never hire her.

They might, in fact, spread the word that she was indiscreet, which would be a career killer. Not that she'd have a career to kill if word got back to Palmer that she'd lost his million-dollar painting.

Brynne climbed onto the stool next to her. "You can trust

us not to share whatever you reveal. Once you're part of the Sisterhood, your secrets are our secrets."

Sisterhood.

The word freaked her out even more than "help." It implied a bond, one impervious to a lifetime of stupid comments, late arrivals, missed birthdays, bad dates, and missing shoes.

But Lena knew—*knew*—bonds were as fragile as snowflakes. One degree up the thermometer and the meteorological piece of art would melt away.

She would never allow herself to bond with someone like that again. She wouldn't survive it.

"Y'all barely know me," Lena heard herself saying. "Why would you want to include me in your trusted circle?" She speared them all with a look of suspicion. "Especially since most of you are related, either through blood or marriage, to the Blackwells."

"Randi and Carlie Beth have vouched for you," Evie said, climbing onto the other stool next to her. "That's good enough for me."

"Me too," Riley echoed, joining them at the bar.

Carlie Beth slid a plate with a fat omelet, hash browns, fruit, and a tin cup of salsa in front of Lena. "Sounds like it's settled." She winked at Lena. "Spill it, girl."

Desperation kept Lena rooted in place rather than reverting to her normal MO, which would have been to exit the building and never return.

She'd had to master many things over the years, but finding missing objects wasn't a skillset she'd needed to develop yet. If she had time, she could figure it out. Figuring things out was one of her superpowers.

But she didn't have time. Soon, she would have to notify Palmer—and the police—about the theft. The longer she waited, the worse the senator's response would be.

She picked up the tin of salsa and poured it over her omelet. "Fair warning. I don't need to change Rohan's mind about something trivial. What I need from him will also impact the family business."

"In a nefarious or illegal way?" Randi asked.

Lena shook her head.

"Excellent," Riley said, accepting a slice of warm banana nut bread from Randi. "An actual problem to solve. I was afraid we would have to save him from making a fatal error in his boot buying."

Brynne shivered. "Lord, save me from men with no fashion sense."

Despite the anxiety coiling in her stomach, Lena smiled. She had never been part of a sisterhood before. She liked these women, but she didn't love them. Would never love them. She wouldn't allow herself to develop such a deep connection.

She would take what they so freely offered and walk away.

Piece of cake.

Evie sent her a mischievous smile. "This isn't even all of our gal power. If needed, we could also recruit Roni, Tessa, Joan, Sandy, Micki, Joss, and Maggie."

"Let's not forget Aubrey," Carlie Beth said. "She's old enough now to wreak havoc."

Everyone laughed, except Lena. She was surrounded by kind, funny, generous women. Women who had accepted her—someone they barely knew—into their sisterhood. Lena found herself wanting to join them. If only to observe how functioning friendships worked.

But experience had shown her that linking her heart to

others was the surest way to getting it broken. Which she'd endured far too many times already in her two-and-a-half decades.

So she did what she'd trained herself to do. Be present, put on her game face, and disengage her heart.

WEARING A LOOSE PAIR OF SWEAT SHORTS, ROHAN PADDED out onto the patio outside his suite of rooms. He loved this time of the morning, when silvery light washed over the landscape, cleansing away the previous day's hardships.

He unrolled a gray mat and positioned it toward the distant mountains, where the sun would rise above the gentle peaks soon. The morning was calm, quiet. Even the birds had yet to rise.

Two doors down, a light flicked on, casting a soft orange glow over the pavers outside the suite's French doors.

Soon, Grams would emerge with her own mat, though it wouldn't be made of foam. His grandmother would perform her morning meditation on a small rug her Navajo mother had handwoven after surviving the Long Walk. Twice.

In the mid-1800s, the United States government hungered for the land west of the Mississippi and took brutal measures to acquire it. The traditional homelands of the Navajo—or Diné—extended across portions of what is today considered Colorado, Utah, Arizona, and New

Mexico. The Diné called this sacred land Dinétah—Among the People.

When the Diné refused to give up their land, the government employed a scorched earth campaign, led by frontiersman and Army Officer Kit Carson. Carson burned their villages, destroyed their water sources, and killed their livestock, all in an effort to starve them off their land.

It had worked.

In the winter of 1864, the Army forced thousands of Diné from their ancestral lands to Bosque Redondo Reservation in New Mexico, which was nothing more than an internment camp at a military outpost known as Fort Sumner.

Hundreds died during the Long Walk, an eighteen-day, three-hundred-mile trek, either from the elements, starvation, or Army execution. Four years later, the U.S.-Navajo treaty was signed, allowing those who survived the deplorable conditions at the camp to return, on foot, to some of their ancestral lands, a much smaller area in Arizona and New Mexico.

It was there that Rohan's great-grandmother had woven the details of her story into her rug. A rug Grams used every day in honor of her ancestors and to never forget their many sacrifices.

Rohan went through a series of stretches before settling on his mat and facing the spot where, in the distance, soft silver-blue melded with a warm amber. Watching the dawning light and listening to the forest around him yawn to life lulled him into a meditative state.

For about five seconds.

No matter how hard he tried, his mind wouldn't let go of all that had happened in the past twenty-four hours.

After leaving Miss Kamber's loft, he'd returned to the

Friary, intent on delivering his recommendation to Zeke and Lynette.

But his mother hadn't been on the property and Zeke had been tied up in video conferences all day. Frustrated, he'd spent the rest of the day and far into the evening behind his monitors, searching for Miss Kamber's digital footprint. She had to have one. Everyone did at their age.

Gen Z. The generation who would embrace the smartphone's wonders and nosedive into its pitfalls.

If anyone was going to put out a post or video that would later haunt them when applying to colleges or interviewing for jobs, it was this eager bunch of Like-Share-Follow seekers.

But no matter how deep he'd dug, he found nothing but ether before Angelena Kamber's fifteenth birthday.

He stretched his neck, left and right, releasing the gathering tightness. He had to let this go. Now wasn't the time for distractions. No matter how beautiful or mysterious.

Once he shared his recommendation with Zeke and Lynette, he would forget about the forger and double his efforts on safeguarding BARS and his family.

Resolve in place, he calmed the ticker tape in his mind for ten minutes.

He'd take it.

When he got to his feet, he spotted Grams perched on a thick pillow, which sat atop her mother's handwoven rug. A serene, patient expression on her beloved face as she waited for the first rays of the sun to spill over the treetops.

Rohan rolled up his mat and, without another glance to the east, strode back inside.

· · ·

TWO HOURS LATER, AFTER ROHAN'S WORKOUT AND SHOWER, he found the entire crew in the Theater, the open conference room where his family planned and strategized their asset recoveries.

Zeke sat at the head of the table. Liv Westcott, BARS's new provenance consultant and the love of Zeke's life, was to his right, along with Cruz, Phin, and Maddy Carmichael, the love of Phin's life. Grams occupied the seat to Zeke's left and Lynette was next to her.

The chair at the foot of the table was empty.

Shit.

Twirling a pen between his fingers, Cruz smirked, enjoying the novelty of someone besides him stationed in the hot seat for once.

Whoever sat across from Zeke became the focus of his brother's considerable attention. Usually one of the first to arrive, Rohan avoided being Zeked. Until now.

Dropping into the hot seat, he set his laptop, notebook, and pen on the table in front of him. "Did I miss anything?"

Zeke shook his head. "I was filling them in on your concern about the copyist."

A thousand ants marched inside Rohan's stomach, their tiny claws and pincers tearing at the lining. "I'll give my rec to you and Mom after our meeting."

"Whoa-ho," Phin said, leaning back in his chair. "Since when do we silo discussions?"

Fair question.

At all times, they had three or four recoveries at various stages of the process—from initial contact to final payment. Every task played off another, so it was important to keep the team updated any time a recovery's status changed.

Whether they would hire a forger for one of their most sensitive cases to date would be something the team should know about. Which led him back to Phin's question. Rohan didn't know why he hesitated to share his recommendation with everyone present, but his mind constricted against the notion.

"We don't." Zeke leveled Rohan with a hard, brown-eyed stare. "What's your assessment of risk?"

Each question pushed him farther into a shadowed corner. "My visit with Miss Kamber produced more red flags."

"What kind?" Lynette asked.

"For starters, someone burglarized the forger's home this morning and made off with a million-dollar painting." He would leave out the minor detail of his assistance. How could he have known the guy he opened the door for was a thief instead of a resident?

"Forger?" his mother repeated, her expression darkening.

The wall at his back softened into quicksand, sucking him deeper into the corner until only his head was visible. "She makes copies of masterpieces, then sells them. It's the very definition of art forgery."

"When she sells them, does she try to pass them off as an original?" Liv asked. While with the FBI, the former special agent had worked primarily on art and cultural crime.

"No," Lynette inserted. "Many online fine art stores purchase her copies to sell to their customers—everyday people who want beautifully rendered art by the masters, like Monet, but could never afford an original." She grasped the handle of her coffee cup and lifted it. "Those who can afford more expensive pieces commission her to make an exact reproduction they can display in their homes, while they lock the original away for safekeeping."

"It's a fine line," Rohan said. The wall of quicksand now framed his face. The pressure around his chest made it difficult to breathe. "But I'll concede the point."

"The same fine line we straddle." Zeke's attention strayed to Phin, reminding Rohan of his little brother's struggle with the company's philosophy about theft and recovery.

The pen twirling between Cruz's fingers came to an abrupt halt. One dark eyebrow climbed into his forehead, revealing blue-gray eyes that could stop women in their tracks.

If Cruz and Angelena ever found themselves in the same room together, their beautiful orbs would be showstoppers.

The thought didn't set well with him.

Cruz said, "Let's back up. A million-dollar painting was stolen?"

Rohan nodded.

Phin whistled.

"What did the thief steal?" Liv asked.

"A painting by Na-lih Catawnee."

Grams sat forward. "Which one?"

"Woman Walking."

His grandmother closed her eyes as if in pain.

"Woman Walking," Maddy echoed, sharing a shocked look with Liv before turning back to him. "Who would be stupid enough to allow their seven-figure painting to stay in an artist's unsecured studio?"

"The building has a fair amount of security," Rohan heard himself say, as if the forger needed a champion in her absence. "Guests have to be buzzed in, which, yes, can be easily bypassed, but Miss Kamber has alarm sensors on her door."

"How did the thief get in?" Phin asked.

Rohan frowned, hating his next words. "I don't know."

In the silence, Grams answered the second half of Maddy's question. "The painting belongs to Blaise Palmer, a U.S. senator and amateur collector."

"The forger"—Lynette sent him a sharp look, and Rohan reshuffled his words—"Miss Kamber was scheduled to deliver the copy by the end of the week."

"How devastating," Lynette said. She met Zeke's gaze and a silent communication passed between them.

Zeke turned to Rohan. "What other red flags?"

"Isn't it obvious?"

"Break it down for us lesser beings," Zeke said in a voice that let Rohan know his patience was coming to an end.

Grams placed a thin hand on Zeke's forearm, and BARS's CEO expelled a breath as he leaned back in his chair.

"Before you go on," Grams said to Rohan, "Tell us how Miss Kamber is doing. Was she harmed during the robbery?"

And just like that, the tension in Rohan's shoulders eased, and the quicksand retreated a few inches. A touch, a word, a look—that's all it ever took for Grams to calm five rowdy boys at the dinner table or five grown men in a business meeting.

"Miss Kamber engaged the thief and suffered a few bruises, as a result, but she's otherwise fine."

"Engaged, how?" Liv asked.

Torn between smiling and frowning, Rohan replayed the scene in his mind. "When she finished showering, she heard an unfamiliar sound and opened the door to find the thief lifting the painting. She attacked him with her hiking stick, then chased him out of her building."

Phin grinned. "I bet that was a sight."

Rohan would like to say he was above noticing the expanse of wet, golden-brown skin above and below her towel. But he wasn't. Not by a long shot. "You have no idea."

"What else you got?" Zeke asked.

The wall closed in on him again. "I spent the better part of yesterday attempting to unearth her missing background. But everything before age fifteen is a black hole." When Cruz and Phin opened their mouths to offer suggestions, Rohan held up a hand. "Yes, it's possible she's in WITSEC. If my recommendation was to move forward and hire her, I'd start looking into major events that happened around the time her file washed out."

"But you're not recommending I hire her?" Lynette asked.

"She's too hot, Mama. Too many unknowns."

"What about the Catawnee painting?" Maddy asked. "Will Miss Kamber be able to track it down by herself?"

"Hopefully, she took my advice and called the sheriff's office."

"A painting that valuable might not see the light of day for a long time," Liv said. "The thieves will take it underground until things cool down."

"Unless they already had a buyer lined up," Maddy said. "If that's the case, the piece is already in someone's personal collection. Likely behind several inches of reinforced steel."

"Nicola St. Martin, anyone?" Phin said, reminding everyone of the Asheville socialite Zeke and Liv had tangled with recently.

"Mom contacted the next two copyists on her list," Zeke said. "Both are booked until January, which won't work for our recovery timeline. We got lucky with Miss Kamber because her next client backed out after his wife unexpectedly filed for a divorce."

Heat traveled up the back of Rohan's neck. "You're going to hire her."

"We all agreed that switching the Caravaggio with a reproduction was the best way to approach the FBI-Payne recovery," Zeke said. "You yourself said we needed the best. Angelena Kamber's work is unmatched and she's available."

"And the rest?"

Zeke shrugged. "As long as she can do the job in the time frame we need, I don't care who she was when she was twelve years old."

"Your call, brother," Rohan said, "but I'm on record saying this is going to end only one way. Badly."

Zeke smiled. "Which makes you the perfect person to take lead on locating the Catawnee."

Dread coated Rohan's throat as he braced his forearms on the table. "What the hell are you talking about?"

"Angelena Kamber hired BARS last night."

"Are you still on schedule to deliver the reproduction next week?" Senator Palmer asked.

Lena's fingers tightened around her phone. *"Shit, shit, shiiit,"* she mouthed to the empty stairwell as her Veronica Beard boots cleared the last step leading to her loft.

Lena hefted the bulky grocery bag higher onto her shoulder and speared her hand into her teal and brown MDBM Cholet bag. Her fingers danced around the bottom of her purse, bending and swaying around her wallet, Fenty refillable lipstick, tissues, ink pen, stray paper clip, and wadded-up receipt.

"That's the plan." *Where the hell were they?* She remembered dropping her keys into their usual pocket. "Unless the paint hasn't dried yet."

"My engagement party is on Saturday."

"Um, yes." Her short nails clicked against metal. "I remember."

"My friends expect to see *Woman Walking*."

A *copy* of *Woman Walking*.

His so-called friends expected to view the painting only

because they had shelled out a thousand dollars for the privilege.

"Displaying the original is out of the question."

Not too trusting of your friends, *huh, Blaisey-boy.*

She reeled her keys from the bag's depths.

"If I don't have a reproduction, they'll have nothing to admire but an empty wall." His voice lowered to a dangerous octave. "I don't like to look the fool, Miss Kamber."

She found the key for the deadbolt, inserted it, and turned.

Nothing happened.

Lena frowned. "Yeah, that would suck."

"I get the feeling you're not taking this situation seriously."

"What? No, of course, I am."

Turning the key in the opposite direction, the bolt slid home.

Locked.

Heat washed over her body, dampening her palms and the area between her shoulder blades. She set the groceries down, never taking her eyes off the thick slab of metal that acted as a buffer between her and whoever was inside her loft.

Another burglar? Who would be bold enough to attempt another robbery so close to the last one? How did they get a key?

A representative from her alarm monitoring company would be here any minute to present a detailed proposal for ways they could amp up her security. She should back away and call nine-one-one. Law enforcement would be here in three minutes, tops.

But what if she'd simply forgotten to lock her door?

Wouldn't be the first time.

How mortifying would it be to call for a safety check, only to realize there was no intruder? Only an idiot tenant.

"I'll do everything in my power to get the copy of *Woman Walking* to you in time for her unveiling."

A mountain of silence slammed up between them. Then Lena heard a muffled female voice in the background, but she couldn't make out the woman's words.

Palmer said, "I'm sending someone to pick up the original."

Lena's heart catapulted into her stomach. "The original? I still need it."

"You said the painting was finished, so there's no need for you to keep it any longer."

"I never said the painting was done."

She had locked the door. She was sure of it. But she couldn't remember the actual act of engaging the deadbolt.

This must be what it felt like when people drove away from their houses and couldn't recall hitting the garage door button, forcing them to drive around the block, or worse— call a neighbor once they got to work.

Better to be mortified than dead.

Even as her logical mind prevailed, Lena reached for the key and turned it in the opposite direction again.

The deadbolt flicked open.

"Waiting for the paint to dry indicates completion to me."

"Almost complete. I'm still working on the eyes."

"The eyes." Palmer echoed in a flat voice.

"Senator, I've never missed a deadline. You'll have the painting Saturday."

"Don't disappoint me."

Lena gritted her teeth. "I won't."

The line went dead.

Lena stared at the door handle. Her heartbeat seemed to echo off the walls.

This is such a bad idea.

She keyed in nine-one-one on her phone and her thumb hovered over the Send button.

With an expert twist of her fingers, she selected another key, inserted it into the handle's keyhole, and eased open the door. Why she bothered attempting stealth, she didn't know. The burglar had surely heard her speaking to the senator and playing tick-tock with the locks.

A sense of déjà vu overwhelmed her as she slipped inside.

"Why am I not surprised you entered instead of calling the police?" a familiar masculine voice asked.

A rush of irritation kicked aside her fear. "I still could." Straightening, she marched farther into her loft. "What are you doing here?"

Her jaw dropped open.

Just . . . dropped.

Dressed in faded jeans, scuffed boots, and a black T-shirt that looked like someone had painted it on his body, Rohan Blackwell stood on a ladder in the corner of her studio and appeared to be installing something.

Shoving her phone in her back pocket and dumping her shoulder bag on the couch, she moved to stand below him. "Is that a camera?"

"Yes, ma'am."

Staring at his broad back, she tried to understand what was going on, even while she followed the play of muscles beneath the thin cotton fabric of his shirt.

She forced her gaze up to where he was putting the

finishing touches on his installation. "Explain what's going on, Mr. Blackwell."

"Rohan."

She waited for the explanation.

It never came.

"How did you get past the building's security?"

"Same way as your burglar."

One-two-three. "Are you going to force me to pull every detail out of that gorgeous mouth?"

His hands stilled, and his head slowly turned in her direction. "You think my mouth is gorgeous?"

She reared back. "N-no! Why would you ask me that?"

"You just said—" He shook his head. "Never mind."

Had she called his mouth gorgeous?

She replayed her words. Although she couldn't recall saying it, she couldn't fully deny it either. His mouth was . . . enticing. Full, yet firm, and surrounded by sexy whiskers. Something about this guy shaved off bits of her hard-earned control every time he was near.

"The café next door is nice." He climbed down from his ladder. "Especially the outdoor eating area."

Lena's last nerve snapped in two. "How about I order you a Reuben *to go*?"

"Would love one, but they're closed on Mondays." He locked eyes with her while he wiped his hands on a blue cloth he pulled from his back pocket. "Sundays, too."

He was trying to tell her something. Lord, she hated backdoor guessing games. But she played along, sweeping through her memory for images of the breakfast-lunch café next door. Metal tables and chairs, live plants in brightly hued pots, sturdy pergola breaking up the sun.

A pergola situated only a few feet away from—

Her gaze shot to the cabinet where she stored her canvases, to the half-opened window just a few feet away.

"You climbed up the pergola?" Not waiting for the obvious answer, she continued, "But the window was locked."

He held up a flat tool she'd never seen before. "Child's play."

Giving herself a moment to think, she retrieved her groceries from the hallway, set the heavy bag on the island counter, and pulled the ingredients for pad thai from its depths.

After a lively discussion with Randi and the other ladies, they had all decided the best way to change Rohan's mind about working with her was to go through official channels.

Which meant sharing her story with Zeke Blackwell.

If he'd decided against taking her case too, she would've been forced to do the unthinkable. But after consulting with some of his team, Zeke had accepted the case, saving her from an awkward conversation with the senator and too many probing questions from the authorities.

When BARS's CEO had told her that someone would be in touch, she had expected a phone call, followed by a meeting. Not a breaking and entering.

Though she would never admit it, coming upon two intruders in as many days had an effect. She'd taken precautions to safeguard her home and had never felt unsafe here.

Until now.

Folding the reusable shopping bag, she met her unwanted guest's gaze. "You've made your point, Mr. Blackwell. I'll pass on your findings to my alarm service. They should be here any moment."

"Rohan." He moved his ladder to another corner of the studio. "The rep arrived ten minutes ago."

She glanced around as if her representative would suddenly materialize. "Where is she?"

"I told her AMT's services were no longer needed."

"You did what?"

"Part of your contract with BARS is to improve your building's security." He gave her a smile that didn't reach the lower part of his face. "Did Zeke forget to mention that during your *meeting*?"

Lena ignored the jab and focused on the first part of his statement.

"You mean my apartment."

"I have to give you credit," he said. "You did a great job of hiding your ownership of this building and manufacturing creditable, nonexistent renters."

"Not good enough, evidently."

This time, the corner of his mouth curled. "See previous discussions about me being good at tech."

The saliva in her mouth seemed suddenly thick and sticky, making it impossible to form words.

"The shell company you used to purchase the building would fool most people, especially an eager seller wanting to offload an old building that's been nothing but a financial sieve for years." He climbed the ladder. "But I like to peel back the layers and poke around in the shadows."

"You did a background check on me?" Terror rippled at the edge of her words.

"One thing you'll learn about me, Angelena, is that I will go to any lengths to protect my family and our business. You're dangerous to both."

"All I want from you—BARS—is to find the man who stole Senator Palmer's painting." She jabbed a finger in his direction. "The man you helped escape. How does that make me dangerous?"

"I don't know yet. But you can be damn sure that I'm going to figure it out."

It was then that Lena realized she'd made *THE MISTAKE*. The one she'd feared for the past decade but knew would one day come.

She had finally tangled with the one person who could destroy the life she'd created.

10

Rohan turned off the vacuum, rolled up the cord, and placed the machine back in the small closet by the loft's front door.

"Full service," Miss Kamber said. "I'm impressed. Most tradesmen leave the mess for the homeowner to clean up."

Rohan ignored her attempt at friendly banter. Even after nearly twenty-four hours, he still fumed about her going around him to get Zeke's approval and his brother's decision to not only take on the recovery, but force Rohan to work with her.

What happened to his brother's policy of getting *everyone's* buy-in before taking on a new job? Given the number of smirks he'd witnessed around the conference table, his family was up to something.

He'd figure out what. He always did.

But first, he had a job to finish. One he'd do even if it killed him. Blackwells didn't let family down, even when they were wrong—or conniving behind his back.

"I've installed motion detectors in key areas throughout

the apartment and cameras to cover the studio, windows, and entrance door."

"Who's monitoring the cameras?"

Rohan's eyes met hers for the first time in an hour. "I am."

"I'm not comfortable with that."

"I'll let Zeke know you're withdrawing your request for our services." He picked up his toolbox and headed for the door.

"Wait."

He glanced back and felt a sharp stab of guilt. She looked more vulnerable in that moment than she had standing in a bath towel on a public sidewalk.

"Are any of the cameras directed at my bedroom or bathroom?"

"I'm not a creeper."

She stared at him, waiting.

Sighing, he said, "No, and the only time I'll be looking is if someone trips the alarm."

Relief softened her expression. A little. She wasn't happy about the intrusion on her privacy.

Tipping his head back, he studied the windowpanes that took up two-thirds of the ceiling. "Those will have to go."

"What will? My greenhouse roof?"

"We'll have to do something about those, too." He nodded at the wall of floor-to-ceiling windows. "I'll get my brother, Cruz, to fabricate some bars for the lower half."

"You're closing me in, like a prison."

"This isn't about you, Miss Kamber. It's about protecting your assets." He knew he was being a shit, but he couldn't seem to stop himself. Despite his suspicions about her connection to the Collective, he didn't want her to feel unsafe in her home. But he'd be damned if he'd admit it.

She scanned her loft—the studio, the security devices, the checkerboard of glass above them, the windows—and shook her head. "The roof stays. I need the natural light."

"You have plenty with the windows."

"Don't you think I'm a better judge of my lighting requirements than you?"

"The roof panes can easily be cut, allowing a burglar to descend."

"At which point, your spy gizmos will sound the alarm."

"Not before the thief leaves with something of value." *Or hurts you.* "You saw firsthand how quickly a million dollars can run out the door."

"No thanks to you."

"How was I supposed to know the guy walking out the front door was stealing a painting?"

"Oh, I don't know. Maybe the black mask covering his face?"

"He wasn't wearing a mask. At least, not that I could see."

"How could you have missed it?"

"Because he angled the painting in a way—" Rohan took a breath, refusing to be bated. "Trust me when I say the roof windows are a major liability."

"The greenhouse roof stays."

Rohan locked his jaw to keep himself from arguing with her any further. "And the windows?"

She considered them for a long moment, and he could see she was on the verge of saying no.

"Don't be pigheaded about this just because you're annoyed with me. Think about how easily the thief and I entered your loft."

She threw him a savage look. "Fine. Install the bars, but on the outside. And I want final approval on the design."

"Design approval?"

She crossed her arms.

"Fine." He shifted his toolbox to his other hand and strode toward the door again. "You're expected at the Friary at two o'clock this afternoon to debrief the team."

"Do I need to bring anything?"

"The truth."

LENA MARCHED INTO THE STEELE RIDGE PUBLIC LIBRARY, with her nemesis's words still echoing in her mind.

The truth. The truth. The truth.

What the hell did he think she was going to do? Lie about the color of the thief's clothes?

She had a vested interest in providing BARS with as much information about the burglary as possible. She needed the Catawnee back ASAP.

Maybe his comment had less to do with the robbery and more to do with what he couldn't find in her background.

You're dangerous.

What made him think so?

For a man who trafficked in data all day long, her missing years would set off some warning bells. But what had caused him to leap into the danger zone?

Lena smiled. The idea of annoying Rohan Blackwell without having to lift a finger made her ridiculously happy.

In the end, he'd be glad his mother hired her to copy the *Nativity.* She hadn't been exaggerating when she'd told him she was the best fine arts copyist.

Many years ago, her mentor Simon Garibay had challenged her to reproduce a painting by Mexican artist Frida Kahlo. She'd copied other pieces by Kahlo's, so she wasn't too concerned about it. Until he informed her that the reproduction had to hold up against three professional authenticators.

It had. Down to using wooden boards from furniture built in the 1930s for the stretcher bars and soaking iron nails in salt water to give them an oxidized appearance.

Lena shot down the fiction aisle, searching for Erica Ferencik's latest environmental thriller. Given the recent events in Lena's life, she should probably check out something a little less nail-biting, but she'd been waiting for this novel for months. She had just enough time to grab the book and make it to the Friary in time for the debriefing.

Debriefing.

Who used that kind of language? You'd think she'd been involved in a covert operation rather than a burglary.

Rohan Blackwell sat at the crossroads of Old and New Worlds. Like having M, Q, and Bond all rolled into one.

"Anderson, Brown, Carbo, Dev, Eldridge, Ellis." Lena read out the names of authors until she reached, "Ferencik." Smiling, she pulled the hardback off the shelf. The cover was even more amazing than what she'd seen on social media.

Electric Blue, Tron Blue, Blue Hosta—or was it Northern Lights Blue?

"Hello, Lena."

The color palette in her mind vanished, as did all the warmth in her body at the sound of the feminine voice. A voice she hadn't heard in over two years.

Cradling the book against her chest, Lena turned to face the last person she'd ever wanted to see again.

"Izzy."

Dressed in a mock neck cashmere sweater, leg-hugging slacks, knee-high leather boots, and a black, lightweight coat that showed off her five-foot-ten frame to perfection, her old friend could have graced any Paris runway.

She'd pulled her long black hair into a low ponytail, setting off her secret-piercing brown eyes, flawless olive skin, and full cruel lips.

"I see you haven't lost your love of books," Izzy purred.

Lena noted the three novels in the other woman's arms. "Neither have you."

Reading had been the one of the few things they'd had in common. That and—

Lena cut off the thought and flicked a finger at the designer jewelry dripping from her ears, throat, and wrists. "Yours?"

Izzy brushed long, manicured nails across the chunky sterling silver necklace. "They're part of my fall collection. Do you like?"

"Beautiful, as always."

"How's business?" Izzy's pleasant expression remained in place, but Lena sensed the simmering fury beneath.

"Never better."

"And Xander?"

Lena's grip tightened around her book. "I wouldn't know."

Izzy's crimson lips stretched into her version of happiness. "He's made quite a career for himself."

Regret, or maybe nostalgia, clutched Lena's heart. The three of them had been friends once. Best friends. Then Lena and Xander had taken their relationship to the next level, and Izzy had never forgiven her.

Lena lowered her arms. Done playing games. "If you knew about him, why ask?"

"To see the pain on your face, of course." Izzy smiled, cold like her heart.

Lena glanced down at the books in Izzy's arms and was struck by a cold realization. "What are you doing in Steele Ridge?"

"Didn't you know?" Izzy's smile grew wider as she turned to stroll away. "I live in the area now."

Lena stared after one of the few people who knew an unhealthy number of secrets about her. Acid burned in her stomach, and she cursed herself for allowing Izzy to turn her into a verbal punching bag.

But she refused, absolutely refused, to allow her thoughts to drift into the past. All of that was behind her now. She wouldn't waste her mental energy on old friends, old flames, or old regrets.

The here and now were what mattered. Nothing else mattered.

Speaking of which—she had a *debriefing* to make.

Following the directions Lynette had texted to her, she made it to the Friary's front gate on time, but their security measures added another ten minutes to her arrival time, which truly made her late.

Like any artist, she considered time a flexible commodity. Even so, she steeled herself against Rohan's censorious stare.

Lynette met her at the door to the Annex, aka Blackwell Asset and Recovery Services' headquarters, and ushered Lena into her office to go over some paperwork, including signing a nondisclosure agreement.

Once they finished, Lynette stood. "Ready to meet the team?"

Lena nodded.

"Grams, Maddy, and Liv are working on other projects, so it'll just be the boys and I."

Lena flinched.

"Is there a problem?"

"No, ma'am. Not really. I just—" Randi and her friends had rallied around Lena to help her come up with a solution to her issue with Rohan. The thought of being surrounded by a bunch of Blackwell men made her head pound. "I didn't get off on the right foot with Rohan, so I would have welcomed more girl power in the meeting."

Lynette's expression softened. "Rohan takes his job very seriously—all my boys do—but Rohan's duties require constant vigilance. The company has grown to a level where the work is more than one person can—or should— handle." She leaned in close. "Don't tell him, but I'm looking for a tech assistant to help him out."

"He believes I'm a danger to his family and the business."

"It's no secret that those in the cybersecurity field are more than a little paranoid." Lynette touched a finger to Lena's arm. "Give him time. Once he comes to know you, he'll see there's nothing to be worried about."

Lena thought of the burglary and Izzy's sudden appearance. She wondered if Rohan's paranoia carried more truth than fiction.

12

"WHO STOLE MY DAMN TUMBLER?" ROHAN ASKED, SEARCHING the Annex's kitchenette for his favorite beverage container.

"No one in their right mind would steal that ugly hunk of metal," Cruz said.

"It might be ugly, but it keeps my ice from melting."

"Another one of Liv's save-Rohan-from-himself products?" Zeke asked.

"I don't doubt it," Phin said. "She probably got tired of hearing the ice machine's racket all afternoon."

Rohan moved to the lower cabinets, eliminating hiding locations one door at a time.

"Dude," Cruz said, "grab another cup. There are only a hundred to choose from."

"None of them have double-walled insulation."

"Someone's uptight this afternoon," Phin murmured.

Rohan sent them all a shut-it look, hating that they were right. But damn, he loved his orange tumbler. Sweat-proof exterior, twelve-hour hot/cold retention, double-walled stainless steel, BPA free, shatter-resistant, thirty-two fluid ounces . . .

"Did you check the dishwasher?" Zeke asked.

Rohan gritted his teeth as he opened the appliance door and spotted a patch of orange on the top rack. "Dammit. Who put it there? I told you guys it wasn't dishwasher safe."

"I did."

Rohan straightened, best tumbler in the world in hand, to find his mother standing near the Theater's conference table, one gray-shot eyebrow raised.

Shit.

"Wash that thing every once in a while," she said, "and I won't mistake it for a dirty dish abandoned on the counter."

"Apologies, Mama." He blasted his brothers with a sweeping glare for not warning him of her approach, which prompted three unrepentant grins.

Lynette motioned to an empty chair, and Lena moved out from behind her to take the Hot Seat.

Their eyes locked, and Rohan forgot all about asshole brothers and ugly tumblers.

The jittery sensation in his stomach both intensified and settled at the sight of her. Ever since he'd left her apartment, his insides had been in full-tilt rebellion. Which had a powerful impact on his mood.

No distractions.

He broke eye contact, busied himself with washing his drink cooler, and refilled it while Lynette introduced Miss Kamber to the team.

"Call me Lena. Everyone does."

Rohan ignored the stab of jealousy. They'd been alone on two separate occasions, and she hadn't offered him the choice of using her first name, let alone her nickname.

What the hell was that about?

He brushed off the irritation and joined everyone at the table, sitting between Zeke and Cruz and as far away from their client as possible. Pulling his laptop closer, he flipped it open.

"Thank you for meeting with us, Lena," Zeke said. "Rohan has filled us in on the details of the robbery. If you've thought of anything new since the incident, please share it with us. The more we know, the better chance we'll have at locating the Catawnee."

"I have nothing new."

"If a memory dislodges, even days from now, let us know."

She nodded.

Rohan used his wireless mouse to click through a couple of screens. "This is what we know about the painting."

The large TV display behind Phin flicked from the BARS logo to a scanned copy of the painting's historical chain of ownership, known in the art world as provenance.

"Painted by Na-lih Catawnee in 1929 at her studio in Cherokee, North Carolina. She sold *Woman Walking* to the president of a shipbuilding company four years later. The shipbuilder willed it to his daughter upon his death in 1970 and she passed it on to her daughter, Ava Sanson, in 1988. After returning home from an event, the shipbuilder's granddaughter discovered *Woman Walking,* along with three other pieces from her collection, gone."

"Insurance?" Cruz asked.

Rohan shook his head. "They disappeared the same evening Ava took possession of the Catawnee. The FBI recovered the other three pieces within months of the burglary, but *Woman Walking* remained missing for over thirty years until several months ago, when the family received a tip."

Rohan clicked the mouse, and a screenshot of a website slid onto the monitor. "Several years prior, Gridmore Fine

Arts Recovery had approached Ava and offered to search for the painting. She declined, believing the FBI were doing all they could to recover it."

"Is Gridmore like BARS?" Lena asked.

"Near enough," Zeke said. "They specialize in artwork. We don't have any limitations on what we'll recover. If someone steals it, we'll find it."

Rohan continued, "Seventeen months ago, the holder of *Woman Walking* contacted Ava and conveyed their desire to return the painting."

"For a fee," Lynette said in a flat voice.

Rohan nodded. "They likely got duped into purchasing it, then found out it was hot when they tried to resell it. They were probably hoping to recover their losses from an owner desperate enough to buy back their own property."

Selling high-profile artwork on the black market was harder than most people realized. Ask any unorganized thief who didn't do their homework ahead of time. Stolen art was worth a fraction, less than ten percent, of its market value. Which made a million-dollar painting far less attractive when they were looking at a ten-thousand-dollar payday.

"Let me guess," Lynette said. "Fed up with the FBI's lack of results, she hired the recovery firm to coordinate the transaction?"

"Unfortunately for her, yes." Rohan pulled up an excerpt from Gridmore's contract, which showed they took a percentage of the market value of the recovered art as their fee.

A chorus of groans rippled around the table.

"What am I missing?" Lena asked.

Cruz said, "The more notoriety attached to an artwork, the greater its value."

"When Ava's mother owned *Woman Walking,* the painting appraised at $75,000," Rohan said. "Now it's worth twenty times that amount."

"Who had the painting?" Phin asked.

"Unknown. The firm worked through an intermediary. One of the holder's conditions was to remain anonymous."

"How did Palmer come into possession of the piece?" Zeke asked.

"In order to pay Gridmore's fee, Ava had to put her family heirloom up for auction last month."

"Damn," Cruz said, verbalizing the sentiment everyone was feeling.

Rohan's attention shifted to Lena. "Palmer's $1.2 million bid won." She stared down at her thumbs, which seemed to be engaged in a Duel of the Nails.

What did she make of *Walking Woman*'s provenance? Was she aware of the painting's tragic past? Did she empathize with Ava Sanson's loss? Or did it all mean absolutely nothing to a woman who made her living off the blood, sweat, and grief of others' hard labors?

"Good work, Rohan," Zeke said before turning to Lena. "How did you get involved with Palmer?"

"Someone in the senator's circle read an article in the *Citizen-Times* about the town of Maggie Valley's renovation efforts on Harold House."

"Is that the historic home that got hit by a tornado?"

Lena nodded. "A painting that hung in Thomas Harold's study was ripped away by the storm and never found. The foundation raised the funds needed to commission a copy."

She glanced around the table. "The incident made the senator realize the vulnerability of his new acquisition. He intends to display my copy in his home office and hide away the original Woman Walking in a safe room somewhere in his house."

"There's an unlabeled space off the master suite." Rohan replaced the historical timeline with a schematic of Palmer's mansion and drew a red circle around the area.

"He wouldn't be the first millionaire to stare at his trophies while pulling on his underwear," Phin said.

"Who else knew you had the original?" Zeke asked.

"The only people I know for sure are Palmer, his fiancée, his chief of staff, and the two men who delivered it. But there could be more."

"Do you have their names?"

"Only his chief of staff—Craig Muller." She bit the inside of her bottom lip as her eyes took on that faraway look one gets when deep in thought. "Palmer called me earlier today. He's hosting an engagement party for his fiancée and wants to unveil his newest acquisition—or acquisitions—depending on how you look at it."

"You don't care for your client?" Rohan asked.

She gave him a level stare. "Liking a client isn't a prerequisite to working together."

Touché.

The clenching sensation around his chest suggested he liked her just fine. He simply didn't trust her.

Heads on both sides of the table ping-ponged between him and Lena.

Time to move on. He didn't want to give his relations any fodder for torment.

"Any thoughts on who would want to steal *Woman Walking*?" he asked.

"None."

"What can you tell us about Palmer?" Zeke asked.

"Nothing, other than he's keen on getting what he paid

for by the end of the week. I don't follow politics and we don't have any mutual acquaintances."

"How do ensure your client doesn't resell your copy as an original?" Lynette asked.

"I don't." Her answer raised a few brows. "I'm hired to make a high-quality reproduction. What the client does with my work once they take possession is out of my hands."

"You're not bothered by a client using your work to dupe an innocent buyer?" Rohan asked.

"No."

Rohan leaned back, more than a little disappointed in her answer.

"We're not here to pick apart Miss Kamber's business," Zeke said. "We're here to learn what she knows and track down the painting she hired us to find."

"Look," Lena said. "I know my attitude might seem callous, but no one should ever be duped. Not with today's experts and technology available. Some collectors—professionals as well as amateurs—get caught up in the excitement of owning something rare and go against their better judgment. They trust the seller's word, even when there's a giant red flag flapping in their face."

"I get that it's a copy," Phin said, "but how do you deal with the original author's signature?"

"Depends."

"On?" Rohan interjected when she didn't seem willing to elaborate.

"The client."

"The Caravaggio must look exactly like the original," Zeke put in. "Exactly."

"It will," Lynette said, her gaze on Lena.

"It will to the extent I can use a high-quality photo instead of the original as reference," Lena said.

"Understood," Zeke said.

"If it makes y'all feel better," Lena said, "the back of the canvas will carry my personal stamp as a professional copyist."

"Not on the Caravaggio," Zeke said.

"My stamp is nonnegotiable. It is the one thing I can do" —she held Rohan's gaze—"to ensure the painting isn't misrepresented."

The acid slowly filling Rohan's chest receded.

"Zeke's right," Cruz said. "Once you release the copy into our hands, you don't want to be connected to it."

"Why?" Everyone remained silent. "Please tell me I'm not taking part in something illegal."

A ding sounded, and Rohan stopped sharing his screen before switching windows.

"You're helping to right a wrong," Zeke said. "For your own safety, it's best you remain ignorant of the details."

A brief silence ensued before she said, "Where do we go from here?"

"You replicate a masterpiece," Zeke said, "and we hunt down another one."

"Excuse me," Rohan said, forcing his voice to remain steady, even though his heartbeat hit ten on the Richter scale. He grabbed his laptop and headed toward his office.

"Everything okay?" Zeke asked, concern in his voice.

"Yeah, just something I need to take care of."

He hoped.

13

A BEAD OF SWEAT CREPT THROUGH ROHAN'S HAIR BEFORE IT tickled its way down his right temple.

But Rohan wasn't laughing. He was on the verge of shitting his drawers.

He analyzed the flow of data on his wall of monitors, even while the content of the email he'd received blared its dangerous intent through his mind.

Over and over and over.

"Hello, Rohan. It's time to come back. Or else."

Time to come back.

Come back.

The Collective.

They had truly found him.

He'd expected as much after the attempted breach yesterday and Lynette's encounter with Miss Kamber, but hadn't been sure. Hackers shot volleys across his server's bow on a regular basis. Yet something about yesterday's attack had felt different.

Personal. Angry. Over the top.

How had they found him? What digital clue had he left behind?

Questions, questions. No answers.

Throwing off his shock and recriminations, he waited for Lucy to give the all-clear. The methodical process slowed his heart rate and, when he swiped the perspiration from his temple, no more followed in its track.

By the time Zeke entered his office ten minutes later, all the security layers had updated to green.

PROTECTED.

Lucy had done her job.

He had done his job.

The knowledge did nothing to disintegrate the knot in his gut.

Zeke waved toward the monitors. "Something going down?"

Rohan swiveled back to his desk and closed the laptop. "Everything's fine. Just some time-sensitive information I needed to follow-up on."

Zeke studied him. "You're not trying to avoid Lena?"

"Why would I?"

"You made your feelings about her clear."

"And yet here we are." When Zeke opened his mouth, Rohan waved off whatever company explanation his brother was about to give. "As Lena said, I don't have to love and admire her to do my job."

Zeke sent Rohan a knowing smile. "Good thing we didn't have dry wood lying about with all those sparks flying between the two of you."

More like flaming daggers.

"I'm not letting down my guard around her. She's hiding something and I intend to find out what."

Zeke shook his head. "Your relentlessness is part of what

makes BARS successful. But I need you to divert your mental energy toward background checks on Palmer and his associates."

"Can you have Cruz do the backgrounds? I'm going to be tied up with this for a while."

"What is *this*?"

"Follow-up on the Gardner case." The lie burned all the way down to his gut.

"I thought that case was done."

"Not quite."

Zeke knocked a knuckle on his desk. His expression conveyed extreme unhappiness. "I'll ask Cruz to work on the background checks. You have until tomorrow to finish the Gardner case, then I need you focused on Kamber's."

Rohan gritted his teeth, then nodded. No sooner had Zeke disappeared down the hallway, Rohan's laptop dinged again.

He lifted the display, and an image flashed on screen.

He frowned, not understanding what he was looking at. The orientation was . . . wrong. Then it hit him, and every cell in his body trembled with dread. The camera shot was from high above. A woman sat in a red chair, with her feet buried in a peach Ottoman and a sketch pad propped on her knees. Sheets of discarded paper littered the floor around her. Three easels lined up before her. The middle one empty.

Angelena Kamber.

Someone, or some thing, like a drone, had taken a picture of her through the glass roof.

Last night.

14

"STARTING SOMETHING NEW?"

Lena looked up from the clerk's rhythmic scanning of paint tubes, brushes, and various other items she needed for the Blackwell project to meet the older woman's gaze.

A good four inches taller than Lena's five-and-a-half-foot frame, the clerk had a quiet, yet helpful, way about her. But Gayle spoke to a lot of people and shared bits of information she gleaned from one customer to the next. Not in a judgy, gossipy way. Just conversational.

Lena didn't like parts of her life traveling from one stranger to the next. Who knew if word of her would make it to the wrong person.

If Lena answered yes to Gayle's question, the clerk would want more details. Which would result in Lena delivering a mountain of lies or prevarication. She wasn't above doing either to protect her privacy, but these days she tried to stick to the truth as much as possible.

As a general rule, she didn't discuss her clients. But this was a small town, and she figured someone had noticed

Rohan coming or going from her building. Which meant Gayle was more likely fishing for information.

"Restocking supplies," Lena said.

"When are we going to see an original of yours hanging in the Triskelion Gallery?"

Never.

"Hard to say. Right now, I'm concentrating on perfecting my technique," Lena said, keeping to the story she'd manufactured six months ago, when she'd moved to Steele Ridge. "I figured, if it worked for Picasso, it might work for me."

"I've seen your reproductions. They're quite extraordinary."

Lena's mind drifted back to her meeting with the Blackwells a few hours earlier. She could think of only two reasons why they wouldn't want an identifying stamp on the back of a reproduction. They either intended to sell it as an original, which she doubted, given the way they'd grilled her, or they were going to use it to replace an original.

Which begged the question—who had a stolen Caravaggio?

She shook her head. None of her business. She had more pressing things to worry about right now.

"Thank you." Lena paid for the supplies and exited the arts and crafts store.

In the old days, Lena would have spent weeks searching for the exact paints Caravaggio had used to paint the *Nativity* and roamed antique shops and flea markets, looking for old frames and stretcher boards.

A career forger, with a lot at stake, might even go to the extreme and find a seventeenth-century painting by a lesser-known artist, strip it down, and use the canvas.

Lena didn't have to worry about her copy passing professional or scientific scrutiny. All she had to do was get the painting's colors and texture and mood close enough to fool the untrained eye. Something she'd mastered a decade ago.

Next stop, the office supply store. She needed to sweet-talk the printer into doing a rush job for her. She wanted to get started on the Caravaggio as soon as she delivered Palmer's painting.

Pausing at one of the few stoplights in downtown Steele Ridge, she waited for the walk symbol to light up while eyeing the line of stormy clouds billowing her way. Snow-white clouds morphed into different shades of gray—silver, then steel, then a roiling, angry iron.

A current of electricity that had nothing to do with the oncoming storm fired down her spine, lighting up her senses.

With a casualness she didn't feel, she surveyed her surroundings, searching for the source of her unease as she drew a small, white-and-black-handled umbrella from her handbag. The weather could turn on a dime in the mountains, so she always had it with her—to keep her dry and to help ward off any unwanted attention.

Someone approached on her left, and her fingers tightened around her makeshift weapon.

She looked up to find a stocky man, wearing dark sunglasses and a long-sleeved T-shirt beneath a flannel overshirt. He stood a little taller than her, with gray hair speckling his sideburns and temples. His cheek bore the telltale signs of once having suffered from severe teenage acne.

He nodded toward her umbrella. "Looks like you came better prepared than me."

The man seemed familiar, but she couldn't place him.

Unlike most people who lived here, Lena avoided introducing herself to everyone she met. She wasn't interested in making friends. Friends asked a lot of questions.

"Life in the mountains," she said.

"At least we're getting the rain. Folks out west haven't been so lucky."

A megadrought was sweeping over the far western states, eating away at crucial water sources for an agriculturally dense region and rising populations who had no access to groundwater. Throw in escalating temperatures, which contributed to even more evaporation and melts snowpacks earlier in the season, and you had a recipe that no one wants to make.

"Guess I should have listened to my husband and worn my raincoat," a female chuckled on Lena's right.

The woman's pale, upturned face watched the darkening sky with concern. Wind whipped her ponytail around, freeing curly wisps of hair.

The walk symbol finally lit, and Lena said, "Be safe, y'all," and, a little reluctantly, handed the woman her favorite umbrella.

The woman's eyes widened in surprise, and she darted a look at the man before accepting the gift. "Thank you."

"Can't have your husband saying 'I told you so,'" Lena said before darting across the street.

The first fat raindrop hit her dead center on the crown of her head, but she ignored it, putting everything she had into guiding her body through the normal motions of preparing for a downpour.

Zip up her jacket.

Hunch her shoulders.

Pick up speed.

Look for her stalker.

THE RAIN BEAT DOWN ON LENA, TURNING HER WORLD INTO A gray slate of continuous static. All thoughts of visiting the office supply store had washed away.

When the wind whipped another set of tiny liquid knives into her face, she cursed her random act of kindness in giving away her only protection to a stranger.

She ran up the walkway leading to her building, angling her head to the left to keep the rain out of her ear. And nearly barreled into Rohan on her stoop.

"Fine weather," he said, straightening from his slouched position against her building. His gaze traveled over her as if he were inspecting her for injuries.

Unlike her, not a drop of rain had trampled his clothes.

Damn him.

She brushed a sodden lock of hair out of her eyes. "I told you all I know about the burglary at the *debriefing*."

Rather than be irritated by her testy tone, he smiled.

Smiled!

"I brought you a present."

"No, thank you." She passed her proximity card over the reader and heard the faint click of the door's locking mechanism disengaging.

He reached down to pick up a cardboard cylinder resting against the brick building at the same time he opened the door. "You'll like this one."

"Right now, the only thing I would like is a hot shower and dry clothes." She shot him a glare. "And privacy."

"I'm the soul of discretion."

She strode inside, not bothering to invite him in. He'd

follow. Frankly, she was surprised he'd waited for her at the door rather than in her living room.

Had the situation been different, she might have insisted he come back in an hour. But she could still feel her stalker's malevolent eyes cutting into her back. Being naked and alone didn't strike her as the best idea at the moment.

Once they entered her loft, she grabbed a set of dry clothes and flipped on the bathroom light. She paused inside the door and pinned him with a warning look. "Don't touch anything."

"Yes, ma'am." He looked past her shoulder, at the painting peering out from the bathroom's depths.

Dammit. Why hadn't she slipped into the bathroom and kept her mouth shut? Xander always said her mouth would be her downfall.

While she wallowed in self-recrimination, Rohan had cut the distance between them to mere inches. The heat from his body penetrated her chilled flesh.

He studied every curve, every hue, every detail of the painting inside the climate-controlled box.

Lena's breath clutched at the sides of her throat, waiting, dreading. Hoping.

"Frida Kahlo?" he asked.

Her chest lowered on a slow and steady exhale. *"Self-Portrait with Braided Hair."*

"Artists are rather unimaginative with titling their works."

"Something we can debate *after* I've rinsed off the chill."

He ripped a thick, white towel from the rack and draped it over her wet head and shoulders with a gentleness that surprised her.

"I suppose I can see why she named this one the way she

did. Isn't her hair styled in a chignon in most of her self-portraits?"

Only Rohan would know the French word for the modern day updo. "Many, but not all. Most experts believe she painted this for her husband, who loved her long hair."

"Romantic."

Lena shook her head. "Tragic and unhealthy love."

"What do you mean?"

"Her husband, also an artist, loved women. *All* women."

"Then he was a fool. Why is she in your bathroom?"

"Why not?"

"Seems unusual, even if the painting is protected."

"I disagree. She's the first thing I see every morning and the last thing in the evening." She waved a hand toward the outer room, where her fakes dotted the walls. "I might go days without looking, actually looking, at any of those."

"Good point." He did a hundred-and eighty-degree rotation around the small bathroom. Surveyed her toiletries in the shower and dotting the sink. Skimmed over the bathtub, the candles, and the essential oils. Read the message she'd written on the mirror in red lipstick a few days ago when her doubts of finishing *Woman Walking* got too overwhelming.

You got this.

She closed her eyes. Why hadn't she cleaned off the damning words this morning?

Because she was still struggling. Still in need of the affirmation.

She wouldn't give in to her insecurities. She wouldn't let his scrutiny make her feel ashamed. Whatever worked to motivate a person to be their best self ought to be shouted across the galaxy. Not wiped away.

"Rohan, get out of my bathroom."

Instead of complying, he bent toward the painting. What he searched for, she had no idea, but she was confident he wouldn't find it.

He straightened and turned to her. "Truly extraordinary work, Lena."

The way he said her name—low, intimate, *possessive*—compelled her to look at his mouth as if she could see the echo of it hovering on his lips.

From one slow blink to the next, those amazing lips were closer. Too close.

Not close enough.

Then they were gone.

The bathroom door closed quietly behind him. She stared at the white panels for a long while, wondering why she felt such a keen ache of disappointment. She barely knew him. Wasn't even sure she liked him.

Snapping herself into action, she rinsed the cold out of her skin and let her sweatshirt, yoga pants, and fluffy socks warm up the chill in her bones.

Rather than take twenty minutes to dry her thick hair, she wrapped a towel around it, turban-style. Then she drew in a deep breath and stepped outside, closing the bathroom door behind her.

Rohan sat in her red chair, looking up toward the green-house roof. Lightning crackled through the clouds, putting on an incredible light show.

Many evenings, she'd sat in that same chair, with the same wonder in her eyes. The Heavens in a full-on tantrum were mesmerizing.

But he was in *her* chair. "What are you doing?"

His eyes lowered to hers. "Taking in the view."

Every cell in her body bloomed, ached, heated under his intense scrutiny.

He broke visual contact and nodded at the blank canvas, making her heart slam against her ribcage. "Is that for the Caravaggio?"

"No."

"I didn't think the size looked quite right. What will it be, then?"

If only she knew. For years, she'd been waiting for inspiration to strike.

"I don't know," she said, surprising herself with the truth.

He nodded as if he understood, though she doubted he did. She wasn't sure she understood.

"My present is on the easel behind you."

Next to her nearly completed Catawnee, she found a life-sized print of the *Nativity*. How had she missed it?

Because you were too busy staring at Rohan.

She moved closer, noting he'd attached the print to a piece of foam board with a set of black binder clips, all of which he must have pilfered from her supply cabinet.

"You clearly don't take direction well." Despite her irritation, she was impressed with the quality of the print and the care with which he'd attached it to the board.

"Will it do?" he asked, standing now.

"It's extraordinary." She touched a fingertip to the baby Jesus's glowing forehead. "You must tell me who your printer is in case mine goes belly up." She turned to face him and found him close enough to wrap her hand around his neck and pull him in for a mind-melting kiss.

Years of imposed self-control kept her hands in place. She didn't get involved with her clients. No matter how tempting or handsome.

He stared down at her, his hazel eyes even more vibrant

without his glasses, which hung in the V of his burgundy Henley.

Amidst the rumble of thunder, an unbearable silence stretched between them.

When the area between her legs tingled, Lena stepped away. "Thanks for dropping off the print. You saved me a step."

"You can thank Lynette when you see her." He unclipped the print and began rolling it up again.

"What are you doing?" she asked.

"Helping you pack up."

Lena took a step back and rolled her hands into fists. "Have you lost your mind?"

He picked up one of her sturdier easels and wrestled with folding it up.

"Give that to me before you break it." She snatched it from his hands and set it back up.

"We have a cabin on our property that will meet your lighting needs. No one will bother you there."

When he made a beeline toward her brushes, she rushed after him and placed herself in between him and his goal. "I'm not going anywhere with you."

He shrugged. "I suppose I could move into one of the apartments below."

"Thank you for the print, Rohan, but it's time for you to leave."

"I can't do that."

"Why not?"

"Because of this." He fished out a square of paper from his back pocket, unfolded it, then held it out for her inspection.

She took a cautious step forward. Studied the picture.

Her breath caught, and she lifted her gaze to the greenhouse roof. To the clear window panes Rohan had wanted to replace with something solid and safe.

"Your place or mine?" he asked.

Lena thought about the sensation of being watched, about the break-in, about the picture of her dangling from Rohan's fingers.

"Yours."

15

"CHANGE OF HEART?"

Rohan's attention didn't leave the scatter of code in front of him as Cruz entered his office.

He didn't have to ask what his brother meant. Showing up here with Lena—and her possessions—no doubt had them all snickering behind their office doors.

Bastards.

"We need her to get started on the copy. I'm merely safeguarding our investment."

"You're concerned about her safety, are you?"

Unable to get the Collective's photo of her out of his head, he'd come up with the idea of her staying in one of the on-site cabins. Here, he could protect her in a way that surveillance equipment couldn't.

Rohan sensed the direction of his brother's questions and sent him a don't-fuck-with-me look. "I'm concerned about her productivity. We're on a tight schedule."

"She's a looker. That mass of dark hair, those long, slender—"

"If you're interested," Rohan cut in. His imagination didn't need any help. "She's single."

"Tempting, but I already have another dark-haired beauty in my sights."

Rohan turned around and lifted a brow. "Anyone I know?"

Cruz sank deeper into his chair, hiked an ankle onto his knee, and smiled.

"Did you come here to talk about women? Or do you have a legitimate reason for bugging the shit out of me?"

"I finished the background checks on Palmer's chief of staff and the two delivery guys."

"Anything come up?"

"No hits on them. Palmer's fiancée had some sticky fingers in her teenage years, but that's not unusual."

Rohan grinned. "Evidently, she didn't have a Grams."

Cruz scowled at the reminder.

When he was young, Cruz loved Big League Chew bubble gum. He liked chewing it up, then stuffing the pink wad inside his lower lip like he'd seen older boys do with tobacco.

When Grams found out he hadn't paid for his latest stash, she'd hauled him back to the store and made him apologize to the manager.

To Rohan's knowledge, his brother never stole anything again. Until he got paid to do it for a living.

"As for Palmer," Cruz continued, "he's just another asshole with a lot of money. Did you get anything on the thief?"

"I ran through several escape route scenarios, then focused on the quickest one to I-40 and hacked into security cameras along the way."

"You think he went to Asheville?"

"Asheville or Charlotte seemed the most likely destinations for stolen art."

"Did you speak to Liv or Ash about it?"

"No." If the Collective hadn't been breathing down his neck, he would have thought to tap into their two art crime experts right away.

Rohan considered asking Cruz for his help in fending off the Collective. His brother was like a terrier when it came to tracking down digital prey, but he didn't have the in-depth knowledge he needed to go keyboard-to-keyboard with members of the Collective.

He still didn't know exactly what he was up against. The Collective could be a hundred strong or an organization of one. Besides, his brother would start asking questions he wasn't prepared to answer.

"Might not be a bad idea to tap into their expertise," Cruz said.

"Agreed."

"Want me to work that angle?"

"I got it." Rohan leaned back and pointed at one of his computer monitors. "Recognize that guy?"

Cruz untangled his legs and leaned forward to study an image of a white guy, mid-twenties, medium height, paying for cigarettes and a Mountain Dew at a local convenience store. "No, should I?"

"That's our thief."

"You're sure?"

Rohan hit the Play button, and the guy walked out of the store and got into a black truck. "That's the same Dodge I saw speeding away from Lena's place. It's at least twenty years old." Once the mud-splattered truck backed out of the stall and pulled away, he paused the video and pointed at the driver's side rear quarter panel. "The fuel door was missing on the getaway vehicle. Same as this one."

"Any hits on facial recognition?"

"Haven't gotten that far. This just came through."

"I can take it from here."

"Sure you don't need to clear it with Zeke first?"

"You've heard that one about it being easier to beg forgiveness than seek permission, right?"

"You really want to play it that way?"

Cruz's grin was cocksure. "Don't worry your pretty head about it."

"Thanks, bro."

Cruz pushed out of his seat. "Where's the artist you have no interest in?"

Rohan's appreciation turned to annoyance. "Mom's feeding her."

"You realize we're two-for-two now."

"What are you talking about?"

"Two collaborations with smart, sexy women. Two I-love-yous."

Phin and Zeke had invited Maddy and Liv, respectively, here to collaborate on a recovery and both men had fallen head over heels.

"I'm not falling in love with Angelena Kamber. I don't even trust her."

Cruz strode to the door. "Kinda odd to bring an untrustworthy person to one of the most clandestine places in Steele Ridge, don't you think?" He paused at the door. "I wonder what else"—he pointed at Rohan's lap—"could be motivating you, brother?"

"Get the hell out of here."

Cruz laughed. "Here comes Zeke."

Rohan stared at the empty doorway, listening to his

brothers' quick exchange and chafing at his, evidently apparent, attraction to Lena.

Before he had time to get himself into a full-blown pissy mood, Zeke shoved his head into his office. "Cruz said you've made some headway on the Kamber recovery. Mind coming down to my office to discuss? I'm expecting a phone call."

Drawing in a steadying breath, Rohan followed his brother and sat in one of the two guest chairs before Zeke's desk. He told Zeke about the backgrounds checking out, the lead on the thief, and his intent to talk to Liv or Ash.

"You'll have to talk to Ash. Liv's preparing for trial on the O'Fallon case."

"The one where the guy stole priceless antiques for his kids' inheritance?"

"Yeah, that's all coming to a head. Once the O'Fallon case is in the bag, she can put the FBI behind her. Finally."

"You okay with me bringing Ash into the Kamber recovery?" Although things weren't as tense between Zeke and Ash anymore, they still had some unresolved issues that both men were too stubborn to resolve.

"Keep the details to a minimum. I don't need Special Agent *Cameron* Blackwell complicating this any more than it is already."

And there was the rub. At least one of them. Zeke still hadn't forgiven Ash for leaving BARS and establishing a new persona with the FBI by using his middle name.

"Got it."

The sound of an engine drew Zeke's attention to a window that overlooked the Annex's parking lot. "Oh, shit."

Rohan didn't immediately respond to his brother's exclamation. BARS had a lot of "Oh, shit" moments.

"What's going on?"

Zeke stood. Genuine fear entering his expression. "You gotta stop her."

"Stop who?" Rohan joined him at the window in time to see Grams backing up her utility vehicle—the third one in two years—with Lena in the passenger seat.

Grams hit the gas, and Lena grabbed a handle above her head.

Lynette appeared on the path leading from the Friary, breathless. She stared at him and Zeke through the window, with a how-could-you-allow-this look.

Rohan's heart dive-bombed into his stomach.

"Oh, shit."

16

Lena's right foot bore down on the nonexistent brake pedal while her back pressed harder and harder into the UTV's faux leather seat.

Grams—Johona—blasted them across an open grassy field at a speed that would have left the *Millennium Falcon* in their dust.

When Lynette had stepped away to answer a phone call, Johona had offered Lena a lift to the cabin she would occupy for the next week. Charmed by the miniature matriarch, Lena had readily accepted. She could use the short ride to pump the unsuspecting grandmother for information.

But her brain had switched from inquisitor to survival mode at the first push of the throttle. Now she was afraid to distract her.

"What do you think of our home so far?" Johona asked in a casual voice that belied their hyper-speed.

"Gorgeous," Lena said through clenched teeth as they made a hard left and gravity pulled her toward the open doorframe.

"We care for a thousand acres of property. Most of it left natural to give the wildlife and plants a safe haven."

The UTV flew into a ditch-like thing so fast Lena came off her seat for a heart-stopping moment before the vehicle roared up the other side and onto a gravel-packed road.

Soon they drove through a straight, flat tunnel of trees, and Lena's grip on the handle above her head loosened a little. She took in the astonishing palette of autumn colors—lemony tulip trees, crimson sourwoods, sunrise maples, emerald cedars, and so many others she couldn't identify. A few feet from the tree line, the forest turned dark and impenetrable.

"Do bears live here?" she asked.

"I hope so. We have yet to see any, but we have heard about sightings all around us."

Stalker versus bear. Lena wasn't sure which one she feared more.

The road dipped down and so did Lena's stomach, then the trees cleared to reveal an immense rectangular building on their right. If this was a working farm, she would have assumed they stored large equipment inside. But the Blackwells weren't farmers.

"What's in that build—"

"A red-tailed hawk." Johona pointed to her left. "Do you see it?"

Lena bent low and tried to follow where the woman gestured, but the UTV's canopy blocked her view of the sky. "No, I missed it."

"I will keep my eye out for another."

Lena twisted back around and glimpsed a rotor sticking out from behind the gigantic building. "Do you have a helicopter?"

Johona nodded. "Cruz is an excellent pilot. We have a drone, too."

Lena couldn't envision a single artwork recovery scenario in which either would be required. "I take it the team recovers more than missing paintings."

"Anything and everything."

They continued on at the same breakneck speed for a few more minutes. Lena spotted two preteen kids watching a young man as he lifted and aimed a compound bow and arrow toward a target, maybe fifty yards away. He released the arrow, and the young girl bounced on her toes and clapped her hands.

"Clay brings Sadie and Brodie to the range a few times a week to practice their archery," Johona said. "Clay works for BARS and is a big brother to Sadie. Their mama, Clara, is married to Alejandro. He's maintained the property for years, even before our arrival. Such a wonder. Brodie is Liv's son."

Sadie lifted her own bow and drew back. "Your family doesn't mind?"

"Mind what?"

"Alejandro's daughter using their equipment."

Johona turned dark, probing eyes on Lena. "Why would we?"

"Kids break things." Neil never reacted to her clumsy fingers the way dads did on TV. He would stew in irritation —*for days*—and wouldn't allow her to touch the item's replacement. "Family forgives family. Others, not so much." Lena's eyes widened as the UTV headed for a large oak tree. "Johona. *Tree.*"

The matriarch jerked on the steering wheel, bringing them back to the center of the lane, but Lena didn't stop choking the "Oh, shit" handle.

Silence stretched between them, and Lena worried she'd offended her escort.

"It's true that we would forgive family anything," Johona said a beat later. "My grandsons have a mantra they say when they need courage or inspiration, and sometimes in celebration.

Family first. Through blood. Through hate. Through fear. No exceptions." Johona paused a moment before adding, "As beautiful as it is, their mantra doesn't define family. Because *we* don't define it. Our hearts do."

The older woman's eyes touched on Lena's for an unreadable moment before shifting forward again. "Sadie, Clay, Clara, and Alejandro Rios are part of my family as much as Lynette, Brodie, Liv, Maddy, and the boys."

An unexpected yearning to be added to Johona's list rose in Lena. She quashed the dangerous emotion before it could take root.

It was better for everyone if she kept her distance.

People who loved her had an odd way of winding up dead.

"HERE WE ARE." JOHONA LOCKED THE BRAKES, AND ALL FOUR tires skidded across the gravel. "Welcome to the Osprey cabin."

If they'd been on a dirt road, Lena would be eating their after-dust right now.

Johona disembarked as if she were stepping away from the dining room table and lifted one of the many bags—that somehow survived the wild ride—from the back of the UTV.

Tough lady.

Lena hoped she was still a kickass painter when she

reached her ninth decade. Easing off her seat, she gave her rubbery legs a few seconds to harden up again.

The dark brown cabin sat on a soft knoll, away from the woods. It looked like someone had plucked it from the remote backcountry of a state park. Lena's heart sank, wondering how in the world she'd find any inspiration in a home that resembled a dead beetle.

She grabbed her suitcase and a duffel out of the cargo hold and followed in the matriarch's wake.

In contrast to the unfortunate cabin color, the grounds surrounding the small structure abounded with cheery colors. Half wine barrels full of purple and yellow pansies, enjoying their second bloom of the year, huddled on each side of the front steps. At their feet, white mums with pale yellow centers blossomed in perfect clumps of threes. Camellias flourished along the path leading from the drive to the porch, where twin, handcrafted rocking chairs framed a small table.

Lena could envision herself rocking with a warm cup of tea, while watching the sun make its slow descent beneath the trees.

She set her bags down inside the front door and took in her new home. As she suspected, the cabin contained the requisite bedroom, bathroom, and living room-kitchenette combo.

A stone fireplace took up most of one wall and twelve-inch-wide pine planks decorated the other three sides. In the corner, a daybed sat beneath a square window, with piles of pillows and cuddle blankets.

Matching recliners anchored the fireplace and a small two-person breakfast table sat in a snug space between the living room and what looked like a recently renovated farm-house kitchenette.

All of this she took in on a subconscious level as she rushed across the cabin to the north-facing wall of windows. In the distance, rolling mountains blazed with every autumn color imaginable, giving the Blue Ridge Parkway a run for its money.

Purple aster, yellow goldenrod, and a few tenacious orange butterfly weeds produced bright splashes of color in a tawny grass meadow nearer to the cabin.

Glorious natural light, an inspirational view, and a cozy interior. It was enough to make her forget she would be sleeping in the belly of a dead beetle.

"Will this give you enough light to work?" Johona asked.

"More than enough." She ran her fingers along a gorgeous quilt draped over the back of the couch. "This cabin feels like someone's home. Did I displace somebody?"

Johona shook her head. "We keep two of the cabins ready for visitors at all times, though we don't get many." She gestured to the north. "A few more minutes down the road are two larger cabins. The Rios family occupies one and Henri, the woman who manages the Big House, lives in the other. Don't be surprised if they stop by to say hello."

Lena hoped they wouldn't. She preferred her own company, which was one reason she had purchased her entire apartment building.

"Thank you, Johona. I can't imagine a more peaceful place."

"It is until the boys practice on the shooting range." She smiled. "I'm afraid no amount of insulation or double panes will muffle the sound of gunshots."

"I'm used to working downtown, with all its traffic. A little friendly fire won't affect my concentration."

"Welcome to the Friary." Johona drifted toward the door. "Dinner is at six o'clock. I'll send Rohan to pick you up."

"That's not necess—"

The front door closed, cutting off Lena's protest.

The prospect of seeing Rohan again so soon brought about conflicting emotions. She couldn't deny her attraction to him, which was a problem. She didn't get involved with clients.

She didn't get involved with anyone. Not anymore.

Yet something told her sex with Rohan Blackwell might be worth the risk.

After they concluded their business with each other.

Recalling the rest of her bags in the back of the UTV, she rushed outside, only to skid to a halt at the sight of her stuff sitting on the low porch.

Johona gave her a slow wave, then ripped off down the road.

Silence, unlike any she'd ever heard before, electrified the air around her.

She shifted on her feet. Checked the tree line, the mountain-scape, the road. All were blissfully, unnervingly devoid of humans.

Then, as if the forest released a welcoming exhale, she heard the first sign of life.

A chirp.

Then another one.

And another.

A bright yellow-and-black butterfly floated around her, alighting on a spike of lavender, whose best flowering days were behind it. A fat, hairy bumblebee buzzed overhead, and Lena watched in fascination as it flew into a perfectly round hole in one of the porch's timbers.

"Carpenter bee," a young female voice informed her.

Startled, Lena glanced down to find a girl smiling up at her.

The one from the archery range. Sadie Rios.

She looked to be eleven or twelve. Kindness sparkled in her brown eyes and energy thrummed through her like *Flash* before he took off through the city.

"They make a lot of noise, but they won't hurt you." Her expression was earnest. "Please don't tell Daddy about the hole. He'll plug it, trapping the poor buzzers inside."

Despite herself, Lena smiled and asked the only question that came to mind, even though she already knew the answer. "Who might you and your dad be?"

"I'm Sadie. It's short for Mercedes." She pointed toward the distant cabins Johona had mentioned earlier. "I live down there. Daddy takes care of the grounds and buildings."

"Nice to meet you, Sadie. I'm Lena. Short for Angelena." The girl's attention went to the easels and canvases propped against the porch post. "Are you a painter?"

"I am."

"Who's your favorite?"

"Favorite? Oh, you mean painter?"

"I love Rosa Bonheur."

Lena blinked. Although a prolific painter, the French artist's name wasn't well-known outside the art world. "You know Bonheur's work with animals?"

The girl nodded. "Aunt Liv's been taking me to different art galleries in the area."

"Your aunt knows about art?"

"She tracks down art thieves." Her eyebrows scrunched together. "Or used to. Now she's one of us."

Aunt Liv. One of us.

Another pang. Another longing. Another quashing.

Lena shied away from children like teenage girls avoided

spiders. But Sadie tweaked her curiosity. "Do you want to be an artist when you grow up?"

"Grams said I'm already an artist. I just need polishing. One day, I'm going to be an illustrator and help make animated movies."

"I have an extra canvas and a giant pad of drawing paper," Lena heard herself say. "Stop by tomorrow after school and show me what you've got."

The girl's face lit up. "Really?"

"As long as your parents are cool with it."

"Thank you! I can't wait to tell Brodie. He's going to be so jealous."

"See you tomorrow."

Sadie was already on the run.

Lena's smile faded. "What the hell are you doing, Kamber?"

17

Rohan's heart kicked up a beat as he climbed the stairs to Lena's—the Osprey—cabin. Already, she was taking up real estate in his world. Settling in nice and snug like a chipset on a motherboard.

And he had no one to blame but himself. He raised his hand to knock right as the door opened.

Air stopped flowing in his body at the sight of her. She wore an off-white sweater over brown leggings and low-heeled boots. Gold hoops hung from her earlobes, and her beautiful hair flowed over one shoulder like an ebony waterfall.

Stunning.

"I'm overdressed," she said, taking in his dark gray Henley and tee, blue jeans, and boots. "Give me a moment and I'll change." She motioned for him to enter and turned away.

"Don't," he said, fighting the urge to pull her into his arms.

She glanced back.

"You look great." He cleared his throat and stepped inside. "You won't stand out, I promise. It's always a mix."

"Once I get my car, I can go to the grocery store so I don't have to inconvenience your family."

"It's no inconvenience. There's always more than enough food, and Mom enjoys cooking, especially for new folks."

"Why?"

"Because we're beasts and don't always show the right amount of appreciation." He grinned. "If you want to get on her good side, just ooh and ahh a lot as you eat."

"I'm not interested in getting on anyone's good side. I'm here to find *Walking Woman*."

Rohan's good humor disappeared. "And paint a copy of the *Nativity*."

"Of course." She grabbed a key from a bowl by the door. "Are you in one of those death mobiles or a real vehicle?"

Rohan's mind drifted to earlier in the day, when he'd followed his speed demon grandmother across the estate all the way to the cabin, to make sure Lena didn't get thrown from the UTV. When he'd seen her exit the vehicle, he'd backed away and returned to the Annex.

"Real." He started to smile, then slammed on the brakes. "Don't forget to lock the door."

She jangled the key in front of his face before shooing him outside. He showed her how to set the alarm, and they listened for the telltale click of the lock before heading to his vehicle.

He strode toward the passenger door, checked himself, and continued to the driver's side, ignoring years of conditioning by his father. This wasn't a date and the lady's fingers weren't broken.

Still, he felt like an ass as he settled inside and waited for the system to scan his face and fingerprint. The dashboard lit up.

She settled into the passenger seat. "Is this an electric car?"

Rohan braced himself. He never knew what reaction to expect from people—fascination, disdain, indifference? Nodding, he said, "A Verge TS70."

"How many miles per charge?"

"About three hundred and seventy-five."

"Impressive. I've been thinking about getting one, now that it's easier to find charging stations."

"You won't be disappointed."

By the time they entered the Friary's dining room, Grams, Lynette, Zeke, Liv, Brodie, and Cruz had already assembled.

"Hello, Lena," Lynette said. "Pick any chair."

Lena chose the seat next to Brodie, rather than Cruz, surprising Rohan and earning a raised brow from Zeke.

Many of the women they'd brought home over the years had found Cruz's smoky good looks too irresistible. Literally. After the first few disappointments, Phin and Zeke had used Cruz as a sort of litmus test for their girlfriends' loyalty.

Most had failed.

Crystal had been the only woman Rohan had ever dared to bring home. And she hadn't failed the test.

He pushed away the painful memory and took the seat beside Cruz, earning him a smirk from his older brother.

Cruz leaned in. "Great strategy. Sometimes they're easier to look at than talk to."

"Shut it."

The bastard chuckled.

"Did you talk to Ash?" Zeke asked.

Rohan nodded. "He was on his way to a meeting, but promised to put some feelers out."

"Phin texted. He and Maddy will be down soon," Lynette said. "No sense holding up dinner while they get their clothes back on."

Zeke's head snapped around, and he stared at his mother. Cruz choked on an olive he pilfered from a nearby plate.

"Your father might be long gone, my boy," Lynette said to Zeke, "but I still remember the rigorous demands of new love."

"Stop," Zeke said, downing a bourbon. "I don't want to hear any more about your love life, Mama."

"Or Phin's," Rohan and Cruz added at the same time.

Lynette's lips twitched. "Prudes."

Ten minutes later, Phin and Maddy joined the group. A pretty flush covered Maddy's cheeks, either from exertion, or maybe it was the knowing looks everyone sent their way. Phin's step carried a bit more swagger than normal.

The evening didn't improve. By the time they finished dessert, Rohan couldn't hustle Lena out of the house fast enough. The only highlight of the evening had been watching Lena interact with Brodie. She seemed at ease with him. Much more so than with the adults.

"Good night." Lena wrapped her arms around herself and strode down the path that led to the Annex's parking lot. "I'll take my car back to the cabin."

"Zeke stashed your keys in the Annex. I'll track them down tomorrow." Rohan motioned toward his vehicle. "Get in. I'll take you home."

She turned to head back inside the Friary. "I'll ask him where he put them."

"Lena, leave him be. It's a rare evening when he pulls

himself away from the office long enough to have dinner with the family."

She hesitated, clearly torn about spending more time in his company.

That . . . irked.

"Give me another five minutes, and you won't have to suffer my presence anymore tonight."

She took a visible, deep breath before capitulating.

For the first minute, they drove in stony silence, then Rohan decided to use the time to do some prodding. "Have you started on the *Nativity*?"

"I shouldn't have, but I did."

He recalled how the upper half of the woman's face on the Catawnee had yet to be finished. "Because you don't work on two projects at once?"

She nodded. "Every time my brush hits the canvas, I become the master. I see through their eyes, feel through their fingers, struggle with their emotions. It gets a little crowded inside my head when I work on more than one."

Rohan could relate. When he got deep into code, he no longer saw commands on a screen, but full, detailed images of people and objects and actions.

"I'd only intended to do the *Nativity*'s prep work—constructing the frame, attaching the canvas, and sketching out a rough line drawing. But I couldn't stop staring at the print's Christ child." She shrugged. "One thing led to the next, and I had completed the baby."

"Sounds like a lot of progress for one afternoon."

"After Lynette's initial contact, I began my research. Once I understand an artist's technique and have the supplies I need, my biggest decision is where to put the first stroke."

Rohan couldn't imagine having the ability to create—or

in Lena's case—recreate such lifelike images. An overwhelming need to watch her work barreled through him, but every instinct told him she'd balk at the request.

"Mind if I take a look?" he heard himself ask as he put his vehicle in park.

Lena glanced between him and the cabin before shrugging. "You're paying for it."

18

LENA DREW IN A STABILIZING BREATH BEFORE FLIPPING ON THE light switch. Three table lamps blinked on, casting a soft amber glow over the interior of the cabin.

After finishing for the day, she'd turned the easel toward the center of the room so she could view her work in progress from different angles.

Its position made it the first thing anyone saw upon entering the cabin. That, and its imposing size. At nearly nine and a half feet tall and six and a half feet wide, the canvas was difficult to miss.

Unlike some artists, Lena wasn't shy about showing others her work before she finished. Simon had critiqued the shyness right out of her personality. He doled out compliments and you-can-do-betters in equal measure. Like any apprentice, she had craved her mentor's positive comments. Worked day and night to obliterate his critical feedback until one fabulous day he'd deemed her finished product "perfect."

He'd never used the accolade to describe anyone's artistic talent before. Although she'd enjoyed the novelty, his verbal admiration of her work wasn't what had touched her the most.

What she could recall to this day with vivid clarity was the flood of tears filling his eyes as he looked at her painting. Having one's art spark a deep, emotional connection with its viewer was the ultimate narcotic.

Lena slanted a glance at Rohan while he assessed her painting in progress. Surprised by the nervous jitters setting up shop in her stomach.

She busied herself by stepping out of her tight shoes and stoking a flame in the fireplace. When several nerve-stretching seconds clicked by without a word from her guest, she peered at him over her shoulder. He observed the *Nativity* with a stillness that unnerved her.

She forced the myriad of questions dancing a jig on her tongue backstage.

Fire engulfed the logs, warming her face. She stared at the changing hues—vermillion, burnt sienna, ochre, and dandelion with shocks of ultramarine and brilliant white. Mesmerized by how they swayed together to create the whole. Flames licking the air, gulping down oxygen like starved travelers plowing through a tray of Oreo Thins.

Procrastination complete, she rose and joined him before the canvas.

"I've viewed many paintings attached to your name while conducting my background check," he said in a quiet voice. "All beautiful pieces of art. But none of them prepared me for the real thing."

A wave of relief washed away her anxiety. "As you have observed, there are many real things in my loft."

"Something about witnessing the transformation from this," he pointed at the blank canvas erected a few feet away, making Lena's gut twist, "to this," he air-traced a finger over her pencil sketch of the angel, "to this," his fingers hovered over the painted Christ child, "has given me a new awareness and a new level of appreciation for your talent."

Lena peered at the empty canvas, at the whiteness of her failure, and had never felt like more of a fraud—a forger—in her life.

"It's getting late," she said in a thick voice, "and I'd like to get an early start tomorrow."

"Did I say something to upset you?"

"You praised my work. Why would that be upsetting?"

"Good question." His too-observant gaze landed on the blank canvas, and Lena's muscles locked as if a glacial storm blew through the cabin.

"Thanks for the ride." She marched to the door, opened it, and waited for him to take her not-so-subtle cue.

He gave both canvases another long, considering look before stalking across the room, pausing beside her. He took in her features with a thoroughness that left her breathless.

"Don't forget to set the alarm."

Lena closed the door behind him, sank against the hard surface.

Like lights twinkling across an arid desert, the blank canvas drew her attention again and would not release its taunting grip.

19

"I love you too, baby," Phin crooned into his phone from the back of the van. "What are you wearing tonight?"

Rohan clamped his teeth together. It was bad enough navigating the new love period of Phin's—and Zeke's—cooing at home, but having it blare in Bose surround in such tight quarters was more than he could stand.

Not taking his eyes off the employee entrance of the manufacturing building, Rohan put the ignition in ACC mode and cranked up the radio until he drowned out the conversation in the backseat.

Cruz chuckled from the passenger side. "That's one way of shutting him up."

"Maddy, I gotta go," Phin said, raising his voice. "The guys are being jealous assholes." A short silence. "I'm not sure how long we'll be. We're waiting for the thief to get off work." Another short silence. "Don't worry, I'll be home in time for us to . . ."

Phin's voice dropped, and Rohan was thankful his brother spared them the details of his carnal acrobats. Which, of course, led his lizard brain to thoughts of Lena.

What was she doing right then? Putting the finishing touches on the Catawnee? Or had the Caravaggio distracted her again. After viewing her work last night, he would never think of her as a mere painter. She was a talented artist who should have a gallery dedicated to her own artworks. Why didn't she? Why did she continue copying other artists' paintings?

"Almost three o'clock," Cruz said. "Balor's shift should stream out any minute."

Facial recognition had identified Lena's burglar as twenty-six-year-old Bobby Balor. A McDowell Tech graduate, working as a first-shift machine operator.

"Here they come," Phin said, his voice all-business again.

At 3:02 p.m., employees rushed from a back door like a mass of pissed-off yellow jackets bursting out of their underground hive.

Cruz held up his phone with Bobby's DL photo blown up on his screen.

Rohan didn't need it. The guy's features were etched in his mind. "There." He followed a shaggy-haired, narrow-bodied man fast-walking his way to a black truck, scanning the parking lot as he took a long draw on his cigarette.

Definitely not the mastermind type.

"Skittish," Cruz observed.

"Stealing a million-dollar painting will do that to a fella."

"I'm surprised he hasn't disappeared," Phin said.

"Maybe he figured running would throw a spotlight on his back and decided to carry on for a few weeks or months before enjoying his spoils."

"That plan works only if he didn't get made," Cruz said.

"He probably wouldn't have if our boy," Phin slapped Rohan on the shoulder, "hadn't gone hacking."

Rohan started the van and followed Bobby out of the parking lot. The thief made a brief stop at the ABC liquor store before pulling into a driveway of an eleven-hundred-square-foot ranch where he roomed with two other guys.

"No other cars in the drive," Cruz said. "We going in?"

Rohan killed the engine and scanned the neighborhood from their position a few doors down. He didn't like going into a situation without working through different scenarios. Especially in broad daylight. But the clock was ticking, and he didn't know how long Bobby would stay put.

Nodding, he stuffed his glasses in a protective pocket in his vest and made eye contact with Phin in the rearview mirror. "If anything feels off, get the hell out of there."

"Ten-four."

Phin grabbed a clipboard, straightened his Armani tie, and strode down the sidewalk while Rohan and Cruz headed for the back of Balor's house.

Once they reached their destination, Cruz paused at the corner and listened for Phin's knock on the front door. He nodded to Rohan, who stood on the crumbling cobblestone patio near the rear door.

Once Phin mentioned the stolen painting, Bobby would no doubt bolt. Right into their web.

Drawing his Sig Sauer from his appendix holster, Rohan motioned for Cruz to take up a position opposite him. Their gazes met, and Rohan started a mental countdown.

Five . . . four . . . three . . . two—

The pounding of Bobby's feet through the house preceded the screen door flying open. Rohan caught it, using it to funnel Bobby toward Cruz, who tripped the thief and sent him sprawling.

His brother had about thirty pounds and five inches on

the guy, so it took only a matter of seconds to secure his wrists.

"What the fuck's going on?" Bobby yelled.

"You got this?" Rohan asked, pulling a set of black nitrile gloves from his front pocket and putting them on.

Cruz nodded. "He's not going anywhere."

Rohan entered the residence on soft feet. He stepped into a mudroom, which led into a galley-style kitchen. A noise in the outer room drew his attention.

He eased his head around the doorjamb to find Phin striding toward him from the opposite side of the house.

"Clear," Phin said. "No basement."

The tension gripping Rohan's shoulders eased. "Clear."

Rohan holstered his nine-millimeter and helped Cruz drag Balor back inside. They dropped him in one of the wooden kitchen chairs, securing his hands to the back.

"Robert 'Bobby' Balor," Rohan recited from memory. "Twenty-six-year-old machine operator with Sonoco. Last-born son of Rhonda and Brian Balor. Mom's a director with a local nonprofit and dad's a freelance landscape architect." He cocked his head, considering their prisoner. "You have a taste for high-octane activities and poor investment choices."

"Am I supposed to be impressed with how well you memorized my Wikipedia page?"

Phin snorted. "Lowlifes like you don't have Wiki pages unless it's to recite your rap sheet."

"Fuck you."

Phin smiled. "You can do better than that."

"Where's the painting, Bobby?" Rohan asked.

The thief stilled. "I don't know what y'all are talking about?"

"Why'd you run, then?" Phin asked.

Bobby's gaze dropped to his lap.

"Give us the painting you stole two days ago and we'll walk away. No questions asked."

After a brief silence, the thief lifted his head. Sweat pebbled on his upper lip. "You got the wrong guy. I was watching football all day with my friends."

From his back pocket, Rohan withdrew the print out of Bobby leaving a convenience store and held it up to him. "This truck matches the one I saw leaving the scene of the crime."

Bobby squinted at the picture. "How can you tell? Picture's pretty grainy."

"Amateur move to stop at a store in the middle of a heist, Bobby."

The thief stared back.

Rohan nodded at Cruz and Phin, and his brothers split off to search the house.

"Keep your fucking hands off my stuff!"

"Tell us where the painting is and we'll leave your cache of cocaine alone."

His eyes widened.

Rohan hunkered down on his haunches, out of kicking distance. "I know everything about you, Bobby, except this one little piece of the puzzle." He flattened his voice. "I like puzzles. I'll find the painting with or without your help."

Bobby swallowed. "Who are you?"

"I can be your friend, or your adversary. You decide." He leaned forward a few inches. "I recommend the former."

The thief shot to his feet, chair and all, and rammed his shoulder into Rohan's face.

Cartilage cracked, and Rohan's vision blurred. He lost his balance, but twisted at the last second and grasped the bottom half of the fleeing man's pant leg. He clutched the material, jerked hard. The thief crashed to the floor. Wood splintered.

Before Rohan could get his legs underneath him, Bobby kicked out of his grasp and scrambled away, leaving the destroyed chair behind as he threw open the screen door once again. This time, his mad flight met with no resistance.

The door banged shut.

"Dammit!" Rohan blinked hard to clear his vision and staggered to his feet. Blood streamed from his nose and his face felt like a sledgehammer had hit it.

Cruz and Phin stormed into the kitchen. When they moved to help him up, he ordered, "I'm fine. Get the bastard."

Grabbing a dirty hand towel off the counter, Rohan pressed it to his bleeding nose while he stalked through the house. In the main bathroom, he rummaged through drawers and doors until he found a few cotton balls up he could stuff up his nostrils.

In one of the bedrooms, a laptop sat open on a rumpled bed as if Bobby had been using it when the doorbell rang. A godawful odor emanated from the bed that even his cotton barriers couldn't ward off.

He carried the laptop to the kitchen counter. Since the computer hadn't gone to sleep, he didn't need Bobby's password and was already scanning emails by the time Cruz and Phin hauled the thief back inside.

The bastard cackled when he saw Rohan's face.

Cruz shoved Balor into a seat. "Shut up. You don't look any better."

"Good luck, Rocky," Bobby sneered at Rohan. "You won't find anything on there. Everything's gone."

"Thanks for the tip." Rohan redirected his attention to uncovering deleted files. So many computer users operated under the misbelief that when you deleted a thing, it was gone. Forever.

But a good hacker could recover just about anything.

It so happened Rohan was one of the best.

Five minutes later, he looked at Bobby. "Tell me about Mr. Byrne."

20

"WE'VE LOST OUR LIGHT," LENA SAID, SETTING DOWN HER paintbrush.

Sadie did the same, but her weapon of choice was a charcoal stick. The girl stretched her fingers wide, then shook out her wrist.

"Is your hand bothering you?"

"No," came the quick response.

Lena used a rag to wipe the paint from her fingers. "I'll show you some exercises you can do to help preserve your back and arm."

"I've never drawn this long before."

"If you're serious about improving your craft, you'll be putting in many more hours than the two we worked today." She moved toward Sadie's workspace. "Think of your body as a work tool." She thought a moment. "Does your dad use a chainsaw?"

The girl nodded. "A few weeks ago, he had to cut up a tree that fell across the road."

"Did he sharpen the chain cutters before he used it?"

Another nod.

"Did he clean it afterward?"

"Yeah, there was a lot of sawdust gunked up inside."

"Why do you suppose he went through all that extra effort?"

Her brows knit together. "So the chainsaw would work?"

"Work *safely*. Sawdust can catch fire and a dull blade can increase the chances of kickback." Lena demonstrated an imaginary saw jerking back toward the user's head. "Kick-back can be deadly for sawyers." She lifted her paint-stained hand. "It's the same with your drawing arm. If you don't care for it properly, you will, over time, destroy it—and your career."

Sadie opened and closed her hand several times. "Okay."

She handed the girl a new rag. "Clean off the worst of it, then tidy up your supplies."

"A cluttered workspace creates a cluttered mind," Sadie quoted.

Lena smiled. "Who said that?"

"Nana Lynette. She used to be in the military."

"You seem very close with the family." Lena began putting her own art supplies away. "Calling Lynette Nana and Liv aunt."

"We've all sort of adopted each other. I call the guys uncle, too."

A small piece of Lena's heart clutched with envy. For nearly a decade, she'd called Neil Dad, but it had always felt like more of a label than a connection.

Once they had finished cleaning up, Lena nodded toward Sadie's easel. "Do you mind if I take a peek?"

The girl glanced at Lena's painting in progress. "I'm not good yet."

"No artist ever is in the beginning. Practice, heart, and perseverance will get you where you want to be."

"What about talent?"

"If you've got a speck of it, PHP will take care of the rest."

Relieved, Sadie nodded her assent.

Lena moved to stand before Sadie's sketch, and her breath caught. Not because she looked at the renderings of the next daVinci, but because she stared at a familiar figure.

Her.

The charcoal-rendered Lena wore a pensive expression. The tip of her paintbrush pushed against the center of her bottom lip as she contemplated the construction of an angel's left wing.

Staring at herself, at her work, through the eyes of another, left Lena feeling unsteady, as if she perched on the top rail of a fence during gale force winds. Then something snagged her attention.

Charcoal Lena's eyes were . . . wrong. They seemed to be directed at a blurred rectangle in the distance. A rectangle with three legs.

A rubber mallet slammed against her ribcage.

Sadie hadn't captured her scrutinizing her brush strokes on the *Nativity,* but staring at the bloody blank canvas that plagued her every waking hour.

Why had she brought it with her?

Some would call the affliction masochism.

Lena called it hopeful idiocy.

All the roiling emotions inside her must have showed on her face, for Sadie rushed out, "I'm sorry. I should have asked." She made to rip the sheet from the sketch pad.

"Wait." Lena put a hand on the girl's arm. "This is incredible, Sadie. You . . . surprised me, is all."

She pushed her own fears back into their box and

focused on her young student. "You have an eye for detail, an extremely valuable trait in an artist. Have you taken any classes?"

The girl shook her head. "I just like to draw."

"People?"

"People, animals, plants, buildings. Everything, really."

So much about this girl reminded Lena of herself at her age.

"Do you have a sketchbook?"

"Sort of. I use a bullet journal I got for Christmas."

"I'd love to see your sketches."

"Okay." Sadie cast her an uncertain look. "Tomorrow?"

"And the day after, and the day after." She smiled. "Let's wash our hands, then I'll walk you home before I fetch my car from the Annex."

"I can show you a shortcut."

"Won't your mom wonder where you are?"

"Not until six." She skipped-ran to the bathroom.

Lena used the kitchen sink to clean her own hands, then located two flashlights. Expecting to follow the vehicle track for much of the way, she hesitated when Sadie immediately set out for the woods.

Noticing Lena's lagging steps, Sadie waved her forward. "I've taken this shortcut many times. It's okay."

Night sounds pulsed around them. Lena had never heard anything so loud, so amazing, so freaking eerie in her life. "Johona mentioned there were bears in the area."

"Bears, coyotes, copperheads. Lots of cool animals," Sadie said with excitement, then seemed to realize Lena didn't share her love of predators in dark places. "I've never seen a bear on the property, and it's too cool outside for copperheads to be moving around."

"And the coyotes?"

"Flying champagne corks kill more people each year than coyotes. If one comes near us, make eye contact and a lot of noise. They scare easily."

Lena recalled the scene in the movie *The Rundown* where Seann William Scott's character tricked Duane Johnson's character into establishing dominance with a troop of angry monkeys.

That hadn't worked out so well.

"Are you sure about the eye contact?"

"Yep." Sadie continued down the trail.

During the fifteen-minute walk through the woods, Lena checked the footpath behind her no less than one hundred and two times. The relief she felt when they finally broke through to the other side could not be measured.

She spotted her car, then remembered Zeke had her keys. "Crap."

"What's the matter?"

"Zeke took my keys."

"His office light is still on. I'll get them." The girl ran off, leaving Lena in the dimly lit parking lot.

Alone.

Somehow, it was worse than strolling through the woods. A wall of solid black existed outside the small circle cast by the lone solar-powered parking lot light. She imagined this must be what it felt like for a lobster inside one of those restaurant tanks before the chef dropped them into a vat of boiling water.

When she was a little girl, Neil would take her camping at the local state and national parks. But after they moved to Asheville, those trips had dried up. It had been years since she'd spent much time outside the hustle and bustle of her urban environment.

But amid the eeriness of her situation, hovered wonder. Standing below a dark sky full of twinkling diamonds called to her creative side. She now had a better understanding of van Gogh's obsession with the night sky. It wasn't simply black and white, but several degrees of blues, yellows, and greens. Maybe one day she'd make it to the far northern climes and paint the borealis.

A twin set of lights crept down the road leading to the Annex. She backed into the shadows as the vehicle—a dark van—rolled into the lot. Her heart crowded into her throat until the driver's side window slipped down.

Rohan stared back at her.

Relief and excitement speared through her mind, then confusion as his features registered.

Something was wrong. She couldn't put her finger on what, exactly, in the dark, yet a stab of fear edged out her other emotions and propelled her forward.

He turned away from her, spoke to someone inside the van. A few seconds later, a door slammed, and Cruz rounded the back of the vehicle as Rohan drove away.

"Hey, Lena," Cruz said. "What are you doing out—?"

"What happened to him?" she interrupted, pointing a finger at the departing vehicle.

"Who?"

"Did someone attack Rohan?"

"We ran into a little trouble."

"Little? Did you see his face?"

"Honestly, I tried not to look at it." He shivered dramatically.

She took off toward the Annex.

"Lena," Cruz called.

Phin stepped in front of her. "Now's not a good time." He

gave her what she supposed was his disarming smile. "We have some business to deal with."

"Did you *deal* with whoever did that to your brother's face?"

Mr. Charmer disappeared and steel laced his words. "Yes."

"Step aside, Phin."

"Go home, Lena. Rohan will see you in the morning."

"Sadie went inside to get my car keys."

"*Shit.* Cruz?"

"I'm on it." Cruz stormed into the building.

"Does your business have anything to do with my stolen painting?"

"You mean Palmer's stolen painting?"

"I mean don't-be-an-ass-answer-the-damn-question painting."

His smile reappeared. "I can see why you're ripping Rohan's guts from the inside out. If Maddy didn't already own my heart, I'd sweep you off your feet."

"The only thing you'd be sweeping is my dust."

She shouldered past him, only to be blocked yet again by Cruz ushering Sadie out of the building. Phin joined his brother, shoulder to shoulder, while the girl held out her keys.

Lena took the keys and stared at the two immovable objects before her. It would be a waste of time to argue with them further. They were in full-on protect-the-family mode.

"If he's not on my doorstep in one hour, I will be on his. And no pint-sized bouncers are going to stand in my way."

Frowning, Cruz glanced down at his Thor-like body, then at his brother. "Pint-sized?"

Phin shrugged, even as he squared his shoulders and expanded his chest.

If Lena wasn't so concerned about Rohan, she would have found their confusion and posturing hilarious. Right now, they were irritating barriers.

"One hour," she repeated and turned toward her vehicle, Sadie at her side.

21

Rohan's head felt like an oil rig had taken up residence in his skull. His brain hurt. His nose throbbed. And he wasn't thrilled about facing one of the most beautiful women he'd ever met with two shiners and a swollen honker.

But he believed the threat his brothers had passed on for Lena. So here he was.

When he raised his hand to knock, the door jerked open. Again.

"Do you have a sixth sense about my arrival or something?" he asked.

"You mean like hearing tires on gravel?"

As before, she left him at the door. He could feel the heat of her anger in the air.

Maybe he should have spoken to her when they had arrived at the Annex, but he'd been focused on two things—an ice pack and tracking down the lead they'd pulled from Bobby Balor. In that order.

He closed the door and strode to where her current reproduction sat. As before, his gaze shot across the canvas, gobbling up every brush stroke and admiring how she played light against dark.

"The reproduction is coming along nicely."

"Yes."

She leaned a hip against the back of the couch, arms crossed, eyes narrowed in a way that foretold a verbal storm was imminent.

He left her to her stewing. She would blow off whatever was on her chest when she was ready.

A charcoal sketch propped against another easel caught his eye. He moved closer and realized it was a picture of Lena. "Practicing self-portraits?"

"Sadie."

Surprised, he studied the image. "Great likeness."

Her expression softened. "She's quite talented."

"It's nice of you to share your space and supplies."

"Who hurt your face?"

Heat singed his ears. "The guy who stole the Palmer painting. Bobby Balor. I tracked him down to a house on the east side of town. He was reluctant to name the person who'd hired him."

"He punched you?"

"His shoulder ran into my face."

She sucked in a breath. "How badly does it hurt?"

Nuclear.

"Not too bad. Ice helps. Until my brain freezes."

"Have a seat."

"Can't."

She paused halfway to the refrigerator. "Why not?"

"I'm on my way to Atlanta."

"To do what?" She opened the freezer.

"Bobby didn't want to talk, but his computer sang like Michael Bublé."

She grasped his hand as she walked by and guided him to the couch. "Sit."

"I can't—"

"Five minutes. You can ice your nose while finishing your story."

"I can't tolerate any weight."

"This is soft and not too heavy. I use the sachet on my wrist when I've stayed at the easel too long."

"Five minutes."

"Or until you finish your story."

Rohan sat, reluctantly.

"Lean your head back." Once he complied, her knee sank into the cushion beside him and he caught a whiff of whatever soap or shampoo she'd used that morning.

Fresh. Feminine.

Quite a contrast to the hard-edged artist.

He liked both.

The cold pack looked like one of those aromatherapy hand-sewn bags. He braced himself for impact, but she gently lowered it over his nose. The cool material combined with a scent he couldn't identify eased the tension in his body and head.

It felt so damn good. He groaned.

A light touch smoothed over his hair. He was so caught up in the cold penetrating all the aching layers that he almost missed it.

With the pack covering his eyes, he couldn't check her expression. Had the contact been an accident? Or intentional?

The part of him whose craving for her increased with each encounter prayed for the latter.

"Talk," she said, bringing him back to reality.

Definitely accidental.

"Balor bragged about deleting his files, thinking he'd covered his tracks."

"But you recovered them?"

He nodded, earning him a sharp pain through his skull. "Most people don't realize how easy it is, thankfully."

"You're a hacker. Of course, it's easy."

Rohan kept his breathing even and his hands loose. "Ethical hacker."

"A modern-day Robin Hood, huh?"

"I don't cause harm." An image of Grams's hitched-up eyebrow surfaced. "Unless they deserve it."

"And who determines who deserves your digital wrath? You?"

"Sometimes, but mostly we decide as a team."

"How does one become a hacker?"

Somehow, being unable to see her made it easier to talk about what many people likened to online theft or perversion.

"I was always good at figuring out things on the computer. Once I took a coding class, a whole new world opened up to me."

"In what way?"

"There was no door that I couldn't open, no shadow I couldn't penetrate. But what kept me enthralled for many years, what pushed me to become better—the best—was gaming."

"Gaming? You really are a nerd."

He lifted one corner of the ice pack. "Proud card-carrying member."

She lightly smacked his hand, and he released the pack.

"You created games like Zelda and Minecraft?"

"High fantasy was my favorite. There's no greater rush

than creating a new world, building story after story, or finding the perfect color palette for a character's sword."

"A digital canvas." She grew quiet. "I guess we aren't so different after all."

For a guy who prided himself on his excellent communication skills, he couldn't form a single word.

The heat of her body infiltrated the layers of his clothing, and he got a strong sense she was staring at his mouth.

Because that's what he would've been doing if their positions had been reversed.

She continued. "We both ride that razor sharp line of being law-abiding citizens and outlaw renegades."

Rohan pulled off the ice pack.

She was close. So damn close he could see the variations of gray in her eyes. Close enough to hear the rapid intake of her breath. Close enough to lean forward a few inches and taste her glossy, red lip balm.

Into her arms.

Into her very essence.

He lifted his head and a dagger of pain drove through his right eye, straight through his skull. "Dammit," he hissed, fighting a wave of headache-induced nausea.

"Close your eyes," she said in a soft voice, as if speaking in a normal tone might shatter him. The cool bag returned to cover his damaged face. "Just stay there for a few more minutes."

He swallowed. "Thank you, but I need to get to Atlanta."

"Can't one of your brothers go instead?"

"One of the pint-sized bouncers?"

If it didn't hurt so much, he would've smiled. Unable to help himself, he'd watched the whole exchange through his video feed. For as long as he lived, he would never forget

Cruz's and Phin's shocked expressions as she and Sadie strode away.

"Are they really upset with me?" she asked.

He shrugged. "Knowing those two, you probably elevated yourself on their likability scale."

"That's messed up."

"That's being a Blackwell." He yawned. "They can't go to Georgia. They're tied up with other things."

"A few minutes of quiet won't kill your schedule."

"Saturday is fast-approaching. Every hour counts."

"What's in Atlanta?"

"Not what." His eyes drifted shut. "Who."

"*Who's* in Atlanta?"

"Bobby's art dealer."

"Do you have a name?"

"Killian Byrne."

A heavy silence fell between them. One Rohan wanted to explore, but fatigue finally took hold, and his thoughts scattered like startled cats every time he reached for them.

"I'm coming with you," he heard her say, as if from a distance.

He shook his head and winced. "Your painting."

"I'm coming," she insisted.

The thought of being in a vehicle with her for hours calmed his mind. She would be with him. Right beside him. Safe.

At some point, his hand had moved from his stomach to her knee, where it rested against his thigh. He gave it a squeeze in acknowledgment before giving in to the relief of oblivion.

22

THIRTY MINUTES INTO THEIR DRIVE TO ATLANTA, FBI SPECIAL
Agent Asher "Cameron" Blackwell called.

"Hey," Rohan said, "I'm in the car with Angelena
Kamber, the copyist. Is it okay if I keep you on speaker?"

Lena dragged her attention from the winding state
highway to glance at her traveling companion in the
passenger seat. The restorative nap, cold compress, and two
white pills had done wonders to reduce the swelling around
his nose. Not much could be done about the bruising near
the corners of his eyes.

"Speaker is fine," Ash said. "Sorry, bro, but I don't have
great news for you."

"Let me have it."

"None of the local authorities I've contacted have heard
rumor of the stolen Catawnee."

Rohan shared a look with her. "Okay, thanks for checking. We're headed to Atlanta to follow up on a lead we got
from the thief."

"The thief?"

Rohan winced, as if he'd said too much or revealed

something he shouldn't have. "Yeah, a machine operator living in Steele Ridge."

"Where is he now?"

"The sheriff's holding cell."

"What story did you tell Maggie?"

"An anonymous caller tipped off the sheriff's office about the thief's stash of drugs."

"Risky."

"Only if Bobby opens his big-ass mouth."

"If I wasn't so damn busy right now, bro, I'd be asking a helluva lot more questions."

The skin around Rohan's jaw tightened. "I'm on information lockdown."

"What the hell does Zeke think I'm going to do? Turn your asses in? Take over your recovery?" Ash sighed. "Never mind. It's best you stay out of it. Just do me a favor."

"Name it."

"Stay safe."

"Always." Rohan disconnected the call.

"Trouble between your brothers?"

He snorted. "Does shit cling to your shoe?"

Questions bubbled on the end of her tongue. Generally, she stayed clear of domestic issues. It was rarely one person's fault, and untangling decades of familial baggage never ended well. So she surprised herself by asking, "Want to talk about it?"

His gaze raked over her features. "Not really. They're adults. They'll figure it out. Eventually."

"But not before giving everyone in the family gray hair?"

He laughed. "Knowing those two chuckleheads, they won't resolve their issue until the ER is filled with Blackwells suffering ulcers."

"I always imagined what it would be like to have a brother or sister."

"You were an only child?"

Stupid, stupid, stupid.

She knew better than to crack open the door to her past. But she found herself answering him, despite years of conditioning.

"Yes."

"Are your parents still alive?"

Lena's hands gripped the padded leather steering wheel. "No."

He turned to her. No doubt assessing how much the admission had cost her. "I'm sorry."

"I barely remember them." An image of a much smaller version of herself being rushed away in the arms of a stranger, her tear-clogged eyes riveted on two bodies slumped inside a vehicle.

Flames.

Screams.

Tears blurring her eyes—

The Verge's tires bounced over the rumble strips at the edge of the road. Lena jerked the steering wheel to the left, forcing the vehicle back in their lane.

"Do you need a break?" Rohan asked.

"Got caught up in my thoughts." She sent him a sideways glance. "I'm not letting you drive, so stop trying to worm your way behind the wheel."

"I'm not good at being idle."

"You should try meditation." She tapped her right temple. "Might slow things down upstairs."

"I do. Every morning."

"Do you work with someone? Or are you practicing on your own?"

"Grams has offered, but I—"

She snort-laughed. "Men are so predictably male."

"Meaning?"

Lena used her baby voice. "If I show weakness, people won't think I'm manly enough."

"Not the reason I don't accept."

"A revelation. I'm on tenterhooks."

His eyes narrowed. "Part of the journey to mastering meditation is conquering the mind's tendency to focus on everything and nothing. No one can help me with that part."

"First off, no one ever masters meditation. It's like most forms of art. They take a lifetime to perfect, yet there will always be imperfection."

"And?"

So much disgruntlement in that one word.

"Not everyone can or should take the journey alone."

Lena let the following silence settle around her as she leaned into each curve of the dark, winding road. She tried not to read too much into her own words. Tried not to think about all the lonely years behind her or the ones stretching out before her.

"I apologize if I brought up a difficult topic earlier," he said. "My curiosity chip is always running."

"Probably why you're such a good white hat."

He gave her a half smile. "Someone's been googling."

"You're not the only one who can background check."

He studied her for a long, pulse-quickening moment. Lena kept her attention on the road. Her body loose.

"Your background is curiously blank prior to age fifteen."

Years of redirecting conversations away from her personal life kicked in. "I moved around a lot after my parents' deaths."

"Did you live in caves?"

"What?"

"Wear deer skins? Communicate by drawing stick figures in the dirt?"

Realizing where he was going, she attempted to throw him off-balance. "As a matter of fact, we did. Pro tip: green leaves make better toilet paper than brown ones."

He angled his body toward her. Leaned in.

Her muscles coiled.

"Because that's what it would take to keep me from finding you." He paused. "That, or witness protection program."

23

IF ROHAN HADN'T BEEN WATCHING, HE WOULD HAVE MISSED the catch in Lena's breath.

"When did you enter WITSEC?" he asked in a quiet voice.

"For a computer geek, you have an active imagination."

"Gaming, remember? There's more to the story than shooting shit up." He considered her a moment. "How did your parents die?"

"Car accident."

"What kind of accident?"

She squinted her eyes as if looking into a murky crystal ball for fragments of her past. The car drifted to the right, and Rohan reached over and fingered the steering wheel, adding pressure until the vehicle glided into the safety zone again.

The adjustment snapped her back to the present. "I don't like talking about that time of my life."

"Why not?"

"None of your damn business."

"While we're working together, everything about you is my business."

"You're a delusional, virus-trafficking, egomaniac if you think I'm going to let you nose around into every corner of my life—"

The dashboard blacked out, and the Verge's engine powered down.

Darkness engulfed them.

For a heart-freezing moment, Rohan couldn't see anything. Not even the pavement.

"What happened?" Lena asked, panicked.

"Did you touch anything?"

"No." The bones in Lena's hand stood out as she gripped the wheel tighter and tried pumping the brake.

Thank God they'd just entered a straight stretch, but it wouldn't last long. No mountain road ever did.

Rohan blinked several times to engage his night vision. Thankful for the three-quarter moon riding the skies tonight. Shadows pulled away from each other, and he could now distinguish the road from the mountainside to their left and the cliff to their right.

"Rohan, the brake isn't working."

"There's no power."

"No power?" she all but screamed. "*Shit!*"

The road curved to the right, while gravity pulled at them, speeding up their momentum. She practically lay on the steering wheel to keep them on the road.

"Put all of your weight on the brake pedal," he ordered, and reached over to help her steer the car.

"I'm trying, but it feels like I'm pushing against a rock."

"Don't let up."

The road switched to the left and their tires crunched

against gravel as the vehicle veered toward a four-thousand-foot drop-off.

"Rohan!"

His arms strained to help keep them on the asphalt. When the road straightened again and the car slowed, he saw their best opportunity to survive this.

"To the left of the steering wheel is a control panel," he said, keeping his voice calm but precise. "Do you see it?"

Her gaze flicked down for a millisecond. "Yes."

"That's where you'll find the parking brake lever. Feel for it."

"Got it."

"When I tell you, hook your fingers beneath the lever and draw it toward you." He pointed to the right side of the road. "We're headed for that pull off." He wrapped his fingers around the door's grab handle and braced himself.

"That's not a pull off. That's a sliver of dirt."

"Now!"

She yanked on the brake lever, and the Verge came to a jarring halt.

A thank-you-Jesus silence fell around them.

"Turn on the hazards," he said over the blood pounding in his ears.

She did as instructed. "Has this ever happened before?"

With the danger behind them, he had time to think, analyze. Conclusion reached. He would fucking murder whoever had disabled his vehicle and put Lena in danger. "Come on. We need to get out of here."

"What's the plan? Stand here and wait for someone to come by?"

He checked his phone. "No service." He shoved the device into his front pocket. "Grab your bag," he said, doing the same.

"Why?"

He motioned downhill. "Hope you wore a comfortable pair of shoes."

"We're walking?"

"Unless you know how to fly."

As it happened, Lena's ankle-boots weren't ideal for downhill hiking.

"How far is the next town?" she asked, repositioning her large shoulder bag across her body.

"I'm guessing about five miles."

"You don't know?"

"Do I look like a GPS?"

"I would have thought someone like you would have memorized the route."

"Someone like me?"

"Techy. Prepared. Anal. Don't you get off on data?"

"Interesting data, maybe."

"The distance to the next town is pretty damn interesting about now, isn't it?"

"Eight."

She blinked. "Eight miles?"

"On the pain in the ass scale. You land on eight."

"Sounds like I have room for improvement."

"Damn straight."

"I'm still two points off the mark of being a full pain in the ass."

He threw her an annoyed look, but she didn't miss the slight curve at the corner of his mouth.

They fell into silence for several minutes.

"Tell me about this Bobby Balor," she said over the rhythmic slap of their soles against pavement.

"What do you want to know?"

"How'd he learn about the painting?"

"All we could get from him was that a friend overheard Palmer talking about hiring you to make a copy of *Walking Woman*. Balor learned it was worth over a million dollars and decided to make quick work of his debts."

"Friend? Sounds unlikely. There are several degrees of separation between Balor and Palmer."

"Agreed."

"He sold the painting to this Atlanta art dealer?"

"So he said."

"You don't believe him?"

"He's a criminal. Everything he says is suspect."

Lena's chest tightened. "What if his little sister has cancer and the funds from the sale would help pay her medical bills?"

"He doesn't have a sister, let alone a sick one."

"But what if he did? Would he still be a criminal in your eyes?"

"Are you feeling sorry for this guy?"

"I'm just pointing out that not every situation is black and white. As you should know."

"Why is that?"

She held her breath as she veered around a pulverized roadkill that was now little more than tufts of fur. "Based on what I've seen around the Friary, BARS will do whatever takes to recover an asset and return it to its owner." Helicopter, drone, outdoor range, mysterious building Johona hadn't wanted to talk about.

"You'd be right."

"But what if the owner you're so dedicated to serving had stolen the asset in the first place?"

A pained expression crossed his face.

"It's already happened?" When he didn't confirm, she pushed on. "What separates what you do from someone who's desperate to survive?"

"Is that why you copy other artists' work instead of filling that blank canvas with your own original?"

The question slammed into her. Tore at her insides like a ravenous wolf.

For a moment, she couldn't breathe. It was as if a vacuum had sucked out every molecule of oxygen streaming through her blood.

How had he figured out her greatest fear? Or was it a regret? Somehow, somewhere, she had lost herself in the beauty created by others.

It took her a solid minute to realize that Rohan hadn't figured out anything. His goal had been to throw her off-balance, and he'd succeeded. Because she'd allowed her insecurities to overwhelm her.

Again.

Lena eyed the extreme drop off on her right, wondering if she could maneuver herself around to his left side without raising his alarm bells.

"If you want to end me," he said, guessing the direction of her thoughts, "I'd prefer a less painful mode of death than toppling down the side of a mountain."

"Let's stick to business conversation from here on out. Deal?"

"Anything to keep your finger off the trigger."

"Back to Bobby Balor. *If* he's already sold the painting to this dealer in Atlanta, wouldn't that mean Bobby had a buyer lined up ahead of time?"

They came around a bend, and Rohan put out a hand to stay her, pointing ahead of them. Four silhouettes of various sizes stood in the middle of the road.

Spooked, they shot forward, bounding down the road, their white tails catching the moonlight as they waved side to side in order to confuse and distract. The deer continued for a while before dashing off to the left, into the forested mountainside.

Delighted to see wildlife that didn't eat people for a late-night snack, Lena grinned at Rohan. He stared at her mouth as if he'd never seen her smile before.

Maybe he hadn't.

His scrutiny made her look away. "Did Balor strike you as someone intelligent enough to pull off a heist on his own *and* have a buyer in his back pocket?"

"Not even close. Burglarizing your loft while you were there proves he's an idiot."

"But I wasn't supposed to be there, remember? You came to my loft because I was late for our meeting."

Rohan stopped. "Who knew about the meeting?"

"You, Lynette, and the rest of your crew, I presume."

"You didn't tell anyone?"

"Who would I tell?"

"Social media?"

Only a guy would ask a single woman who lived alone if she posted her schedule online. "Really?"

He cursed under his breath.

"What?"

"I'm one hundred percent certain the meeting didn't leak out of BARS."

"And if I didn't tell anyone . . ."

His eyes met hers through the gloom. "You've got a bug problem."

24

FORTY-FIVE MINUTES LATER, LENA STILL COULDN'T BRING herself to believe someone had planted a listening device in her loft or had somehow tapped her phone. First, a stalker. Then ghosts from her past haunting her. Now, this.

Why her? She didn't live in a James Bond world. She painted, she ate, she slept. Queue up boring music. Repeat.

But as absurd as it sounded, she couldn't come up with a more plausible reason for how Bobby Balor knew she was supposed to be at Triple B the morning of the burglary.

With every downward step, her toes crammed into the V-shaped toe well of her boots. God only knew what subcutaneous damage she was doing to her nails.

Besides the possibility of losing her toenails, the sliding motion hurt like hell.

To take her mind off the pain, she refocused on the bug business. An idea started to form. One too ridiculous to consider, but too credible to discount.

Where had she been the moment she'd received Lynette's call?

Halting, she lifted her phone to check her call log.

"Problem?" Rohan asked.

"Checking to see when your mom first reached out to me."

"You need this information while we're standing on a dark mountain road?"

Ignoring his sardonic comment, she scrolled through her short list of incoming calls, while trusting him to keep an eye—and ear—out for traffic. Once she found Lynette's name, she tapped the information icon.

12:22 p.m.

Lunch time.

After a bout of physical therapy for acute shoulder pain, Lena had forced herself into the habit of taking a walk midday to stretch out her muscles and give herself a mental break. She used the time to run errands, grab something to eat, or browse the library's shelves.

Lena pushed through her memories, searching for that day, that conversation, that time.

12:22

12:22

12:22

A blurry image of her sitting on a barstool, waiting for Grady, Triple B's smooth-headed bartender, to deliver her to-go order surfaced. A phone call. Lynette Blackwell. A conversation. Switch to speaker phone. Check calendar. A date and time agreed upon.

All while sitting amid a busy lunch crowd.

"Dammit!"

"What's wrong?"

"I set up the meeting with Lynette while waiting for my lunch order at Triple B."

Rohan motioned for them to continue walking. "Someone who knew you, or knew of you, with a nefarious mindset, overheard your conversation, set up a heist and a buyer in . . . how many days?"

She glanced down at her phone. "Two."

"Stretches my belief of what's possible." He switched his duffel bag to the other hand. "However, if Balor was already watching you, waiting for an opportunity to snatch a painting, I suppose he could've pulled it off."

Watching you.

Lena's steps slowed as she recalled the tingling sensation at the base of her neck when she walked home from the art store.

"What's going on in that head of yours?" Rohan asked, stopping again.

The art store incident happened after the burglary. Why would Balor stalk her once he had the painting? Had he been gearing up to hit her loft again?

She rubbed at the pressure building in her temple. It had been years since she'd felt this unnerving helplessness. She didn't like it.

Not one whit.

Rohan tucked her hair behind her ear, startling her. "Headache?"

"It's a lot to think about."

"I'll help you figure out what's going on. We'll eliminate the possibilities, one by one."

His reassurance loosened the tight knot of uncertainty in her stomach. "I want to speak with Bobby Balor."

"When we get back. Right now, let's keep our focus on Killian Byrne. Get the painting from him and/or squeeze whatever intelligence we can out of him."

She nodded her acknowledgment.

Searching for a new topic of discussion, she asked, "How do you like working for the family business?"

He raised a brow. "Didn't we agree to avoid personal questions?"

"I asked about your family business."

His brow hitched higher.

"Consider it a gray area."

He shook his head, but amusement curled at the corner of his eyes.

"Most of the time, I like it. Can't beat the commute and I can set my own hours." He looked up the road as if searching for his feelings on the matter. "I care about BARS's success much more than I would some other corporation, and leadership respects my opinion." He sent her an aggrieved look. "Most of the time."

"Why do you suppose they didn't follow your recommendation regarding me?"

"I imagine they thought my judgment was compromised."

"Was it?"

"No." His voice lowered. "Maybe."

Despite the warning bells ringing up and down her spine, Lena asked, "You're not sure?"

"I'm sure you're hiding something and I'm sure it's going to come back to take a chunk out of BARS's collective ass."

Lena stiffened, feeling the truth in his words.

"But what I'm not sure about." He cut the distance between them. "What I can't seem to stop wondering about," his attention dipped to her mouth, "is if your lips taste as good as they look."

Out of instinct, Lena sucked in her bottom lip, eliciting a growl from Rohan.

By the time she released her lip, he was mere inches away. His broad chest filled her vision and his scent wrapped around her.

"Tell me this is a bad idea," he whispered, dropping his bag.

"This is a bad idea."

"Tell me to step away."

She opened her mouth, but no words of command emerged.

His hand slid around the side of her neck, tilting her head back even farther. "Tell me, Lena."

"I want to," she whispered, "but I can't."

It was all the permission he needed.

25

Rohan cursed his idiocy all the way to Lena's mouth.

The first touch confirmed it was everything he'd imagined it would be.

Soft. Hot. Intoxicating.

He deepened the kiss. Their tongues tangled, the slick warmth sending tingles down his spine.

He wanted her. Wanted her so damn badly that he started mentally assessing places along the road where he could drag her farther into the shadows. Instead, he wrapped a hand around her waist and drew her in close. Trembled at the way her slight curves melded with his body.

A perfect fit.

Too perfect.

Too . . . distracting.

He broke off, backing away several steps. But it wasn't far enough. He could still taste her. On his lips, on his tongue.

Her scent whirled in his nostrils. A living, breathing reminder of what he couldn't have.

Of what disaster smelled like.

"This was a bad fucking idea." His hands rolled into fists

to keep from reaching for her again and finding the nearest tree.

He turned and continued down the hill. His heart thundering so loud he imagined the beat echoed off the towering mountainside. Because of this, he didn't immediately hear the truck's approach.

When the rumble of a diesel engine finally registered, the vehicle's headlights had already spotlighted Lena, who stood looking after him. With the lights behind her, he couldn't assess her expression.

But he had a fairly good idea he wouldn't be on her Christmas list this year.

He rushed back to her side as the silver truck slowed to a crawl.

"What's the plan?" she asked.

"Don't have one." He nudged her behind him and approached the open passenger side window.

"Looks like you folks had a bit of car trouble."

The driver wore a wide-brimmed Tilly hat and a pair of camo chest waders. He appeared to be in his upper thirties, solidly built, and tall, given how little headroom he had left in the cab.

The handle of a large hunting knife poked out from beneath the closed visor.

Rohan rested an elbow on the window frame. "Battery, I think."

"Dead battery on such a fancy new car?" He grinned. "Sounds like you got yourself a lemon."

"Can't argue that fact."

"I'd let you use my cell phone to call a tow, but this is a dead zone. Not gonna get any service until you hit the outskirts of town."

"How far's that?"

"About five miles."

Rohan tapped his palm against the sill and straightened. "Thank you, sir."

The driver's attention settled on Lena, lingered there for a beat too long, before sliding back to Rohan. "I gotta drive right through town to get to my place. I'd be happy to give y'all a lift."

Rohan considered the knife, the man's outdoor garb, and the trailer hitched to the back of his truck, carrying a fishing boat. He was clearly returning home after a long day trolling the shoreline of one of the many lakes in the area.

But there was something a little off about the way the guy looked at Lena. Appreciation he could understand. She was a beautiful woman.

The hunger worried him. Most men could control their baser urges, yet there were far too many who couldn't. Or simply wouldn't.

"Thanks, man, but I think we'll—"

"Be happy to accept," Lena said, stepping up beside him. "I'm Lena and this is Rohan."

The driver nodded. "Dean."

Rohan smiled at the driver. "Would you give us a moment?"

"Don't take too long. Folks drive like maniacs through here."

"I'll keep it brief." He drew Lena away a few feet. "I don't trust him."

"You seem to have trust issues in general."

"Only for people who give me good reason. He does."

"Why? Because he's hot and appears to like the look of me?"

Rohan blinked. "You think he's hot?"

She made a disgusted sound. "There's no way I can walk another five miles in these boots. My toes are killing me."

He noted the three-inch heel and narrow toe. "Why didn't you say something?"

"No sense in both of us worrying about it."

"When you've gone as far as you can, I'll carry you the rest of the way."

"Are you kidding me?"

"He has a knife."

"What angler-hunter-mountain man doesn't? I bet you have one in your front pocket."

Leatherman Skeletool. He never left the house without his multi-tool.

She smirked. "Boys and their toys."

"Hey," the driver called, watching them through the sideview mirror. "Y'all coming or not?"

"The next town is five miles away," she said, before turning back to the truck. "It'll all be over in ten minutes."

Rohan followed. His mind running through a dozen "then bad shit happened" scenarios and how he would respond to each one with nothing but a two-and-a-half-inch blade for a weapon.

Rohan followed, drawing his "boy toy" from his pocket. "This is a bad fucking idea."

LENA PRESSED AGAINST THE TRUCK'S OPEN DOOR AS ROHAN shouldered her aside and climbed into the back of the extended cab, sliding to the center of the bench.

He gave her a long, hard look before transferring his attention to Dean, whose smiling green eyes watched her climb inside.

The knife Rohan had mentioned was nowhere in sight.

Its absence both relieved her and filled her with a low hum of anxiety.

Once they were underway, Dean asked, "Where're y'all headed?"

"Atlanta," Lena said, seeing no reason to prevaricate. A-Town was a big city.

"Don't hear about too many folks going down there. Normally, those people are coming up here to escape the heat." He gave her a knowing smile. "Must be something special. An anniversary, maybe?"

Lena forced a conspiratorial grin. "I wish, but we're headed down for business."

"Well, that ain't no fun." He eased his truck and trailer through a series of sharp switchbacks with an expert hand. "I work in real estate when I'm not on the water. My daughter, Holly, had the day off from school, so I was gonna take her and her mama out on a picnic." He grew silent for a moment. "But Holly got sick and her mama didn't want me underfoot, so I hitched up my boat and made a day of it."

"Sounds like you got the best end of the deal."

He reached for his wallet lying in an open nook beneath the dashboard and fished out a small picture. "This is my girl. About two years ago."

Lena took the tattered, much-loved photo and held it beneath her phone's flashlight. A smiling girl with brown, curly hair stared back at her. She sat in a wheelchair.

The sight relieved some of the tension she'd been harboring since entering Dean's domain. A man who shared pictures of his disabled daughter to strangers wasn't likely to go on an impromptu murdering rampage.

"She seems like quite the character."

"She's that and more. Got a lot of her mama in her. Thank the Good Lord."

Lena showed the picture to Rohan, receiving nothing but a short nod in return, before handing the picture back to their driver.

"Got any kids of your own?" Dean asked, dropping his billfold back into the nook. A bold move given he had two unknowns in his vehicle.

"No, we're not—"

Lena hesitated revealing that she and Rohan weren't involved. First of all, after their explosive kiss, she wasn't sure what they were. But mostly because having a virile, knife-wielding guy—no matter his marital status—believe you were taken provided a certain amount of protection against unwanted advances.

"You're not . . . ?"

"Married."

"These days, the young and in love—or not so in love—don't need the vows to have kids."

"When—if—I have children, there will be a husband in the picture."

"He'll be a lucky man." Dean draped his left wrist over the steering wheel and tapped his thumb against the dashboard. "At your age, I bet your mama's pestering you about grandchildren. My mother-in-law was damn—excuse my French—relentless about it until we got pregnant with Holly."

Sweat broke out on Lena's palms, and she wondered how many more miles until they hit civilization. "I don't have that problem. My parents passed away many years ago."

"I'm right sorry to hear that. No little girl should have to grow up without her mama."

Emotion clenched the back of her throat, and Lena turned to her window. Studied her reflection from the dash lights, though another image, one she hadn't seen in twenty years, stared back at her.

The woman had features similar to Lena's, but sharper around the edges. The eyes hard, yet intelligent and kind. Soft hands for wiping away Lena's tears. An encouraging voice when her little girl got lost reciting the alphabet.

"Mind me asking what happened to them?" Dean's voice was gentle.

Lena swallowed, regretting her decision to accept this man's assistance. He seemed nice enough, but his prying unnerved her. She supposed this is what most people called chitchat.

Lena called it nosy.

"Lights up ahead," Rohan said, breaking his silence.

Gratitude for his intervention filled her chest, and she had a sudden urge to pepper his handsome face with kisses.

Dean waited a heartbeat as if he were expecting her to answer his question, before nodding. "You should be able to pick up a signal now."

Lena woke up her phone and noticed a new text message from Lynette.

After pulling into the nearest gas station, Dean pointed down the road. "Tough Luck Towing is a half mile that way." He hooked his thumb at an establishment across the street. "Blanche's Motel. It don't look like much, but the sheets are clean and the water is hot."

As Lena jumped out of the vehicle, a dark gray BMW pulled into the first stall in front of the Quik Mart. A sturdily built man and woman with dark, wavy hair exited the car, stretching extravagantly, as though they'd been driving for hours, before entering the convenience store.

Lena stared after them for several seconds. Something about the woman seemed familiar, but despite the blinding parking lot lights, she hadn't gotten a good look at either of their faces. Besides, she didn't know anyone who drove a Beamer.

She shrugged, used to snatches of memory hitting her at the oddest times. Turning back to the truck cab, she heard Rohan offer their savior gas money.

"Keep your money. Something tells me you're going to need it." He nodded to them both, his gaze taking in Rohan this time, then drove away. Boat trailer bouncing in his wake.

"You were right," she said. "There was something a little off with him."

"Come again? Did you say I was right?"

"Don't ruin this rare moment of like-mindedness." She peered down at her phone. "I got a text from your mom."

"Can't be good."

"Why?"

"Because I got one, too." His thumb flashed across his screen, pulling up the text.

Curious, Lena opened her messaging app and tapped on Lynette's name.

A second later, her phone went dark.

She tapped the screen to wake it up, thinking she got knocked out of her messaging app. Nothing. She hit the screen again. This time, harder.

Nothing.

"*Sonofafuckingbitch!*" Rohan exploded, right before he threw his phone across the parking lot.

26

Rohan stared at Lena's disabled phone, still processing this latest strike by the Collective.

The photo, the car, and now their phones. Fun and games? Pressure for him to return to the group? Or the beginnings of a cat-and-mouse game, where all the mice die?

"What's wrong with you?" Lena looked at him as if half of his brain had picked up and left home.

He raked shaking fingers through his hair. "The bastards disabled our phones."

She snatched her phone back and stared at the logo hovering against a black background. She tried turning it on and turning it off, everything he'd already attempted. The logo didn't move.

"Who did this?" she asked. "How did they do it?"

"It's a type of smishing—phishing via text messages. Only they weren't after our personal information. They just wanted to screw with our phones."

"They can kill my phone without me clicking a link or opening an attachment?"

He nodded. "All you have to do is bring up the message."

"But it was from your mom."

"Display name spoofing. If we could pull up the sender's information, you would see the message didn't come from Mom's phone number. Spoofing is common with email, but this is the first time I've come across it with text messages."

"Everything on my phone is gone?"

"Not gone in the sense that it's deleted, but you no longer have access."

"Can they get to the cloud?"

"Doubtful, if it was password protected."

She released a sigh of relief.

"Although," he stared at the phone in her hand, at the logo, going through his mental database.

"Although, what?"

"The phone is in a type of stasis. They could be mining it for passwords and usernames." He met her gaze. "You don't keep your login information in a notes app, do you?"

The relief melted from her features.

"Fuck," he said, feeling the weight of responsibility. He should have anticipated something like this. Should have warned her to be extra cautious.

Yet he had fallen victim to the same scam. The hacker part of his brain admired the technique for its brilliance. Opening up a text message from a familiar contact was as instinctual as blinking. No one would suspect a message from "Mom" to be anything else.

The human side of his brain silently, relentlessly flailed him for not being three steps ahead, for not preventing the attack.

"I'm sorry, Lena. I really am."

"You know who did this."

"In a manner of speaking, yes."

"What's with the ambiguity, Rohan? You either do or you don't."

"I know the players responsible, but not the individuals themselves."

"You're speaking in circles."

A harsh reply flew to the tip of his tongue, but he forced it back. His attention had snagged on the station's surveillance camera above them.

"Come on," he said.

"Where are we going?"

"To see Blanche."

As it turned out, Blanche had died a decade ago from complications of COPD, or so her daughter Ruthie, a plump, jolly, quite gossipy woman, had informed them—in excruciating detail—when she'd handed them the key to her last available room.

Rohan had to force himself not to think about the kiss he'd shared with Lena. Not when they'd entered the small room, not when he noticed the full-sized bed and no couch, not when Lena kicked off her boots, and especially not when she emerged from the bathroom wearing a form-fitting T-shirt and ass-molding running shorts.

It was going to be a long, agonizing night.

He had enough on his mind to balance at the moment. Adding thoughts of a smoking hot client's body to the list would tip the scale toward disaster. He wouldn't let that happen again.

Promising to find them some food, he'd backed away from temptation and sprinted across the street to the Quik Mart.

. . .

Rohan set two soggy-bread sandwiches and two bottles of water on the counter. "I didn't see any prepaid phones on the shelf," he said to the pimple-faced clerk.

"No, sir. Sold my last two not ten minutes ago."

Coincidence or had the Collective followed them?

He shot a glance across the street. Every nerve ending screamed at him to get back to Lena.

Turning his attention back to the clerk, he noticed the large rectangle in his front jeans pocket.

"My phone died, and I need to make a phone call." He nodded toward the kid's pocket. "I'll give you twenty bucks to use your phone so I can call my brother."

The clerk looked uncomfortable. "Uh, I don't know—"

"Forty bucks," Rohan interrupted. "Please, it's important."

With evident reluctance, the young man slid his phone from his pocket and unlocked it before handing it over.

Rohan placed the forty dollars on the counter, plus another twenty for the food. "I'm just going to step outside for some privacy. I'll be back in five to get my food."

"Don't make me call nine-one-one, sir." The clerk pocketed the two twenties, then scanned a bottle of water.

"I won't."

Once Rohan finished his call, he removed the number from the clerk's phone and returned the device. "Thank you." He collected their dinner from the counter and rushed back to the motel.

Sitting cross-legged on the bed, Lena reached for the food and drink, her dark eyes fixed on him.

"Thanks, now explain to me what's happening."

Rohan ripped off his glasses, tossed them on a night-stand near the Holy Bible, and plopped down in the most uncomfortable chair ever built.

He had thought about how this moment would play out over the past decade, but never once had he imagined sharing the darkest moment of his life with an artist, in a motel room, in the middle of nowhere.

"In my senior seminar course, my team was assigned to a budding energy bar company, owned by Troy Neff. They tasked us with building a system that would protect the company's secret recipe along with the rest of its intellectual property and assets. The seminar helped small businesses get off the ground, while giving students real-life experience."

"Interesting story, but what do energy bars have to do with someone hacking my phone?"

"Patience, Grasshopper. It will all make sense in a second."

"Grasshopper?"

"Never mind." Rohan bent forward, rested his forearms on his knees. "I got elected to the team leader position, which basically meant I got stuck doing eighty percent of the work. Not only did I have to ensure the three other students stayed motivated and liaison with the company president, I also had to keep my instructor updated, write my share of code, and check everyone else's work."

All the old frustrations bubbled in his stomach like fermenting kimchi.

"Neff's sister, Crystal, who was also an investor, attended the meetings. A month into the project, we began seeing each other."

"What'd everyone think about the new arrangement?"

He shrugged. "I didn't care. I was young and arrogant and, by that time, fed up with my teammates doing minimal work and getting the same credit as me."

"Did you talk to them about it?"

"Not in any formal, sit-down way, but they all knew I wasn't happy with their performance. Soon after the project started, one of the guys—Bruce—began subverting my directions."

"Let me guess," she said. "You were either a supreme asshole or Bruce was pouting because he didn't get the leadership position."

Ignoring her first suggestion, he said, "I voted for him to take the lead. He was smart and talented, and I sure as hell didn't want the role. Unfortunately, he was less likable."

"What happened to the sister? Did you break her heart?"

He raked a thumb over the calluses on his palm. A result of building and breaking down props in the shoot house, a large building on the property where they set up detailed scenarios for their recoveries before executing them in real-time.

"We got pretty hot and heavy, which meant spending less time with the team, less time checking their work. When they realized I'd kicked them off my coattails, they got more serious about contributing. Bruce fielded questions that came up. Everything seemed to be going great until I returned from a long weekend in the Outer Banks with Crystal."

All these years later, the memory of walking into the owner's conference room still had the power to produce sweaty palms and a racing heart.

"At our weekly check-in, I learned that not only had the company's server been breached, but the hacker had stolen the energy bar recipe and blasted it across the Internet."

Lena sucked in a breath. "Their proprietary IP was no longer a secret."

"The company was ruined, and my teammates stared at me as if I'd betrayed them. Worst of all, Mrs. Holland, my instructor and mentor, looked at me with a mixture of disappointment and empathy."

"Why empathy?"

"She knew—" He swallowed back a sudden lump that formed in his throat. "She was the one who'd encouraged me to socialize, to make more friends, to date, to do something besides write code and play video games."

"So you did," she whispered.

"My selfishness cost a good man his livelihood and my mentor retired early to take the heat off the school."

His gaze caught hers. "Know what happened to me?"

She shook her head.

"Nothing. Not a damn thing I didn't force."

"What do you mean 'force'?"

"I insisted on getting an F for the project."

"But it was your senior seminar, your last class."

Instead of walking the stage with the rest of his classmates, he'd taken the class over and received his diploma in the mail a year later.

"I paid a small price for ruining a family."

"And Crystal?"

"I broke it off."

"Why?"

"I just...couldn't any longer." He raked his right thumb against his left palm, over and over, as if he could rub away the past. "Every time I looked at her, she was a reminder of what I had done. What I had failed to do. The guilt became too much."

"Did you love her?"

"I could have, I think. Had things been different."

Lena slid off the bed and knelt before him, wrapping her warm hands around his. "It wasn't your fault."

Her simple act of compassion squeezed his heart until

he was sure not a single bead of blood moved through the damaged organ.

"The hell it wasn't. My team, the instructor, the owner—they all put their faith in me to do what I do best."

"And you did."

"You don't understand." He shot out of the chair, ripping his hands from her grip. He didn't need her empathy. Didn't deserve it. "I left them to finish the last of the project. Practically dared them to try to do it without me." He gave her a level, unfiltered look. "I knew they didn't have the collective know-how and was damn smug about it."

"Your teammates were responsible for their own actions—or lack thereof. If they didn't know how to finish the project, they should have spoken to Mrs. Holland."

"As team leader, it was my responsibility to see the project through to completion and to protect the client's assets."

"Was it? Seems like a lot of responsibility to put on the shoulders of one student."

"I could've handled it. But I failed because I allowed my dick to swim in the deep end too long."

"Don't," she said in a harsh voice. "Don't cheapen what you had with Crystal because shit happened. You're allowed to have a life."

Rohan squeezed the back of his neck, wishing he'd kept the past where it belonged. "You won't be so generous when you hear how I went from one bad decision to another."

27

LENA ROSE FROM HER KNEELING POSITION AND CROSSED HER arms to prevent herself from sliding them around Rohan's waist. The urge to press her ear against his thundering heart was so strong her hands shook.

More than a decade later, and he still hadn't forgiven himself for the stolen IP. The entire incident sounded like a perfect storm, one where no one triumphed and no one survived without deep, visceral scars.

"Rohan, please sit and finish your story. What happened next?"

After a moment's hesitation, he sat on the corner of the bed and stared at the worn-down carpet as if he watched scenes from his past being played out on the rust and black checkered pattern. "Something about the hack felt personal."

"In what way?"

"Why attack Troy Neff's company? Although things were coming together for him, his was still a small business. Hardly worth the effort. Blasting the recipe across the

Internet rather than selling it to Neff's competition or holding it for ransom smelled a lot like revenge to me."

"Let me guess, your teammate, Bruce, decided to knock you out of the game."

"Good presumption, but it wasn't Bruce."

When he remained silent for a full minute, Lena prodded, "How did you track down the hacker?"

"By becoming one."

"A hacker?"

He nodded. "I followed the thief's digital footprint to a guy named Cal Simmons. Turns out, Troy had hired him prior to partnering with the university. But their personalities didn't jive, and Cal's technical skillset had its limitations. After a few months of head-to-head combat and disappointing performance, Troy finally fired him."

"Classic disgruntled employee retaliation. If Cal's skillset sucked so badly, how did he manage to hack his way to the secret recipe?"

"He must've had help."

"Evidently, his hacker friend was only slightly better, since they failed to cover their tracks."

Rohan shrugged. "Don't know, don't care. Cal was the one who had set things in motion. I held him responsible for the attack against the Neffs."

"How much time did he serve for the cyberattack?"

"None."

"Seriously?"

"I didn't turn him in."

A note of savagery entered his voice, kicking up Lena's pulse. In an instant, she understood. An eye for an eye. What comes around goes around.

Cal Simmons had ruined the Neff family, so Rohan had responded in kind. "What did you do?"

"I tore his life apart, page by page, until there was nothing left of it but chaff." He met her eyes. "And I don't regret one damn bit of it."

Lena thought she should feel *something* for Cal Simmons's plight, but not so much as a twinge of sympathy surfaced. "Does Troy Neff know what you did?"

Rohan shook his head. "He received a sizable, anonymous donation, which he used to jumpstart a successful plant-based meal delivery service."

"I don't see what you did as being a poor decision."

"I don't regret what I did to Simmons. The bastard had it coming. What I regret, what's led us to this motel in the middle of nowhere was my decision to join the Collective."

"Why does the word *cult* immediately come to mind?"

"It was, in a way. A twenty-first-century faction of hackers from across the globe. All anonymous."

"What did they believe in? Did they have a particular ideology?"

"When the law failed or the political will was nonexistent, the Collective served out its version of justice."

"Vigilante justice?"

"That's one side of the fence."

"And the other?"

"Guardian justice."

"Sounds like a great glob of contradiction to me." Lena picked up one of the water bottles, ignoring the sandwich, and dumped the contents into her tumbler, then took a long drink. "I thought the guardian mentality believed in communication over use of force."

"By the time the Collective gets involved, a lot of talking has already taken place. Even so, we gave the target two options with their associated consequences. Some—many —choose the wrong path."

"Then what?"

"Digital apocalypse."

What she knew about Rohan and his family could fit inside a paint tube. But something told her he'd joined such a group on the strength of a young man's fury and guilt, not because he wanted to become judge, jury, and digital executioner.

"Is the Collective like the mob? You're in until death do you part?"

"Yes and no."

She dropped her chin and gave him a professorial over-the-eyeglasses-rim look. "Are we really going to do this again?"

He kneaded the muscles at the back of his neck. "I got out, and now they're letting me know they didn't agree with my decision."

"How long ago?"

"About six months."

"Are they responsible for disabling our phones?"

He nodded. "I got the first hint they'd uncovered my identity yesterday when I had to fend off a strong cyberattack against BARS."

The Verge was nothing but a computer on four wheels. Vulnerable like any other device plugged in to the Net. "Your car?"

"Seems a little too coincidental to be anything else. I should never have purchased a vehicle manufactured in this century. They're too connected, too vulnerable. I knew the Collective's reach."

"But you thought you could outwit them?"

"Maybe." His gaze caught and held hers. "Or maybe I was too attracted to her sleek lines and her intuitive interface."

Lena released a shallow breath. She couldn't get caught up in this man's hotness right now. A lot of questions were stacked up in her mind, and Rohan had the answers.

She looked toward the drab green-and-red striped curtains covering the windows. "Do they know where we are?"

"It's doubtful they know our exact location."

But not out of the question, she thought, reading his body language.

"Is this how hackers get their jollies?" she asked. "By making their targets feel helpless and alone?"

"It's one way."

"Is that why you paid cash for the room? Our credit cards are dead, too?"

"More than likely. Plus credit cards leave a digital trail."

"They're online terrorists."

"That's not how they see themselves. That's not how I saw myself."

She recalled the term he used earlier. "White hat."

"Activist."

The situation reminded her of something she read online about a group of organized hackers who'd disrupted Russia's state TV channels by broadcasting footage of the war in Ukraine.

"You're part of a hacktivist group?"

"Was."

"Do you wear a white mask while lurking in the digital shadows, collecting bits and bytes of information to use against your prey?"

He gave her a sidelong glance. "My preference leans more toward Scooby-Doo pajamas."

Lena's stomach felt like the Mystery, Inc. van was doing doughnuts inside. "How far will this prank go?"

"This wasn't a prank, Lena. Hacktivists are serious about their craft. They're some of the most tenacious people on the planet and won't stop until they achieve their goal."

"Which is?"

"My best guess? They either want me to return to the fold or they're intent on total destruction. Me, my family, our business," his voice lowered. "You."

"Me?"

"Unfortunately for you, they believe you're important to me. We've spent time together, you're staying at my family's estate, and now we're road-tripping together."

She couldn't help but wonder if a tiny part of him cared about her. Their kiss had felt real enough. But maybe he was once again slaking his curiosity.

"I've become collateral damage in a techno-geek pissing war."

"I'm sorry, Lena. This is the last thing you need to be sucked into right now."

She waved off his apology. "Tomorrow, we'll find a car rental place, and I'll continue on to Atlanta while you head back to Steele Ridge."

"Not happening."

"I'm perfectly capable of feeling out the art dealer on my own and you need to get to a computer."

"Give me some credit here. I didn't leave the Collective with blinders on. I took precautions." He glanced at his watch. "They'll hold until I can get my hands on a computer."

"Which could take hours, if not days. Who knows if the mechanic's shop will even be equipped to fix your car. It's doubtful if they have a lot of experience repairing seventy-five-thousand-dollar hacked vehicles."

"Getting a computer won't take days."

A sick feeling swirled in Lena's stomach. "How long?"

The smile he sent her was warm and sexy and knowing. Her brain lit up like a firework. "This place might be clean, but I'm not staying here beyond tomorrow."

"Agreed."

He toed off his shoes.

"What are you doing?"

"Making myself comfortable. I suggest you do the same."

Lena inventoried the furniture in the small room for the hundredth time since entering. One full-sized bed and two nightstands. A chair that looked more like a torture device. No couch. Not even a cushy carpet to lie on.

She would either have to sleep standing up or share the bed with Rohan. Since equestrian DNA didn't grace her body, she only had one true option.

Sleep beside Rohan.

Frustratingly, the idea didn't disturb her as much as it should.

Slipping beneath the covers, she rolled to face the center of the bed, not wanting to put her back to him. "Keep your hands to yourself, or I'll remove your ability to make little Rohans in the future."

When silence met her threat, she opened her left eye and found him staring down at her. A secret smile, bordering on cocky, tilted one side of his mouth.

He pulled off his shirt, revealing a broad chest and ripped abdomen.

All the saliva in her mouth disappeared as he reached for the bedside lamp and plunged them into darkness. She half expected him to call her bluff. But all he did was ease his big body onto the bed and wish her a good night.

Lena ignored the stab of disappointment and closed her

eye again. With him so close, she didn't think she could fall asleep.

Hours later, a door slammed and jolted her awake. She glanced up from where she slept on a sliver of the bed, then at the gorgeous, sleeping man who reclined against the headboard next to her.

Rohan.

His bare chest rose on even breaths. One thumb hooked around his jeans belt loop, as if to prevent his arm from dangling off the side.

Near his hip, their fingers had tangled together, and she wondered who had reached for whom. Lena tried not to think about how warm his skin felt against hers or how nice it was to wake up beside such a powerful body.

It had been a while since she'd made a physical connection with a guy, and she was grateful she hadn't strayed from her side of the bed in some nocturnal search for comfort.

Rohan cracked open an eye. "Morning."

She eased her hand away and repositioned her pillow before sitting next to him. "I forgot how inconsiderate people staying in places like this can be."

"Inconsiderate guests aren't limited to sixty-nine-dollar motels."

"I suppose you're right." She reached for her phone, then remembered it had been hacked. "What time is it?"

"Almost five." He considered her a moment. "Have you spent many nights in motels like this?"

"A few. When I was younger." She brushed her hand over the bedcover that appeared to be made out of the same fabric as the curtains. "But most of the time, a room like this didn't fit into my budget."

"What happened when you were fourteen?"

An image of Neil's pain-filled eyes and her mad dash

into the night flashed through her mind. She closed her eyes for a moment, pushing back the fear, the pain, the uncertainty that never seemed to be far away.

"I'm going to take a shower." She swung her legs off the bed and rose. "Then I'll ask Ruthie if there's a car rental place nearby."

"Still determined to ditch me, huh?"

His sleep-roughened voice slid down her spine like a velvety touch.

"Our responsibilities are pulling us in opposite directions. Not me."

Over the last two years, she'd grown used to being alone. So the reluctance digging at her insides confused her, and she shut the bathroom door with more force than necessary.

ROHAN STARED AT THE BATHROOM DOOR, LISTENED FOR THE shower to start before he scooped up Lena's oversized bag.

An arrow of guilt thunked against his chest, but didn't penetrate. She was hiding something from him. Something that might help him track down the Catawnee.

Sifting through her wallet, he found nothing but cash, credit cards, and old receipts. He bypassed clothes, feminine products, and snack bars before he came across a sketchbook. Lifting it out, he flipped it open and a small disc fell out.

He picked it up and knew immediately what he was holding. A GPS tracker.

Had the Collective planted this in her bag? Was this how they knew the perfect moment to disable his vehicle?

The water in the other room shut off, and Rohan cursed. He fanned through the sketchbook, pausing on one page before dropping it back inside. He rearranged her possessions into some semblance of order. Seconds later, a hair dryer revved up.

It would take a while to dry that beautiful mass of hair, so he continued his search. "If I were Lena, where would I hide something important to me?" he whispered.

He ran his hands over the outside of the bag, testing the leather material for anything that felt out of place. Something crackled beneath the flat bottom, and he froze. He glanced between the bathroom door and her bag. Knowing he wouldn't have another opportunity, he searched for a false bottom inside and came up empty.

Laying the bag on its side, he knelt down and eyed the stitching, looking for inconsistencies.

Nothing.

The hairdryer shut off, and his hands froze until the sound of a toothbrush against teeth reached him.

Time's up.

Frustration exploded in his head. Something was at the bottom of her purse, hidden away. There had to be an opening.

Unable to admit defeat, he pressed his fingers along the seams, feeling for the opening he couldn't see.

There, on one of the longest seams the material was slightly more raised than the other side. He manipulated it until the material finally separated enough to reveal the smallest zipper he'd ever seen.

The faucet turned on, followed by the double tap of hard plastic against porcelain.

Wasting no more time, he unzipped the secret compartment, removed its contents, and set the bag to rights again. By the time Lena appeared seconds later, Rohan stood at the window, peering through a small crack in the drapes.

The wail of a siren echoed in the distance.

He turned away from the window to find her wrapped in a damp threadbare towel. His body responded to the sleek golden flesh exposed by the narrow white barrier. The sight reminded him of the first time he'd seen her—barreling down her apartment building's stairs in nothing but a Scooby-Doo towel.

Amusement twitched at the corner of his mouth—until she strode toward her purse. His breath caught.

She hefted her bag onto her shoulder and gave him a quick glance. "Forgot my clothes."

The bathroom door shut behind her again.

Rohan released a long, shuddering exhale.

28

"Something's going on," Lena said as soon as Rohan emerged from the bathroom, twenty minutes later.

She made a valiant attempt to keep her attention on his face and not on his bare chest and feet or the area where his jeans rode low on his hips, showing off the deep grooves of his delicious abs.

She failed, miserably.

"What do you mean?" Finger-combing his hair, he joined her at the window.

Gathering herself, she pulled the curtain back a few inches. "Two cop cars and an ambulance just pulled up to the office."

He leaned in and his fresh-out-of-the-shower scent filled her nose. "I don't like the feeling of this. Did you speak with Ruthie?"

Lena nodded.

"Did she appear sick or distressed in any way?"

"She was the same as last night. Happy, helpful. Offered me some bagels." Lena angled her head for a better view.

"Maybe one of the guests had a heart attack or overdosed. Or maybe a couple's domestic dispute went haywire."

"It's possible."

A light knock at the door startled her, and she backed into Rohan's chest. He placed a reassuring hand on her shoulder before shifting to the other side window to look outside.

"It's okay." He unlocked the door and Cruz slipped inside.

On the tail of her initial surprise at seeing Rohan's brother, Lena glared at her travel partner. "You have a phone?"

He shook his head. "I paid the Quik Mart clerk forty bucks to make a call."

Lena stared him. "And I'm just now learning about this?"

"You were determined to go your own way—"

Cruz cut in. "Argue later. Right now, we need to wipe everything down and get you the hell out of here."

"What's happened?" Rohan asked.

"Someone stabbed the owner to death."

Ruthie was dead?

"I left her not ten minutes ago," Lena said.

"Someone must have called the authorities before murdering her," Rohan said, his expression grim.

Lena tried to process what was going on, but it felt like a thick steel wall blocked every avenue of logic. "Are they trying to frame us for this?"

"I wouldn't have thought they would take the game this far, but I can't rule it out."

"Who are we talking about?" Cruz asked.

"Later," Rohan said. "We need to get out of here. It's only a matter of time before the police start knocking on doors."

Rohan donned a T-shirt and stabbed his bare feet into his boots. "Did you bring everything I asked for?"

"Have I ever failed you, brother?"

"What about the Verge?"

"Already towed back to Steele Ridge."

"We accepted a ride with a local last night."

"If it becomes an issue, we'll deal with it."

"Why run?" Lena asked, following orders even as she questioned them. "Won't that make us look guilty?"

"It'll buy us time to track down who's behind this," Rohan said. "I can't do that stuck inside a police station answering a thousand questions."

Once they were ready to depart, Cruz tossed Rohan a key fob for their rental. "Black Wrangler at the east side of the building."

Rohan caught them easily. "Who's with you?"

"Neuman's hovering at the edge of the growing crowd. Gathering intel."

Rohan looked at her. "Ready?"

Questions boiled on the edge of her tongue, but she only nodded. This wasn't the time for delays.

Cruz eased open the door, checking both ways before he glanced at Rohan. "Family first."

"No exceptions."

The serious expression on Cruz's face turned mischievous when his eyes met Lena's. "He's a pain in the ass, but I love him."

Rohan made like he was going to throw the keys at Cruz's head. His brother ducked and slipped outside, a large smile on his face.

Lena lifted her bag and positioned the strap across her body, instinctively running her hand over the bottom for the familiar crackle of paper. Satisfied, she followed Rohan out of the room. They turned left where Cruz had turned right.

Taking advantage of the predawn shadows, they stayed close to the building. Lena expected to hear shouts for them to stop at any second, but the only thing she heard was the low hum of voices and the staticky chirp of radios.

But that didn't stop Lena's pulse from warping through her veins. She chanced a glance around and noted several vehicles in the parking lot, including a silver truck that looked like the one Dean had been driving last night, except this one didn't appear to have a trailer attached.

Her steps slowed. The morning gloom obscured the interior of the vehicle's cab. She couldn't tell if it was empty or if someone sat inside, watching them escape.

The situation had that kind of vibe.

"Lena, hurry up." Rohan motioned to her from the corner of the building. His hand made a flicking motion, as if he'd thrown something. Whatever it was disappeared in the low light.

Shrugging, she rushed forward and jumped into the passenger side of the Wrangler as Rohan slid behind the wheel.

Turning the automatic lights off, he started the engine, put it in drive, and let the vehicle coast toward the back of the building.

Once again, Lena held her breath, listening for signs of pursuit. This time, she did look behind her.

Unease gripped the walls of her chest.

No uniformed officers chased after them.

No lights and sirens.

No silver truck.

Forty minutes later, they crossed the border into Georgia

and stopped at the Valley Café in Dillard for breakfast and Wi-Fi.

Cruz had not only come through for them with a vehicle, but the back of the Wrangler contained a change of clothes, a wad of cash, new phones, and a laptop.

To her immense relief, all her business files were still on the cloud. The moment she could tap into a secure network, she would begin the painful process of changing her passwords. She'd already notified her bank and credit card companies.

Sweet Mary, she wished hackers would focus their energies toward something more productive like locating missing kids or tracking down serial killers. Wouldn't that be more rewarding than terrorizing strangers?

While she downed a serving of eggs Benedict, Rohan alternately pounded away at the keyboard and ate a stack of pancakes like slices of pizza.

"Aren't you concerned about security?" Even she knew free public Wi-Fi wasn't safe.

"I'm using a double VPN."

"English, please."

"A virtual private network." He continued to type as he spoke. "The information is encrypted, twice, and my IP address is masked. The extra layer of security also protects against a brute-force attack." He looked around, no doubt noting that most of the customers sported gray hair and rounded middles. "Might be overkill, but I've underestimated my foe one time too many."

Lena pulled out the sketchbook she kept in her bag, frowning when she noticed it was opened to a drawing she'd done of Rohan a few nights ago when she couldn't sleep. She was always careful about closing the sketchbook to preserve the drawings inside.

She glanced at Rohan whose gaze remained fixed on his screen. Had he searched her bag? The thought didn't set well for a multitude of reasons.

Then terror set in.

Keeping her breathing steady, she walked her fingers along the bottom of her bag again and pressed the tips into the pliable material until she felt the crinkle of paper. Relief washed over her, and she cursed the part of her brain that liked to scare the shit out of her.

She had simply forgotten to close her sketchbook. The end.

Flipping to a new sheet of paper, she let her lead pencil fly. The routine calmed her nerves better than any five-hundred-dollar-a-day spa. By the time Rohan finished, Lena had filled three pages with faces she'd come into contact with over the past week.

Rohan paid the bill with the cash Cruz had left them, and they were back on the road in minutes.

Two hours later, they strode into Killian Byrne's art gallery, and excitement added an extra buoyancy to her step.

Roaming along the walls, viewing the artworks, analyzing the lighting—it all soothed her soul. Then an image of the blank canvas sitting inside her cabin surfed through her mind, dampening her enthusiasm and reminding her of what she could never have, never achieve.

"I'll search for Byrne on this floor," she said, needing some alone time. "You take the second."

"Or I could flag down a staff member and have him brought to us."

"Are you really going to deprive me of this opportunity to peruse the gallery?"

On the drive down, Rohan had gone through a laundry list of facts about the art collector and his gallery. The forty-thousand-square-foot building housed the largest collection of art from Irish artisans in the U.S.

Byrne had traveled the world in search of emerging artists of Irish descent, looking for unique pieces to add to his collection. Which made his interest in the Catawnee curious.

"If you see him," Rohan said in a tone that conveyed his displeasure at splitting up, "text me. Otherwise, we'll meet back here in fifteen minutes."

A quarter hour wouldn't be enough time to explore the entire lower level. She opened her mouth to tell him so, but he cut her off.

"Fifteen minutes, Lena. This is a business trip, not pleasure. We'll come back another time to roam the gallery."

"*We* will?"

He set his jaw and strode off.

Pleasure pushed aside some of her unease at the realization Rohan imagined spending time with her beyond their business relationship.

The notion shouldn't make her want to run after him and fling her arms and legs around his body like a chimpanzee. It should put her feet in motion, not stopping until a thousand miles separated them.

"I remember when you used to look at me that way," a warm, familiar voice said near her ear.

Startled, Lena turned and stared into the pure blue eyes of the first man—the only man—she had ever loved.

29

THE MOMENT ROHAN REACHED THE SECOND FLOOR, HE flagged down a petite, pixie-haired attendant, wearing a sharp black business suit and six-inch hot pink heels.

"Good morning," he said, channeling his inner Phin. "Could you tell me if Mr. Byrne is available?"

"Mr. Byrne's schedule is . . . irregular. He pops in and out, as he wishes."

"Would you see if he has time to speak with me?"

"You are?"

"Rohan Blackwell."

She eyed him as if trying to determine whether he merited a face-to-face with her employer. When her expression turned sympathetic, he knew he hadn't made the cut.

"I'm sorry, but Mr. Byrne is quite busy. It would be best if you called and made an appointment."

"All I need is five minutes of his time."

"The gallery's number is on our website." She teetered off.

Rohan set his jaw and made a pass through the second floor on the chance Busy Byrne might make an appearance.

When no art dealer surfaced, he sat down on a wavy white bench that he hoped was for resting and not for viewing.

He would give Lena the full quarter hour. She deserved it after the harrowing events of the past twelve hours.

Opening his messenger bag, he pushed past the laptop to get to the side pouch where he'd stashed the items he'd pilfered from Lena's bag. Guilt stabbed at his chest again. This time, it didn't bounce off. It slid between his ribs and pierced his black heart.

A better man wouldn't look inside the protective pouch. He would give it back to Lena and ask for her forgiveness. Or, if he couldn't quite muster complete goodness, he would return it to her bag.

But Rohan was a hacker, with the requisite curiosity and compulsion to unearth information. He was also a Blackwell and he couldn't quite set aside the fact that Lena had appeared in his life at the same time the Collective had struck.

Could she be hiding more than her past?

He removed the plastic cosmetic bag and unzipped it. Drew out the first thing his fingers touched. A thick folded piece of paper with a downy texture, indicating it had been handled many times.

With great care, he unfolded the sheet and stared.

It wasn't a letter, but a sketch. A good sketch. A promising sketch.

A sketch by a young hand.

In the foreground, a doe and her twin fawns frolicked through a meadow of wildflowers against the backdrop of rolling mountains. At the top, in imperfect letters, read, "Best Trip Ever." The signature at the bottom read, *Angela Jones.*

Why would Lena carry this around like a treasure? Was Angela a childhood friend? Someone she'd lost? Could this be a link to Lena's missing past?

The second item was a four-by-six photo inside a zippered plastic bag. A white multigenerational family stared back at the camera. Based on the outdoor environment and balloons in the background, he guessed the picture had been taken at a backyard birthday party.

Since none of them, not even the toddler, had brown skin, he assumed this wasn't Lena's family. Who were they? And why were they important to Lena?

Could they be her adopted family?

Setting the picture aside, he reached for the final item, a folded handkerchief.

Inside the brightly colored cloth, he found a teardrop-shaped gold pendant about the size of a quarter. The loop at the top signaled that it had once been part of, or made for, a necklace.

On the back was a symbol. One he didn't recognize.

He took out his phone and snapped a picture, front and back, of each item before carefully returning them to Lena's pouch.

He rubbed his finger over the colorful bag.

"Who are you, Lena Kamber?"

30

XANDER DOUGLAS WAS KILLIAN BYRNE.

Lena would have liked to pretend the revelation surprised her, but she couldn't. On a subconscious level her mind must have been working the angles, calculating the odds, because crossing paths with her former best friend and lover again seemed inevitable.

"You've done well for yourself, Xander," Lena said, as they strolled by several paintings in the art nouveau style.

"As have you." His southern accent now masked behind an Irish burr he'd adopted for his new persona. "Killian, if you please. Best not to confuse the hired help."

"Speaking of confusion." She turned to face him. "Why did you steal my painting?"

"Steal? Look around you, darling. I have no need to steal anything."

"Nor do you peddle anything besides Irish artwork. So why take a Catawnee?"

"I don't know where you got your intel, but your painting isn't here."

"Because you've already moved it?"

"You're relentless, Lena." He gazed at her as if everything about her delighted him. "It's one of the qualities I've always adored about you. A quality that made you an excellent forger. But a quality that makes you a pain in the ass at this precise moment."

"You really shouldn't have communicated with Bobby Balor through email. Quite sloppy of you. Simon would be quite disappointed."

"A perpetual state for him, when it came to me. Or Izzy. Or the rest of the gang." His voice took on an edge. "Not you, though. You were the sole benefactress of his attention, his talent, and his—"

"What do you want?" she interrupted, not wanting to rehash old arguments. Pure willpower kept her attention centered on the man before her and not scanning the area for Rohan. The last thing she wanted was for him to catch her and Xander in an intimate tête-à-tête.

"Want?"

"I don't have time for your games. Tell me what you want in exchange for the Catawnee and let's be done with this."

"Afraid your new lover might see us together? Would he be jealous?" His voice hardened. "Or are the two of you just fuckmates?"

"He's not my lover," she bit out.

"Yet. You have an appetite that cannot be suppressed for long—"

"Xander, shut up."

A smile spread across his handsome face. "He doesn't know about your past."

The icicle growing in the pit of her stomach blossomed into a full-fledged stalagmite.

She took a step toward him. "And it's going to stay that way."

He held up his hands as if to ward her off. "Of course, Angel."

She ignored his term of endearment. It used to melt her bones—right into his bed. Now it just pissed her off.

"You created this elaborate scheme to get me here, so cut the crap and tell me what you want."

His blue gaze traveled over her features, down her torso, and along her hips before making the slow trip back up to her eyes.

What he'd intended as an erotic suggestion made her skin crawl. Quite the opposite response than when Rohan's eyes lingered on her longer than was appropriate for colleagues.

"You give me far too much credit, Angel," he said. "But I've never been able to pass up a golden opportunity."

"Xander—"

"A painting for a painting."

She frowned. "A paint—" Then she understood. "No, I don't do that kind of work anymore."

"Don't kid yourself, Angel. What you do as a copyist is only one lie away from how you spent your youth."

She thought of the blank canvas in her cabin and the copy of the Catawnee sitting next to it and felt the truth of his words.

"Where is the Catawnee?"

He considered her for a long moment. "Someplace close. You have my word that it will stay there until you deliver."

She wanted to snort, to tell him that her paintbrush was worth more than his word.

But despite Xander's failings, he had never flat-out lied to her.

Betrayed her, yes.

Lied to her, no.

"What painting am I . . . copying?"

"*The Fountain* by John Singer Sargent."

"A transition piece?"

He smiled. "From 1907."

Many art experts considered Sargent as one of the finest portrait painters of his generation. He not only captured his model's likeness with an accuracy that could bring tears to a viewer's eyes, but he infused their essence into every brush stroke. Literally bringing the portrait to life for a single moment in time.

Lena recalled when she'd first viewed Lady Agnew of Lochnaw's portrait. Sargent's mastery made her believe the young barrister's wife had been on the cusp of an action during their session. Maybe she'd been about to ask for a glass of wine or rush off to her next engagement.

But after years of painting portraits, Sargent had stopped doing formal sittings and began exploring watercolors, landscapes, and people in their everyday lives. Many considered *The Fountain* as his transition piece to plein air painting, which captured a balance of portraiture and natural setting.

Not in a thousand years could she do justice to a John Singer Sargent.

"Are you out of your damn mind?" she asked.

"Not even a little."

"Has anyone ever successfully replicated his work?"

"Don't tell me Angelena Kamber is afraid to take a crack at a Sargent."

A part of her welcomed the challenge. The thought of succeeding where so many others had failed excited her, made her hand itch to get started, but the logical part of her mind—no, the emotional part—knew she would fail like all the others.

However, the survivalist in her sealed the deal. "Once I deliver my current commissions, I'll get started."

He shook his head. "Sorry, Angel. I need the painting ASAP. I have a studio stocked full of supplies."

She still needed to complete *Woman Walking* and deliver the painting by Saturday. No way could she paint a Sargent *and* finish the Catawnee in the same time frame. The Sargent alone would require two weeks to do it justice. "Your timeline is impossible."

"As I recall, you always did your best work under pressure."

31

Rohan returned to the main floor, hoping Lena had had better luck at locating the art dealer than he did.

"Byrne's a bust," she said, whizzing past him and slamming through the gallery's front doors.

Rohan followed. "Wait a second. What do you mean he's a bust?"

"He's off looking for his next masterpiece."

Why hadn't the upstairs attendant used Byrne's acquisitions trip as a viable excuse to get rid of him? She seemed to believe he'd be making an appearance today.

Lena tapped Wrangler's tailgate. A silent request for him to unlock it. When he did, she started pulling out her belongings.

"What are you doing?"

"Checking into a hotel while I wait for the art dealer to return."

"When will that be?"

"Friday."

"Cutting it close, don't you think?"

"I don't have a choice, do I? Byrne holds the key to getting the painting back."

"What about the Caravaggio?"

"I'll get back to it on Sunday."

Rohan rubbed his temple while he worked through a plan. "Okay, we'll hole up here until Byrne returns. I'll let Zeke know about the delay with the Caravaggio."

"I can handle Byrne on my own. There's no need for you to stay."

"I'm not leaving you here to question the art dealer on your own. That's what you're paying us for, remember?"

"My contract with BARS is done. I hired your company to find the Catawnee and you have. I can take it from here."

Something was off. On every level. Yet Rohan couldn't decide what had his pulse racing more—the realization that Lena was keeping something from him, again, or the fact he wasn't invited to her sleepover.

"You hired BARS to recover the Catawnee. My job isn't done until the painting is back in your possession."

"Your job is done when I say it is." She twisted her wrist, checking an imaginary watch. "Which is now."

Anger boiled his blood. "You know nothing about this Byrne guy. You start snooping around and asking questions, he might take extreme measures to protect his investment."

"A scenario that might play out whether you're here or not."

"I have a set of unique skills to protect you."

"What are you going to do? Bash him over the head with your keyboard, then tie him up with a power cord?"

Rohan forced back his instinctive response. She knew nothing about the special training he and his brothers went through to ensure each recovery was a success. A secret few knew about outside the family.

"Go home, Rohan," she said in a quiet voice. "Protect your family from the Collective."

He stepped closer, placing a hand on the laptop inside his messenger bag. "I have everything I need to do battle right here."

She seemed to sway toward him, prompting him to place a hand against her cheek. Anger still simmered there, just beneath the surface.

"Let me stay." He didn't recognize the low, urgent quality of his voice. "We'll figure this out together."

She squeezed her eyes shut for an aching moment. When she opened them again, the softness he'd imagined seeing there was gone.

"This thing you think is growing between us is nothing more than a distraction." She stepped away. "Something neither of us can afford right now. Go home, Rohan." She strode away with all the leisure of a window shopper.

Distraction.

Yeah.

Right.

Rohan tapped on a name in his cell's favorites list. Waited for the call to connect.

"What's up," Zeke asked.

"I need your help."

32

AFTER THE THIRD GROWL FROM HER HOLLOW STOMACH, LENA
set down her paintbrush and rubbed at her gritty eyes with
the heel of her hand.

Lifting her head, she scanned Xander's studio for her
phone, finding it on the white, squat-back leather couch.

As she'd done a thousand times since fleeing Blanche's
Motel, she scrolled through the local news for information
on Ruthie's death. Other than the initial report of officials
vowing to bring her murderer to justice, the web had been
silent.

Lena rubbed her temple, trying to puzzle out the reason
behind Ruthie's death. Was it related to the break-in at her
apartment or an isolated incident?

The police had been on-site with lightning speed. That
was unheard-of in rural areas, adding weight to her suspicion that it might be premeditated murder.

Her stomach ripped off another reminder, and Lena
decided it was time to feed the machine. Italian? Sushi?
Pizza? Indian?

A big bowl of linguini puttanesca didn't sound too bad.

But not as good as a stack of savory samosas. Her mouth watered at the mere thought of sinking her teeth into the pastry's crispy outer shell and all that warm, potato-y goodness and explosion of spices hitting her tongue.

Definitely Indian tonight.

While she waited for the browser to load the nearby eateries, Lena's skin prickled.

She'd had the feeling several times throughout the day, but no amount of searching the building across the street had uncovered anyone with a spyglass watching her. Nor had she located hidden cameras inside Xander's studio.

Once, she'd caught a blur of movement near the balcony. But with her being five stories aboveground the most likely culprit was a pigeon.

First Steele Ridge and now Atlanta.

Paranoia or a sixth sense?

If the studio had drapes, she would've closed them, despite what it would have done to her natural lighting.

Especially now.

The more the sun set, the more prominent her reflection became in the windows. A sense of vulnerability and eeriness tangled in her stomach.

Her thumb raked through nearby dining options. Best of India Cuisine was only a half mile away. Perfect.

Palmer's deadline was fast-approaching, and she still had so much more to do on *The Fountain*. She forced back the panic.

Eat first.

Paint later.

She pulled up her ride-sharing app and typed in her destination. Before she could hit Select, a knock sounded at the door.

Only one person knew she was here. Xander. And she'd

made it clear to him at lunchtime that she was here to work, not reminisce.

Maybe one of Xander's friends saw the light on and decided to drop by. She blew out an exhausted breath, not in the mood to engage with other humans.

Unless the human was Rohan. But he was long gone. She'd made sure of it.

Even though she'd done some questionable and, at times, downright unethical, things to survive since she'd fled Neil's house all those years ago, she had few regrets.

But she regretted her parting words to Rohan. He'd flinched as if she'd sliced his chest open. In a way, she had. She'd taken something he'd told her in confidence and thrown it at him like a weapon.

For her, it had been a shield. She wouldn't allow herself to bond with someone again.

It was too dangerous.

Another knock. This one harder. Irritated.

The door handle rattled, and Lena was glad she'd flipped the lock and dead bolt after shooing away Xander earlier.

As quietly as she could, she moved toward the door. Her pulse pounding through her veins like an ancient drum. She pressed her ear to the barrier in an idiotic attempt to divine who was on the other side.

Silence.

"Dammit, Lena," Xander said a heartbeat later. "Open up, or I'll feed this pasta to the rats in the alleyway."

Pasta. She hoped it had big fat meatballs and red sauce.

And pickles.

She loved eating pickles with her marinara.

As soon as she opened the door, he pushed inside. His hands were empty.

She checked the hallway. No carryout bags.

"Where's my food?"

"I'll treat you to dinner after I see your progress."

Her fingers rolled into fists, and she indulged in a mental bout of boxing. She laid him out in two seconds flat.

"I was right to pick you for this job." He admired her canvas as if he observed a Rembrandt in progress. "As much as I hate to admit it, your skill is a league above my own."

More like ten leagues, but Lena kept her assessment to herself. Xander's skill was adequate enough to fool the untrained eye, which made up ninety-eight percent of the population.

"Your originals sell well enough," she said.

"Unbelievably well." He sent her a mischievous smile, the one that had always had the power to melt the icicles around her heart. "Street rats to legitimate entrepreneurs. Who would have guessed three kids randomly plucked off the streets would have our level of success? Not Simon."

Simon's selection hadn't been completely random. Unlike some of the homeless living in Pritchard Park, she, Xander, and Izzy had set up a small business of drawing caricatures of tourists with popular landmarks in the background like Biltmore House, Tupelo Honey Café, Blue Ridge Mountains, or Malaprop's Bookstore. Whatever the tourists wanted to help commemorate their time in Asheville.

One of them would draw, while the other two carried caricatures of themselves around downtown. People would inevitably ask, "Hey, where'd you get that done?"

In the beginning, Lena had done most of the drawings. She'd been sketching her whole life. It was the one thing she didn't have to leave behind. Her burgeoning talent had traveled with her from one new town to the next.

Eventually, Xander and Izzy had tired of their pandering roles and talked Lena into giving them drawing lessons. She worried they would want to work with the tourists before they were ready. But they both recognized they had to create a quality product or the customer wouldn't fork over the twenty bucks.

Which would've killed their budding business.

On busy days, they had sat behind her and drawn their own caricatures. On rainy days, Xander had roamed local art galleries and Izzy made jewelry.

Cheap beaded stuff at first, then as their enterprise grew, Izzy transitioned into sterling silver. As it turned out, she made better bling than caricatures and Xander slowly became an expert on everything from the Renaissance masters to emerging techniques.

Lena had spent her free time painting. Anything and everything. A bird's nest, a storefront, a distant mountain peak. She played with colors and textures and light.

Simon had watched all of this unfold. Had observed them for two years, hustling nonstop through the tourist season and scrounging their way through the off-season.

His selection had been far from random. It had been strategic.

And thank the mountains for it.

"If your business is rocking," Lena asked, unable to tamp down her curiosity, "why do this?" She pointed to her forgery-in-progress.

"More."

She raised a brow.

"I have expenses. The gallery, this studio, my penthouse condo downtown, a flat in Dublin, plus I just signed a lease for a new gallery in New York City."

"New York? Aren't you spreading yourself a bit thin?"

"Only until the new gallery gets established." A soft look entered his eyes. "You've always been content with just enough. Such an existence would wither my soul."

Maybe when she was younger, but not as an adult. However, the difference between her and Xander was that she had abandoned the criminal side of her old life.

Until now.

"I saw Izzy the other day," she said, monitoring his features. "She asked about you."

Surprise flickered before his expression soured.

She had never quite understood the two. When Lena had finally given in to Xander's relentless pursuit of her, Izzy had grown distant and angry. A year later, Izzy had set her sights on Xander. Pursued him in the same relentless way he had Lena.

But Xander hadn't held out for years, as Lena had. His love for her had kept him strong for nine whole days. And Izzy had detached her tentacles from him twelve hours later.

Turned out, Izzy had been right. She should have resisted Xander.

"Don't mention her name in my hearing," he said.

"It's been two years, Xander. Let it go. You'll be much happier."

His expression hardened. "Like you let it go?"

"I did."

"Then why don't you ever call me back? Why didn't you accept my invitation to the gallery's grand opening?"

"Because I've put that time of my life behind me."

"Including me?"

"Especially you."

He took a step forward. "We had a lot of good times, didn't we?"

Keeping her feet planted, she said, "Yeah, we did."

Another step closer. "Why do you want to forget everything?"

Forget me, his eyes asked.

"I never wanted that life. Never wanted to be a forger or street thief. I did those things to survive. To get through a night without food, to get through a winter with minimal shelter." She lifted her chin, deepened their visual connection. "Now I have everything I need." Except someone to fill the loneliness. "I don't need to remember those times."

His beautiful eyes went flat and he stepped back.

"I have one thing you need from me, sweet Lena. The Catawnee. Finish what you started, or I'll sell it on the black market and you'll never see it again."

He stormed out.

Her stomach growled.

"Guess that means I need to get my own dinner."

Across the studio, her work-in-progress drew her eye. The lighting wasn't quite right on the fountain's waterspout. She picked up her paintbrush.

33

"*Two minutes to insertion,*" Cruz said through Rohan's headset. His brother's attention remained focused on the cockpit's control panel.

Wind barreled through the helicopter's cabin, forcing Rohan to keep his feet braced apart as he stood. "Copy." He met Neuman's eye, and the new recruit nodded his readiness for his first operational fast rope.

Liv clutched a handle above her head and gave him a thumbs-up. With Zeke occupied in the stakeout van and Phin doing surveillance, they were short one insertion team member. Liv had jumped on the opportunity to be the one to pull up the rope after their descent.

"Phin, target's status?"

"*About half staff,*" came his staticky, amused reply.

"Come again?" Rohan asked over the *whomp whomp* of the helicopter's blades.

"*Target is fully occupied with a beautiful woman and an endless supply of bourbon.*"

Rohan removed his headset and gestured for Neuman to

do the same. He didn't care what the hell Killian Byrne was doing at the club as long as he stayed there for the next hour.

They had thrown a recovery plan together faster than any other, and Rohan knew it was laced with holes the size of Massachusetts.

"One minute," Cruz said.

Rohan double-checked Neuman's gear, then his own.

Ten seconds.

Ten seconds for him and Neuman to fast rope down to the roof, and for Cruz to disappear. The sixty-story building was tall enough and the night was dark enough to hide two specters shooting out of a helicopter from onlookers below.

But curious folks in the other high rises worried him. They would have an unimpeded balcony view.

Would they act like ninety-nine percent of the population and resume their lives? Or would they be among the rare one percent who would listen to their instincts and call in the unusual activity above Liddington building?

Cruz gave the go sign.

Rohan kicked the coil of thick rope out, made sure the end dragged the ground below, then motioned Neuman forward. The recruit placed a hand beneath Rohan's on the rope, then swung out, clasping the rope between his gloved hands and boots, then let gravity do the rest.

Then Liv stabilized the rope for Rohan as he followed Neuman three seconds later. Wind from the rotor down-wash pushed against his shoulders and whipped at his face, cleansing away the last of his uncertainty. The jarring contact of his boots against the rooftop completed the transition from plan to execution.

They bolted toward the stairwell door. Rohan glanced

back to see Liv expertly retrieve the rope as the helicopter drifted away.

Neuman took a knee and went to work on the deadbolt, while Rohan's fingers blazed across his tablet, disabling the building's security cameras.

Seconds later, the door clicked open. Neuman waited for Rohan's thumbs-up before plunging down the stairwell. Like many after-build penthouse apartments in these old high-rises, Byrne's apartment didn't have a direct connection to the stairwell.

The penthouse had one ingress and egress—the elevator. In order to access it, they had to go down a level, then back up, increasing their exposure.

Once inside the lift, Neuman held a keycard Rohan had made before the proximity reader. The red light turned green, and Neuman hit the penthouse button.

For hackers like Rohan, technology was like a red carpet. Follow it, and you'll gain access to the most exclusive places.

"Eyes and comms good?" Rohan asked Zeke, who sat in their surveillance van two blocks away and followed their progress through small cameras attached to their shoulder harnesses.

"All good," Zeke responded through Rohan's earpiece.

The trip up a single floor was practically over before it got started. When the elevator doors binged open, lights inside the apartment flickered on.

Not ceiling lights or sconces or floor lamps. But tiny pin lights strategically placed over works of art scattered on the walls and carved out nooks.

Zeke whistled. *"Byrne has pieces that would make Kayla salivate."*

Kayla Krowne, Liv's best friend, successful lobbyist, and

Phin's new boss, had amassed an impressive collection of priceless artworks. Although Rohan appreciated art in its many mediums, he preferred his world of zeroes and ones.

They started their search at the back of the apartment, in the master bedroom. The penthouse's schematics showed a large walk-in closet. It was as good a place as any to start. Most thieves liked to keep their treasures close to their underwear drawer.

The master suite was a sizable space, with a sleeping area and sitting room. When Byrne sat up in bed, he could look down the entire length of his suite. Straight at a large painting on the other end.

Rohan stilled as a wave of familiarity washed over him. Then his feet were in motion, eating up the distance to the far wall.

"Hey," Neuman said. "The closet is this way."

"Go ahead. I'll be there in a second."

The closer Rohan got to the portrait, the thicker his throat grew. When he stood a few feet away, he could see he'd been wrong. It wasn't a painting, but an enlarged photograph.

A couple, snuggling on a couch. Their hands covered in multihued paint. Big smiles aimed at the camera.

Lena and Byrne.

THE SMALL LOCKED ROOM ATTACHED TO BYRNE'S CLOSET didn't house *Walking Woman,* but an incredible array of weapons. The quantity and variety were so great that Rohan had to wonder if there was something more to Killian Byrne than his pretty art collection.

"Clear," Neuman said, coming out of the spare bedroom.

"Clear," Rohan said after sweeping Byrne's office.

Frustrated, Rohan paused in the kitchen as he studied the penthouse's floor plan on his tablet. "There has to be another hidden room. Byrne would want to keep the painting close."

"Maybe he already put it on the black market," Neuman said.

Rohan shook his head. "It's here. I'd bet my best keylogger on it."

"How can you be so sure?" Zeke asked.

Rohan thought about the enlarged picture in Byrne's bedroom. The one of him and Lena happy and full of life.

Had she been part of the heist? Had she been giving the performance of ten lifetimes since they'd first met?

He recalled her expression as she chased Bobby Balor out of her apartment building. The fear, the anger. Not even Meryl Streep could pull off such genuine emotion.

"I'm *not* sure," Rohan said. "But something tells me he wouldn't leave it at the gallery, or a similar location, where someone might come across it. The painting is too important to him."

And Lena.

Had he taken the painting to lure her here? Had he banked on the fact she would eventually call him for advice? Her former lover turned art dealer?

Rohan's attention locked on an undesignated space behind the pantry. It was large. As big as the kitchen and living room put together. How had they missed this?

Because they'd thrown the recovery together faster than Lynette could whip up her famous yogurt pancakes.

He zoomed in on the area, then shoved the tablet into a sleeve on his tactical vest before yanking open the pantry door. Speaking of large.

Cherrywood shelving reached from the floor to ceiling,

each one ten feet wide. Dozens—hundreds—of canned goods filled several shelves, three deep and four high. Bags of flour, rice, and sugar lined up, side-by-side, their square chests thrust into the air.

"Is this guy one of those survivalist types?" Neuman asked.

Rohan glanced over his shoulder at the luxury penthouse. "If he is, he took a wrong turn at the crossroads." He scanned each shelf. "Look for a mechanism that will open a hidden door."

They ran hands beneath each shelf, along the trim work on the double doors, and toed the baseboard.

"Nothing," Neuman said.

"The painting is back there. I can feel it in my bones."

"Target is on the move," Phin reported in Rohan's ear. *"He's stumbling out of the club."*

"Dammit."

Rohan moved containers and cans and bags away from the wall, searching for anything that looked out of the ordinary. He grabbed a bottle of ginger soy sauce, but it didn't budge.

Excitement kicked up in his chest. "Help me clear everything away from this bottle." They worked in tandem until Rohan had plenty of elbow room.

"Give it a shove," Zeke said.

Rohan pushed.

Nothing.

"Pull it."

"I did."

"Harder."

Rohan braced a hand against the shelf and tried again. It gave way and a distant click sounded.

The wall slid inwards several inches, then rotated forty-five degrees.

Rohan flicked on his Maglite. Words clogged in the back of his throat.

Neuman added his light to Rohan's. "Holy shit."

34

THE MAN WHO NOW CALLED HIMSELF KILLIAN BYRNE PARKED in one of the many handicapped spots in the multilevel garage at the back of his building. A fucking black Jaguar had taken his reserved spot, and Killian didn't have the stomach for driving in circles in search of a nonexistent empty stall.

Number 507 must be shaking the walls again. Why couldn't the bastard party at a club, like he did, instead of inviting all of his loudmouth, stall-stealing friends to their building?

He pushed out of his vehicle, then had to stand there a moment and wait for his head to catch up.

Damn, that last bourbon fucked up his body.

Blinking hard several times, he cursed his inability to recognize the warning drink. The one that said, "Order another, asshole, and you'll regret it."

He remained in place an extra ten minutes, knowing it wouldn't be enough time to wash away the evidence of the last few hours. But even hard-asses like him drifted into fairytale land on occasion.

When his world clattered together in a single image again, he exited the garage and made his way to the service elevator at the back of the building.

Although the elevator had an industrial feel and had the faint scent of fermented cabbage, the ride was fast and smooth. But most of all, no one else would be inside at this time of the day.

The doors binged open, and Killian smoothed his black hair back into place. For a moment, Camille had tempted him in the dim light of the club, with music pounding through his veins and her fingers trailing along his thigh. Onyx hair like Lena's brushing his cheek.

But Camille wasn't Lena.

None of them were.

He'd sampled every shape, age, size, and color. No one had come close to taking her place.

Their smiles didn't make his heart sing. Their bodies didn't make him crave more. Their presence didn't make his rotten soul reach for the light.

He hadn't realized the treasure he had until he'd screwed things up with Lena.

He understood now. Understood the life he was born to live and who he wanted to share the journey with.

Somehow he'd win Lena back. He'd talk her into giving him—them—a second chance.

Then he'd make some changes. Reset some things he'd put in place when his grief from losing her had nearly consumed him.

Lost in his own thoughts, he went through the familiar movements of entering his place without knocking. The darkened studio sent a stab of disappointment all the way to his knees. Walking was difficult. Like his joints needed a good dousing of WD-40.

"Lena?"

Several hours had passed since he'd stormed out of here, like an ass. Promising her dinner, then reneging.

Threatening her.

He blew out a breath. Not the best approach for a man trying to win back the woman he loved.

Where had she gone? For a walk and fresh air? Had she gone out for food?

Another thought wrapped around his gut and squeezed. What if his outburst had chased her away? What if his self-absorption had destroyed his second chance at happiness?

He flicked on the wall switch, intent on searching the studio for her belongings.

Two bodies moved toward him.

The one on the right said, "You should have stayed at the club and fucked the brunette."

Before he could utter a response, something hard slammed into his skull. He heard a loud crack. Then something warm washed over the back of neck.

As he crashed to the floor, his eyes found *The Fountain*. His soggy brain grew sluggish, but two words clawed to the top, one after the other.

Extraordinary.

A tear rolled off his nose and plopped onto the hardwood.

Lena.

35

Rohan found a light switch and flipped it on. The pantry was like a portal into another realm. A realm you heard about on the news, but could never quite bring yourself to believe.

Easels stood in two concentric circles at the center of the enormous room. The inner ring contained works-in-progress, the outer an original masterpiece. A tall table, stool, and an array of paint supplies accompanied each WIP.

Workstations, he realized.

Three dozen vertical drying racks filled with finished canvases rested against an adjacent wall. Blank canvases of every shape and size waited along the opposite wall for their moment of transformation.

Beyond the easels, Rohan spotted a haphazard arrangement of metal cots. Six, maybe seven, young bodies scrambled from beneath thin blankets, shying away from the light as if it would scorch their tender flesh. They sought the corners, where shadows still lingered, or scrambled for the meager protection of a plastic chair or cardboard box.

Only one remained visible. A teenaged girl, holding something long and narrow in each hand like a street fighter who was ready to slice and dice, stood between Rohan and her fellow prisoners.

Fierce. Determined. And scared shitless.

She reminded him of Lena.

Thick tentacles wormed around Rohan's stomach, squeezing his guts until bile shot to the back of his throat. He clenched his neck muscles, fighting back the nausea.

"It's a fucking sweat shop," Zeke said, echoing Rohan's own conclusion.

Nothing Rohan had ever learned from the moment he'd slid from his mother's womb to the second before they'd opened the pantry's hidden door had prepared him for what to do next.

He had a recovery to complete, but he could not—would not—leave these kids to this fate. How he would explain this discovery to the authorities, he didn't know. He'd worry about that later.

Right now, he needed to assess the situation and locate the painting.

"Find the painting," he said to Neuman. "I'll take care of this."

Out of the corner of his eye, he caught a swift movement, then something white and heavy rocketed through the air toward them.

"Get down!" He ducked a nanosecond before a ceramic mug whizzed by and crashed into an easel behind him, sending a masterpiece to the floor.

Rohan heard a dull *thunk* right before Neuman cried out and crumpled to one knee. A second mug dropped to the concrete floor, shattering.

"Stop!" He yanked off his face mask and searched the

room for the culprits with the wicked fast mugs. "We're not here to hurt you."

The young woman's stance remained tense, and the air grew thick with everyone's uncertainty, including his own.

When no more projectiles raced toward his head, Rohan backed up to the recruit's side and removed the younger man's face mask to assess his injury. "It's not deep, but it's a bleeder." He pressed the woolen material against the wound and guided Neuman to a cot. "Sit down and keep pressure on it."

"What about the painting?"

"Don't worry about that right now. Get the bleeding under control."

Rohan rose and pointed to the long wood-handled paintbrushes the girl gripped in each hand. "You can put those down." The tapered ends could cause some serious damage if wielded by a skilled hand.

Instead of lowering her weapons, her hold tightened until her knuckles pushed against taut flesh.

"What is your name?"

Silence.

"Why are you here?" As if the answer wasn't hammering him in the face. But his mental clock was ticking down the minutes and he hadn't the slightest freaking idea what to do with this feral girl—or her compatriots.

Still no response.

Was she keeping quiet out of caution? Or was there a communication barrier?

"Phin," Rohan said, "where's the target?"

Three seconds ticked by.

"Phin, what's the target's status?"

"He's back at the studio."

Somewhere in the depths of Rohan's chest, glass shattered.

The enlarged photo in Byrne's bedroom filled his vision. Lena laughing, covered in paint. Leaning into Byrne's side like it was her natural habitat. Like she . . . fit.

In the times he'd come across her painting, she had never worn a drop, a smudge, or a splatter of paint. A little on the pads of her fingers, but nowhere else.

It was as though she'd lost the joy of it.

Because she lost Byrne?

Would the two be reminiscing about old times? Would they be snuggling on the white leather couch? Or entangled on the king-sized bed?

Yeah, thanks to Cruz's drone, he knew exactly what the inside of Byrne's studio looked like. Knew the hours of concentration Lena had committed to Byrne's project when she should have been back at the cabin working on Rohan's —BARS's—commission.

But he'd needed to know.

Needed to know she was all right.

Needed to see her.

"Copy, Ro?" Phin asked, drawing him back to his current crisis.

"Copy." Good thing Cruz wasn't still in the area, he might have sent the drone up again to keep an eye on them —Byrne. "Stay with him."

"Copy that."

Rohan could now see six distinct faces emerging from the shadows or peeking out from their protective barriers.

If he were to guess, they were all mid-teens. Their skin tones ran the gamut, from darkest black to palest white, and everything in between.

A smaller figure than the rest pulled away from his

hiding place. A harsh voice hissed a warning, and an arm made a mad swipe to corral the little body.

The boy darted forward and latched onto his protector's waist. A pained expression crossed the young woman's face. It was the same look his mother would get when one of her boys had done the opposite of what they'd been told.

Although she didn't look old enough to be the little guy's mom, the warrior gave him the same comfort any mother would in this situation. She brushed a palm over his hair and whispered reassuring words Rohan couldn't make out.

Placing a hand against his chest, he said, "My name is Rohan." He pointed behind him. "And that's Clay. We're here to locate a painting that was stolen from a friend."

The other captives emerged from their safety zones and slowly approached until they had gathered around their protector in a loose V.

"The sooner we find the painting," Rohan said, "the sooner we can help you leave this prison."

"Leave?" Someone to the right said, trepidation in their voice.

"Prison?" Another echoed.

Rohan nodded. "I know someone who can assist us with finding your parents. My brother Ash. He's with the FBI."

His words didn't have the effect he'd intended. Rather than melt away that last of their caution and bring hopeful smiles to their faces, his mention of the FBI whipped them into a frenzy of tears and terror.

"There's no need to be scared," Rohan said. "My brother is a good man."

The young woman raised her hand, and the cacophony around her quieted. She pinned Rohan with a centuries-old look, one that harbored wisdom beyond her years. "Mr. Rohan—"

"Sonofabitch," came Phin's alarmed voice.

Rohan held up a finger to the girl and turned his head to the side while he pressed a finger to his earpiece. "What's happened, Phin? Is the target on the move?"

"Oh, he moved alright."

"Dammit, Phin. What's going on?"

"You need to get down here. Now."

36

WITH LEFTOVERS IN HAND, LENA FOLLOWED THE SIDEWALK leading back to the studio with her eyes fixed on a distant spot. Her mind was already back at the easel, blending colors, thinking about her next brush strokes.

After Xander—Killian—whatever—left, she'd spent a few more hours at the canvas. First working on the fountain, then trying to perfect the drape of Jane deGlehn's dress beneath her painter's smock. The first throb of a hunger headache told her it was time to set down her paintbrush and map out her route to the Indian restaurant.

Past experience had warned her not to ignore her body's need for sustenance. Unless she enjoyed being curled up in the fetal position, nursing the migraine of a lifetime.

The hour away from the studio had not only replenished her energy reserves but her enthusiasm. Despite the reason behind her current project, the copyist in her loved the challenge, loved figuring out the master's technique. Loved every small victory on the canvas.

If only she had more time to do the forgery justice. Then

again, did she want some unsuspecting buyer to purchase her John Singer Sargent knockoff?

Far too many forgeries were hanging in museums and private collections across the world as it was. Some of them hers.

With her mind winding through the rugged roads of her past, she didn't immediately register the spangle of blue and red lights against the neighborhood buildings until she reached the studio's street corner.

A crowd of onlookers craned their collective necks to see beyond the yellow crime scene tape. Lena joined the curious, rubbernecking with the rest of them. "What happened?"

"A dude jumped off the roof," a twenty-something man with a shaved head said.

"He didn't jump," another said. "Someone pushed him."

A third person chimed in. "Nah, it was a hit-and-run."

The group grew louder with their guesses, but the one thing each story had in common was that a man had died. By gruesome means.

Lena pushed through the masses until she reached the police tape. She moved along the line until she found a gap between law enforcement bodies on the other side. Until she spotted a broken body draped over the curb, with the lower half on the sidewalk, the upper half on the street.

Blood pooled beneath a familiar dark head.

Xander.

Lena stumbled into the restless onlookers around her.

"Watch it, bitch."

"Get off my damn foot."

"Hey, you okay?"

Survival mode kicked in, and Lena steadied herself. She couldn't afford for anyone to remember her.

Adjusting her bag across her body, she tunneled through the gawkers and strode away from yet another murder victim who'd loved her.

LENA HOOKED A LEFT ON THE NEXT INTERSECTION, GLANCING over her shoulder as she did. No one was in pursuit, and the only person looking at her oddly was the homeless woman who now held Lena's leftovers in her lap.

The relief she'd hoped for didn't come. In fact, the more distance she put between her and Xander's shattered body, the more labored her breathing became.

Until she saw him. Heading straight for her.

Rohan.

Something inside her broke.

No, collapsed.

One moment she was strong. The next, she was running.

The armor she'd built around herself disintegrated, piece by piece.

By the time she flung herself into Rohan's arms, there was only blood and bones and flesh left. Every inch diseased or damaged beyond repair.

"I got you," he whispered against her hair.

"Xan—Killian's d-dead," she said in a breathless rush, still unable to believe he was gone. "I think someone threw him off the balcony. Or he fell. I don't know. He was on the ground. The blood. His face—"

"Sshh-shh. Shh. I know, I know."

In the distance, a siren's *woop woop* sounded.

"Come on," Rohan said, "let's get you off the street."

He motioned to a large black van idling not far away. When the vehicle came abreast of them, one of the back doors flew open, and Zeke extended a hand toward her.

She didn't even have time to be shocked. Simply accepted his assistance. The moment they were all inside, the door slammed shut, and Phin eased the vehicle back into traffic.

Lena didn't know what to do with herself. Electronics lined each side of the van. Monitors and keyboards and flashing buttons made her feel as if she'd stepped onto the set of a Jason Bourne movie.

Zeke patted the back of a swivel chair. "Have a seat."

She sat, though she continued to take in her surroundings. "Is this a surveillance vehicle?"

Rohan glanced at Zeke behind her before nodding.

"Who were you tracking?" She recalled the unnerving feeling of eyes on her all day and several times in Steele Ridge. Now that she thought about each instance, Rohan was never far away. "Me?"

"We'll circle back around to your lack of faith in me in a moment. Right now, I need to know what you left behind in Byrne's studio."

He knew what she'd been up to since their explosive parting outside the gallery. Shame scored a fiery path up the back of her neck. Not for her decision to protect him against Xander's machinations, but for him seeing her for what she really was.

A forger.

"Lena, focus. What belongings of yours will the police find in the studio?"

The mention of police snapped her right-headed again.

Lifting the shoulder strap over her head, she sat her bag on the van's rubberized floor. "Everything I brought with me is in this bag."

"Everything? You sure you didn't leave a toothbrush behind?"

She couldn't tell him that keeping her life in a bag made moments like this so much easier. The confession would lead to more questions.

Dangerous questions.

"The police won't find physical evidence of my presence, but I didn't wipe down the place."

He gave her a steady look. "Why would you?"

She stared back, silent.

"Are you in the system?" Zeke asked, cutting to the chase.

She rotated in her chair. "What do you mean?"

"Your prints. Will the police get a hit?"

The lie sprang to her lips, but she stopped it there. She could give them the answer that would make herself look good now, but they would learn the truth as soon as the police came knocking on her door.

First Neil, then Ruthie. Now Xander. Three suspicious deaths with her fingerprints on-site. The cops were sure to connect the dots.

"Yes."

To Zeke's credit, he didn't flinch at the revelation. She did not check Rohan's reaction.

Zeke turned to Rohan. "Can you zap them?"

Blood froze in Lena's reins. "Zap my prints? Have you lost your mind?"

Rohan stared at his brother for a long moment, though she could tell he was already making calculations and assessing the risk.

"If I had more time, maybe," he said at last. "But not before APD processes the scene and uploads the prints to NCIC."

Lena's lungs expanded with air again. Her past would

catch up with her and she didn't want Rohan anywhere near the blast zone.

"We need a plan," Zeke said.

Rohan' eyes bore into hers. "Did anyone see you coming and going from Byrne's place?"

"I don't think so. Other than my arrival, which was via the service elevator, this was the first time I've been outside the studio."

"At least we have that on our side," Zeke said. "If they get a hit, the police won't be able to prove when you were there."

"Maybe the waitstaff at the Indian restaurant, where I just had dinner, would remember me."

"There might also be CCTV footage confirming you were either at the restaurant during the time of the murder or walking to and from it," Rohan said.

"I'll have Cruz look into it," Zeke said.

"What about your painting-in-progress?" Rohan nodded at her bag. "Are your brushes in there?"

"What makes you think I was painting anything?"

"I sent a drone up to check on you."

"I knew it." She slapped a palm against the metal ledge holding their computer equipment. "All day, I had the feeling of being watched." She glared at Rohan. "Ever heard of a phone?"

"First of all," Rohan said, "I didn't call because you made it clear you didn't need any *distractions*. And second, I sent the drone up once."

"Only once?"

"Once."

Could her instincts be faulty? Had the burglary and Ruthie's murder thrown her into full-on paranoia?

"Maybe Byrne was monitoring the studio," Zeke offered.

"Did you notice any cameras?"

She shook her head. "I searched."

"Some surveillance cameras are the size of a house key," Rohan said. "Easily concealed against the untrained eye."

"But this wasn't the first time I've felt watched." As soon as the words were out of her mouth, Lena wanted to rope them back in. The last thing she needed right now was Rohan thinking she was unstable.

"When was the first time?"

"Back in Steele Ridge."

"Before or after the theft?"

"Just before, then right after."

Rohan shared a look with Zeke.

"I'm not losing my mind—"

"I believe you."

She blinked. "You do?"

"We'll sort out who's stalking you later. Right now, we need to understand your exposure." He nodded toward her bag. "Did you stash your paintbrushes in there, or are they still at the studio?"

"The studio."

A heavy silence followed her statement.

"Don't worry your gorgeous heads about this," she said with forced confidence. "I've been in stickier situations and came out on the other side."

"Stickier than murder?" Rohan asked.

"As you've pointed out before, there's much about me you don't know."

He waited several taut seconds for her to elaborate. When she didn't, he asked, "Any ideas who killed Byrne?"

"Don't you want to ask if I did it?"

"No."

"Why not?"

"Because you're not capable of murder."

The absolute certainty in his voice wrapped a tingle of warmth around her heart.

"And Phin's been trailing Byrne all night."

The tingle evaporated. "Why? What are you even doing here? I fired you."

"Blackwells never fail to finish a job."

How could she be mad at him for ignoring her wishes? If he hadn't shown up when he did, she'd be in freak-out mode right now.

"I don't know who would want to hurt Killian. I haven't spoken to him in two years."

"The shrine in his bedroom would suggest otherwise."

"I have no idea what you're talking about."

"An enlarged photo of you and him, covered in paint and laughing, is hanging on the wall in his penthouse." Rohan's voice dropped. "You're the first thing he sees every morning."

Was that jealousy she detected in his tone?

Lena knew the picture he was referring to. Xander used to keep it on his bedside table as a reminder of how one could overcome the limitations of one's upbringing.

Considering the upward trajectory of Xander's business, both legit and not-so-legit, she could see why he'd super-sized the photo.

"It was taken the day Killian and I passed our GED exams. A celebratory moment shared between two friends." She pinned him with a look. "We were lovers for a short while."

"What happened?"

"He found solace in another's arms." She lifted a brow. "What were you doing in Killian's bedroom?"

"Searching for the Catawnee."

Excitement bubbled. "Did you find it?"

"Among other things, yes."

She stilled, glancing between him and Zeke. "What other things?"

"Seems your boyfriend-not-boyfriend was quite the entrepreneur."

"Are you talking about his gallery expansion or his more illicit business?" She had a good idea of which one he meant, but it seemed like a good idea to clarify.

Rohan's face darkened.

"Easy, brother," Zeke said.

"Don't tell me you're squeamish about forged paintings," she said. "You just confessed to breaking and entering, plus surveilling people."

Rohan opened his mouth, then closed it. Opened it, closed it. Opened, closed.

Zeke asked in a careful voice, "Were you aware he built his business on the backs of imprisoned teenagers?"

Every drop of blood leached from her face. "He wouldn't."

How many times had he complained about being enslaved to Simon? Not literally, but to leave Simon's employ would have meant leaving safety and security behind.

And Simon wasn't above exploiting the fact.

"He not only could," Rohan said. "He did."

Lena shook her head, unable to believe Xander could do something so inhumane. "I don't believe you. He would never be so cruel."

"The kids we found in a hidden room off his penthouse's pantry would argue otherwise."

The samosas stirred low in her stomach. Pressing a fist to her mouth, she glanced at Zeke, needing confirmation.

He nodded.

"Where are the kids now?"

"One of our team members stayed back until DFCS arrives." Rohan's voice hardened. "Why were you painting in Byrne's studio, Lena?"

She squeezed her eyes shut. All of her lies felt like sawdust in her mouth.

Kids.

Xander had held kids in a locked room to paint forgeries for him. The man she remembered would never have done something so disgusting.

Even Simon, for of his faults, had allowed them the freedom of coming and going as they wished. His bondage had manifested in subtler ways. But they could have left at any time.

Could money truly have been the motivating factor?

With Xander dead, she might never know for sure.

"Lena?" Rohan prodded.

She drew in a deep breath and unbarred the door leading to her past.

37

SENSING LENA WAS READY TO TALK, ROHAN JERKED HIS CHIN
at his brother, and Zeke joined Phin in the front cab.

The two could still hear everything she said, but having
one less Blackwell hulking over her would give the illusion
of privacy.

"When I was fourteen," she began, "I ran away and lived
on the streets for close to a year before joining forces with
Killian—I knew him then as Xander Douglas—and a girl
named Izzy DeCarlo."

"Why did you run away?"

"Things at home got . . . heated. It became clear that I
wouldn't be safe there any longer."

Rohan picked up on the stockpile of missing information in her explanation, but he'd let it go. For now. "How did
you join forces?"

"We set up a stand in Pritchard Park, where we charged
twenty dollars to draw caricatures of tourists in front of their
favorite landmark."

"All three of you were artists?"

"To a degree. My work generated the most word of

mouth. Izzy moved into designing jewelry and Xander leaned into the business side." The tips of her blunt nails seesawed back and forth across the plastic arm of her chair. "It all worked. We made enough money to last us through the winter when tourism died down."

Rohan pulled out a low stool and sat down. "Impressive." He wrapped his fingers around her fidgety hand.

"Terrifying." Her knee started to jackhammer. "We came to the notice of Simon Garibay. After observing our enterprise for a time, he offered each of us an opportunity we couldn't refuse."

He rested his other hand against her knee and soon the pistoning slowed, then stopped. "Let me guess—copying artwork."

"Nothing so legit." The smile she sent him held no humor, only a reflection of decisions made and a life lived. No matter how flawed. "I told you once that I was one of the best."

"*The* best, as I recall."

"I earned the title by forging several hundred paintings, which sold to reputable museums and avid collectors, even through premiere auction houses. To my knowledge, no one has questioned any of their authenticity."

"How is that possible?"

Humor lit her eyes. "Because I'm the best." She flicked her fingers in the air. "And because Simon and Xander became expert storytellers. The provenance they wove together for each piece was a work of art in and of itself."

"Where's Simon now?"

"He died from an accidental overdose three years ago."

"Accidental?"

"Simon suffered from chronic back pain and had been taking OxyContin for years, one in the morning and one in the evening, like clockwork. Toward the end, Izzy mentioned several times seeing him take the meds throughout the day. Despite his questionable business choices, he wasn't a man of excess."

"Who found him?"

She glanced away a moment before continuing. "The three of us. On our way to lunch, we stopped by his office to see if he wanted anything."

Fighting the urge to comfort her, he said, "What happened to the business?"

"He left it to me."

Rohan whistled low. "A lot of responsibility for a—"

"Twenty-two-year-old."

"How'd the others take your anointment?"

"Let's just say, they drowned their misery in each other's arms." She stared down at where his hand held hers in a loose grip. "About a year after I became the owner, the three of us agreed it was time to go our separate ways. That was two years ago and the last time I saw them until this week."

"The three of you had survived the streets together. Their betrayal must have been painful."

"To hear Izzy tell the story, I was the one who betrayed our friendship by getting romantically involved with Xander."

"Because Xander had nothing to do with the change in your relationship."

"Love is blind, right?" Lena shrugged. "I took Simon's money, set up my own studio, and became a certified copyist." Her attention fell on one of the blank monitors, and she grew silent.

"You missed your friends."

"For a time. Everything turned out for the best. For all of us." She pinched the bridge of her nose. "Xander said something about me not returning his calls." She met his gaze. "This sounds farfetched, but what if he had the painting stolen in order to force me to seek him out."

Rohan had wondered the same. "To what end?"

"A second chance."

A steel band cinched around his chest. "Why not just show up in Steele Ridge and woo you back?"

"A fair question." She sighed. "I can't shake the feeling that the theft was more than a theft. Something seems calculated about it. Something Bobby Balor probably had no clue about."

"So Byrne was the 'friend' who heard Palmer talking about hiring you?"

"Maybe." She threw up her hands. "I don't know. But it's another angle the sheriff could question Bobby about."

Rohan nodded, then asked a question that was burning a hole in his chest. "Would you have?"

"Would I have, what?"

"Given him a second chance?"

She studied him for a long moment before answering. "One thing you'll learn about me, Rohan, is that when my life gets too hot, I leave it behind and start fresh somewhere else."

She was going to run. As soon as they returned to Steele Ridge, she was going to take off and go so deep underground that no digital highway would lead him to her.

Anger and fear and something unidentifiable filled his chest. "We paid you to do a job," he reminded her.

"Which I'll fulfill now that we have the Catawnee back."

Then she'd be gone and would never look back.

"Where is the Catawnee, by the way?"

"Headed back to the Friary with Cruz." He rubbed a

thumb over the back of her hand. "What bargain did you strike with Byrne?"

"Copy a Singer in exchange for the Catawnee."

"Copy or forge?"

She stared at him. Her silence answer enough.

An image of the fierce teenaged girl standing up to two commando-like men with nothing more than paintbrushes for weapons speared through his mind. Why hadn't Lena fought against Byrne's manipulation? Why had she given in to the bastard?

"You're a coward."

She shot out of her chair, sending it crashing into the low counter. "You don't get to fucking say that to me."

"I already did."

"What do you"—she jabbed a finger into his chest— "know about bravery?" Another jab. "You, with your big house and loving family and mounds of money."

"I know I'd choke off my right testicle," he grabbed her finger mid-jab, "before selling my soul to someone like Byrne."

She yanked her hand away. "Because you've never had to choose."

"Choose what?"

"Between surviving and dying."

"And you have?"

"Everybody who has ever loved me is dead. Every. Single. Person. So yes, I've been a survivor my entire life."

Died and left her alone. Rohan heard the painful admission even though she chose not to share it.

"How did your parents die?"

She blinked and reared back. "I told you. Car accident."

"Bullshit."

They lapsed into awkward silence, and a few minutes later she and Zeke swapped places.

Once they reached the Annex, Rohan handed Lena her shoulder bag from where she'd left it in the back of the van. "After I finish unloading the equipment, I'll drive you back to the cabin."

When he didn't receive an acknowledgment, he turned around in time to catch Lena vanishing into the woods.

38

At the sound of an engine, Lena wiped the paint from her hands and groaned as her muscles uncoiled from their prolonged positions. Everything hurt. Her eyes, her brain, her back. Everything.

After finishing *Woman Walking,* she'd dedicated the rest of her day to the Caravaggio. The faster she could complete the Blackwell commission, the faster she could whitewash this page of her life.

It had taken hours for her mind to settle down last night. Every harsh word from her argument with Rohan kept replaying, over and over. Each retelling worse than the last.

Yet despite the way their conversation had ended, Lena didn't regret sharing part of her past with Rohan. Without judgment, he'd held her hand and listened to her story. His mood had changed from supportive to combative only after she'd spoken about starting fresh someplace else.

Before she made it to the door, Sadie burst into the cabin. Big smile lighting up the room. Brodie Westcott entered more slowly, cautiously.

But it was Rohan's broad shoulders filling the doorframe that made her heart stutter. She didn't know what to say to him. How to feel around him.

All the fury she'd felt last night had dissipated during the wee hours of the morning. Replaced by sadness and a keening, hollow ache in her chest.

Rohan gave her a tentative smile, as if he was unsure of her welcome. She didn't exactly smile back, but she didn't incinerate him either. He seemed to take that as encouragement and stepped inside, closing the door behind him.

"Brodie doesn't believe I can paint," Sadie said by way of greeting.

The brown-haired boy's ears turned red, and Lena smiled. "It's nice to see you again, Brodie."

"Hello, Miss Lena."

"Can I show him?" Sadie asked.

"Of course. It's yours to show." She expected the boy to take one look at his friend's amateur effort and either make a face or outright laugh, as boys were wont to do.

But Brodie did neither. He stared at it from far away, then moved in for a closer inspection. The longer he kept quiet, the more Sadie's smile dimmed.

The boy shook his head. "Is there anything you're not good at, Mercedes Rios?"

She smiled. "Well, I haven't mastered shortstop yet."

Brodie's eyes widened. "Crap." He fished his phone out of his jeans and checked the time. "I gotta go. Mom's waiting."

"Take the UTV," Rohan said, opening the door again. "Keys are in the ignition."

"Thanks, Uncle Rohan!" He lifted a hand and rushed outside. *"Bye."*

Sadie followed her friend's progress through the window. "He has a baseball game."

"At this time of the year?"

Rohan said, "Liv found him a travel team that plays tournaments in the fall."

Sadie grew serious. "After his dad died, he wouldn't even pick up a bat. But Uncle Zeke helped him get back in the game. I hope he stays in for as long as it makes him happy."

"You're a good friend, Sadie."

The girl blushed. "Oh! You finished the eyes." She dashed over to the Catawnee. "They look wonderful."

"Thank you. I think being away from it for a few days allowed me some perspective."

"Let's celebrate. How about we take our easels outside?"

Lena glanced at the *Nativity,* and a cloud of sadness settled around her. Maybe a change of scenery would do her good. She'd been cooped up with nothing but tension and heartache as her companions for far too long. A studio without walls sounded glorious.

"You've been staring at that stuffy painting all day." Sadie grabbed the blank canvas and its easel. "It's time to put some paint on this, and I know the perfect spot to inspire you. Grab your supplies."

The girl was out the door before Lena could blink. She eyed Rohan. "Did you put her up to this?"

"No, ma'am. I came across her and Brodie on my way here and gave them a lift." His gaze shifted from the empty doorway to her. "She's worried about you."

A tide of emotion rose in her throat. She forced it back down. "Did you need something?"

He stared at her for a heart-thumping moment. When he finally spoke, his voice was rough. "Yes, to apologize." He took a step closer, then checked himself. "I shouldn't have said what I did."

"You mean about me being a coward and a liar?"

He nodded, wincing. "I lost my head a little."

"Over what, exactly?"

He looked at the ceiling, then released a resigned breath before meeting her eyes. "Thoughts of you in Byrne's arms, and my fear that you'd disappear the moment we got back to Steele Ridge."

Lena's heart kicked up its pace. "Why would either of those things upset you?"

"Byrne doesn't—wouldn't have deserved you."

"And?"

"You have a commission to finish."

"Coward."

"Pardon?"

"Liar."

His nostrils flared. "You think Byrne would've deserved a second chance?"

"No."

"How is my statement not true?"

"I didn't say it wasn't true. I called you a liar. Big difference." She folded her arms across her middle. "Tell me the real reason you didn't want me to be with Xander."

He stepped closer, and she could feel his harsh breaths graze her cheek. "Because I don't like the idea of another man touching you."

"Why?"

"I care about you, dammit."

If her life wasn't her life, she would've taken the step separating them and crushed his mouth with hers. But her victory was ephemeral and hollow.

When she remained silent, he whispered, "Lena, say

something." His voice held ache and need and maybe a little fear.

She unfolded her arms. "You had something right, Rohan." Her throat tightened at the spark of hope in his expression. "I'm leaving Steele Ridge once I've finished the Caravaggio. Like the Blackwells, I don't stop until the job is done."

Something raw passed over his features. Although she hated seeing it, she understood. Had expected it.

He'd put himself out there, and she'd cut the wire he stood on.

It was a fall few could forgive and even fewer could recover from.

"Copy loud and clear." He strode away, paused on the porch, and jerked a chin toward Sadie and the blank canvas. "I hope you're inspired."

Something in Lena's chest cracked. She thought it might have been her heart, but that organ had been destroyed long ago.

She shuffled from window to window until she found Rohan heading toward Sadie, who had set up an outdoor studio beneath a large tulip tree. Open meadow all around them. The sun-burnished mountains in the distance.

Rohan paused to place a hand on the girl's head and say a few words before continuing on toward the Friary.

Lena closed her eyes as a great pressure bore down on her chest. Breathing became difficult and a fine sheen of sweat smothered her from head and waist. She grabbed a nearby *Outside* magazine and fanned herself as she fought to stop the rising tears.

Sadie glanced back at the cabin, a worried expression on her sweet face.

Guilt cramped Lena's stomach. She dropped the magazine, wiped the sweat from her face, and snatched her work-in-progress off its easel.

She had nothing to give the blank canvas.

Nothing.

39

"Park in the first lot," the security guard said to Lena after verifying her cargo. "Someone will come assist you with the paintings."

Lena accelerated past Senator Palmer's entrance gate, surprised the guard hadn't checked her for weapons. He seemed to be more interested in whether she'd brought the paintings than if she was packing.

As it turned out, Xander had been right. She really did do her best work under pressure. When she'd stood before *Woman Walking* this morning, she saw the brush strokes play out in her mind as if they were musical notes flowing across a sheet of music.

Thirty minutes later, she was done.

With Palmer's guests arriving soon, she imagined the senator had cut a deep groove in his Italian marble entryway with his pacing. Not that she'd ever seen that part of the mansion. The one other time she was here, she'd entered through a side entrance.

Parking areas occupied each side of the drive that led up

to the two-story brick mansion. Its enormity reminded her of the Friary, though Palmer's house didn't have the same welcoming atmosphere.

Everything here, from the uniformed guards to the exotic flowers in the enormous planters lining the walkway, served a specific purpose. To impress. To project power.

There wasn't one wild hair to be found.

As instructed, Lena chose the nearest parking area and opened the back of her Bronco. Two thick-chested men, wearing black suits and military-style haircuts approached and, without a word, they reached inside her vehicle for the two sturdy shipping boxes.

As she waited for them to retrieve the original Catawnee and her copy, she noticed another vehicle, a silver SUV, backed into a stall in the other lot.

The sight shot Lena back to the night she and Rohan had fled Blanche's Motel. A similar vehicle had been in the motel's parking lot. She'd thought it looked like Angler Dean's truck.

But now, she wasn't so sure. She hadn't been able to see the back end well enough to say for sure if it had been a truck or a utility vehicle.

With the amount of fear-induced adrenaline rushing through her body at the time, she couldn't be certain of anything about that night. Besides, there had to be a million silver truck-like vehicles on the road, right?

She stared at the SUV as if she could bully it into spewing its secrets out the front grate. When the suits started for the house, she nodded at the vehicle. "Looks like the senator's guests have already started arriving."

Suit Two shook his head. "Boss's fiancée."

Feeling ridiculous that she had allowed the events of the

past week to play circus with her imagination, she closed up the Bronco and followed the procession of paintings inside.

Fifteen minutes later, Lena's copy hung in a place of honor in the mansion's enormous reception room, while the original sat propped against the wall below it.

"Exceptional work, Miss Kamber," Senator Blaise Palmer said. "Quite worth the wait."

Dressed in a tuxedo and shiny black shoes, the amateur art connoisseur smiled at Lena's creation as if he had something to do with the finished product.

When Lena looked at the copy, she could see the flaws as well as the mastery. It was always so with her work and one of the myriad of reasons she'd been unable to paint an original. When copying old and modern-day masters, the imperfections lent to the piece's authenticity. No painting was ever perfect.

But Lena couldn't seem to apply the same logic when contemplating an original. Every cell in her body deemed the work crap before she placed the first brush stroke on the canvas.

"Thank you, sir."

The senator motioned for Suit One to take the original away, then turned back to Lena. "You must stay for the unveiling."

"Stay?" She glanced down at her T-shirt and jeans. "I don't have time to go home and change."

"My fiancée has a closet full of dresses." He gave her body a full assessment. "She has a few inches on you, but the rest is proportionate."

Lena started backing away, two decades of keeping a low profile kicking in. "Thanks, Senator, but fancy dinner parties aren't really my thing."

"Consider your future, Miss Kamber. Some of the region's wealthiest residents will be in attendance tonight. All of them appreciators of art."

Suit Two draped a ribbon of red silk over her copy.

"You intend to tell your guests I painted this?"

"Not all of them. A select few will be invited to view *Woman Walking* in my private study." He smiled. "At which time they will become very interested in who painted this one."

"I've got a stack of business cards I'll leave with you."

"Your cards can't answer questions. Of which I'm sure there will be many."

The senator's insistence was starting rub her in all the wrong places. "Questions I'll be more than happy to answer over the phone or at my studio."

She smiled to take the edge off her refusal. Even though she had no desire to be a display piece at his party, she needed to stay on the senator's good side. Word of mouth kept her in Veronica Beard boots and designer purses. "Now that I've delivered your commissioned work, I look forward to receiving the second half of my fee."

"I'll have my assistant send it straightaway."

She nodded, turning away. "Thank you—"

"If you stay."

Every muscle in her body went taut. She met his gaze. "If I don't?"

"The transfer could take some time, I'm afraid."

"That's blackmail or extortion or something equally shitty."

"That's cooperation, Miss Kamber."

Lena wanted to slam her fist into his smug face. But it would only land her in jail. The senator could spin the tale any direction he chose and folks would believe him.

Because politicians were so damn trustworthy.

"One night of your time, Miss Kamber. I guarantee you'll leave here with commissions tucked in your back pocket."

The click-clack of high-heeled shoes on marble broke through Lena's vivid mental dissection of the senator's manly parts.

"Ah, here is my beautiful fiancée now. She will help you get ready for the party."

Lena transferred her attention from the senator to an exquisite olive-skinned woman in a white silk gown, with draped off-the-shoulder sleeves, and pearl-drop earrings. More than a few inches differentiated Lena's body from this goddess's.

Shock ripped the breath from Lena's throat as she stared into a pair of familiar brown eyes. Eyes she'd seen smiling, crying, judging.

Hating.

Izzy DeCarlo's eyes.

"Bella. Father," Senator Palmer said. "Come meet the artist who reproduced Catawnee's *Woman Walking*."

Izzy floated alongside an older gentleman whose face appeared as smooth as a twenty-year-old's and whose blond hair had somehow escaped that passage of time. However, no modern science could mask the sharp intelligence simmering behind his still bright blue eyes.

Senator Palmer held out an arm, and *Bella* transferred her willowy body from one man's protection to the next. The hello kiss she pressed to the politician's mouth was so erotic, Lena had to look away.

A throaty laugh echoed through the room. "Look, darling," Bella said with a knowing smile. "I've embarrassed our guest."

"You've embarrassed me, my sweet," Palmer said. "Best we save such exhibitions for later."

Bella's self-satisfied expression dimmed under his rebuke. "Of course, my love."

Palmer nodded at the Catawnee. "What do you think, Father?"

"Extraordinary." He smiled at Lena and studied her for a long second before he held out his hand. "Gerard Palmer."

She accepted his hand. "Lena Kamber."

Senator Palmer said, "Bella, Miss Kamber needs your assistance."

"Oh, really?"

"Senator," Lena protested, "I told you—"

"Take her upstairs, my sweet, and prepare her for the dinner party."

"Excellent idea, son."

"I thought you would agree."

Bella's dark eyes took in Lena's sloppy bun and casual clothes. "It's a lot to ask in forty-five minutes."

Palmer kissed her forehead. "I have complete faith in you, my beauty. The pale yellow with the diamond teardrop necklace, I think."

"But I'm wearing that to—"

"Pardon the interruption, Senator," a new voice said, "but I need a few minutes of your time before your guests arrive." The man's sharp gaze strayed to Lena, and he nodded.

Lena recognized the newcomer as Craig Muller, the senator's chief of staff.

"Father," Palmer said. "Will you join us?"

"Of course." Gerard looked at Lena. "I hope we find time to chat later."

The trio strode away without a backward glance. Which suited Lena just fine.

She moved to stand sneaker-to-stiletto with the senator's fiancée. The height difference didn't bother her.

It never had.

"What are you up to, Izzy?" Lena asked her old friend in a snarled whisper.

40

Lena stripped out of her clothes while she waited for Izzy to emerge from a walk-in closet the size of a New York City apartment.

Shock still vibrated in Lena's body at seeing her old friend in the senator's mansion. At learning she was engaged to the man who could be the next president of the United States.

Even as a teenager, Izzy had always had a heavy dose of ambition and the intelligence to recognize opportunity and capitalize on it. She had a refinement and poise about her that had always been well beyond her years.

But First Lady level?

Had the senator's people done a background check on her? Had they discovered her penchant for nicking items from the arts and crafts store? And jewelry and clothing departments?

"Here we go," Izzy said, holding up a plain black gown. "This should fit your diminutive stature."

"I thought your fiancé ordered the pale yellow." Not that Lena cared. If Izzy hadn't made an unexpected appearance, she'd be soaking in a bathtub right now—despite the senator's threats—with a good book rather than enduring Izzy's razor-sharp insults.

"Little moments like this give me an opportunity to reinforce what my fiancé does and does not have control over." Izzy motioned with two bejeweled fingers. "Undergarments, too."

Lena almost felt sorry for the senator.

Almost.

Holding her nemesis's gaze, Lena dropped her bra and panties.

Izzy cast an admiring, if reluctant, eye over Lena's toned body before flicking her fingers again. "Arms up."

Lena did as instructed, and the cool material slipped over her bare skin. The front halter straps, open back, and shirred front slit saved the black chiffon from obscurity and the Grecian cut offset the tightness around her hips.

What they would do about the five inches of extra material pooled around her feet, she didn't know.

Izzy dropped a pair of strappy stilettos that looked as though they were covered in black diamonds before her. "You're lucky my feet are small," she smirked, "and yours are large."

Sliding her feet into the beautiful shoes, Lena said, "I'm surprised your background passed political muster."

The moment she stood six inches taller in her borrowed Christian Louboutins, Lena felt her confidence resurge.

"Ten years ago, my past would have limited me to a couple of nights in the senator's bed."

She indicated an ornate chair before a mirrored dressing table and waited for Lena to sit. She removed the band from Lena's hair and began brushing out the tangles.

"But times are different now. Woman are more powerful

than ever and the right marketing campaign can turn youthful indiscretions into a triumph over poverty."

Lena met Izzy's eyes in the mirror. "If you hadn't taken more than you needed, you wouldn't have been caught and arrested."

"A minor detail that only two people in the world know."

"One," Lena said with some effort.

Izzy paused in her use of a flat iron. "What do you mean?"

"Xander's dead."

The flatiron clattered to the floor.

"What? How?" Izzy demanded.

Lena swiveled on her chair and picked up the hot iron. She placed it on the glass-top table, giving herself time to sift through what she could and couldn't share.

"The authorities believe he jumped from his balcony."

"Bullshit. Xander loved his life. Besides, he would never do something so . . . so—" Her voice caught.

"Drastic?"

"Messy. He loved his face far too much to pulverize it against the pavement."

"In pursuit of his ambitions, Xander had amassed quite a bit of debt," Lena said. "Maybe he received some bad news about one of his new investments and acted on impulse."

"By flinging himself over a railing and plummeting six floors?" Izzy shook her head. "He could have come to me for a loan." She picked up the flat iron, her motions swift and jerky. "Or you."

Everything Rohan had discovered pointed to suicide, yet Lena couldn't believe it either. Not only for the reasons Izzy mentioned but because Xander thrived on challenge. He had been the guiding force of their teenage enterprise. Constantly tweaking how they had operated.

A new thought struck her. Had she been the killer's intended victim and Xander showed up at the wrong place, wrong time? Lena pressed a hand against her stomach, sick at the possibility.

"He didn't need a loan. He had things in play that would cover his debts many times over."

"Like what?"

"Like indenturing kids to forge paintings."

"Don't be ridiculous. Xander chomped at the bit the entire time we worked for Simon."

"I thought so, too, but the evidence is indisputable."

Izzy's narrowed eyes met hers in the mirror. "How do you know all of this?"

Lena couldn't tell Izzy the real reason her life had intersected Xander's again, after years of absence. The last thing she needed was for the bitter woman to whisper in Palmer's ear that Lena had lost the Catawnee. Not to mention the fact she'd been in Xander's studio not long before someone flicked him over the balcony like a cigarette butt.

"How I know doesn't matter. If you don't believe me, dig out your phone and do an Internet search."

"Did you see him . . . before he died?"

Lena said nothing.

A long silence stretched between them.

"It's true then." Izzy's hands paused for so long that the smell of burning hair reached Lena's nose.

She tapped Izzy's hand. "What's true?"

Izzy snapped out of her trance and released Lena's hair from the iron and began pinning it in place. "You never truly know the ones close to you."

An image of Rohan surfaced, and Lena knew with absolute certainty that he would never endanger or take advantage of a child for his own gain.

She didn't understand why she was so certain about a guy whom she'd known for less than a week. But she was. "Xander's ambition made him a complicated person." Lena's eyes roamed around Izzy's elegant boudoir, then at the woman herself. "As are you."

Izzy inserted the last pin that forced Lena's thick hair to waterfall over her right shoulder. She rested her chin on the crown of Lena's head, and smiled. "You have no idea."

41

"Why does Lena keep that blank canvas blank?" Sadie asked, reeling in her fishing lure a few inches.

Rohan had wondered the same thing. Had even poked at her about it the night of their hike down the mountain.

He'd come to the conclusion that Lena didn't believe she could make a living off selling her original works. The belief was paralyzing her creativity, becoming the proverbial self-fulfilling prophecy.

But he couldn't share his suspicions with Sadie. "Maybe she's searching for the right inspiration."

"I don't think she's going to find it inside that stuffy cabin."

"Stuffy?"

A flush crept into the girl's cheeks.

"Some people find safety and comfort within four walls," Rohan said in an amused voice.

Sadie made a face. "Walls make me itchy."

"I'm well aware." He plucked a sprig of yellow aster from a nearby plant and wove it into the long braid hanging down her back. "Now that she's finished with the Catawnee, maybe she'll be more open to tackling the blank canvas outside."

"What if she says no?"

"I've never known you to let that two-lettered word deter you from a mission."

A conspiratorial smile blossomed on the girl's sweet face. "Operation Paint It."

"Nice." Rohan's phone rang. "Let me know if you need backup."

Sadie's eyes widened, then laser-focused on her pole. She gave it a quick jerk and began reeling in either a big fish or a healthy clump of moss.

He checked his phone's ID. Frowning, he answered.

"I have some additional information on the Palmer theft," Sheriff Maggie Kingston said.

As soon as he'd returned to Steele Ridge, Rohan had notified Maggie about the recovery and the situation in Atlanta. "Hold on a sec." To Sadie, he said, "You got this?"

She rolled her eyes, reminding him that this wasn't her first angling rodeo.

Grinning, he kissed the top of her head and whispered, "I hope it's a big one." He turned toward the Annex. "What'd you got, Maggie?"

"My detective wrung some more information from our boy Bobby."

"Must be something good if you're calling me."

"The jury is still out on how good. I'm hoping you can help me decipher the information."

"I'll give it a shot, but don't get your hopes up. I know about as much as you do."

"Bobby claims he was supposed to snatch two paintings."

"Two? I don't recall any mention of a second painting in his emails between him and Byrne."

There had only been three messages, which led Rohan to believe they had moved their conversations to WhatsApp or another encrypted communication service.

"According to Bobby, Killian Byrne added *Woman Walking* only a few days before the burglary."

"Added?" Rohan considered this new information. "That would mean Palmer's painting wasn't the original target."

"Ding, ding. He said he couldn't get the other piece once he realized Lena was home."

"How was a single man going to steal two paintings?"

"His partner called in sick that morning."

"You're shittin' me?"

"Nope."

"All the other paintings in Lena's loft are fakes she's painted. Other than the value of her artistry, they're worth nothing."

"Maybe Killian thought otherwise."

"Did Bobby name the second artwork?"

"I'm in my squad and couldn't write down the name my detective gave me. It was produced by a woman. Freya, or something similar."

"Frida Kahlo?"

"Sounds right. Do you remember seeing it?"

"The painting hangs in Lena's bathroom. Bobby wasn't able to get to it because she was taking a shower when he arrived."

"The bathroom seems an odd place to hang a painting."

Especially one protected within a climate-controlled case.

"But what do I know," Maggie continued. "Since I moved

in with Jay, the only decoration I've managed is a toilet brush."

Rohan was no longer listening. His mind blasted through various images and fragments of conversation, making connections.

"Thanks, Maggie, I gotta go."

"Do you have something?"

"I'm not sure. Maybe."

"Keep me in the loop, Rohan."

"Will do."

He disconnected and ran the rest of the distance to the Annex.

42

A FISSURE OF UNEASE CRACKLED DOWN LENA'S SPINE.

"Are we done here?" she asked the woman whose smile made her want to check for trip wires in her hair.

"I've done what I can," Izzy said, putting the finishing touches on Lena's makeup.

Lena shot out of her chair and headed for the door. She didn't like leaving her belongings behind, but she had little choice.

Something about their conversation bothered Lena on a level other than frustration. But she couldn't put her finger on it. Especially since she had to devote her mental power to defending herself against Izzy's verbal attacks.

"I'll leave the gown on the bed. The shoes, I'm keeping, as an inconvenience fee."

Izzy followed her from the room, the measured clip-clop of her high heels in stark contrast to Lena's rapid staccato.

Lena cursed herself for allowing Izzy to get under her skin. In the last year of their working relationship, she'd grown adept at ignoring Izzy's sly barbs.

But something about this new Izzy—Bella—felt more

sinister. Darker. Like every word she spoke carried a dangerous double entendre.

"Angela," Izzy called. "Are you forgetting something?"

Lena stopped.

Angela.

Blood thundered in Lena's ears as she turned around.

Izzy held up Lena's phone and a tube of lipstick. Dropped both into a silver clutch and held it out to her.

Now Lena understood the darkness surrounding Izzy. The senator's fiancée had information that could destroy Lena. Relished having the knowledge, yet chafed at the necessity of keeping it under wraps for reasons Lena had yet to discern.

She'd bet ten-to-one that Izzy hadn't intended to reveal it at this precise moment. But dear, impulsive Izzy could never stick to a plan.

Putting one stiletto in front of the other, she met Izzy halfway and accepted the accessory.

"I must say," Izzy purred, "the simplicity of your real name—Angela Jones—suits you far better. Which does your new beau, Rohan, prefer?"

A thousand questions clattered through Lena's mind. How did Izzy discover her former identity? She had only ever known her as Angelena Kamber. Why would she go snooping in that direction? How did she know about Rohan? Was Izzy stalking her? Did she kill Ruthie and try to pin it on Lena?

Somehow, through the mental barrage, she kept her expression neutral, unaffected by the deep crevasse now splintering her life.

"The prescription meds you're so fond of have finally broken your brain, Izzy. You should see a professional before your fiancé realizes his mistake."

Heat crouched on Izzy's cheeks, giving credence to Lena's wild guess.

"You should be nicer to me, Lena."

A part of Lena's brain registered the slow approach of footsteps.

"Why's that?" Lena shifted until her back was to the wall. "I thought you enjoyed our verbal MMA matches."

"What I'm going to enjoy is taking your life apart piece by piece."

A large figure materialized from behind Izzy. He wore a well-cut suit and a small amount of product to tame his brown, wavy hair. Not a single whisker bladed his strong jawline or ounce of fat graced his toned body.

But no amount of polish could camouflage the handsome, keen-eyed features of her savior.

The fisherman.

"Dean?"

Ignoring her, he leaned in to kiss Izzy's cheek. He lingered there for a beat too long.

Izzy gave him a sideways glance. "I take it your . . . meeting went well?"

He turned his dead-eye stare on Lena. "Unfortunately, I had to sever the relationship."

Izzy laughed, and it sent a chill down Lena's spine.

"This is Desmond," Izzy said, enjoying Lena's confusion. "He sees to an element of the senator's security." The backs of her fingers caressed the man's chest. "And performs other duties for me."

So much for her barometer on bad men. "How's your dear little daughter, Holly?" Lena asked, disgust coating her every word.

Izzy laughed. "Didn't I always tell you not to believe every sad story you heard?"

Lena had trouble processing the web Izzy had spun around her. Images of her and Rohan's time on the road flashed bright behind her eyes, blinding her to a truth her mind wasn't ready to accept.

She met Desmond's cold gaze. "You killed Ruthie."

"No, darling," Izzy said. "You did. Just as you killed Simon Garibay, Xander Douglas, and Neil Jones."

At the mention of the only father she had ever known, Lena's entire body iced over.

"Imagine my surprise—and delight—when Desmond uncovered your secret identity and an order of arrest for Angela Jones." She smiled. "For the murder of her father."

Lena edged away from the pair, who stared at her like they'd come off a weeklong GI cleansing and she was a large slice of Tiramasu.

"Did you know there's no statute of limitations on murder in North Carolina?" Izzy continued.

"What do you want?"

"What should have been mine," Izzy sneered. Pent-up rage sent her pearl drop earrings swinging.

"Xander?"

From one blink to the next, Izzy's stormy emotions settled. "Don't be absurd. We shall talk about the price of my silence later." She motioned to Desmond, who gestured for Lena to precede him across the catwalk balcony. "Enjoy the party."

Paralyzed to her core, Lena allowed Desmond to guide her away. How would she ever be able to socialize with the senator's guests with her life unraveling all around her?

She couldn't. At the first opportunity, she would retrieve her things from Izzy's room and sneak away. She wouldn't return to the cabin or her loft. Everything she needed to start over was in her Bronco.

Within the hour, she could be across the Tennessee border. She'd figure out the rest once she put some distance between her and Izzy.

A lump hardened in her chest at the thought of not saying goodbye to Rohan—or Sadie. They both deserved better than wondering for years what had become of her.

But she couldn't think about all of that now. At the moment, she had to devise an escape plan. She strode across the catwalk with purposeful strides.

"Oh, and Lena?" Izzy called.

Lena turned and met the other woman's eyes. Hate filling her heart.

"Don't even think about disappearing. It would be a shame if little Sadie vanished in those woods she loves so much."

43

"Ash," Rohan said, dictating a text message. *"Did you get anywhere on that name I gave you? Send me what you have, no matter how small. Maggie found out Balor was originally hired to pinch a Frida Kahlo piece from Lena's loft. Woman Walking was a damn afterthought."*

Rohan hit the Send button on his phone and stared at the Frida Kahlo in Lena's bathroom, aware the painting's owner could return home at any moment.

Yet the mental war raging inside his head kept him rooted in place. Did he truly want the answer to his question? Or would it be better to continue on in blissful ignorance?

Walking away from an unfinished puzzle wasn't in his DNA.

Setting his jaw, he flicked open the locking mechanism to the climate-controlled case. Removed the painting from the wall and set it on the kitchen's island counter.

The pad of his finger glanced over the artist's signature and year painted in the lower righthand corner before he flipped it over. Between the stretcher bars lay a vast expanse of untouched canvas.

No *Fine Art Fakes by Lena* stamp.

No synthetic DNA marker.

Only a yellowed-with-age envelope wedged beneath one of the wooden bars.

He detached the envelope and carefully opened it. Inside, he found a folded Certificate of Authenticity and the painting's apparent provenance, or chain of ownership.

The last name on the list was not Garibay, Kamber, or even Jones. In fact, the final owner wasn't a person at all, but a museum.

Rohan set aside the paperwork and turned the painting back over. He stared at it with a growing sense of dread and awe.

An original Frida Kahlo. A masterpiece worth millions.

And it was displayed in Lena's bathroom.

44

"You have an admirer."

Lena turned toward the owner of the velvety voice and found a gorgeous blonde eyeing Dean—Desmond—who stood not far away, sipping champagne from a crystal flute. All her attempts to lose him had so far failed.

"More like a stalker."

The blonde raised a brow, her attention zipping between Lena and her appointed guard dog. "Shall I contact security?"

"He's part of the senator's security team, so I don't think lodging a complaint will do much good."

"Sounds like I've encountered a person of fascination." The blonde smiled and held out her hand. "Kayla Krowne."

Lena transferred her nearly empty wineglass to her left hand in order to shake the other woman's surprisingly firm grip. Every other woman she'd encountered tonight acted as though they were about to handle a slimy fish.

"Angelena Kamber. Call me Lena."

"What brings you to Senator Palmer's engagement party?"

Lena suppressed a snort. "Interesting that no family, other than the senator's parents, were invited to his *engagement party*."

Kayla eyed the crowd. "Yes, I see what you mean. This gathering appears to be more for his special friends."

"Friends who can afford thousand-dollar Swedish meatballs."

"They're quite good. Have you tried them?"

"I'm not that special."

Kayla laughed. "I take it you're not here to help further the senator's political interests?"

"I'm here to answer questions."

"About what?"

Lena nodded toward the illuminated *Woman Walking*.

"Are you the artist?" Kayla asked, sounding delighted.

"You can tell it's a copy?"

"Of course." The dismay that surged through Lena must have showed on her face, for Kayla rushed to reassure her. "I'm an avid collector, and Na-lih Catawnee happens to be one of my favorite local artists." The hand holding her glass of white wine swept over the gathering. "No one else here has such a discerning eye. Not even the senator."

"Are you associated with a museum?"

"My interest in art is not so altruistic, though my collection could fill a small museum." She took a drink of her wine. "I'm a lobbyist."

She held Lena's eye as she made her declaration, as if she expected Lena to be put off by her profession.

"No judgment here. I'm a professional copyist."

"I like you, Angelena Kamber."

Lena's spirits lifted for the first time since setting foot on Palmer's property. She finished her wine and grabbed another from a passing waiter.

"Ditto, Kayla Krowne." She gave the lobbyist a sideways glance. "Mind if I ask what you're hoping to get Palmer's support for?"

"What makes you think I am?"

"Thousand-dollar meatballs."

Kayla laughed. "Stellar investigative skills."

"Details matter in my line of work."

Kayla rubbed her bottom lip against the rim of her wine-glass while considering the senator, who stood across the room with Izzy latched onto his arm. He shook the hand of a gray-haired, Coco Chanel-wearing donor. "Palmer and I don't see eye-to-eye on issues."

"Then why contribute to his campaign?"

"A necessary reconnaissance fee."

Lena stared at the couple, considering Kayla's words. "You think to get to him through his new fiancée?"

"He wouldn't be the first politician to be managed by his spouse." She cast Lena an assessing glance. "But Palmer isn't like most politicians. He doesn't boast. Doesn't jack up his ego with pillow talk. I'm told he has a plan and follows it. To the letter."

"You want the plan," Lena said, thinking out loud, "so you can derail it."

An appreciative smile spread across the lobbyist's face. "What a diabolical stratagem. Wish I had thought of it."

Lena lowered her voice. "Do yourself a favor and steer clear of Isabella DeCarlo."

"You speak from an unpleasant experience?"

"One that's years old and, because I didn't learn my lesson, another one only a few minutes ago."

The lobbyist's brows knit in concern. "Anything I can do?"

"Thank you," Lena said with meaning. "But I'm not someone you should entangle yourself with either."

"I disagree."

What was it about the women in this town? Every one of them seemed to have an overpowering need to fix her problems.

Unfortunately, she could think of only one way to take care of her situation with Izzy, and she doubted Kayla would go that far for a stranger.

"Lena?"

A familiar masculine voice pulled Lena from her dark thoughts. She focused on the handsome man who now stood at Kayla's side.

"Hello, Phin."

"Hello." He searched the crowd. "Rohan here?"

"Not that I know of."

"You two are acquainted?" Kayla asked.

Phin's smile turned conspiratorial. "A recent, but mutually beneficial, acquaintance."

Kayla turned curious eyes on her.

Lena glared at Phin. "Don't let the Blackwell Charmer misdirect you. Ours is a business arrangement."

"I wonder if Rohan would agree."

Lena recalled their recent exchange in her cabin. "Absolutely." Wanting to shift the conversation to safer ground, she asked, "How do you know each other?"

"I work part-time for Kayla."

"You work for her?"

"At Krowne and Associates. The largest lobbying firm in North Carolina. Maybe even the entire Southeast."

Lena turned wide eyes on her new friend. "And you still do your own reconnaissance?"

"I lead from the trenches. It's the most effective way to

uncover opportunities and"—her eyes twinkled—"make new alliances."

At that moment, Palmer caught Lena's attention and waved her over. She released a long sigh of resignation.

"Show time?" Kayla asked.

Lena nodded. "Be prepared to watch one of the greatest tragedies of the twenty-first century."

"Is your phone in that Gucci clutch?"

"Yes."

Kayla held out her hand. When Lena hesitated, the lobbyist waggled insistent fingers.

Lena glanced at Phin.

In perfect Captain Picard pitch, he said, "Resistance is futile."

She fished out her phone, unlocked the home screen, and placed it in Kayla's outstretched hand.

The lobbyist's fingers flew over the keys, then a muffled ring resonated from her own clutch.

"You have my number now," Kayla said. "And one favor credit. Use it. No judgment. No questions asked."

Lena swallowed back the hard ball of emotion in the back of her neck. "Thank you."

Lifting her chin, she glided toward an uncertain future.

45

AFTER A FEW INITIAL INTRODUCTIONS, SENATOR PALMER HAD instructed his fiancée to escort Lena into his private study, with assurances that he and his passel of admirers would follow once his celebrity friend arrived.

Before Lena entered, she had caught Kayla's eye and conveyed the timeless message that every woman understood. A message that one word or one feeling couldn't define. It was a message that pleaded with the receiver.

Don't leave me.

Now, Lena hovered near the fireplace, while Izzy poured them drinks at the sideboard and Desmond's malevolent stare chewed into the back of her neck.

The original *Woman Walking* hung over the mantel and her copy was propped on an easel to the right of the fireplace. She had to admit the lighting, location, and ambiance suited the Catawnee. Her certainty about the senator's and Izzy's worthiness to have exclusive access to it every day was another matter.

For a moment, Lena's surroundings faded into the background. The woman in the painting seemed to beckon her forward with the power of her gaze alone. All the tension from the past hour eased from her muscles, and Lena forgot, for a split second, that her former best friend had threatened Sadie.

Other than their rift over Xander, Lena couldn't figure out what else had caused Izzy's deep animosity toward her. Then again, love triangles have been the death of many literary characters over the centuries, so maybe the loss of Xander had been enough.

But to threaten sweet Sadie? That just pissed her off.

Even though Lena's instincts urged her to put Angelena Kamber away in a box and run, Izzy's warning about what she would do to Sadie kept her rooted in kiss-ass hell.

Only a little while longer.

Once she escaped Izzy's net, she would go to Rohan and tell him everything. Whatever was going on inside Izzy's head was growing like a fast-acting malignant cancer, and Lena needed Rohan's beautiful brain to help her figure it out.

Izzy handed Lena a flute of champagne. "I cannot see why Blaise thought it was a good idea to set your attempt at a copy so close to the original," Izzy said. Venom slithered around every syllable, though a passerby would find her tone conversational. "Your hues are all off. The model's dress is lifeless, and her eyes are flat." She leaned forward. "And what is that on her right cheek? A tick?"

Many artists struggled with self-confidence, anxiety, depression, and imposter syndrome at different times in their career. Lena had experienced them all. Sometimes to crippling effect.

But not today.

Today, she observed the painting she'd spent hours on with a fair eye. One that spotted the flaws, but also recognized she had produced an excellent copy. A copy that most Catawnee experts would mistake for the original. One day, she would ask Kayla which brush stroke gave it away.

Lena lifted the glass to her lips and finished half her drink in one long gulp. "Don't you have an ass to kiss somewhere, Izzy?"

"Bella," she hissed back. A few seconds ticked by before Izzy's explosive emotion receded. "There's nowhere I'd rather be than right here. Right now."

"I'm afraid I don't share your warm and fuzzies."

"Which makes me even happier."

Lena turned to face her nemesis. "What have I done to make you dislike me so much?"

"Dislike?" A small laugh, filled with darkness, rippled up her slender throat. "Such a confined word for what I feel for you."

"And yet the question remains the same."

"You stole my life."

"What alternate universe have you been dwelling in? You're the one who slept with my boyfriend and screwed up our friendship."

"No, Lena. You broke everything the moment you crawled into bed with Xander."

"Because you wanted him for yourself?"

Anger ignited in Izzy's dark eyes. *"Because I wanted the three of us to stay together forever."*

Lena blinked. "Do you know how out there your statement is?"

"Together, we were unstoppable. We beat the streets, the drugs, the prostitution. The starvation." Her manicured hand jabbed the air with each point. "With a little ingenuity, we could have ruled the art forgery business for the entire east coast."

"Simon might have had something to say about your master plan."

Their mentor had treated his young forgers with a guiding, but firm hand. Simon didn't take any crap from the homeless teenagers under his protection, and anyone who messed with one of his protégées had a habit of disappearing.

Simon wouldn't have taken kindly to the three of them splitting off and starting their own forgery business in his town.

"You always gave Simon more consideration than the tyrant deserved." She made a pinching motion against the silken material draped over her long thigh. "He was nothing more than lint. Easily plucked and discarded."

A chill trickled down Lena's spine. If Simon had died under mysterious circumstances, she would now wonder about Izzy's role in their mentor's death. But he hadn't. His death had been nothing but a stupid, tragic accident.

Izzy's eyes shone like polished onyx. "But you couldn't keep your damn legs closed."

"It wasn't like that and you know it."

"You knew—*knew*—Xander wasn't the one, yet you still tossed away everything we'd built together like it was nothing."

"Keep rewriting history to fit your own demented narrative."

"I rewrote nothing."

"Rather than have a civil conversation about your hurt or anger or whatever it was you were feeling, you decided the best way to deal with the situation was to lure Xander into your bed. You're the last person to be casting any damn stones."

A heavy silence, but for the ringing in her ears, settled

around them. Lena searched her memory for clues. Clues that Izzy had dropped about her dreams for them. As hard as she tried, she couldn't pull a single one from the depths of her mind.

Izzy had one thing right though. Getting romantically involved with Xander had been a horrible idea. But she'd been young and stupid and lonely, and Xander had been so willing and patient and gentle.

A sudden weariness rolled over Lena. "What do you want from me?"

"Only what I'm owed."

"Which is?"

"Life for life."

46

A PERFUNCTORY KNOCK SOUNDED ON THE DOOR BEFORE CRUZ entered Rohan's suite of rooms at the Friary. "What's up?"

"I need a favor," Rohan said, sliding a bare arm into a crisp, white dress shirt.

"If you want me to knot your tie, you're shit out of luck."

"I need you to do some research on a painting by Frida Kahlo."

"Which one?"

"Self-Portrait with Braided Hair."

"Are you looking for something specific?"

"It disappeared from the Asheville Museum. I'm not sure when. See what you can find out about the robbery and where the piece might be now." He tucked the tail of his shirt into his black trousers. "Liv or Maddy might have some insights."

"I could tap into Ash, too."

Rohan shook his head.

"I have him working on something else for me. Best not to dip into that pool too often."

"Is this connected to Byrne's death?"

"I believe so. To what extent, I'm not sure." He worked his feet into a pair of Santoni dress shoes. "Maggie told me Bobby Balor revealed his original target was the Frida Kahlo hanging in Lena's bathroom. A few days before the heist, Byrne added *Woman Walking* to the order."

Cruz whistled. "Shit just got real complicated. Where are you headed in that getup?"

"Palmer's engagement party. Something's going down with Lena that has Kayla spooked."

"Kayla knows Lena?"

"She does now."

Cruz sat on the arm of a chair and glanced down at the plate holding a half sandwich on the nearby table. "Phin with her?"

Rohan nodded. "He's the one who texted me."

Just as he'd returned from Lena's, Rohan had received a message from Phin. Lena hadn't just dropped off the paintings. She was gowned, jeweled, and at Palmer's side.

A part of him wanted to smash his fist into Palmer's handsome face. The other part wondered what the hell else Lena hadn't told him.

"Why go through all the trouble?" Cruz said. "Phin's right there. Have him dig deeper."

"I need to be there."

"Ah." Cruz grinned, picked up Rohan's sandwich, and sniffed. "You shouldn't have brought her here."

"That's my dinner."

Cruz's smile grew wider as he took a large bite. "My hypothesis is now a theory. Three out of three Blackwell men have gone bonkers over the women they've collaborated with."

Considering Rohan's thoughts had been running along

the same lines of late, he had to give credit to his brother's observation. Damned if he'd tell him, though.

"I need the information on the Kahlo yesterday." Rohan pulled his suit coat off a hanger and motioned for Cruz to precede him from the room.

Cruz laughed. "Yes, ma'am."

Once they were outside the Friary and about to go their separate ways, Cruz turned serious. "How are you getting into Palmer's?"

"Haven't worked that out yet. I'm hoping Kayla can give me an assist."

"Be careful, Ro. I don't know what's going on between Palmer and Lena, but there's a good chance he'll be our next president. Men like that have squashed more than a few pissants to get to the top."

"You calling me a pissant, brother?"

"It wouldn't be the worst insult I've slung at you."

Rohan's mind turned toward Lena as he slid behind the wheel. The sense that she was in danger grew with each passing minute.

47

"WHERE IS SHE?" ROHAN ASKED KAYLA AS SOON AS HE AND Phin reached her side.

"How about we start out with something like, 'Thank you, Kayla, for convincing the senator's aide to let you join the party,'" Phin said.

"It's okay," Kayla said. "I recognize the Lost Blackwell look by now."

Rohan snapped out of his surveillance of the room. "Lost Blackwell?"

"Once a Blackwell man loses his heart to a woman, he wraps his entire, protective universe around her." An emotion Rohan couldn't interpret weighed down Kayla's knowing smile. She tapped a red nail against the center of his chest. "You, as a single being, an individual entity, gone forever."

Rohan frowned, having no idea what she was talking about.

"You're synced with another," Phin interpreted. "Like I am with Maddy."

Kayla grinned. "And Zeke is with Liv."

"First Cruz, now you." Rohan's features softened. "But Phin is right." He kissed her cheek. "You have my sincere thanks for your help."

Given the type of gathering, Rohan suspected she'd had to contribute another grand to the senator's campaign in order to get the aide's cooperation. He would offer to pay her back, but knew she would refuse. "I owe you a debt. Don't hesitate to claim it."

Heat entered her fair cheeks.

"Kayla Krowne is blushing," Phin said, reaching into an interior coat pocket. "I need to get a picture of this."

"Do it, and I'll send you to meet with Mayor Henley instead."

Phin shuddered and clasped his hands behind his back.

Kayla nodded toward a set of doors at the far end of a hallway. "Lena's down there, with a group of the senator's biggest donors, in what I understand is the senator's private study."

"Why?"

"To show off his million-dollar painting."

"Why did he include Lena?"

"He has Lena's copy in there as well. It makes sense that he would invite the artist to be on hand. The exposure could take her business to a whole new level."

"I sense a *but*."

"Lena seemed reluctant, almost nervous, about attending the private gathering."

"She's not a big people person," Rohan said. "Could her reaction have been social anxiety?"

"It's possible." Kayla thought for a moment. "What put my antennae on alert was how she spoke about the senator's fiancée."

"Something specific?"

"She told me to steer clear of her."

"Did she say why?"

"I got the impression there was some old, bad blood between them."

"What is the fiancée's name?"

"Isabella DeCarlo."

"Izzy DeCarlo?"

"I've not heard anyone use that nickname. She goes by Bella."

Rohan would bet his best ultra-wide monitor that Bella DeCarlo was Lena's former business partner.

"How long has it been since they disappeared into the senator's study?"

"Forty-five, maybe fifty, minutes ago. I doubt there are many people left inside. Several of the donors have already returned to the party."

"Stay here." Rohan checked himself. "Please."

They nodded, and he left to extract Lena from the senator's lair.

48

"Finally, I have you all to myself."

Startled, Lena tore her attention from the paintings to find the senator next to her. She glanced around and noted only a few people remained in the room. Izzy, Desmond, Gerard and Elizabeth Palmer, and the senator's chief of staff, Craig Muller.

The latter studied her with an unnerving intensity. During their few encounters, Craig had treated her respectfully, but with a somewhat dismissive air. As if he always had higher priority issues to deal with than an artisan. He probably had.

Seconds after Izzy had delivered her cryptic life-for-a-life remark, the senator and his entourage had entered the study. The senator had regaled the group with the story of how he came into possession of the artwork and why and how he commissioned Lena. Then he set them loose on her, and she'd spent the next forty minutes answering questions and swapping contact information.

"My apologies, Senator. I got lost in thought. I'll get out

of your hair so you and Iz—Bella can have some time alone."

"No need." The senator's gaze settled on Izzy, where she stood near the sideboard in private discussion with Desmond and Gerard. "She's happily engaged at the moment." His polished smile appeared. "Besides, it's about time I got to know you better, don't you think?"

No.

Getting too chummy with her clients led to inquiries about her family and friends and schooling—or lack of. All things she needed to keep buried.

At times, her self-imposed isolation truly sucked. Loneliness made fools of everyone, at some point. Searching for information on Neil a few weeks ago had been the height of foolishness.

One familiar face. One morsel of new information. Her heart had ached for both, yet her search had produced nothing.

It was as if someone had erased him from history. Her memories seemed to be the only thing left of him and those were growing grayer and grayer with each passing day.

She might not remember everything about her adopted father, but she recalled her previous conversation with the senator with perfect clarity.

"If I don't stay," she said, "will you threaten me with nonpayment again?"

"Forgive me, Miss Kamber. I was desperate to introduce you to my guests, and you left me with little choice."

"For future reference, I respond well to *please*."

"Duly noted."

"Great. If you'll excuse me, my next commission is waiting."

"But we haven't had our chat yet."

"Some other time." Lena turned to leave.

"Please, Miss Kamber."

Lena closed her eyes and mumbled every curse word she knew in one long, unbroken sentence. She blew out a breath and pasted on her broadest I-hate-you smile. "Not fair to use my own words against me."

"Not from my perspective." He noticed her empty glass and called across the room. "Bella love, bring us some champagne, will you?"

"Of course."

Izzy brought three flutes of sparkling wine. Once Palmer and Lena claimed their drinks, the senator handed his fiancée Lena's empty glass. "Thank you, sweetheart," he said in a tone of clear dismissal.

The icy look *Bella love* settled on Palmer, then her, could have shored up the Doomsday Glacier.

Izzy hovered at their side for another breath before pivoting on her stilettos and downing her champagne.

"Is your talent God-given or did you have to work hard to develop it?" Palmer asked.

Lena's bicep squeezed the silver clutch tucked between her arm and body. "Both. I've been painting or drawing for as long as I can remember. But it took many years of practice —and a few patient mentors—to get my skills to their current level."

"It's a gift to know at such a young age what you want to do for the rest of your life. Some people might not find their true talent until well into adulthood. Others will go to their grave without crossing paths with their true destiny."

The thought of such an existence hurt Lena's heart. She couldn't imagine never having drawn her first picture and experiencing that moment where the world, and all its possibilities, seemed endless.

All of a sudden, her fingers ached to run along the hidden seam of her shoulder bag upstairs, to hear the familiar crinkle of paper. "It is a blessing."

"I'm sure your parents are quite proud of your accomplishments."

Lena took a long swallow of her champagne. "They would be, if they were still alive."

"Forgive me. I didn't realize."

"Why would you? They've been gone a long time."

"They died when you were young?"

"Yes, a car accident."

"My condolences. Losing one's parents is never easy. But for them to be taken away while you're a child, has to be the hardest of all."

Lena said nothing. She couldn't. A long-buried emotion burned her throat. She didn't understand why she was being so forthcoming with the senator. She wasn't even sure she liked him.

Yet he drew her in by his calm presence, by the surprising sincerity in his voice.

She took another long drink of champagne.

The same voice he used like a weapon to persuade constituents to vote for him, big corporations to support him, colleagues to compromise—or outright set aside— their fundamental beliefs for him.

The alcohol she'd consumed hadn't dulled her wits enough to mistake his polished small talk for compassion. Every word out of a politician's mouth was a stratagem for reelection. A technique Palmer had perfected over his long political career.

But why would he bother? He had the painting. She had nothing left to offer him.

When he asked if she'd gone to live with family after the

accident, she startled herself by shaking her head. "A nice man named Neil adopted me."

"Did he know what happened to them?"

"Maybe. I don't know. I grew curious about them in my teens and asked a few questions."

"But he didn't have any answers?"

An image of Neil in his chair, struggling to breathe flashed through her mind.

Run.

She shook her head.

"What is Neil up to these days now that you're all grown up and have a successful business of your own?"

Tears filled Lena's eyes, and she looked away.

"No, please don't tell me your adopted father is dead, too."

Lena lifted the champagne to her lips again.

"What happened to him?"

An image of Neil in his office, foam bubbling at the corner of his mouth shot to the top of her memory bank.

"It doesn't matter. He's gone. Just like everyone else I've ever loved."

A silence spread around them, and Lena cursed her alcohol-loose tongue. For someone who rarely drank, three —or was it four?—glasses did funny things to her survival instincts.

"Once again, I ask for your forgiveness," Palmer said. "I gave my curiosity too much free rein."

"It's time for me to go, now that I've fulfilled my end of our so-called bargain." Lena set her empty glass down on a side table. "I hope you enjoy, *Woman Walking,* Senator."

She strode to the door, only to be intercepted by Craig Muller.

"Leaving, Miss Kamber?"

"Yes, please excuse me." She attempted to go around him, but he placed a hand on her arm. Not a restraining hand, just an attention grabber.

"Now that your business with the senator is over, I wondered if you'd be interested in having dinner with me."

Shock threw her body into a temporary paralysis while her mind worked through his words.

The chief of staff was a relatively fit man in his forties, with brown flecks in his blue eyes and a small scar on his chin. He went about the senator's business with an enviable quiet confidence. A catch for any woman.

"The timing of my invitation might not be ideal, but I thought better here than me showing up on your doorstep." His thumb smoothed over her forearm. "I've admired you from the moment Bella brought the news article to our attention, but I felt it best not to complicate matters until you concluded your business with the senator."

He referred to the *Citizen-Times* article about the reproduction she did for the Harold House after one of their prize paintings got swept away in a tornado.

Izzy had brought the article to their attention.

Lena's soggy mind swam around, searching for connections. Izzy wouldn't have recommended her out of the goodness of her heart. She'd had a reason. A nefarious one.

The answer came to her in a flash.

She drew her arm away. "Thank you, Mr. Muller, but I'm late for another appointment."

Recognizing a brush-off, the chief of staff stepped back, his features tight. She could still feel the arctic cold of his gaze when she shut the study door.

And looked straight into Rohan's suspicious eyes.

49

"WHAT ARE YOU DOING HERE?" LENA ASKED, MOVING AWAY from the study door.

Rohan took in her sexy-ass dress, shimmering hair, and sparkling jewels and experienced an intense desire to both kiss her senseless and throw his coat around her shoulders.

"Taking you home." He braced himself for an argument, but she nodded her consent.

"My things are upstairs."

Rohan sent a quick message to Phin as he followed Lena to the west wing of the mansion, where the family slept.

Once the partygoers' voices receded, Lena asked, "Why are you here?"

"Kayla was concerned about you."

"That doesn't explain why you're here. Your role in recovering the Catawnee was over the moment you delivered it to me."

"Three people have died since I met you."

"Three?"

"On my way over here," Rohan said, as they entered a large feminine bedroom, "I got a phone call from the sheriff.

Bobby Balor's roommate found him dead about an hour ago. Strangled in his living room."

"How long had he been dead?"

"The coroner's estimating between two to three hours."

Lena paused in the midst of gathering her clothes. Recalled the look that passed between Dean and Izzy. His reference to severing a connection. Her laugh. "Do you think the same person killed Ruthie and Xander?"

"I don't know. If it was just the thief and the art dealer, I'd say someone is trying to cover their tracks. But I haven't figured out how Ruthie plays into all of this."

"Maybe she doesn't."

"What do you mean?"

A pained look crossed her face, and she shook her head. "I'm not sure." She kicked out of her stilettos. "Turn around."

"Why?"

"Because I'm naked beneath this ridiculous gown and I want to put on some underwear."

"Wait until we get home."

"It'll only take a minute."

"Lena, we don't have—"

A feminine laugh sifted through the door before a tall, dark-haired woman in white entered. "Is this your first lover's spat?"

Lena sighed. "Go away, Izzy."

So this was the infamous Izzy DeCarlo. She was pretty, but Byrne had been an idiot to stray away from Lena for this hard-eyed woman.

Izzy's gaze traveled over Rohan, and a low hum of appreciation vibrated in her throat. "Lena, you always were clueless when it came to guys. You should be fucking this one instead of arguing with him."

Holding her mound of clothing against her chest, Lena moved to stand in front of him. With their height difference, Lena's presence did nothing to prevent the other woman from looking her fill. But Lena's attempt to protect him made his heart swell with an emotion he'd only come close to once before.

Love.

Somehow, this artistic spitfire of a woman had crawled into his chest and taken up residence in his heart. The realization should have scared the hell out of him, given his battle with the Collective, and maybe it did, a little.

But more than that, he wondered if she felt the same about him.

Lena's gown left a good portion of her back bare. He rested his palm against the warm flesh of her right shoulder blade, hoping she'd interpret his touch as a gesture of solidarity and not him being an opportunistic perv.

"We're leaving," Lena said.

"Not until you and I have had our chat."

"We've chatted enough."

Izzy moved farther into the room, and a man entered behind her.

Rohan's attention zeroed in on the newcomer. There was something familiar about him. "Dean?"

"They call him Desmond," Lena said. "He's part of Palmer's security team—and Izzy's pet dog."

Desmond clenched his fists and stepped toward Lena.

Rohan lunged forward, forcing Lena behind him. "You like to hit women, do you, Des? Is that what happened to Ruthie? She wouldn't give you what you wanted, so you showed her what happened to ladies who say no?"

"There's the fire I adore," Desmond said in a red velvet

voice. "Beautiful, but you're still holding back." He brushed a fingertip along Rohan's whiskered jaw. "Don't."

Rohan grabbed Desmond's finger and bent it backward. "I won't." He exerted pressure until the other man's body yielded to the pain, then he slammed a foot into Desmond's chest, sending him crashing into the wall.

Desmond smiled as if the violent action was exactly what he'd wanted. He pushed off the wall and drew a gun from inside his coat. He didn't point it at them, just let it hang from his hand at his side. A sick-fuck smile on his face.

Rohan split his attention between Desmond and Izzy. "Expect a visit from the sheriff."

"I wouldn't get the police involved, Rohan." She purred out his name. "I'm not the worst predator Lena needs to fear."

Desmond slanted a hard glance at Izzy.

"Lose the Seductive Bella act," Lena said.

"Afraid I'll turn his head, like I did Xander's?"

Rohan opened his mouth to set her straight, when Lena's fingers wove between his.

"No," Lena said, keeping her attention on Izzy.

He infused all of his newfound feelings into one long squeeze of her hand.

"How adorable." Izzy clasped her hands in front of her. "I wonder if you would still be enamored of our Angelena if you knew—"

"Let's get out of here," Lena said, tugging him toward the door.

He didn't budge. "Knew what?"

"Rohan, please. You can't believe anything she says."

"Knew what?" he repeated.

"She's wanted for murder."

50

THE ABYSS LENA HAD BEEN APPROACHING FOR DAYS—*YEARS*—was suddenly beneath her feet.

She tumbled. Crashed into the sharp edges of her life. Bled out all of her regrets until there was nothing left but a hollow, endless ache.

No life's blood.

No fight.

No hope.

She jerked her hand from Rohan's and left Izzy to seed her poison. To kill Lena's first prospect of happiness and a normal life in years.

Barefoot, she walked through the mansion, ignoring Kayla's call, Gerard Palmer's hand signal, and potential clients' scandalized stares.

Her eyes stayed dry the entire drive home. They didn't well with tears once while she mentally constructed her exit strategy. It wasn't until she pictured Rohan's reaction at finding her gone tomorrow that she felt the first sting of loss.

After unlocking the dead bolt, she shouldered her way inside and went to her wardrobe. She pulled out the backpack she'd been wearing the night she'd fled Neil's home and crammed two sets of clothes inside.

She tamped down the urge to pack up her studio, but the countdown clock ticking in her head trebled now. Zipping up her pack, she rushed to her bathroom, flipped on the light, and stared in shock at the empty display case above the toilet.

The Frida Kahlo was gone.

"Looking for something?" a distant voice asked.

Lena turned toward it with dread and a battalion of other emotions. Heavy on the dread.

Beyond the bathroom's glowing light, the loft's colorful palette had dulled to a thousand shades of gray, obscuring her intruder's presence.

Even without seeing him, she knew who'd burglarized her apartment. Again.

She felt no fear. Just a soul-killing inevitability.

Flipping off the light switch, she waited for her eyes to adjust.

A gust of wind ripped fading leaves off trees and carried them past her enormous windows. Lightning strobed through the loft, and she spotted a figure sitting in her favorite chair, facing her.

Still dressed in his finery, Rohan stared at her through black-rimmed glasses. He sat with his legs spread wide, one outstretched. His elbows braced against the armrests. The lower part of his face hidden behind his clasped hands.

He looked as if he were trying to work out a complicated mathematical equation and was failing.

Her attention flicked to the painting propped against the chair beside his right knee. Anxiety coiled like a viper in her stomach.

She nodded toward the Kahlo. "What do you plan to do with my painting?"

"Your painting?"

Her last bit of hope shredded like a delicate strand of saffron.

"Depends," he said when she remained silent.

"On?"

"How truthfully you answer my next question."

Anger sparked. She wasn't a liar. She was a survivor. A pawn sliding across a board game she'd never wanted to play. Who was he to judge her?

"How will you know if I'm being truthful?" she prodded, moving closer.

"I won't." His gaze seemed to probe into the dark, broken corners of her heart. "I'll accept your word."

"Why? You've clearly been suspicious of me from day one. Why do you have faith in me at a time when you shouldn't have any?"

"My initial suspicion had to do with your sudden appearance at the same time I was fending off a cyberattack. I was concerned the Collective had sent you and that you would destroy me and everything I cared about."

Lena wanted to ask how things were going with the Collective, but knew he wouldn't appreciate the distraction. Frankly, neither would she. Although she cared about the outcome of his cyber battle, she was more concerned about where he was going with this conversation.

"Your question?" she asked, getting back to the root of their discussion.

"Who are you?"

Lena didn't flinch or show any outward sign of the adrenaline rushing her body. "I see Izzy filled your ears with juicy bits before you left."

"I didn't need Izzy's sensationalist comment to know you weren't born Angelena Kamber." Rohan had broken into her apartment, removed the Kahlo, and made himself comfortable in the time it had taken her to make a ten-minute detour to her bank's ATM.

Izzy wouldn't have just blurted out every sordid detail she'd uncovered about Lena. She would have drawn the moment out. Enjoyed the power she held over Rohan for as long as possible.

Much longer than ten minutes. Which meant—

"You didn't stay and hear Izzy out?"

His serious expression turned annoyed. "Do I look like a guy who would listen to such a vain and vengeful woman trash on someone I care about?"

Lena stared at him, unable to mask the shock caused by his declaration. Did he realize what he'd said? Had something short-circuited in that brilliant brain of his?

He set his glasses on a nearby table and pushed out of his chair. "Do I?"

The violence in those two words caused her to take an involuntary step back. "No, not really. But she delivered a rather effective cliffhanger. Few would've been able to contain their curiosity."

"I admit, she piqued mine." His eyes burned into hers. "But not quenched. I prefer to sip directly from the fountain, not a broken glass." He advanced a step. "Who are you?"

She swallowed. "I don't know."

"Ehh." Another step. "Wrong answer."

Lena backed up, uncertain about this raw, feral side of him. "It's the only one I've got."

"Who is Angela Jones?"

"A name I used for nearly a decade."

"Then you became Angelena Kamber?"

She nodded.

"We'll come back to Angelena in a moment."

His head tilted to the side, considering her. "You were known as Angela Jones from the time you were what, five to about fifteen?"

"Yes."

"When did your parents die?"

Lena's palms grew moist, and she couldn't think over the rhythmic pulse slamming against her eardrums.

"Don't lose your courage now," Rohan said in a gentle voice. "I'm not going anywhere. No matter what."

Considering their situation, she could have taken his comments as a threat. But Lena concentrated on his tone and the way his gaze caressed her like delicate fingers trailing through her hair.

"Four turning five, I think."

He shortened the distance between them and took one of her hands in his. "They died in an auto accident?"

"That's the story Neil told me. But I—"

"Who's Neil?"

"The man I called father for ten years."

"He adopted you?"

"I suppose so. I'm not sure."

"His last name was Jones, too?"

She nodded. Lena had always hated her last name. It was so . . . generic. Ordinary. It had never felt right.

"But you, what?" he asked.

"Pardon?"

"You don't believe your parents died in a car accident?"

51

R ohan's legendary calm fractured with each second he waited for Lena's reply.

He had imagined many scenarios to explain her hidden past, some involving a witnessed crime that would require her going into WITSEC, but not once had he considered that the violence had been against her family.

A frustrated growl erupted from her throat, and she strode to the bay of windows, where nightfall's talons sank deep into the landscape.

Moving to her side, he watched her reflection light up with each successive bolt in the sky. Though it nearly killed him, he waited for her to formulate words she had likely never dared speak while she struggled with the eroding effects of time. Memories, especially ones managed by a nervous system not yet able to comprehend certain audio and visual communication, were transitory beasts.

"My parents and I had gone to my grandparents' house for a birthday party." She rubbed her temple as if to bring into focus images obscured by a thick fog. "Maybe mine. I

remember being excited and pleased by everyone's attention." She sent him an apologetic glance. "But it might
simply have been that I was basking in the spotlight of
attentive, loving grandparents."

He pulled her fingers away from where she attempted to
drill a hole in the side of her head and massaged away the
tension in her hand. "Understood. Go on."

"I remember the rich, spicy aromas of my grandmother's
kitchen. I remember standing on a stool beside her. My
chubby hands covered in white flour." She lifted her free
hand and spread her fingers wide. "But I can't recall my
dadi's face."

"It happens. There are nuances to my father's features
that I can no longer recall, and I had a lot more time with
him than you did with your grandmother."

She curled the fingers of her free hand into a fist.

"What else do you remember?"

"Driving in a vehicle. My mother trying to comfort me
from her position in the front passenger seat." She paused,
staring at his reflection, but her mind was decades away.

Thunder punched the building, sending a shiver down
the panes of glass, a split second before a snap of lightning
forced her back to the present.

"Why was she comforting you?"

"I might have been crying." She shook her head. "My
mother handed me something. It was shiny, I think. Then a
bright light illuminated her face. Her eyes widened. Then
nothing. My memories go dark, except for a brief flash of
being carried away from the car."

Rohan turned toward her. Without releasing her hand,
he brushed her loose hair behind her ear. He wanted her to
look at him, but knew she was still deep in the past.

"Where were your parents?" he asked in a low voice.

She closed her eyes a moment before her tear-drenched gaze met his. "Burning."

52

Twenty years ago

FLAMES CONSUMED THE VEHICLE, AND HER LITTLE HAND reached for the two unmoving figures inside.

"*Maa! Pita!*" She screamed at the top of her four-year-old lungs and kicked at the stranger carrying her farther and farther away. But her parents didn't move, didn't stop the strange man from shoving her into the backseat of a big truck.

Another man, with scars covering his face, got behind the wheel and a woman with short, curly hair climbed into the front passenger seat.

"You stupid fuck," the driver growled, as they sped away.

She scrambled up to stand on the back seat. Tears made it difficult to see, especially in the dark, but she stared at the burning vehicle through the rear window. Any moment, *maa* and *pita* would come for her.

Why hadn't they let her stay with her grandparents like they had promised?

One moment she'd been blowing out the candles on her birthday cake and the next pita was scooping her up and running out the door, without putting on their winter coats.

"I don't kill kids," the stranger sitting beside her said.

"You should have left her behind," Curls said.

"Where? It's freezing outside, and the vehicle is going to blow any second—"

A huge ball of fire shot into the air at the same time the flames consumed the two figures in the vehicle.

"No!" She shrieked and shrieked until her throat hurt and her legs gave out.

The stranger who saved her laid her down on the backseat and something warm covered her shivering body.

"What was the girl doing with her parents?" Curls asked. "Our intel indicated she was going to stay the weekend with her grandparents."

"Something spooked the Kumars," Savior said. "They'd barely been there fifty minutes before Team A reported them hauling ass out of the house."

"Someone must have tipped them off," Scarface said.

"We'll work out what went wrong later," Curls said. "Right now, we need to decide what to do about the girl."

"Let's look for a church and leave her on their doorstep," Scarface said.

"We're not leaving her outside," Savior said. "It's twenty degrees and dropping. She doesn't even have shoes on."

"What about a hospital?"

"Cameras," Curls said.

"Then there's only one other thing we can do," Scarface said.

"No," Savior said in a mean voice.

"We're not taking her with us, which means we're out of options."

"Do you have the stomach to put a gun to this girl's head, Lonnie?"

Scarface said nothing.

"Do you, Zora?"

Silence.

"Where does that leave us?" Scarface asked.

"I'll figure something out. For tonight, she can stay at my place."

"Not a good idea," Curls said. "Someone might see her."

"I've got a garage. No one will see her, coming or going."

"Kids are sneaky," Scarface said.

"I want my *dadi*," she croaked out through her dry, scratchy throat.

"You will. If you're a good girl," Savior said. "Can you be good, Anjali?"

She looked into the stranger's face for the first time. His eyes weren't kind, but they weren't cold like his partners'.

Maa always made her promise to be good if she wanted an extra cookie or new toy. Anjali could be good again in order to see her grandmother. *Dadi* would know how to help *maa* and *pita*.

She nodded.

Savior used the cuff of his long sleeve to dry her tears. To the driver, he said, "Drop us off at my house."

The woman shook her head. "Dispose of her before the boss finds out, Neil."

"I will."

THE MEMORY REMAINED CLEAR IN LENA'S MIND FOR ANOTHER heartbeat before it dissipated back into its protective vault where it had slumbered for two decades.

Rohan's thumbs swiped across her cheeks, then he drew

her into his arms. His shirt absorbed the tears that continued to flow. At any other time and with anyone else, she would have felt embarrassed about the avalanche of emotions overtaking her body.

Instead of cutting off her tears though, she let them have their day. Freed Anjali Kumar from her twenty-year imprisonment.

Rohan kissed the top of her head and whispered words of reassurance while he rubbed warm circles over her back.

As if the heavens felt her anguish, they too opened the proverbial floodgate. Rain pounded against the greenhouse windows above, like the erratic blast of a machine gun.

Beside her, a steady stream drenched the panes, obscuring the view beyond. How long they stood locked together, she didn't know. Long enough for the raging storm to abate to a gentle drizzle.

Lena swiped at her wet cheeks, yet she was reluctant to release the firm, safety of Rohan's body.

"Can you speak of it?" he asked. His voice low and gentle.

Focusing on his reflection in the window, Lena pulled the memory out of the vault and told him about her parents' murder and her kidnapping, as if she were placing brush strokes on a new canvas. Hesitant at first, then finishing it with a natural confidence.

To her surprise, Rohan didn't probe deeper into her parents' deaths or attempt to pry out more detail about the killers.

Instead, he focused on her.

Anjali Kumar.

"*Dadi*—is that Asian Indian?" he asked.

"I don't know. Why do you ask?"

"Earlier, you referred to your grandmother as *dadi*."

She pulled back far enough to look up at him. "I did?"

He nodded. "You used it quite naturally."

Indian. She was Indian.

A fresh wave of tears sheened her eyes. Hadn't she always had an affinity for Indian food and Bollywood movies?

Radiant joy filled her chest.

Were her grandparents still alive? What if Neil had tried to give her to them but they turned him away?

The thought dampened the excitement bubbling inside her. She hadn't realized how much she'd missed belonging to a family. Being part of a unit. Until this moment.

With some reluctance, Lena stepped away and headed toward the kitchen. "If we're going to dig into my past, I need fortification." She glanced over her shoulder. "How about you?"

"Got bourbon?"

"Henry McKenna okay?"

He nodded, holding his phone. "I take mine neat." He slid onto a barstool. "A quick search reveals *dadi* is a term used in some parts of India for a paternal grandmother." His thumb tapped over the screen again. "Anjali and Kumar are both Indian names."

Lena drew a bottle and glass from one of the kitchen cabinets, placing both in front of Rohan. "Knock yourself out."

While he poured the amber liquid into an empty tumbler and tapped at his phone again, she uncorked a bottle of Merlot. She filled her wineglass to the halfway mark, drained it quickly, and refilled it again.

Warmth soon spread to her limbs and to the tips of her ears. She toyed with the stem of her glass. "My mom was a white woman with beautiful long brown hair. My dad's skin was brown, though darker than mine. He wore his black hair short, military-style."

"Did either have a non-American accent?"

"No, I don't believe so."

"What about your grandparents?"

"Both brown-skinned like my dad." She took a sip of her wine. "I don't recall much about my grandfather, other than his constant smile. As if he found amusement in everything around him."

"Maybe you were hell on wheels even at four."

She grinned. "Maybe."

"You helped your grandmother in the kitchen. Do you remember if she spoke perfect English, broken English, or none at all?"

Everything about her *dadi* had fascinated her—the stories she would tell, the unfamiliar words she would call certain things, the lyrical quality to her voice.

"She had a beautiful accent, but I had no problem understanding her. I think she tried to teach me words from her native tongue."

"Does anything else come to mind?"

"Not right now."

"My guess is that your grandparents immigrated here, and your dad was first generation Indo-American or very young when they arrived."

"Agreed."

"Do you recall anything about your mom's parents?"

She shook her head. "No, nothing. That's odd, don't you think?"

"Not necessarily. They could be deceased or live far away. Or estranged from their daughter."

"I could have family out there. Family who might still wonder what happened to me."

He slid his hand over hers where it rested on the countertop. "If they're out there, we'll find them."

"It appears I'm not through with your services yet."

"You won't hear me complaining."

She squeezed his fingers, and her nose stung with gratitude. "Thank you."

"You're not alone in this, Lena." The intensity with which he looked at her penetrated all the dark places in her heart and lit them up. "Never again will you be alone."

53

ROHAN DOWNED THE REST OF HIS DRINK. AT THAT MOMENT, he wanted nothing more than to vault over the damn island and kiss Lena until he smoothed away the vulnerability consuming her beautiful eyes.

But he couldn't. Not yet. He had a few more questions that needed answers.

"Now that I understand the reason behind your lack of digital footprint, care to tell me what happened ten years ago?"

Her expression changed as if a genie snapped his finger and removed all the warmth from her body.

She slipped her hand from his and took another drink of wine. "I'm not sure you would believe me after what I just shared.

"There's only one way to find out."

"Neil, the man who . . . "

"Kidnapped you," he offered when she seemed to struggle for the appropriate word.

She jerked her head in agreement. "He didn't leave me on a stoop for a kind-hearted minister to find or drop me off on a street corner near my grandparents' house, he raised me as his daughter, Angela Jones."

Rohan thought about the pictures he took of the items hidden away in Lena's bag. A wilderness drawing signed by *Angela Jones* and a photo of a white man with a family. Had the younger man in the photo been her captor?

"I remember little about that first year," Lena continued, "other than that we traveled around a lot. Did a lot of camping. Each time we moved, Neil insisted we get hair 'makeovers,' as he liked to call them."

"Makes sense. He was on the run, from both the law and whoever had ordered the hit on your parents." He winced as soon as the words came out of his mouth. "Sorry, that was an insensitive way of putting it."

"But accurate." She poured him another drink. "Although I feel their loss, I don't remember them. Not really."

"What was life like with him?" Rohan braced himself for whatever disturbing stories she would share.

She shrugged, "Normal."

"Normal?" That hadn't been the answer he would have selected on a multiple-choice question about Life as an Abductee.

"Normal for me." She grabbed her glass and the bottle of wine. "Let's move this hellish slide down memory lane to the living room."

Rohan took his glass, but left the bottle behind. Oblivion wasn't his fate tonight. Whether she knew it or not, she needed his analytical mind running at full capacity.

They settled on the plush couch. Lena curled up in one corner and Rohan sat in the middle, facing her, with his left leg cocked on the couch and his left arm resting along the top of the cushions.

"You were saying?" he prompted.

"Neil soon became 'Dad' and my previous life faded into a handful of screenshots that, on the surface, I understood more as I grew older, but out of context they made no sense."

"Were you happy?"

"Happy like I would've been if my parents had raised me?" She ran the half-full wineglass beneath her nose, but Rohan doubted she registered a single characteristic, so deep was she in her own head.

"It's hard to say. There are millions of miserable kids living in good homes with loving parents." She looked at him, unflinching. "What I do know is that Neil didn't hit me, assault me, and he rarely raised his voice at me. For the most part, I had everything I needed."

She balanced her glass on the side of her knee. "Did he hug me? No. Tell me he loved me? No. Shower me with praise? No. But he paid for my art supplies, picked me up from school every day, and doled out encouraging words and smiles when I needed them most."

Many kidnap victims experienced something known as Stockholm Syndrome, where they developed feelings of love for their captors, because of their dependency on them for everything—food, clothing and, in some cases, permission to talk.

But Lena's relationship with Neil Jones felt a great deal more complicated due to her young age at the time of the murders and her subsequent abduction.

"Where is Neil now?"

"Dead," she said in a low, emotionless voice.

"How?"

"I'm not exactly sure. Poison, maybe. I found him tied to his office chair." She swallowed hard. "Foam bubbled at the corner of his mouth and his eyes were already glazing over."

Her fingers plucked at a loose thread on the couch arm. "I heard footsteps above me, so I knew it would only be a matter of minutes before the killers would return. I clawed at his bindings, but they were so tight. I couldn't—" Her breath shuddered out of her lungs.

Rohan removed her wineglass from her hand and set it on the coffee table. "We can stop."

"No," she said with an emphatic shake of her head. "I'm okay. Just give me a moment."

One hand covered her mouth as if holding back a torrent of sickness. The other lay limp at her side.

Rohan angled his leg farther onto the couch, lifted her hand, and sandwiched it between his knee and warm palm.

"When I finally loosened the first knot, Neil garbled out a single word."

"Which was?"

Her eyes met his. "Run."

54

LENA STRETCHED OUT HER RIGHT LEG, GIVING HERSELF A short reprieve before continuing her story. As difficult as it was to relive that night, talking about it with someone besides the echo of her fourteen-year-old self reduced the ever-present pressure on her subconscious.

"Here." Rohan released her hand, then patted his thigh. "Put those beauties up here."

Lena bit back a smile. Pre-two-bourbon-Rohan would never have called her legs "beauties." She liked this playful side of him.

"There's no need. If my legs start to cramp, I have a sturdy coffee table to park my feet on."

"Does your table do massages?" he asked in a silky voice that made her stomach clench. "I imagine standing all day takes a toll on your feet and legs."

How had he known? Some days, the soles of her feet would go practically numb from the constant one hundred and twenty pounds of pressure on them.

The mere mention of his powerful hands manipulating

her sore muscles made her toes curl. Not just because of the relief they would bring, but because she'd wanted those hands on her since the moment she'd caught him staring at her bare feet.

Rohan might spend a good portion of his day at a desk, but she recalled, with great detail, every chiseled inch of his abs she'd been lucky enough to wake up to in the motel. The man took care of his body just as rigorously as he managed his family's assets.

"You will find, Rohan Blackwell, that I will never say no to a foot massage."

A sexy grin appeared. "Good to know." He made a gimme motion with his hand.

Lena shifted to lean her back against the couch's arm and placed her right leg at a respectable distance from his man parts. The last thing either of them needed right now was an accidental rubbing.

Her black leggings stopped just below her knees, and she hadn't bothered putting on socks. The moment she settled into position, his hands went right to work.

Immediate bliss shot through Lena's entire body as he kneaded her nearest calf. A moan escaped her throat, and the arms she'd unconsciously braced at her sides lost their rigidity.

"See, much better than a cold, hard coffee table."

Despite her efforts, Lena's knee glanced off the growing bulge in his jeans. "I'll give you points for the cold table." She lifted her now heavy eyelids and looked at him. "But, it seems, I can't get away from hard surfaces."

His hands stilled and, for an infinite breath, Lena's heart seized inside her chest.

She reviewed her words, and winced. She'd intended

them to be funny. Maybe a little flirty. But on replay, they sounded inane, like the ridiculous drivel inexperienced teenage girls say in the throes of their first crush.

She really needed to stop drinking in high-stress situations.

"Sorry," she said, preparing to put her feet on the table. Where they should have been all along. "My lame attempt at humor."

He gripped her legs, keeping them in place. "I'm not done yet."

When she opened her mouth to argue, his hand squeezed her foot, ripping another involuntary groan from the depths of her greedy body.

"What happened after Neil told you to run?" he asked as he tended to every pressure point in her foot.

"I couldn't leave him, yet his bindings were too tight." She closed her eyes and all the fear, helplessness, and self-loathing slammed into her again. "Still hearing the intruders above, I ran to the kitchen for a knife. By the time I returned, his heart had stopped."

The backs of his fingers brushed her flushed cheek. "I'm sorry. I can't imagine the range of emotions you must have experienced in that moment."

"Those didn't hit me until hours later. When I was alone with nothing but my thoughts. His death, and my imminent danger, triggered an ignition switch in my head, and my training kicked in."

He slanted her a curious look. "What sort of training?"

"Every six months, Neil would force me to go through an emergency evacuation process. Among other things, I had to grab a small metal safe he kept in the freezer and make my way to one of two go-bags hidden in the house."

"I take it he didn't explain the true reason for the training."

She shook her head. "If he had, I might have hated the drills a little less."

"The order for arrest Izzy mentioned was for Neil's murder?"

Lena nodded. "My prints were all over the crime scene and a neighbor witnessed me going into the house." She watched his hands manipulate her muscles. "Calling nine-one-one, then disappearing, didn't help my case. But I couldn't leave Neil there. It might have been days before anyone checked in on us."

Rohan's warm palm cupped her cheek. "I wish I could have been there for you."

She lifted her eyes to his. "Me too."

The moment stretched, and Lena thought he might lean in and kiss her. A few, electrifying seconds later, he dropped his hand and returned to their discussion.

"Whoever Neil worked for must have had enormous resources for him to have felt the need to keep up his vigilance for so long."

"He never spoke of his life prior to that night, and I never asked. When the memory was fresh, I was too young to care. Then our daily lives fell into a familiar rhythm. I was safe and content and filled my days with school or drawing."

"I sense a 'but' coming."

"Do you have extraordinary sensory detection that allows you to hear my thoughts?"

"Yes." He grinned. "Afraid?"

"More like relieved."

He raised a brow.

"Now I can curse you without expending verbal energy."

He pinched her Achilles' heel. "How about you forgo cursing me altogether and save yourself the mental drain?"

"Not as fun."

"But?" he prompted, guiding them back to their conversation.

"A few months before the attack on Neil, I started having nightmares. The disjointed screenshots I mentioned earlier."

When her hair fell over one side of her face, she smoothed it back with an efficient hand, then draped the thick mass over a shoulder. "Once the nightmares began, I started experiencing this overwhelming need to know more about my mother."

"Not your father?"

"Yes, of course, but it was my mom's face that came to me, again and again."

"What did Neil tell you about her prior to the nightmares?"

"Only that she had died in a head-on collision caused by a young woman under the influence."

"He stuck to a version of the truth."

Lena glanced at her bed, where she'd dropped her shoulder bag on the way to her wardrobe. More puzzle pieces clicked into place, and a sick feeling crawled into her stomach.

She jumped up and sprinted across the room. Shoving her purse onto its side, she ran her finger along the bottom.

"What are you doing?" Rohan called.

"I think I understand why Neil kept me."

She located the tiny seam and started unzipping the secret compartment.

"Lena," he said, an odd note in his voice as he reached her side.

"What's the matter?"

"I, uh, need to tell you something."

"Just a second. Let me show you this first."

She reached inside to retrieve the cosmetic bag of treasures she'd been carrying since the night she'd left Neil tied to a chair.

Rohan's heart thundered as he watched her pull the bag from its hiding spot.

On their journey back to Atlanta, he'd slipped the items into the hidden pocket of her bag while she had napped in the front seat.

From the moment he'd taken her possessions, guilt had festered in his gut. No matter how he justified his need for knowledge, the feeling had persisted. Returning the items had done nothing to assuage his condition.

He'd decided at the lake to confess his betrayal the next time they were alone. It was one of the many reasons he'd arrived at her loft unannounced.

Lena removed the photo from the plastic bag and held it out to him. "The small metal safe I retrieved from the freezer the night of Neil's murder contained several keep-sakes. Some I recognized, others I didn't. Until now."

A couple in their mid-fifties occupied lawn chairs beneath a giant oak tree draped in Spanish moss. Their hands clasped together and their smiles wide. Colorful balloons attached to a pink draped table in the background suggested they had been celebrating a big event, like a birthday or anniversary.

On the grass in front of them, a young woman, wearing a party hat, sat cross-legged with a toddler hellbent on escaping her lap. The scramble for supremacy didn't dim the delight on the woman's pretty face.

Above the triangle of happiness stood a blond-haired man. His hands rested on the couple's opposite shoulders. Unlike the rest of the group, the guy's impassive features hid from the viewer his state of mind.

Lena pointed to the man behind the couple. "Neil Jones. The man who abducted me."

Reflexively, Rohan placed his hand on the small of her back. For her support or his, he didn't know.

"Blond and good-looking wasn't the image I had of him in my head."

She glanced up at him. "How did you imagine him?"

Rohan shrugged. "Different. Less like a dad."

But his ability to blend in, to not draw attention to himself had aided in his avoidance of detection for ten years.

Lena's finger traced over the woman with the toddler. "I always wondered who the other people were in this photo. From the way they're positioned, I had imagined the older couple were his parents and the woman was his sister. The child, his nephew or niece."

"And now?" he asked, though he could guess the answer.

"I still believe the people are his parents. Neil's resemblance to the man is unmistakable." She drew in a slow breath. "But I think the other two individuals in the picture were his wife and child."

"Were? You think they're dead?"

She nodded. "What if my parents' car crash triggered his own wound? A fresh one. One he hadn't come to terms with yet?"

"When he saw you in the backseat, the loss of his own daughter came rushing back."

"He reacted on instinct, saving me from the burning vehicle." Tears rimmed her eyes. "I replaced his little girl."

Setting into motion a series of events that even Neil Jones couldn't have foreseen. "It would explain why a killer would take on the responsibility of raising a small child—and treating her well."

While they unraveled the mystery of the picture and Neil's motivation for upending a little girl's life, Rohan had been plying soothing circles over her back and shoulders.

She dropped the photo on the bed and turned into his arms. "I think it might be too much," she whispered against his shoulder.

"I meant what I said earlier." He kissed the top of her head. "We'll get through this together."

"Why is this all coming to light now?"

"Talking about your parents must have dislodged an old memory."

"Yes, but—" She pushed out of his arms and began pacing. "Why would Izzy even contemplate that Angelena Kamber wasn't my true identity?"

"Maybe she didn't. Maybe she stumbled upon the information." The thought rankled, but it had to be considered.

She made a dismissive gesture. "If a white hat—"

"Ethical hacker," he corrected.

"If you couldn't uncover my previous identity, there's no way Izzy DeCarlo just found the information."

"Agreed." He sat on the edge of her bed. "Why does she hate you so much?"

She emitted a noise that sounded like a hard drive on the fritz. "Evidently, she viewed us—Izzy, Xander, and I—as a sort of modern-day Three Musketeers. She was pissed that I broke up the Knights of the Round Table by getting involved with Xander."

"Chevaliers."

"Pardon?"

"The Knights of the Round Table were English. The Three Musketeers were French."

She blinked. "How many terabytes of data live inside that brain of yours?"

"More than some, less than others." His smile faded. "Because you stole some happiness for yourself, she orchestrated an elaborate scheme to destroy your reputation?"

She shrugged. "These days, people kill for a lot less."

With his hands braced on the edge of the bed, he drummed his fingers against the side.

"I can hear your internal processor churning from here."

Rohan blinked and refocused on her. "I can't put my finger on it. But my gut tells me there's more at play here." He considered her for a long moment. "Can you think of anything you did out of the ordinary leading up to the burglary or before you got the sense of being watched?"

"No," she insisted. "I eat, paint, sleep. Repeat. My life is one big predictable—" She broke off and her eyes widened.

"Tell me."

"A couple weeks ago, I took a break and walked to Barron's Park. I passed a man on the trail who reminded me of Neil. Which led me to realize his birthday was the very next day. I thought about him all the way home. When I got there, I—"

Rohan's breaths clogged in his chest while he waited for her to finish her tale. When she didn't, he demanded, "You what?"

"I did an Internet search on his name."

56

From Rohan's expression, Lena got that her search on Neil's name might have set some things in motion. Terrible things.

But how, exactly, she didn't know.

"What did I do?" she asked, when he continued to stare at her. Scratch that. Stare through her. She was getting good at identifying his Think Mode.

"Whoever ordered your parents' deaths is still out there."

"That, I'm loud and clear on. What am I missing?"

"We've already established they likely have significant resources at their disposal."

"Yes, yes." She motioned for him to get to the point. Rude, but she couldn't stand the gaping hole in her knowledge. "And?"

"They likely have trigger words in place."

"Trigger words?"

"When someone enters a series of words or phrases into a search engine, they're alerted."

"People can get access to that kind of data?"

"If they're clever enough or have money to buy friends in crucial places, yes."

"But wouldn't that be an enormous amount of data to mine?"

"A good program would weed out most of it."

"If my search triggered someone's super algorithm, why haven't they attempted to kill me yet?"

"A good question."

Another thought struck her. "Why hasn't the APD tracked me down yet? My fingerprints were all over Xander's studio."

"Not if whoever killed him wiped down the place."

"If we're talking about Izzy, why would she have Desmond undo what he did? She made it clear today that I would pay with my life. I thought she meant to kill me, but what better way to make me suffer than spending the rest of my days in jail for a crime I didn't commit?"

"What if Izzy's pet wasn't the one who murdered Byrne?"

Izzy had been livid about the police declaring his death a suicide. For his sake? Or because death by his own hand would've screwed up Izzy's plan to ruin Lena's life?

Lena cupped her hands over her nose and mouth as she recalled the moment she broke the news to Izzy about Xander's death. Izzy had always been a superb actress, but she'd never been able to fool Lena. Izzy's shocked reaction to the news had been real.

"If not Desmond, who?"

Neither of them spoke for a long while. The weight of the situation seemed too heavy, too complex to decipher.

"It's been a long day," she said. "My bed is calling."

"Agreed." He brushed a hand over his whiskered face. "I'll take the couch."

"The independent side of me wants to tell you I don't

need a babysitter." She strode toward him, stopping an arm's length away. "But my practical side—the side that's kept me alive all these years—would be thankful for your company."

He reached for her hand, brushed his fingers over each of her knuckles before kissing the back of her hand. His eyes met hers. Waited for her decision.

"Survival always floats to the top."

The corners of his eyes tilted upward, yet something in his gaze—a sadness or maybe regret—made her heart stutter to a halt.

"What's wrong?"

"There's something I need to tell you."

The heaviness in his voice told her it wouldn't be something they could talk through in five minutes. Call her a coward, but all she wanted to do at that moment was to sink into the sheets and let Rohan drive away the pain of the last twenty-four hours.

Stepping between his legs, she framed his face with her hands. "Later." She pressed her lips against his, exploring them with gentle nips and evocative scrapes of her teeth.

While responding in kind, his hands surrounded her hips, drew her closer.

Lena's fingers pushed into his hair, cradled his head, and deepened the kiss. When she leaned in to rub her aching breasts against his chest, he broke free of their kiss.

"Lena, please," he panted against her throat. "I need to confess—"

She lifted his chin. "Tomorrow."

"But—"

"Tomorrow, we can discuss your lack of boundaries with my personal possessions."

He stilled. "What specifically do you mean by personal possessions?"

"The ones in my purse's secret compartment."

"You knew I'd taken them?"

"I had my suspicions the moment I emerged from the hotel bathroom." She gave him a stern look. "But the torn pages from the Bible fooled my initial inspection."

"I should probably apologize, but it would lack full sincerity."

"Oh?"

"For one, I found a device in your purse."

"What sort of device?"

"My guess is GPS. I pitched it into the motel parking lot."

Lena recalled him flicking something as they fled from their room. The confirmation of someone keeping tabs on her whereabouts made her queasy.

"And another thing," he sent her an aggrieved look, "those items helped me piece some things together." His expression shifted again. It wasn't quite contrite, but a close cousin. "But I didn't like betraying your trust. I would prefer to never have a reason to do it again."

"Is that your bizarre way of telling me I need to be more upfront with information?"

A hint of a smile. "It would save us both a lot of trouble."

He clasped a hand around the side of her neck and brushed his thumb over her cheek. "Despite my extreme measures to unravel this mystery, you can trust me. I swear it."

She covered his hand with hers and turned to press her lips to his palm, then looked him in the eye. "I know. Why else would I allow you to keep priceless fragments of my life?"

His hard swallow was audible. He exerted pressure until her forehead touched his. "I'm sorry, Lena."

"You put them back, as I had hoped."

He gave her an appreciative smile. "Leaving your bag in the back of the van on our return trip to Steele Ridge wasn't an accident, I take it."

"No, it wasn't."

"Lena—"

She placed a finger over his lips. "Save the groveling for tomorrow."

He smiled and lifted his head. "Only if you promise to explain why you lied to me about the Frida Kahlo's provenance."

Lena's heart sank. "Omission isn't a lie." When he opened his mouth to disagree, she stopped him with a kiss. Savored the slick glide of his tongue against hers.

He pulled away. "Trying to distract me?"

"Not working?"

"Let's say, at the moment, I have a more powerful need to hear a bedtime story. One about how you came into possession of the original *Self-Portrait with Braided Hair*."

Lena sat on the edge of the bed, and Rohan joined her, twining his fingers with hers. She soaked in his warmth, knowing it would be the last time he offered her comfort.

"Several years ago, Simon and I had a good-natured argument about whether or not I could create a reproduction that could fool the most discerning auction houses in New York City. My forgeries had already fooled our local art museums and private collectors, so I was feeling a bit full of myself."

Rohan smiled. "I can relate."

"I didn't think much about it until a few weeks later when Simon brought me a high-quality print of *Braided Hair* and another painting from the same era."

"What did you do with the other painting?"

"I stripped the paint off and reused the canvas and backing materials." She braced herself for his judgment.

"To lend authenticity to the Kahlo?"

She nodded, even as a vise tightened around her chest.

"As an artist, you must have felt the impact of that down to the bone."

Surprised he would understand, she stared at him, speechless.

"I know you, Lena. You wouldn't have taken pleasure in the destruction of another's art."

"It wasn't the first time, nor was it the last."

"You met his challenge?"

"Yes," she whispered. "I put everything of myself into that reproduction." She stared at the Kahlo propped against her red chair. "A week later, Simon came back with letters of authenticity from three separate authenticators. One of them from Sotheby's."

"Quite an accomplishment."

"One of the best moments of my life. Only capped by Simon's decision not to go through with the auction house sale. Instead, he hung the piece in his office."

"When did you learn he'd switched your copy with the original at the Asheville Museum?"

"After he died. I found the provenance in his safe."

"Did you never think to notify the museum of your discovery?"

She shook her head, knowing her story had killed any budding feelings he had for her. His family had built their business on returning stolen objects to their rightful owners. He'd become a hacker to right other's wrongs.

Lena was the epitome of everything he must despise.

"I—I liked the idea of my work hanging in a museum. Pathetic, huh?"

"I imagine it's every artist's dream to view their work on a museum's wall, much like it's every author's wish to see their book on a shelf in a bookstore."

It was true. Even more so for someone like her who couldn't seem to paint an original concept. "If you've changed your mind about keeping me company, I understand."

"I haven't."

She glanced down at their clasped hands. "Rohan, I want you to know that I'm not proud of the work I did for Simon. Or rather, I'm not happy about the people we hurt. I wanted out, wanted to stop, but painting was all I knew. All I cared about."

"Why did you never try to paint your own originals?"

Embarrassment squeezed her heart. "I tried after Simon died. But I had nothing. Still have nothing. It's as if copying others' work for so many years has stripped me of my creativity." She smiled. Or tried to. "A just punishment for my sins."

"You survived the best way you knew how. At the first opportunity, you set up a legitimate business and used your talent to bring joy into peoples' homes." He brushed a lock of hair away from her face. "Give yourself some grace."

"I will, if you will do the same."

The corners of his eyes lifted. "I'll try."

She rose and faced him. "Are you sure you want to stay?"

"Positive."

"I could use someone to help me warm up this big bed."

He rose to his feet and leaned toward her. "Any someone?"

Unlike Izzy, Lena didn't have a seductive bone in her body. Not one. But at the disgruntled note in his voice, she released a slow, knowing grin. "You'll do." She buffed her nose against his. "For now."

"For always," he growled before grasping her beneath the arms and launching her into the air.

Her backside had barely hit the mattress before Rohan's large frame covered hers, blocking out the lamplight and the world beyond.

Tracing a nail along the length of his jaw, she said, "Desmond was right. There is an untapped wildness in you."

"Only for you, love."

His mouth angled over hers. Their tongues tangled, lips mashed, teeth clinked. To get closer, deeper. To reach that pinnacle of pleasure their bodies craved, needed.

Lena's hips arched upward in an instinctual drive to possess and be possessed. To connect.

To take.

To consume.

"Clothes," she demanded. "Now."

He reared up on his haunches and shucked off his dress shirt while she sat up and shimmied out of her top.

Unable to resist all that bare chest mere inches from her face, she pressed her lips against the expanse of skin covering his heart. The organ thundered beneath her touch, and she reveled in her ability to have such an effect on this big, beautiful, brainiac.

His hand came up to clutch the back of her head, encouraging her with the lightest pressure. Her tongue swirled around his hard nipple, and he sucked in a sharp breath.

"God, Lena. You have no idea what your touch is doing to me."

Moving to his left nipple, she gave it equal attention

while her palm caressed the extraordinary length of him through his trousers. She glanced up, aware of her glistening lips. "I have some idea."

Another animalistic sound reverberated in his throat as he unfastened her bra and bore her back down on the bed.

Balancing his weight on his left elbow, his other hand cupped her breast. Massaged it. Tested its meager weight and size.

Lena had never been ashamed of her breast size, nor any other part of her body. But at that moment, with this man, words of apology rose to her lips.

There, they froze.

Right next to her breath.

57

A RAW, UNGOVERNED EMOTION SWELLED INSIDE ROHAN'S chest as he took in the woman beneath him.

She was so beautiful, so perfect in every way.

From her thick, black hair to her expressive gray eyes to her soft brown skin to the tips of her ruched nipples.

He couldn't stop taking in every square inch of her.

The pressure inside his chest grew, pushing upward into his throat, bear-hugging his airway before storming his skull and shooting straight for his eyes.

He squeezed them shut, clamped his teeth together, and flared his nostrils to accommodate the rapid flow of air. The assault raged for what felt like an eternity, but was in reality mere seconds. Long enough to bend his will and break down his defenses.

Tears gathered, ballooning until gravity sent them cascading down his cheeks.

Lena was there to catch them, to whisk them away with her thumbs.

Others followed.

"Rohan," she said, alarmed. "Baby, what's wrong?"

The words he needed to speak trenched into his throat. No amount of swallowing would force them out of their protective shells.

Until his eyes met hers.

The pressure eased enough for him to force out the hardest words he'd ever uttered.

"I never thought," he said in a guttural voice, "that I would ever," he kissed the hollow of her neck, "have this." He pressed his lips to the delicate skin below her chin.

Her hands shook as she dried away the last of his tears. "I know, baby." She kissed his chin, his cheek, his forehead. "I know."

Then she reached between them and unfastened his trousers, and Rohan forgot all about second chances.

In between more kisses and laughs and unintended elbow jabs, they wriggled out of their clothes until heated flesh met heated flesh. It was the most exquisite moment of Rohan's life, and he never wanted clothes to come between them again.

Lena hooked an ankle over his ass, and her wet heat cupped his length. A hiss escaped Rohan's lips, and he swore he'd spend hours drawing out their pleasure.

Next time.

He removed a condom from the wallet he'd tossed on the bed and prepared to roll it on.

She stayed his hands, and his attention jerked up to her face.

"Old or new?" she asked with a lifted brow.

He smiled. "Brand new."

"Hopeful, were you?"

"You have no idea."

Spreading her arms like a seductive angel, she clasped

her fingers around the iron bed posts above her head, and waited.

In a few short moves, he was covered and nudging her legs wider.

LENA SQUIRMED WITH AN ACHING COMBINATION OF NEED AND anticipation as Rohan positioned himself at her entrance.

But rather than ease all those tantalizing inches into her, he laid a scorching path of open mouth kisses up her torso, over her breasts, and along her neck.

She grasped his bottom and angled her hips in a way that he could not misinterpret.

Take me.

Now.

His lips glided along her jaw, and his tongue toyed with her earlobe before he drew it into the warm cavern of his mouth.

"Rohan," she panted.

"Hmm?"

"Put the USB drive into the port."

He stilled and drew back to look at her, a roguish grin on his face. "Sexy tech talk?"

"Whatever it takes to get you inside me." She shifted her hips and sucked in a satisfied breath when an inch slid home. "Now." Her hands smoothed over his broad shoulders until she cradled his head. She brushed her lips against his and whispered, "Please."

"With absolute pleasure."

He pushed into her, and Lena's ability for rational thought vanished. Her lover set a gentle pace at first. She assumed it was to give their bodies time to acclimate to one another.

Whatever the reason, it was maddening. She wanted to feel his passion for her, taste it in his hard kisses, smell it in the sweat coating his skin.

His scary mind must have keyed in on her body's clues, because he began pounding into her with an intensity that had them both coming in seconds.

As the last pulse rocked her body, Rohan kissed her with a tenderness that brought tears to her eyes. He shifted his weight to her side and, with the lightest of touches, brushed her hair away from her face.

"Did I hurt you?" he asked.

"Not even close."

"Come here, then."

He rolled onto his back, and she snuggled against him. His fingers trailed through her hair, over and over, until finally they stilled, and his breaths deepened as sleep claimed him.

Lena itched to pick up her pencil and sketchpad so she could memorialize the novelty of having Rohan Blackwell's beautiful body naked tangled in her sheets. But she couldn't bring herself to move from the warmth of his embrace, and soon fell into a deep sleep.

They spent the next two days indulging their bodies, making elaborate meals while wearing bath towels, showering—lots of showering, and sharing stories about their childhoods while cradling their drinks of choice.

By silent consent, they kept the outside world at bay and simply enjoyed each other. No TV, no computers, no phones. Just themselves.

Thankfully, Rohan kept a change of clothes in his car, though he had little need of them. On the final night of their sabbatical, Rohan made love to her again, drawing out the moment with tender kisses, reverent caresses, and long, slow, powerful thrusts.

When the climax of all climaxes speared through her, she yelled out her pleasure and hung on to his broad shoulders until he followed.

Rather than stroke her hair, as he had the previous two nights, until they both fell into satiated oblivion, Rohan rested his shoulders against the headboard and drew her into his side. He splayed one hand over her naked hip and propped his forearm on his upraised knee.

"I need to go back to the office tomorrow," he said.

"I know." She brushed her fingers over the ridges of his abdomen. "The Caravaggio awaits me as well."

"These past two days have been . . . great."

She smiled against his chest. "Agreed."

"Ready for another confession?"

The rapid beats inside her chest slowed to one hard *thunk*. "Is it going to ruin my afterglow?"

"Undecided."

"Maybe you should wait—"

"I think I'm in love with you."

Lena's mind blanked. It was as if a stranger had smacked her upside the head and she spent the next several seconds trying to figure out what she'd said to offend them.

Slowly, she sat up, allowing the sheet to spool around her waist. "Rohan, I—" Words. She had no words.

He flinched. "Looks like I need a reset button." He moved to get out of bed, but Lena caught his arm.

"No, wait." She swallowed, not sure what to say, but knowing the absolute worst thing she could do was allow him to leave her bed. "I—you caught me off guard. I expected more bad news or intrusive questions. Not—"

"A confession of love," he prompted, with a sad smile.

"You have to admit, our relationship hasn't exactly been normal."

"Neither of us could be labeled normal." The backs of his fingers trailed along the inside of her arm. "Why would you expect falling in love to be anything but unique?"

Lena felt as if two winch hooks had latched onto her heart and a set of enormous chains began drawing the thick irons in opposite directions.

A part of her wanted to turn into him and let her body convey all the newfound feelings bubbling inside her. But another part of her wanted to grab her bag and run for the highest mountaintop.

People who loved her died. Not just any old death, but violent ones.

And Lena knew, to the ends of her soul, that if she lost Rohan in the same manner, it would annihilate her.

There would be no coming back from such a loss.

He must have sensed her conflict, for he kissed her forehead, strode into the bathroom, and closed the door with a soft click.

It was the click that did her in. The firm finality that she'd ruined one of the most precious moments of her life.

She rolled to her side, buried her face in her pillow, and wept.

58

ROHAN FLIPPED OPEN HIS LAPTOP AND USED THE BATH TOWEL draped around his neck to swipe away the bead of water that splattered onto Lena's island countertop.

He slid the towel over his wet hair and did his damnedest to ignore the scent of Lena's shampoo as it wafted past his nose. He glanced over at the bed, where she lay in a fitful sleep. The urge to go to her and banish whatever demons visited her dreams was strong.

But the fifteen feet of distance separating them seemed like an Indiana Jones brand of quicksand. One wrong step, and he'd be eyes-deep in trouble.

He'd said the words. Words he'd never expected to utter to a woman, and she'd stared at him with an expression that a long, hot shower hadn't been able to clarify.

Whatever she'd been feeling, she hadn't returned the sentiment, and that hurt like a motherfucker.

His phone dinged and Rohan realized he'd been staring at the laptop's login screen. After tapping in his ten-digit passcode, he picked up his phone to see who'd texted him.

Ash: *Get my email? I got the goods on your girl. Brace yourself.*

Goods?

Rohan checked his computer's clock.

9:22 p.m.

His workaholic brother must have capped off a long day of cold case investigating with a celebratory bourbon or two or three.

Setting his phone down, he brought up his email app.

Ash's name stood out in bold letters at the top of the page.

His pulse thundered in his ears. Since Atlanta, he'd been feeding his brother information on Lena's various identities, trying to piece together who he was slowly falling in love with.

He'd sent his most recent update after Lena's break-through Saturday night. In hindsight, he should have let her know then that he was looking into her background. But he'd been in get-it-done mode and sent the text off without a second's thought.

What had started out as his duty to protect his family from this mysterious, unknown woman had evolved into a profound desire to help her discover what really happened that fateful night and track down Anjali Kumar's family.

If anyone could help fill in the blanks on Lena's birth family, it was special agent Asher Cameron Blackwell. Missing persons might not be his brother's specialty, but Rohan knew Ash had used every resource at his disposal and pulled every favor he had at the Bureau for this one.

Partly because who wouldn't want to help right such a terrible wrong. But mostly because his perceptive brother had divined how important Lena was to Rohan.

He fully expected his older brother's email to be riddled

with his signature grumbles and admonishments and cautions, but that was par for the course. Ash simply couldn't shut down the big brother chip.

Rohan's finger hovered over the laptop's touchpad. A strange uncertainty filled his chest and pushed into his stomach. His gaze shifted to Lena's sleeping form.

Should he wake her? Get her permission to delve into her past?

But what if Ash had sent information they had already uncovered? Why get her hopes up unnecessarily? Or worse, what if he'd found something even more soul-destroying?

She had suffered so much already. Adding another blow seemed cruel.

He couldn't do that to her. A quick read of Ash's findings would tell him if he should wake her or not.

Decision made, he clicked on the email, read Ash's intro about the attached document being self-explanatory, and opened the PDF file.

Seconds later, an alarm on his computer blared out a warning.

Then all hell broke loose.

59

LENA BOLTED UPRIGHT IN BED AT THE SOUND OF AN ALARM that would do a prison breakout justice.

It took an extra second to pry her gritty, tear-stained eyes apart. When her vision cleared, she found no rioting prisoners, no swiveling spotlights. Just Rohan's shocked face illuminated by the glow of his laptop's screen.

Before she could ask what was going on, his expression changed to one of fury. On an epic, multiverse scale.

"Fucking bastards."

His fingers flew across the keyboard. She'd been around computer users her entire life and had never seen anyone type so fast.

She got out of bed and slipped on the clothes she'd been wearing earlier. Before she'd had the best sexual experience of her life—and then ruined one of the most precious moments when she snubbed Rohan's declaration.

A new set of tears burned her eyes. She pushed Sobby Lena away. Based on Rohan's reaction to his computer's alarm, now was not the time to address her stupidity. She'd serve that up to him later on a dessert platter.

After securing her hair in a sloppy bun at the back of her head, she laid a hand on his bare shoulder. His skin was cool, but the muscles beneath felt like they'd been forged from molten steel.

He didn't acknowledge her touch. His entire focus was on the gibberish flashing across his screen.

"The Collective?" she asked.

His head jerked in acknowledgment.

"What are they attempting?"

In answer, his jaw tightened, and he appeared to redouble his efforts on the keyboard.

His phone vibrated on the counter, and she glanced at the screen.

Zeke.

Rohan mouth firmed into a thin line before he slashed a finger across the Accept button. "Cruz and I are on it."

"Yeah, he just flew by my office in his underwear, saying something about a serious breach," Zeke said. "Talk to me."

"Are you with Cruz?"

"Hold on." Three seconds passed. "Okay, you're on speaker."

"This could be scareware," Rohan said, his fingers not missing a beat. "Check the file extensions."

Cruz said, "Copy that."

Lena could hear violent keyboard tapping on the other end.

"Where are you?" Zeke asked.

Rohan winced. "Lena's."

An ocean's deep silence followed. Then Cruz said, "It's not scareware. The files are switching over to crypt extensions."

Rohan's computer stopped responding.

"Sonofbitch!" he roared, pushing off his barstool and

sending it clattering across the floor. "I'm dead in the water. Take the server offline. Lock down the network. Do whatever you have to do to stop the spread. I'll be there in ten minutes."

"Copy."

Lena could hear the strain in Cruz's voice and the bionic key tapping in the background.

Rohan stomped away and grabbed a wrinkled shirt from the floor by the bed.

Lena watched him with a wary eye while she spoke to the men on the phone. "Zeke, what's happened?"

"All I can give you is the footnote version."

"That's more than I have right now."

"A hacker has taken control of our proprietary database —our company's lifeblood—and is now demanding a ransom."

"There's no way around this?"

"The files have been encrypted, and the hacker is the only one who has the key."

"There's no way to decrypt the files?"

"Not without the hacker's private decryption key."

The full, disastrous weight of the situation settled around Lena. No wonder Rohan was consumed with helpless fury. The Collective had him—and his family business —at their mercy.

"*Fuck!*" A loud thump, like a fist hitting a desk, followed Cruz's furious exclamation.

Jamming his feet into his dress shoes, Rohan's head whipped up. "What's wrong?"

A heartbeat of silence. Then Cruz bit out, "The ransomware deleted the backups."

"Both sets?"

More typing and clicking. "Both," Cruz confirmed.

Rohan closed his eyes, and Lena could almost hear the shattering effects of Cruz's words. She took a step toward him, but he stormed into the bathroom, shutting the door.

Lena lowered her voice. "How did the hacker get by all of Rohan's systems?"

"Probably through phishing," Cruz said.

Lena was familiar with the term. Anyone with an email account probably received a dozen emails every day, encouraging them to click a link or open an attachment.

A lot of times they were easy to spot and users deleted them right away or the email provider sent them straight to spam. But some bad actors have devised remarkable imitations of correspondence one might receive from a favorite retailer or social media app.

All it would take is one moment of inattention or someone in too big of a hurry and they click on a malicious link or file.

Then Wham-o.

A viral infection.

But the BARS team didn't strike Lena as a group who would fall victim to such schemes.

"I don't understand," Lena said. "How did the ransomware get activated?"

A deep, tortured voice behind her answered. "Because I opened a file I shouldn't have."

"You?"

Rohan reached past her to collect his phone. "Zeke, I'm on my way." He disconnected, then pulled up a message from Cameron Blackwell.

Or at least it looked like an email from his brother.

The email address didn't contain an obscure URL and the body of the message was free of typos, strange wording, or anything else that would have set off his alarm bells.

"Did the Collective hack into Ash's email and send you the message?"

He shook his head, while hitting buttons on his phone. Then he held it up for her to read.

He'd pulled up Ash's contact information. At first, she didn't key in on what he was showing her. Then she zeroed in on the email addys, specifically the work address.

cblackwell@fbi.gov

She bent toward his laptop and squinted at the Sender's email address.

cameronblackwell@fbi.gov

Her hand drifted to cover her mouth, then she looked up at him. "Anyone could have missed this, Rohan."

"Not someone like me."

There was something in his eyes. Some message there that she couldn't decipher. Until he broke visual contact to stare daggers at the message on his laptop.

The two previous times she'd looked at the message, she'd focused her attention on the Sender field, not wanting to invade his privacy.

Now she looked. Read the message from "his brother" and a cold knot in her chest formed. It wound tighter and tighter with each word. He'd asked the FBI to investigate her.

Her. The woman he'd purported to love.

She'd told him everything. Hauled out every piece of dirty laundry and dropped it at his feet.

Of anyone he could have betrayed her to, why had he chosen the FBI? His brother would be duty bound to investigate anything he found. What if his investigation had led to Angela Jones and the arrest order?

She scraped a fingernail over the PDF icon in the lower

left corner of the message. "What did you hope he would find?"

"Answers."

"That's obvious," she ground out, fisting her hands at her side as she glared at him. "But to what questions?"

He leaned past her and snapped his laptop shut. "I'll explain on the way to the Friary. Right now, I have another mess to clean up."

"Mess?" Scalding heat erupted across her entire body. "You consider me a mess that needs tidying up?"

He suppressed an expletive from bursting out of his mouth. "No, that's not what I meant."

It hit her then. The last time Rohan had gotten serious about a woman, a man had lost his livelihood and Rohan had shouldered the blame. From that point forward, he'd viewed romantic relationships as *distractions.*

Lena knew he was now regretting their sabbatical and his declaration of love. His mind was probably telling him if he hadn't been preoccupied by his feelings—if his logic hadn't been compromised by lust—he would have caught the email address discrepancy.

She touched the hand holding his laptop. "You're not Superman or Cyberman or Technoman. You're Human, with all the accompanying limitations and irritating flaws."

He squeezed his eyes shut and raked a hand through his hair. "Look, I have to get back to the Friary. Grab your shoes and purse."

Shifting back a step, she shook her head. "You don't need me there—and let's face it. You don't even want me there, at the moment."

"The hell I don't."

She put more distance between them, then nodded at the door. "Go."

"I'm not leaving you alone," he said, stepping back into her space. "Three people associated with you have been killed, and your friend Izzy seems to be out for your blood."

"Izzy's bitter, not a murderer." At least she hoped not.

"I'm not convinced. Who do you suppose ordered Desmond to kill Ruthie? Palmer? For what purpose?" He shook his head. "My money is on Izzy. Zeke filled in Maggie, and she's going to see what she can find out from the local authorities."

Lena was glad they'd requested Sheriff Kingston's help. Maybe, just maybe, whoever murdered Ruthie would be brought to justice.

"I appreciate you contacting the sheriff, but Izzy and Palmer are no longer your problem."

His eyes narrowed. "What do you mean by that remark?"

"Our business, professional and personal—" The word caught in Lena's throat. She cleared it and tried again. "It's over, Rohan. Now, go deal with your family crisis."

A muscle worked in his jaw. "Not until you get your damn shoes on and grab your purse."

"I don't want to be anyone's mess to clean up."

"You're not." He pointed to the rumpled bed. "I all but said three words to you I've never said—and will never say —to another woman. Unless you find a life with me repulsive, Anjali, Angela, Angelena, you're stuck with me."

She sucked in a breath. "Was that a proposal?"

"Neither one of us is ready for that yet." He stepped closer and brushed a thumb over her chin. "But it's a commitment to get there. If that's our destiny."

She leaned into his touch. "A tech guy talking about destiny?"

"It seemed like a romantic thing to say." He placed a gentle kiss on her forehead, the tip of her nose, then her lips. "Get your things." His thumb caressed her cheek. "Please."

Lena could see the uncompromising determination in his eyes. He wasn't leaving without her and every second he stood here arguing with her put his family's livelihood at greater risk.

She nodded and turned to collect her belongings. "I'll stay the night at the Friary, but no guarantees beyond tonight."

As she marched toward the exit, she heard him murmur, "We'll see."

60

ROHAN STRODE INTO THE ANNEX. EVERY STEP PUSHED A GLOB of bile higher and higher into his throat.

The moment he'd been dreading for years had arrived.

He'd failed his family. Just like he'd failed Troy Neff's family.

But not in the way he'd feared.

The Collective hadn't bested him because of a missed software patch or inadequate detection systems or by a dozen other more technical and complex means.

He'd fallen for a damn phishing scam.

How many warning emails had he sent to his family about phishing and social engineering tricks? How many times had he cautioned them to double-check a sender's email address—even if it's a family member—before clicking links or opening attachments?

Dozens.

It was the ultimate embarrassment.

Rohan rounded the small reception area and halted. Trailing behind him, Lena slammed into his back and emitted a surprised, *"Oomph."*

"How about a rolling stop next time—" Her words faded away as she stepped to his side and took in the seven people milling around the Theater's conference table.

Zeke, Phin, Cruz, Lynette, Grams, Liv, and Maddy. The entire crew was there to observe his humiliation.

Perfect.

Everyone was on their feet, except Grams and Cruz. The latter's nose was stuck in a laptop, no doubt trying to find a digital miracle.

When he realized that Lucy had failed to stop the files from being encrypted, Rohan knew the game was up. No one had ever been successful at uncovering a hacker's private key. Many in the business estimated that it would take a thousand years to unlock the correct mathematical sequence.

Cruz knew it, too, but his mule-headed brother was slower to concede defeat.

While Rohan stood there, waiting for his family's judgment, Lena slipped her hand into his. The action startled him as much as seeing his entire family assembled.

He glanced down and found her, not looking up at him with an encouraging smile like he'd expected, but glaring at the other occupants in the room. His attention shifted from her to the others to her again, trying to understand what had upset her.

When he looked at his family a second time, he became even more confused by the burgeoning smiles on Maddy's and Liv's faces. Then Phin's and Lynette's joined in. Zeke remained his stony-faced self. Grams's perpetual serenity was on full display.

"We clear?" Lena asked the other occupants.

Smiles grew wider. Even Zeke's stoicism cracked a tiny bit.

Rohan squeezed her hand, but she kept her hard gaze on the group.

Grams said, "As clear as the starlit sky outside." She indicated two empty seats at the end of the table. "Please."

"Clear about what?" Rohan asked, feeling like a kid eavesdropping on an adult conversation about sex.

"Your guardian angel just warned us not to assign blame for what happened earlier." Zeke's lips did twitch then. "An unnecessary threat, but it's good to know she'll be able to hold her own with us."

The last bit of his brother's comment wiped the scowl off her face and replaced it with wariness.

If Rohan's emotions hadn't been so pinned tight, he would've enjoyed the moment when his family gave their blessing for his choice.

Instead, he thanked Lena with a kiss.

He'd meant it to be a quick peck. But his lips never popped off hers like he'd intended.

They lingered. Explored.

Possessed.

"For the love of God, Rohan," Phin said. "Are you really going to make me watch this with Grams sitting two chairs down?"

Lena broke away, a flush painting her cheeks. He hadn't thought she could be more beautiful. He'd been wrong.

Rohan pulled out one of the empty chairs for her and he took the one next to hers. The others followed suit.

A weighty, dread-filled silence settled between them.

Drawing in a breath, Rohan said, "Despite my angel's warning, I owe you all an apology."

"No you don't, Rohan," Lynette said. "The technological world is changing at a never-before-seen rapid pace. Too fast for one man to guard against." She glanced at Lena. "Especially if he wants to also have a life."

"I don't disagree," he said, catching his family's surprised looks. "But my apology is for keeping y'all in the dark on a past misdeed that's come back to bite us all in the ass."

Lena put her hand on his thigh and gave it a light squeeze of assurance.

"Misdeed?" Phin said, "Like modifying a formula in Zeke's spreadsheet and watching him spit fire until he found it."

Zeke's pivoted his head toward the youngest Blackwell and narrowed his gaze.

Cruz made a sharp movement beneath the table, and Phin sucked in a breath as he reached down to rub his injury. "No need to get violent. I was just trying to judge the level of Rohan's *misdeed*."

"Which I'm sure he's about to explain if you'd keep your trap shut for a few minutes."

Zeke made a motion for Rohan to continue.

He filled them in on his senior project and the Neff family. About his relationship with the company president's sister and how their family's secret energy bar recipe got broadcast across the Internet. He told them about his revenge on the hacker and how that caught the Collective's eye. He shared with them the excitement he first felt in working with the Collective, then his concern about the group's apparent shift from their original ideals.

"I wasn't comfortable with our last two hacks, so I left," he finished.

"When was that?" Zeke asked.

"About six months ago."

"From how you described the Collective," Liv said, "I get

the impression that it's an organization you can't just walk away from."

"The hacker who recruited me wasn't happy about my decision, nor my resistance to their entreaties to stay." He braced his elbows on the table and stared at his clasped hands. "I know their history, their methods, and their means, which makes me a threat to their continued anonymity."

"Hackers are competitive, paranoid beings," Cruz said, closing his laptop and shoving it away. "Some, a lot more than others. If nothing else, they would work to uncover his identity and use it to ensure he didn't betray them."

"Which they did." Rohan covered Lena's hand on his thigh. "They made sure I understood they'd found me by throwing volleys at our network, sending me threatening messages, and disabling my car. Nearly killing Lena in the process."

"And you," Lena added.

"Worst-case scenario, notwithstanding sending you both off a mountainside," Cruz winked at Lena, "would be destroying everything and everyone important to you."

"Which they're doing." By locating and burning backups he had kept on two separate clouds. Why hadn't he saved a third one offline, completely disconnected from their network? Stupid, fucking mistake.

Losing control of BARS's database and business files would set their multimillion-dollar company back years. Their technological infrastructure and knowledge base would have to be rebuilt from the ground up, while they continued meeting new clients, planning recoveries, and executing those plans.

"What's the ransom demand?" Zeke asked, cutting

straight to the question that was no doubt on everyone's mind.

Lena's thumb rubbed along the inside of his thigh, somehow knowing this would be the hardest question he would answer.

"They want eleven million eight hundred and fifty-two thousand four hundred seventy-three dollars and twelve cents in seventy-two hours."

Phin surged forward in his chair. "You got to be fucking kidding."

Maddy ran a comforting hand over his arm, then wove her fingers between his. A heartbeat later, Phin lifted their joined hands and kissed the back of hers.

Everyone displayed their shock in different ways. Zeke's jaw was clenched tight, Cruz made for the liquor bar, Lynette closed her eyes, Liv stared at him wide-eyed, and Grams wore a strangely expectant look.

Like she expected Rohan to pull out a silver bullet.

He didn't have one.

Sensing an unspoken undercurrent, Lena asked, "Why such a specific amount?"

Everyone, including Rohan, turned toward Lynette, BARS's office manager and keeper of the books.

"Because," his mother said. Her voice was full of fear and uncertainty. A state Rohan had never heard in twenty-nine years. "That's the exact amount in our bank accounts."

61

LENA'S BREATH CAUGHT IN THE BACK OF HER THROAT.

Financial ruin.

A group of off-the-rails keyboard warriors were going to destroy an entire family because one of their members chose not to play in their polluted sandbox anymore?

The destructive plan was unconscionable. Evil on a level that Lena had trouble grasping.

"In order to get the files back, you have to bankrupt the business?"

Rohan nodded.

And lose everything.

Their crisis hurt her far more than it should. She barely knew these people.

But the thought of Grams never tearing down the road in her utility vehicle again, Sadie having to leave the only home she'd ever known, and Rohan living with such unbearable guilt tore a softball-sized cavity right into her chest.

She couldn't do it. She couldn't watch them lose everything, like she had. Twice. No one should have to rebuild their lives from scratch.

Some people had a romantic notion about erasing their past and moving some place where no one knew their name. For some, it would be an exciting adventure—for about three days.

Then boredom would set in, followed by fear of getting sick or hurt or, God forbid, dying. What would strangers do with their corpse?

What no one considered, though, even diehard introverts like her, was how endless loneliness eats at your mind, blackens your enjoyment of your new world.

Her gaze took in each occupant of the room before settling on Rohan. If his inadvertent action bankrupted his family, he would never forgive himself, never open himself up to love again.

There would be no *them*. He would cut himself off from everyone, including her.

She couldn't let that happen. Couldn't let Rohan dwell the rest of his days on a blank canvas.

Lena withdrew her phone from her shoulder bag and tapped through several screens with her free hand.

Confirming what she already knew, she said, "I have a solution."

Rohan didn't at first register Lena's words. His mind kept churning through plausible scenarios that would get them out of this nightmare he'd created.

All his fail-safes hadn't been enough to protect BARS. The bastards had even found the offshore accounts.

It was so clear to him now that he should have gone on the offensive the moment they started making jabs at his security defenses. He should have uncovered each of their identities and had a counterattack ready to go.

But he'd been too self-assured, too certain he knew their tricks well enough to deflect any attack. Too confident in Lucy's abilities. Too eager to open a damn email.

When Lena's words finally penetrated his inner turmoil, he asked, "What did you say?"

"I have a solution." He wanted to be civil and listen to whatever ridiculous suggestion she made, but he didn't have it in him. He couldn't produce even a kernel of interest.

If he and Cruz hadn't found a way out of this mess, there wasn't a chance in hell she had a viable solution. But he hadn't displaced every brain cell yet, so he muttered, "Oh?"

Even to his own ears, the word sounded more grunty than encouraging. A part of him winced, another part couldn't even manage a shrug.

Lena removed her hand from his leg, and a bone-deep cold moved in.

"Please forgive, Rohan," Grams said. "He is not himself. Share your thoughts with us, Lena."

His grandmother's admonishment socked him in the balls, but his eyes remained fixed on his clamped hands.

Beside him, Lena released a low, shuddering breath. But when she spoke, her voice was strong and all business.

"For some time now, I've been researching investment opportunities. Nothing I've come across has been enticing enough to make me want to take the leap. Until now."

Heart rocking in his chest, Rohan turned to stare at Lena. She ignored him, keeping her attention on Zeke and the others.

"I'd like to invest twelve million dollars into BARS."

The background check he'd conducted on her had revealed a healthy bank account, but not twelve mil healthy.

He could think of only one other asset she possessed that would fetch enough cash to save BARS. But it wasn't hers to offer.

"You're not selling the Frida," he said.

The look she sent him could have burned water. "I have no intention of selling *Self-Portrait with Braided Hair*. I have other plans for her."

Rohan would circle back around to that comment later. "I did a thorough background check on your financials. Although a wealthy woman, you don't have that kind of change."

"You might be good at tech, but I'm good at hiding things. I assure you, I have the money."

"Why BARS?" Zeke asked.

"Because you return things to their proper place. Because you don't stop until you've righted the wrong. Because," she opened her hand and set the gold pendant on the conference table, "little girls need heroes like all y'all."

Rohan stared at the pendant she'd been carrying around for twenty years, not because of its beauty or value, but for the simple reason that it linked her to her family.

The pendant blurred as the full force of what she was offering him—them—set in.

One tear, two, three tears splattered against the table below him.

Jeezus, he was becoming a watering pot.

He squeezed his eyes shut and drew in a bracing breath, then raked a hand down his damp face. He looked up in time to see Zeke glance around the room. Each person present gave him a sharp nod. Then they all rose and filed out, one by one.

Cruz, being Cruz, strode away with his normal confident

stride, not affected by the fact that he was still in his underwear.

Grams paused between him and Lena. A hand on each of their shoulders. She kissed Rohan's temple, which nearly set off a fresh wave of waterworks.

Then she did the same to Lena. "We accept your generous offer, Angelena Kamber, and you have our collective gratitude for all the days we walk this Earth."

Lena nodded, struggling with her own emotions.

"We accept your *loan* with interest," he corrected in a guttural, yet firm voice. "I'll get our money back, Grams. I swear it."

The family matriarch brushed her fingers over the back of his neck before returning to his shoulder. "Rohan."

It took a moment before he could look at her. When he did, he saw nothing but love in her eyes.

"If your grandfather were here, he would no doubt say something wise that you would eventually pass down to your son and he to his." Her fingers dug into his shoulder with surprising strength. "But your grandfather is not here. I am. And I seek a promise from you."

In the depths of her dark eyes, Rohan recognized the same unwavering strength and resolve their ancestors must have had in abundance to survive the Long Walk over a century ago.

"Anything, Grams."

"Find the ones who did this to us and make them pay."

62

T HE FOLLOWING MORNING S HERIFF M AGGIE K INGSTON showed up at their gate.

"She's asking to speak with Lena."

Rohan stared up at Zeke, straining to see his brother beyond the ghostly imprint of code.

After the family meeting, he'd planted himself at his desk with a fully independent laptop he kept in reserve for emergency breakdowns. It was time—past time—for him to go on the offensive. He would track down the Collective's identities and make them pay. The same way he had Cal Simmons for screwing over the Neffs,

Only minutes ago, he'd found something disturbing. Really freaking disturbing.

Rohan reached for the cup, sitting on the warming dish. It brimmed with a coder's magic elixir.

Coffee.

"Why does Maggie want to talk to Lena?" he asked, taking a tentative sip to test the temperature.

"Might have something to do with the string of dead people you and Lena left behind on your road trip."

Rohan stared at his brother, not in the mood for his ribbing.

"Touchy this morning, I see." Zeke shrugged. "She didn't say. I assumed she had an update on Ruthie's murder to share."

"Did Maggie ask for me, too?"

"No."

"Why not? I was at the motel."

"Maybe the local authorities lifted one of Lena's fingerprints. In Atlanta, she admitted to being in the system."

"So am I."

No Blackwell had made it to age twenty without at least one brush with the law. For some, like Zeke and Cruz, multiple swipes.

"Can you hold her off?"

"What do you think?"

The sheriff was tenacious. A great quality for those on her good side, not so great for the other ninety-five percent of humanity.

"How the hell did she even know Lena was here?"

"Me," a new voice said.

Zeke whipped around, as surprised as Rohan, to find a disheveled Lena throwing aside a blanket as she sat up on his office couch.

The last time he'd seen her was right after the meeting, when she and Grams had followed Lynette into her office. The private meeting had certainly piqued his curiosity. But he'd been too focused on his own personal mission to give their cloak-and-dagger activities any further thought.

Had she been on his couch all night, catching fragments of sleep while keeping him in coffee?

If he hadn't been a hundred percent sure about his feelings for her before, he was now. Once again, the timing sucked, so he stayed rooted in his damn chair and took in every wisp of her wild hair, every wrinkle in her red top, and every dark smudge beneath her sleepy eyes.

"You called Maggie?"

"Sort of." She smoothed her hair off her face and swept it into a familiar bun. How it stayed in place without a hair band was a mystery. One he hoped to solve soon.

"I held a video conference with Maggie, Grams, Lynette, and a few other ladies I trust." She glanced between him and Zeke. "They helped me come up with a plan. Maggie's part of the solution."

Now he understood why she'd been cooped up in an office with Lynette and Grams.

"A plan for what?" Zeke asked, an edge of warning, or was it wonder, in his voice.

"Nothing either of you need to worry about. This isn't a BARS issue, this is *my* issue."

Now that he'd cleared the code from his head, another part of his brain kicked in. He rose from his chair, feeling every minute of his inactivity for the last six hours.

"We're partners now, Lena. Your business is our business, and vice versa."

"Even if mine included another dead body?"

Zeke raised a brow in Rohan's direction, then dropped into one of the guest chairs.

Rohan nodded toward the empty space next to Lena. "May I?"

"What about Maggie?"

"I got it." Zeke tapped several buttons on his phone's screen to remotely open the entrance gate.

Lena nodded at Rohan and shifted away a few unnecessary inches.

Despite her care of him last night, she was still hurting from the way he'd reacted to her investment offer.

He didn't blame her. She would've expected some response from him. Something besides silence. But none of the words he thought of seemed right. *Thank you* sounded too paltry for her level of generosity. *I love you* would have created another awkward void.

Rohan would make it up to her, but not with Zeke gawking at them.

Sitting a respectful distance away, he rested his arms on his knees and turned his head to look at her. "What's this about dead bodies?"

"Something Izzy said to me got me thinking." She wrapped her arms around a burgundy throw pillow.

Rohan looked at Zeke. "Isabella DeCarlo, a childhood friend and Senator Palmer's fiancée."

His brother nodded, a slight frown between his eyes, as he waited for Lena to continue.

"Unbeknownst to me, Izzy had created a grand idea in her mind that she, Xander," she paused for Zeke's sake, "you know him as Killian Byrne, and I would take over the business where we all worked, until a few years ago."

"Which was?" Zeke prompted.

With a resigned glance at Rohan, she told his brother about her parents' murders, her kidnapping, her mostly normal upbringing, her adoptive father's killing, her time on the streets with her friends, and her work for the man who had given them all a new life, then lost his.

Zeke sat in stunned silence for a full ten seconds before he said something that would have brought Rohan to his knees if he hadn't already been sitting.

"I heard about the lessons you've been giving Sadie. She's laid claim to you, as part of her intimate circle." A small smile appeared. "As I suspect my brother has." His smile faded. "For them, you will always have a place in this family. However, what you offered to do for BARS last night, what you're doing for all of us, has garnered you the full force of my family's protection. You're safe here, Angelena Kamber. Never doubt it."

63

Lena swiped at the lone tear before it made its way down her cheek.

Never in a million years would she have believed this big gruff guy could bring her to tears with words alone.

The Blackwells. A surprise. Every last one of them.

She rose from the leather couch and placed a kiss on Zeke's cheek. "Thank you."

He gave her an almost shy smile. "Welcome." Then he lightened the moment by winking at his brother.

She stepped on his foot, earning her a satisfying grunt.

Plopping back on the couch, she continued. "Izzy made it clear that I would pay for ruining her life. I think—" She tapped the side of her forefinger against her upper lip. "I think she might have killed Simon."

"Didn't he overdose on prescription painkillers?" Rohan asked.

"According to the medical examiner's report, yes."

"Why do you believe Izzy might have murdered him?"

"A few weeks before he died, she made a point of telling us she'd seen him popping pills during the day, and up until that point he'd only been dosing in the morning and evening."

"Maybe his back pain got worse."

"It's possible, but I remember now that it had been Izzy who'd suggested we check to see if Simon wanted us to bring him back something for lunch. I recalled being surprised, yet proud, about her thoughtfulness. Izzy had never concerned herself with Simon's welfare before."

"Not sure those two recollections would be enough to convince a jury that she's guilty of murder," Zeke said.

"Yesterday, she compared Simon to lint. Something easily 'discarded.'" She glanced at the two men. "I know it sounds ridiculous, but it was the way she said it. Her body language. She was without remorse. Proud, even." Lena hugged the pillow to her chest again. "She all but gloated about Desmond killing Ruthie, and I have a strong suspicion he killed Bobby Balor."

"Who's Desmond?" Zeke asked.

"Izzy's lover and God knows what else," Rohan said. "He's also head of Palmer's security."

Zeke frowned again and rose. "Be back in a second." His thumbs flew across his phone as he left Rohan's office.

Lena stared at the open door. "Where's he going?"

"No idea."

Rohan angled his body toward her. One hand clutched the back of the couch, the other reached for hers.

After her cold recollections of Izzy, his touch warmed her, comforted her. Bolstered her in a hundred different ways that would see her through the challenging hours ahead.

"Why do you think Desmond killed Bobby?"

"To ensure his silence." She glanced down at their hands. "Bobby said a friend of his heard about Palmer getting a copy made of *Woman Walking*." She lifted her gaze to his. "What if his *friend* was Izzy?"

"Even with Izzy's past, I can't see the two of them running in the same circles."

"No, but Izzy knows a lot of people. She's a networking queen, just like Kayla. How do you think she wound up engaged to a senator?"

Rohan's eyes widened as if struck by a thought. "Before Balor died, Maggie got him to reveal that *Woman Walking* wasn't his original target."

"What was?" Even as the words left her mouth, she had a sinking feeling she knew.

"The Frida." He gentled his voice. "Could Izzy and Killian have known it was the original?"

Lena ignored the stab of betrayal. "It's possible, but I don't think so." She gave it some thought. "They both knew three experts had authenticated my copy."

"Maybe they stole the Frida and sold it as an original, knowing the auction house wouldn't be able to tell it was a fake."

"They knew I wouldn't say anything."

"Because you were the artist." Rohan caressed her hand as he spoke, keeping her grounded. "Why did they add the Catawnee to the theft order?"

"Izzy saw an opportunity to discredit me. A way to slowly erode my business. Who would hand over their precious artworks to someone who lost a million-dollar painting?"

"With Killian gone, Balor was the only other person who knew Izzy had organized the theft of her fiancé's expensive painting."

Lena nodded. "When I first saw Desmond at Palmer's, he'd just returned from a meeting that Izzy seemed inordinately pleased about. I remembered thinking the entire exchange felt off, somehow. You said Bobby had only been dead for two or three hours by the time his roommate had found him. So I think the timing fits."

"Desmond kills Balor, tying up a loose end, and returns to the party, giving himself dozens of alibis."

"If I didn't hate her so much right now, I'd be impressed by her diabolical plan."

Silence fell between them, and Lena's thoughts shifted away from betraying friends to the man next to her. It had been difficult to watch him pound away on his keyboard through the long hours of the night, searching for malicious phantoms.

When her two-hour videoconference with the ladies had ended, she'd strode by his office and noticed that his desk was devoid of food or drink. Not knowing the last time he'd had either, she'd located some energy bars and did her best to keep his coffee cup filled.

She didn't even try to talk him into getting some rest. If their situations had been reversed, she would have been as determined as he to chase down the digital terrorists.

How long would it take for him to forgive himself? Would he ever?

"Lena," Rohan said in a low, guttural voice. "Thank you for taking care of me while I worked."

Lena's stomach did a little flip-flop at the love shining in his eyes. "I wish I could've done more."

"I'm sorry about how I acted last night. About not showing you how much I appreciated your offer to invest—"

"*I love you.*" The words tumbled out of her mouth, awkward and wobbly, like a litter of preweaned pups checking out their new territory.

His eyes flared and his breath caught mid-inhalation, as

if someone had punched all the air out of his lungs. Then a smile broke across his face, and he cupped her cheek. "I love you, too." He kissed her, soft and reverent, before lifting his head.

For the first time in over a decade, terror blinded Lena against what the future might hold. More fragments of memory had come to her since last night. Dangerous fragments she wished had remained buried deep in her psyche.

But she was tired of running. Tired of starting over. She wanted what she saw in Rohan's eyes. She wanted the happy ending.

"Thanks, gratitude," he said. "They will never be enough for the sacrifice you're making."

"It's not a sacrifice. It's a sound business investment."

"Loan," he corrected. "With interest."

Smiling, she lifted her free hand to trace the edge of his jaw. "What I seek is not your thanks or gratitude."

"Name it, and it's yours."

"What I need is your forgiveness."

"For what?'

"Loving you."

A VAST WAVE OF CONFUSION SWEPT OVER ROHAN, THRASHING him around like a surfer without the balancing weight of his board.

"Why would I need to forgive you for such a gift?"

"Because everyone I've ever loved, everyone I've ever cared about has died. Not left me. But died." Her grip on his hand tightened. "Those are lousy odds for you."

"Another thing about Blackwells"—he moved in closer —"is that we beat the odds"—he slid his nose along hers— "every time."

She made a distressed sound before covering his mouth with hers. Tingling warmth spread across his chest, pushing away the fear, the uncertainty. He slid his tongue along her lower lip, a silent request. A plea to recapture the same closeness they'd both reveled in last night.

Before his world came tumbling down.

His beautiful painter opened the door, and he slipped inside, exploring, enticing, worshiping.

When her body surged forward, pushing him back into the cushions, Rohan's mind splintered and he reached for the hem of her top.

"I knew Desmond didn't sound right," Zeke said, striding back into the office. He froze.

They froze.

Zeke blinked, then averted his eyes. "About time y'all made nice." He made a show of sitting down and pulling a piece of paper from a beige file folder.

Once Lena settled in next to him again, Rohan placed a hand on her thigh, needing the contact. "What do you have on Desmond?"

Zeke thrust the paper at Rohan.

"What's this?"

"Page three of Palmer's background check."

Rohan's lust-glazed eyes did a quick scan, but every word looked foreign, indecipherable.

He could still taste Lena, smell her, feel her. The paper shook in his hand.

"Give me a damn clue here, Zeke."

His brother ripped the page from his grasp. "Section Twelve, Direct Reports—"

Rohan snatched it back. "I don't need to be spoon-fed. Just focused."

Zeke grunted and murmured, "Could've fooled me.

Palmer's chief of personal security is a Nepali-American woman by the name of Sreva Rai."

Lena frowned. "Who is Desmond to Palmer then? The senator clearly knew him—and had no problem with his fiancée having a cozy tête-à-tête with the man."

"Desmond Locke," Rohan read. "Chief of Cybersecurity."

"Cyber?" Lena rose and paced away a few feet, then turned back to them. "Now I understand how Desmond uncovered my Angela Jones identity."

Rohan shook his head. "No, something more is at play here, but I can't put my finger on it."

"Give me what you've got," Zeke said.

"Both Ash and I failed to uncover even a slice of Lena's life before she hit fifteen. I don't buy that Desmond pulled a section of her life out of a hat at the snap of Izzy's fingers."

"I'm with you," Zeke said. "So how'd he do it?"

"He had a piece of the puzzle that we didn't."

"Like what?"

"The identity of my adoptive father Neil," Lena chimed in. "It's the only thing that makes sense. He's the one and only link between Anjali, Angela, and Angelena."

"How did Desmond discover Jones?" Zeke asked.

"The billion-dollar question."

"Sounds like y'all could use some help," an amused female voice said.

Kayla Krowne leaned against the doorframe, arms folded across her middle. She wore a lightweight black sweater, slim gray pants, and practical leather boots.

"Thanks for answering my text on such short notice," Zeke said. "You really were in the area."

"Are you kidding? I wouldn't miss this opportunity for

the world." She turned brown eyes on Lena. "Twice in twenty-four hours. We're destined to be friends."

"Being friends with me is dangerous."

"I thrive in high-risk situations." She smiled, then leaned back to look in the outer room. "Is my BFF joining us?"

Zeke shook his head. "Travel baseball. Liv took Brodie to an overnight baseball tournament in Gaston." He nodded toward the front of the building. "Did you see a pony-tailed sheriff loitering outside?"

"In the parking lot. She appeared to be in a Texas show-down with Grams and her utility vehicle."

Zeke groaned.

"Care to tell me what's going on?" Rohan asked, itchy to get back to the keyboard. Maggie could hold her own with Grams.

Zeke motioned for everyone to sit. Rohan and Lena returned to the couch and Kayla lowered herself into the other guest chair.

"I recognized Isabella DeCarlo's name from Palmer's background check."

Kayla hitched up a brow. "Doing a background check on a sitting senator. This is getting better and better."

"Although Liv and Phin vouched for you," Zeke said, a warning note in his voice, "I want to make it clear that anything we discuss today stays in this room."

Kayla's lips twitched. "What would you do if I discussed it with all my closest pals? Hang me up by my toes until I apologized?"

Rohan could almost see his brother's blood pressure shooting into the next galaxy. Normally, outsiders heeded Zeke's commands with little or no pushback. But Kayla swam in an ocean of sharks on a daily basis. She recognized the different between a nose bump and a bite.

Zeke's features took on the same expression he used to get when his younger brothers had pulled off a successful prank. "I'll make a stop at every one of your fancy houses and piss on your fancy beds. How does that sound?"

"Revolting." She exhaled. "I'm so glad I don't have any brothers."

Grinning, Lena wound her fingers between Rohan's. He tried to smile back, but the passage of time drummed in his head. He needed to get back to his hunt.

"As I was saying," Zeke threw Kayla an annoyed look before turning back to Lena, "your mention of Isabella DeCarlo also reminded me of a comment Liv made a few weeks ago, after she read about the senator's engagement."

Lena's nails pressed into Rohan's flesh, as if preparing herself for bad news.

"Liv said her former colleagues in the FBI's white-collar squad had been monitoring the senator's campaign finances since before his first election, but they've never been able to nail him down on anything."

Rohan looked at Kayla. "Are you here to fill in the gaps on Palmer?"

Kayla's lobbying firm no doubt had reams of research on Palmer, and every other politician in North Carolina, making BARS's background check look like a shopping list.

"Blaise Palmer comes from an extremely wealthy family," Kayla said. "His late grandfather made millions in the coal industry and his father is now making bank in renewable energies." She crossed one long leg over the other, settling into her story. "Gerard Palmer is a shrewd businessman and, at seventy-four, still holds a great deal of influence over his son."

"Keen for his son to become the next president of the United States," Rohan concluded.

Kayla nodded. "I'm certain the senator's engagement to Miss DeCarlo was his father's doing."

"Why certain?" Zeke asked.

"Bella DeCarlo doesn't have the right equipment to hold Blaise's interest in bed."

After a moment of speculative silence, Lena said, "Izzy further legitimizes the persona they've molding for years."

"Rumors have been circulating for years about the senator's sexual leanings," Kayla said, "and not just that he prefers men, but men with certain shared kinks."

"Desmond," Rohan said, recalling the man's provocative words to him in Izzy's boudoir.

"He started working for the senator about a year ago. My source inside the senator's household has observed Desmond leaving the senator's bedroom more than once." Kayla tapped her nails against the chair's arm. "What I don't understand is how Bella DeCarlo fits into all of this."

"What do you mean?" Rohan asked.

"Bella's like a black dress amidst a circle of pastels. She doesn't fit into the picture that Gerard Palmer has painstakingly staged." Kayla considered Lena. "Any thoughts on what value she would bring to the Palmer empire?"

Lena shrugged. "Izzy's gorgeous and intelligent. Adaptable and cunning. She's a rags-to-riches success story. She's also extremely ambitious."

"Ambitious enough to overlook her husband's lovers?" Rohan asked.

"If a loveless marriage garnered her the title of First Lady, Izzy would likely escort the men to her husband's bed."

"She sounds delightful," Kayla said. "I almost wish you hadn't talked me out of approaching her the other night."

Lena grinned. "Me too. It would've been entertaining watching the two of you spar."

The conversation around Rohan faded as his mind whirled with possibilities and connections and a hundred different scenarios. Yet he still couldn't figure out how Desmond knew about Lena's adoptive father.

Rohan caught Kayla's eye. "Does the name Neil Jones ring any bells with you?"

She took a moment to think, then shook her head. "Who is he?"

"A man who played a part in murdering my parents, then raised me as his own," Lena said. She summed up the first half of her life in a no-nonsense voice. But Rohan knew what it must have cost her to share such a painful past with someone she'd only just met.

Empathy softened Kayla's features, but she didn't offer condolences or other platitudes people awkwardly conveyed in moments like this. She stuck to being Kayla.

"Damn girl, you really are a person of fascination."

64

"Where's everyone hiding?" Maggie called from the outer room.

When Rohan's hand tensed in Lena's, she sent him an encouraging smile—or tried to—before rising to meet the newcomer.

When she cleared Rohan's office and got her first in-person look at Sheriff Maggie Kingston, Lena wondered if she was about to make the biggest mistake of her life.

A drab beige uniform encased Maggie's long, athletic build, which somehow magnified her attributes. If her brown hair had been five shades darker and she had traded out her crisp polyester uniform for a red leather bodice and blue skirt, she would've blended in well on the island of Themyscira, along with Princess Diana and the other Amazonian warriors.

Lena inwardly smiled at her Marvel-influenced imagination, even while straightening her spine and cursing her comfortable, but grounded, On tennis shoes. Right then, she would've sacrificed a month's worth of chocolate for the extra four inches her Veronica Beard boots would've added to her height.

Extending a hand, Lena said, "Thanks for coming, Sheriff Kingston."

"Just Maggie. Please." Steele Ridge's top officer smiled as she shook Lena's hand. "You made quite an impression on my sister Riley. She talks about you as if you're already one of the 'girls.'" Maggie glanced behind Lena and lowered her voice. "Considering Rohan's growing scowl, I'd say she sized up the situation pretty well."

Lena peered over her shoulder and, sure enough, Rohan stood at his office door, eyeing the bulky duffel bag the sheriff carried with suspicion.

Maggie released Lena's hand. "Ready?"

"Ready for what?" he asked, moving to Lena's side.

The sheriff lifted a puzzled brow in Lena's direction.

Clasping a hand around his forearm, Lena said, "Go back inside and finish hearing what Kayla has to say. This," she motioned toward Maggie, "is personal, as I mentioned."

"What's in the bag, Sheriff?" Rohan asked, a rare hardness in his voice.

Maggie's chin lifted, and her already square shoulders sharpened. "This is a police matter."

"Why aren't you having this conversation at the *police station* then?" Zeke asked, inserting himself into the discussion.

"I try hard not to be disrespectful to ninety-year-old women." Maggie took in the offices, then the open conference room. "The Theater might be better than using Lynette's office. It'll give us more room." She looked at Zeke. "Okay with you?"

"Sure. I love it when law enforcement takes over our

office. Can I fetch you some coffee? Show you where the restrooms are located?"

"I'm sorry, Zeke," Lena said, wishing she'd followed her gut and met Maggie at the loft. "As Maggie suggested, your mother and grandmother insisted we use the Annex." She sent the sheriff an apologetic smile. "We should go."

Rohan grasped her hand before she could take a step toward the exit and stabbed a "behave" look at his brother. "You're welcome to use the Theater."

Kayla appeared and held up her phone to Lena, screen side out. "Bella DeCarlo accepted my invitation to lunch."

"What the actual fuck is going on?" Zeke said, his annoyance climbing to a full boil.

Kayla settled amused eyes on Lena, and the friendship the lobbyist had hinted at took root in Lena's chest. Anxiety wormed its way into her heart, but Lena didn't have time to worry about the consequences to those who got too close. Not with Zeke's head about to pop off, and Rohan's patience thinning.

"Maggie and Kayla, would you bring Zeke up to date, while I speak with Rohan?"

Zeke narrowed his eyes on Kayla. "In the area, my ass."

"True statement."

"Don't pull your lobbyist mumbo jumbo on me."

Maggie followed Zeke and Kayla into the Theater, grinning as she listened to the two warheads continue their back and forth bickering.

Rohan stroked a finger along Lena's jawline. "Tell me what you girls have cooked up. Please."

"I can't let Izzy get away with killing Simon, Ruthie, Bobby, and quite possibly Xander."

"You've decided she had something to do with Byrne's death?"

"I don't know, but Desmond was obviously following us. If he was willing to kill Ruthie and Bobby, why not Xander?" With all the recent revelations, Lena no longer bought into Izzy's shock and outrage at hearing about Xander's death.

"For what purpose?"

"Maybe Desmond made a mistake. Maybe he had expected me to walk into the studio, and Xander surprised him."

Rohan rested a hand on her hip, and she felt the warmth all the way to the soles of her feet. "Is that what you think? Izzy sent Desmond to hurt you and wound up killing Xander instead?"

"Again, I don't know. But all of this feels connected, and there's only one way to find out for sure."

His fingers tensed around her hip. "How?"

"By asking Izzy."

He said nothing. Just stared at her, waiting.

"While wearing a recording device."

He closed his eyes, as if her answer had dealt him a mortal wound. "Please tell me you're joking. Tell me you're not talking about attempting to get a confession out of a presumed killer. One you've said will stop at nothing to become the nation's First Lady."

When he put her plan in those terms, it did sound a bit iffy. For a moment, a brief moment, she considered calling it off. Then a collage of faces that Izzy and Desmond had hurt filled her vision. "I'm equally motivated."

No doubt hearing the determination in her voice, he nodded. "Let's do this."

"Wait, what about the ransom demand?"

"Later."

"Rohan—"

"Thanks to you, we have a strategy to deal with the

Collective." He brushed a wisp of hair behind her ear. "We'll deal with Izzy together."

"But I thought you wanted to hunt down the Collective."

"I do and I will. First things first." He kissed her, hard and fast. "Let's see what kind of shit surveillance equipment Maggie brought with her." He winked and placed a hand on her back as they joined the others.

For the first time in two decades, Lena felt loved and safe and not alone.

65

"EVERYONE MEET AT THE VAN IN NINETY MINUTES," ZEKE SAID, wrapping up their strategy session and heading to the kitchenette.

Lena leaned toward Kayla, who was sitting next to her. "Would you mind giving me a lift back to my place? It's downtown."

"Absolutely. Are you ready to go now?"

"Right after I use the restroom."

"Why do you need to go to your loft?" Rohan asked, overhearing their conversation.

"In case you hadn't noticed, I'm still wearing the same clothes I had on yesterday."

"Don't you have something at the cabin you can change into?"

"Yes, but I need to take care of some things at the loft."

"I'll drive you."

"You have too much to do here," she said. "I'll be back in an hour."

The conflict raging inside him was real, and Lena nearly gave in. He'd already lost two hours and would likely lose several more by helping Lena take down Izzy. But she couldn't have him tagging along. Not on this trip.

"I'll stay with her until she's ready to return," Kayla offered.

Rohan raked a hand through his hair and nodded. "Okay, okay. Just call me if anything—and I mean anything—goes sideways."

Lena kissed his cheek, and they both rose.

The Annex's inner door opened and, a few seconds later, a dark-haired man wearing a rumpled blue suit coat, white dress shirt, and dark gray slacks appeared.

Coffee mug in hand, Zeke halted mid-stride. "What are you doing here?"

"Hello to you, too, bro," the man said.

Bro?

Lena frowned, but her confusion lasted only a second. This must be Ash. The eldest brother who had left the family business to pursue a career with the FBI.

Ash glanced around the room until his gaze hit on Kayla, who seemed to be lounging in a far more relaxed pose now than she had been a few seconds ago. His features hardened into suspicion. "What's going on?"

Rohan stood, threading his fingers with Lena's. "You first." He glanced down at Lena, then back to Ash. "Is this about that thing I asked you to look into?"

Ash nodded.

Something about the tenor of Rohan's voice and his fierce grip on her hand fired up Lena's pulse.

Zeke grabbed the nearest chair and rolled it back from the conference table. "Sit down before you fall down."

Ash did as instructed, scrubbing at his face with both hands, as if trying to wake himself up. "Got any coffee in this joint?"

Zeke clunked his full, steaming mug on the table in front of his brother.

"Thanks." He took a tentative sip and waited for everyone to resettle themselves. Although the eldest Blackwell's eyes were bloodshot, they were no less penetrating when they landed on her. "You're Lena, I take it."

She nodded. "Ash?"

His gaze shifted to where Rohan's hand covered hers on the table. "That's right." He lifted a chin toward Maggie. "Cameron to my colleagues."

"My aunt's married to your uncle," Maggie said, speaking for the first time. "Not sure what that makes us, but more than a damn colleague." She frowned. "You look like hell, Cam. What's happened?"

"Late yesterday afternoon," Ash said, redirecting his attention to Lena. "I drove down to Charleston to speak with an elderly couple, a Mr. and Mrs. Kumar."

Lena's breath caught. A million questions rushed through her brain, but she forced herself to wait for him to continue.

Rohan prompted him. "And? Are they Lena's grandparents?"

Ash shook his head. "Their son and his family are alive and well."

Disappointment clutched at Lena's chest. She should have known from Ash's haggard features that he hadn't come here with good news.

"For chrissake," Rohan seethed. "Why'd you bring this to us?"

"Because," Ash took another sip of coffee, "the Kumars told me about their second cousins in Hendersonville—Aarush and Saanvi. I met with them this morning, and they told me about the tragic car accident twenty years ago that took their eldest son, Jahan, and daughter-in-law, Morgan."

The names didn't register even a kernel of recognition. Lena excavated her old-new memories, searching for just one name he mentioned.

Nothing.

"Did they say anything about a granddaughter?" Rohan asked.

The agent sent Lena a smile. "Their beloved first-born grandchild, four-year-old Anjali, went missing the night of the accident."

Ash's image blurred, as joy filled her chest.

Rohan's hand tightened, and he kissed her temple.

The agent pulled a four-by-six photo from an inside pocket of his suit coat and passed it down to her. "They don't know about you yet. I wanted to be absolutely sure."

Lena swiped the tears from her eyes and stared down at the familiar faces of her parents and paternal grandparents.

Her family.

Teary again, she looked at Rohan. "My grandparents. They're alive."

Rohan's own eyes glistened with emotion. "Less than an hour and a half away."

"You sure?" Ash asked gently.

She nodded. "Positive."

"With your permission, I'd like to return and tell them the good news," Ash said. "They also deserve to know what really happened to their son and daughter-in-law. It's possible they have a stray bit of information that could lead us to their killers."

His request touched Lena. She knew he didn't need her permission to investigate a cold case, but she appreciated the gesture. "Of course."

A thought struck her, and she reached between her legs to retrieve her shoulder bag from the floor. Unzipping the secret pocket at the bottom, she took out a folded silk square made of blue, red, and yellow swirls.

She burrowed her fingers inside the folds and removed a gold teardrop pendant. Rising, she walked over to Ash. "I think my mother gave me this the night of the crash. It has a symbol on the back. Maybe my grandparents will recognize it."

Ash held out his hand, and Lena somewhat reluctantly placed the keepsake in the center of his palm. It was the only true connection, if that was what it was, to her biological parents. Neil had protected it for ten years and Lena another ten. Letting it out of her sight was harder than she had imagined.

Sandwiching her hand between his, Ash vowed, "You can trust me with this. I swear it."

Swallowing, she nodded and bent to kiss his cheek. "I can never thank you enough for the gift of my grandparents."

Ash cleared his throat and stood. "You're welcome, but Rohan is the one who deserves your gratitude. It was his incessant texts and voice mails that set me on their trail."

Lena glanced back at Rohan and poured every morsel of love residing in her heart into her smile.

"Well then," Kayla said, pushing out of her chair. "This was a much happier way to end a meeting." She caught Lena's eye. "If we're to get back here on time, we should leave."

Shifting back to Ash, Lena said, "My apologies, but I have to go."

The suspicious look was back on Ash's face as he

followed Kayla's approach, and Lena wondered what was going on in the agent's head.

She didn't have long to ponder the question.

"Someone want to fill me in on why a lobbyist is sitting in on a family meeting?" Ash asked.

Kayla snaked her arm through Lena's, nodded for Maggie to precede them, and winked at Ash. "Disheveled is a good look for you."

66

Twenty minutes before go-time, Lena peered into Rohan's ever-changing eyes as he adjusted the black glass pendant hanging from a necklace of white turquoise and sterling silver to rest in the hollow of her throat.

During a somewhat heated discussion about how to best outfit Lena, Grams had appeared and presented Lena with the beautiful piece, sans pendant. "For courage and serenity." Then the Blackwell matriarch squeezed Lena's hand, gave Rohan a pointed look, and left them to sort out the rest.

An ache settled in Lena's chest at the thought of growing up in a household with such a strong and loving grandparent. Then an image flashed across her mind's eye, of an older woman holding a cone-shaped pastry dough, encouraging little Anjali to fill it with crumbles of richly spiced potatoes and peas and showing her how to seal up the savory goodness.

Because of Ash's remarkable investigative skills, Lena might be able to make new memories with her *dadi* and *dada*. The special agent should arrive at her grandparents' home in Hendersonville at any moment. Regret arrowed through her, as she wished she could be there when he broke the news about finding their missing granddaughter.

But Ash had a case to investigate, and Lena had a murderer to catch. She would meet them later. If they were willing.

"The pendant contains a pinhole camera and listening device," Rohan said, bringing her back to the present. His all-business techy voice in direct contrast with his gentle touch. "When you see Izzy approach, press the button at the back, and I'll be able to see and hear everything you do."

She searched for the small button with the pad of her thumb. "Got it."

After much back and forth, Maggie had finally agreed to use the Blackwell's state-of-the art equipment and surveillance van with the caveat that she would occupy a seat inside and the Blackwells would be on the sheriff's payroll during the sting operation.

If Izzy confessed to murder, Maggie wanted to make sure everything was by the book.

"This is ready." Cruz dropped a small clear earbud into Rohan's palm.

Rohan held it out to her. "Put this in your ear. It will allow you to hear us."

Lena took the impossibly small bud, with its tiny antenna, and placed it deep in her ear.

Rohan nodded at Cruz.

"Testing one-two-three. Testing."

She jumped at the clear quality of Cruz's voice in her ear. "I hear you."

A smile curled at one side of Rohan's mouth, but it quickly faded. "I don't like this."

"I know." She brushed her hand over his taut biceps. "But Zeke's monitoring the situation from the bar, plus Phin and one of Maggie's female deputies will be sitting a few tables away."

As if on cue, Zeke's voice came through her earpiece. *"Target has arrived."*

Rohan pulled her into his arms and pressed his lips to her forehead. "Promise me you'll stick to the script."

"I promise."

"No going rogue, no taking chances, no putting yourself in harm's—"

She grasped his face with both hands. "I promise."

"Kayla's scheduled to send her 'I'm running late' text in two minutes," Cruz announced.

Rohan pressed closer and whispered near her ear. "I love you. Stay safe."

A hard lump formed in the back of her throat. Before she made a fool of herself by crying, she kissed him quickly, then moved toward the van's back door.

"Fifteen minutes," Maggie reminded her from a task chair next to Cruz's. "That's all the time you have to get DeCarlo's confession before Kayla arrives."

Feeling the reassuring weight of Grams's necklace around her throat, Lena's spine straightened and she shot them all a grin. "I'll have her singing in twelve."

"No getting cocky," Rohan growled.

Lena grinned, turned the door latch, and stepped into the sunlight.

67

ALL OF LENA'S BRAVADO DISINTEGRATED THE MOMENT TRIPLE B came into view. In less than a minute, she would be engaged in verbal warfare with a woman who not only excelled at the craft but had built a life on lies and manipulation.

You've navigated Izzy's peculiarities before. You've got this.

But this Izzy seemed more polished, more self-assured, more intense than the teenager who'd used her smile to draw tourists into their web.

When Lena neared the restaurant, she spotted her old friend sitting at one of the outdoor tables, phone in hand. The warm fall sun glinted off her dark hair and highlighted the perfect line of her delicate throat.

Lena frowned. Rather than occupy the chair with the best people-watching vantage, Izzy faced the opposite direction. Odd behavior for a woman who used to vie for every opportunity to see and be seen.

Briefly, Lena thought about sharing her uneasiness with the team, but decided against it. Preoccupied with her phone, Izzy likely just plopped down at the nearest empty seat.

Shoring up her nerves, she scanned the outdoor dining crowd and located Phin and the female deputy, Kelly Sullivan, sitting before one of the restaurant's large picture windows. No one would know from the look of them that they'd met less than an hour ago.

The sight of Phin in full charm mode brought her the comfort she needed to focus on the mission's goal and not on Izzy's seating arrangements. Lena reached for the pendant at her neck. "Engaging camera."

A second later, Rohan's deep voice responded, *"Image clear. Proceed to the target."*

The moment she was within hearing distance, Lena put her phone to her ear and spoke in an animated voice. "Yes, I would be happy to stop by your house and discuss another commission. Three o'clock is fine. See you then."

She pretended to disconnect from the nonexistent call. When she looked up, Izzy stood before her. A gamer's smile fixed in place.

"Here for lunch?" Izzy asked in a deceptively pleasant voice.

"That was the plan," Lena made a point of taking in Izzy's personal items on the nearby table, "but now I need to rethink my choice."

"I have a few minutes before my lunch guest arrives." She tapped a red nail against the back of a chair at her table. "Sit and tell me about this new commission."

"Now why would I want to do either of those things?"

Izzy smiled wide, then suddenly embraced her. Lena froze, her gaze jumping to Phin's. She could hear the team chattering in her ear, but Izzy's whispered words snagged her focus.

"Because I have a surprise for you, my friend," Izzy said before stepping away. "I've left the best seat at the table for my guest. Take it. The sun feels delicious."

Mystery solved on Izzy's seating choice. Her strategic mind must have been flying at 4Gs since getting Kayla's text last night.

Lena made sure she projected extreme reluctance as she sat down. "I hate to tell you this, but your surprises suck."

A feline smile appeared. "Please don't tell me your boyfriend let a little arrest order come between you."

"Don't you think you're taking this whole 'you screwed me over, now I'm going to screw you over' thing too far?"

"There's no such thing as too far."

"Seems like I did you a favor."

Amusement drained from the other woman's face.

"You're on the cusp of becoming the First Lady of the United States. I'd say that outshines art forger any day."

In the distance, the shrill squawk of an emergency siren echoed off buildings. Lena's attention didn't move off the woman across from her. Living downtown, she'd become immune to screaming emergency vehicles.

"You stupid, selfish bitch," Izzy said through clenched teeth. "You have no idea of the plans I had made, of the things I had done to keep the three of us together."

"Did any of those *things* include murdering Simon?"

Izzy went still. "Simon was like a father to me."

"Bullshit, you could barely stand the man."

"Easy, Lena," Rohan cautioned. *"We don't know if she has a weapon in that handbag at her feet."*

"How did you do it?" Lena asked, ignoring Rohan's warning. "How did you get him to overdose? Did Xander help you?"

Izzy let out a sharp laugh. "What a ridiculous question.

Xander hadn't the nerve for killing the rats stealing our stash of food. Do you really think he could've stomached killing a man he practically worshipped?"

Two fire trucks roared, one after the other, down Main Street. Lena waited for them to pass before amping up the pressure.

"Someone must have helped you. There's no way you would've dirtied your dainty fingers. Not when you have access to men like Desmond, who are easily manipulated."

"Desmond, easily manipulated?" Izzy laughed. "He doesn't do anything unless there's a benefit to him."

Lena inwardly cursed herself, knowing she'd made the fatal mistake of saying too much, of redirecting her nemesis's attention away from the true goal.

"Still so naïve," Izzy said.

A gentle breeze buffeted Lena's face, cooling the sudden heat flushing her cheeks and ears. The air carried with it an acrid scent, and Lena realized the fire must be close.

"Not so naïve that I didn't figure out that Desmond is the one hacking into my life and feeding you information."

Surprise flickered across Izzy's face, then her gaze became more intent as if she were examining every inch of Lena's features.

"He's extraordinary, in so many ways," Izzy said, when whatever she'd been looking for didn't surface, "as I'm sure your boyfriend could attest, but even Desmond hadn't been able to figure out your past until I gave him your other alias."

"Kayla's on her way," Cruz said. *"She'll be table side in two minutes."*

"Time to wrap it up, Lena," Rohan added. *"I'm sorry, but today's not the day."*

Lena's pulse pounded in her ears. With one hundred

percent certainty, she knew this would be her one and only shot of getting Izzy's confession recorded. She let the conversation roll and prayed she could guide it back to Simon in a way that wouldn't raise Izzy's suspicion.

"How did you learn about Angela Jones?"

"Did you really think I wouldn't notice you running your fingers over the bottom of your purse every time you picked it up?"

She'd installed false bottoms in every purse she'd ever owned. Had she really been so obvious? Lena's insides knotted at her carelessness.

Out of the corner of her eye, Lena caught sight of pedestrians and shopkeepers gathering on the sidewalk, sharing comments and looks of confusion as they stared toward the northeast.

The knot in her stomach cinched tighter. The air around her thickened with an unseen menace. She wanted to turn around to see if Phin felt it too, but she dared not take her eyes off Izzy.

Just as her mind began to spiral, Lena's thoughts zeroed in on one of Izzy's comments. "Why would Rohan think Desmond was extraordinary?"

"Who besides someone with extraordinary technical capabilities could have penetrated every one of your genius boyfriend's defenses?"

For a prolonged second, Lena simply refused to believe what she'd heard. But there was no mistaking Izzy's self-satisfied expression.

"Desmond sent the ransomware?"

Did that mean he was part of the Collective? Or was he terrorizing Rohan on behalf of Izzy? Had the cyberattack on BARS been part of Izzy's revenge on Lena? The possibility sickened her.

"Please tell me, how do you console someone after they've lost everything?"

"Lena, disengage now," Rohan said, a breathless quality to his voice.

A shout drew Lena's attention toward the object of everyone's fascination. Above the rooftops, a thick, gray billowing column of smoke soared into the sky. It could only be a couple of blocks away. She studied the location and felt the slow bloom of ice crystals crackle up her spine.

Her apartment building was on fire.

She did indeed have the best seat at the table.

Fingers curling, Lena's gaze shot to the woman who had once been her closest friend.

"Your life," Izzy said, lifting her hand to reveal her thumb and middle finger pressed together.

Snap!

"Up in smoke."

68

RUNNING AT FULL TILT, ROHAN ROUNDED THE CORNER OF THE old Murchison building in time to see Lena launch herself at Isabella DeCarlo.

Dammit!

If only he'd keyed in on the dispatch traffic coming through Maggie's radio earlier, he might have caught the first mention of the fire's location. But he'd been so caught up in Lena's conversation with Izzy that everything else had been background noise.

The two women went crashing to the ground. Lena on top, Izzy below.

Phin and Deputy Sullivan moved in to break up the fight.

Rohan's legs pumped harder. He heard the rapid tread of Maggie's boots behind him. Cruz had stayed in the van to monitor the situation.

Beyond the combatants, a familiar brown-haired man walked past City Hall. Rather than craning to uncover what the commotion was ahead, he kept his attention on the giant plume of smoke. A self-congratulatory smile curled at the corners of his eyes. His lips pursed.

Desmond.

"The little bastard's whistling."

Rohan still reeled from the revelation that Desmond had sent the ransomware. Only this morning, he'd discovered the attack had been one hacker's coordinated effort, leading him to speculate the Collective wasn't a group of like-minded hactivists, but rather a single person's game of vengeance.

"Who's whistling?" Zeke asked.

"Desmond Locke. He's headed your way, approaching the Mad Batter Bakery now."

A short silence.

"No visual yet. Too many people in my line of sight."

Rohan's gaze shifted back to the street fight. Lena rained down blows as if she'd spent a lifetime in the boxing ring. Her fists hammered Izzy's face, chest, stomach, anywhere the other woman's defensive maneuvers left open.

The uproar finally wrested the whistling hacker's attention away from what Rohan could only assume was his latest devastation. Desmond's face lit up, as if the two women were mud wrestling for his entertainment alone. Then he spotted Rohan cutting across the street and his amusement fled.

Desmond's eyes flared in recognition, and he halted. He must have seen something feral in Rohan's expression, because he backed up a step. Then another.

"He's going to run," Rohan shouted.

Lena's bloodcurdling scream of protest rent the air as Phin snaked an arm around her middle, lifting her off Izzy, while Deputy Sullivan moved in to assist the dazed and battered woman on the ground.

"Get away from me," Izzy snapped through split lips.

The deputy backed off, and Izzy eased to her side. In a lightning swift move, Izzy drew a pistol from her handbag and pointed it at Lena's head. The gun shook violently in her hand.

Time slowed, and Rohan's mad sprint sputtered.

"I loved you like a sister!" Izzy struggled to her knees. Her long hair tangled around her face and her yellow button-down top sat askew on her frame. "And you threw it away for a guy who couldn't do what needed to be done."

"Simon didn't have to die," Lena yelled, still straining against Phin's hold.

"Yes, he did!" Izzy lifted her other hand to steady the pistol. "You do, too."

Rohan's eyes locked with Lena's, and the bloodlust in her eyes changed to fear, when she saw his intent.

"Izzy!" he roared.

The woman took the bait and turned toward the new threat.

Lena screamed, "Rohan, no!"

Phin threw Lena to the ground, covering her body with his at the same time Rohan plowed into Izzy, wrenching the gun from her hand.

The momentum sent the two of them tumbling, and Rohan grunted as his face slid across the concrete. The gun flew out of his hand and clattered against the pavement. He heard a hard *thunk* as Izzy's head slammed into the sidewalk, then she went limp beneath him.

Stunned motionless, Rohan blinked several times before rolling into a sitting position. Speaking quickly into her shoulder mic, Maggie pulled a napkin off a nearby table and bent to pick up the weapon at her feet.

Phin released Lena from the barrier of his body, and she rushed to Rohan's side.

"Are you all right?" she asked.

Testing the area near his road rash, he winced. His face burned like hellfire. "I'll live." He gave her body a once-over. "Are you?"

She nodded.

Maggie motioned to the crowd. "Folks, give us some space. The ambulance will be here soon." When everyone continued gawking through their cell phones, the sheriff nodded at the female deputy. "Move them back."

The deputy made shooing motions with her outstretched arms, and the crowd slowly, reluctantly, gave them an extra six feet of breathing room.

Oncoming sirens blared their approach.

Rohan lifted Lena's hand to his lips and kissed her swollen knuckles. "Wildcat, I nearly lost you."

Tears gathered in Lena's eyes. "I'm so sorry."

"For what?"

"My anger. After she bragged about Desmond's scheme, then all but crowed about burning down my home, I—I snapped. I didn't think. I just acted." She swallowed hard. "You could've died because of my outburst."

"If the worst had happened, Izzy, and Izzy alone, would've been to blame." He pushed to his feet and drew her up with him. "Phin, have you heard anything from Zeke?"

"Not since before," he waved toward the gun in Maggie's hand, "all hell broke loose."

Preferring not to use his comms to radio Zeke in front of a gossip-hungry crowd, he asked Phin, "Would you watch over Lena for a minute?"

"Absolutely."

Lena twisted around. "Zeke went after Desmond?"

Even though she'd been in full-on berserker mode, she'd evidently caught some of their transmission.

He kissed her forehead. "Stay with Phin."

Izzy stirred, and Maggie ordered a new-on-the-scene uniformed deputy to guard the injured woman until the paramedics arrived to assess her injuries.

"Come on, Phin," Lena said and headed in the bakery's direction to find Zeke.

Phin barked out a laugh, and Rohan clenched his teeth as he stormed past her to take the lead.

The crowd thinned, then thickened again, just outside Mad Batter. Everyone seemed to be jockeying for a clear view of something on the sidewalk.

Zeke?

Rohan's heartbeat faltered. Had he missed the echo of a gunshot? He searched his mind. No, he would've registered the report.

He picked up his pace, pushing through bodies until he breeched the circle.

Desmond sat on the ground with his elbows braced against his knees and his hands cradling his head. "You cracked my damned skull," he whimpered to the tall blonde, bending to pick up the bakery's often prophetic sidewalk sign.

"You deserved a lot worse for burning down my friend's home." Dressed in a sleek pale apricot jumpsuit and six-inch heels, Kayla Krowne assessed the sign for damage and attempted to stand it upright again.

Today's chalky prophecy read, *You can run from a caramel vanilla shake, but you can't hide.*

"If I were you, shithead," Zeke said, "I'd be thanking

Miss Krowne for using the sign to stop your flight and not one of her stilettos."

Lena rushed into Kayla's arms, and the two women hugged each other for a long while. When they pulled back, Lena said, "Thank you."

"No need," Kayla said. "I took a great deal more satisfaction from cracking his head than I should."

Lena smiled. "Not just for stopping Desmond, but for helping me get Izzy's confession."

Kayla tamed a few wild wisps of Lena's hair. "Any time." She grinned. "Truly, *anytime.*"

"Confession to what?" Desmond whispered.

Rohan hauled the hacker to his feet. "Everything. Now it's time to make arrangements for your one-star, all expenses paid accommodation at Craggy Prison."

69

Inside the sheriff's waiting room, Lena paced in front of the window overlooking Buckner Street, watching Steele Ridge's residents going about their day as if a crazed woman hadn't pulled a gun on Main Street less than an hour ago.

As if Lena's home hadn't burned down.

Everything she owned, gone. Everything except what she kept in her shoulder bag and what she'd brought with her to the cabin.

While she'd watched firefighters waging war against the flames, Rohan had held her in his arms, alternating between kissing her temple, rubbing her back, and assuring her she could use the cabin for as long as she needed.

She'd hugged him to her, taking all he offered. Thankful she wouldn't have to start over alone, this time.

At least this go-round, she had the means to purchase new clothes and art supplies and rent another studio. Thanks to a climate-controlled storage unit she'd rented after landing in Steele Ridge, she had a ready stash of copies to sell as well.

Losing the apartment building hurt. Big time. The loft had begun to feel like a true home. A stable one.

But she'd rise from the ashes once again. Just like the fabled phoenix. It was what she did.

Dark clouds gathered on the horizon, matching her mood.

To her astonishment, no one from the local media had yet shown up. Either another story had taken precedent or the senator's people had so far contained the incident.

After taking everyone's statements, Maggie had ushered the others out the door. But one look at Lena and Rohan's resolute expressions had conveyed to the sheriff that no amount of coaxing would remove them from the station.

Not until they knew for sure that Desmond and Izzy were staying behind bars tonight.

Behind her, Rohan sat in one of the uncomfortable blue floral chairs, tapping away on his laptop. He hadn't looked up from the blue screen since wrapping her hands around a warm paper cup of tea soon after their arrival.

Now on her second tea and racking up steps by the minute, she waited for some small morsel of information. Although Maggie had a pretty open-and-shut case on Izzy, Desmond was a different story. Within minutes of arriving at the station, the hacker had demanded to file a report against Kayla for assault.

The wealthy lobbyist had smiled at Desmond's tactic, then strode into the bullpen, sat down next to the handsomest man in uniform, and began telling her side of the story.

Desmond and Izzy now sat in separate interrogation rooms, and the radio silence was killing Lena.

The only proof they had against Desmond was Izzy's

word. Which, given the spectacle outside Triple B, wasn't the soundest bit of evidence to present in front of a jury.

Boots scuffed against the tiled floor behind her, and Lena turned to find Maggie entering the waiting room.

"They've both lawyered up," Maggie said.

Rohan set his laptop aside and rose to join them. "Did you get anything?"

"Other than to ask for a lawyer, Izzy hasn't said a word since gaining consciousness and Desmond went silent after filing his report against Kayla. Now the bastard wears a perpetual smirk, as if we're all too stupid to catch him."

"Let me speak to him," Rohan said.

"Absolutely not," Maggie said. "We got a search warrant from Judge Naydah, and my deputies are at Locke's place now. I'm sure they'll find something incriminating."

"I don't have the same degree of confidence," Rohan said.

When Maggie's expression soured, Lena offered, "Rohan's not referring to the competency of your employees. Desmond's a professional hacker. He lives in the shadows. It's doubtful he would have left anything for your deputies to find."

Rohan nodded. "And you can be sure he locked down all his electronic devices. It would take days, if not weeks, for your techs to break through."

"Then we're dead in the water," Maggie said.

"Give me fifteen minutes with him."

"To do what?"

"It's best if you don't know."

"You're definitely not going near him now."

He removed his glasses and pinched his nose. "Look, Maggie. I understand you don't have any reason to trust a Blackwell, but I'm asking that you do so now. Just turn your back for a quarter hour, and I'll have enough evidence against him to prosecute."

The sheriff considered him for a long moment, and Lena held her breath. Whatever Rohan had up his sleeve, she hoped it was enough to get Desmond talking.

Maggie shook her head, and Lena's heart splashed into her stomach.

"I'm not letting you into my interrogation room," she glanced around her and lowered her voice, "but Desmond is due for a restroom break."

Rohan's face lit up as understanding dawned. "Thank you, Sheriff."

"Ten minutes. That's all I can give you."

"I'll make it work."

"You'd better. His attorney will be here any second. As things sit right now, I'll have to release him."

Rohan bent to give Lena a quick, hard kiss, then scooped up his laptop and strode away.

"You okay here by yourself?" Maggie asked.

Lena mustered a smile. "I'll be fine."

"If you're not allergic to peanuts, we have peanut butter cookies in the break room. Best you'll ever eat, compliments of my assistant, Shari, who's also covering the front desk today."

Her stomach growled, and she realized it had been hours since her last meal. "Thanks, a cookie sounds amazing."

"I'll let Shari know and she can buzz you through." Maggie made to turn away, but Lena stopped her with a touch to her arm.

"Need something?"

"I wanted to say thank you. Without your help and open

mind, I wouldn't have had the courage to go through with the setup."

"Any time I can remove another bad actor from my town, I'm happy to lend a hand. So don't be shy if trouble comes around again."

Lena grinned. "If there's ever anything I can do for you, please let me know."

"I checked out your website, you know. Beautiful work."

Warmth spread through Lena's chest. "Name it, and I'll paint a copy for you."

"Maybe you could stop by my place sometime and make a suggestion on what might look good on our walls."

"I'd be happy to."

"Time for me to give Desmond his break."

Lena watched the sheriff stride in the same direction Rohan had gone minutes before. Despite the gravity of their current circumstance, Lena felt a paradoxical lightness in her heart as she returned to her vigil by the window.

The media still hadn't yet caught wind of the region's biggest scandal in a decade, which was fine with her. She didn't need or want that kind of exposure.

The clouds opened up, dropping some much-needed rain over the area. Coiffed ladies raised bags over their heads as they scurried for cover and shopkeepers dragged in tables laden with their goods.

A gorgeous blue Bentley with blacked out rear windows pulled into one of the diagonal parking spaces in front of the sheriff's office.

As she watched, a fit woman, wearing a black suit and white dress shirt, emerged from the front passenger side and snapped open an umbrella before turning to the back door, while a male driver, in a matching uniform, did the same on his side.

Something sparked in the back of Lena's mind. A memory she couldn't quite latch onto. A warning she recognized but couldn't identify.

In a choreographed move, Blaise and Gerard Palmer appeared on opposite sides of the Bentley, buttoning their suit coats as they approached the station beneath raised umbrellas. Tall, handsome, and self-assured. They wore their status like a golden mantle for all to see.

The curly-haired woman moved ahead to open the door. Lena narrowed her gaze on the umbrella. On the unique white-and-black handle peeking out beneath the woman's hand.

An exact replica of her favorite umbrella. The one she'd given to the woman waiting at the light with her several days ago.

Lena's attention sharpened on the driver. Scars pocked his face, especially the lower half, as if he'd endured a nasty bout of chicken pox as a child—or severe acne. It was difficult to tell which through the rain-splattered window.

Scars. Curly hair. Driver. Passenger.

Long ago images began to crystalize and take shape.

Neil putting little Anjali in a backseat, a curly-haired woman warning Neil the boss wouldn't be happy, the scarred driver grousing about someone tipping off the fleeing, now dead, couple.

Scarface and Curls might be two decades older, but Lena knew with absolute certainty they had been the ones with her and Neil in the vehicle that night. The ones who'd been contracted to kill her parents.

Her gaze shot to Blaise and Gerard Palmer.

But by whom?

70

As soon as Rohan heard Desmond at the urinal, he exited the stall and set his computer down on the sink counter.

While he let the faucet run, he stared at the man's back through the mirror. All the fear and anger and shame he'd been experiencing since leaving the Collective rushed through his veins and coated his vision with red.

He considered his laptop for a moment. A solid hit to the temple with the aluminum alloy, and a for-good-measure jab to the trachea, would end Desmond's reign of terror over his life once and for all.

The compulsion made his hands shake and his blood roar.

He drew in a lung full of air and slowly released it between his lips, then turned off the water.

It wasn't Desmond's time to die. Not yet. Not before Rohan got some answers.

When the hacker turned from the urinal, his eyes widened in surprise, then lowered as they traveled over Rohan's body. "Bathrooms aren't my personal preference,"

Desmond said, moving closer. "For you, I'm willing to adapt."

The provocative words sat in direct contrast to the simmering rage in the hacker's eyes.

"I've witnessed your adaptation skills. Does Palmer know you're fucking his fiancée?"

Desmond chuckled. "Palmer enjoys my unique skillset too much to protest my side interests, especially since Bella helped me perfect certain," his smiled widened, "techniques."

"You really are a piece of work, aren't you?"

"Poor straitlaced Rohan. You never could tolerate anything but white. No black, no gray. You couldn't even bring yourself to use the term black hat. What did you call yourself? Ah, yes, *ethical* hacker. Tell me, did the more palatable title make you sleep better at night?"

Rohan's jaw hurt from the effort of keeping his anger in check. Desmond clearly enjoyed tormenting him. All Rohan had to do was keep nudging the bastard in the right direction.

"My hacks righted massive wrongs."

Desmond inched closer. "*Ethical* hackers wait for an invitation from an entity before they search for system vulnerabilities. You, my delicious contradiction, not only didn't have an invitation, you crashed the party by conducting search-and-destroy missions on your targets."

Hot bile scoured Rohan's throat at the truth in the other man's words. He *had* sought to destroy the man who'd ruined the Neff family, then set out to shut down several other black hats who'd wrought equally horrific devastation on others with their cyber skills. Until one day he saw his digital vigilantism for what it was—an inadequate salve for failing to protect the Neffs' intellectual property.

He harbored no guilt for his past actions. The hackers got what they deserved. But he no longer had the stomach for the work. He'd leave national cybersecurity to the FBI.

"My past sins are old news," Rohan said, conscious of time slipping away. Maggie probably ordered her deputy to fling open the restroom door at the ten-minute mark. "What I'm curious about is who came up with the plan to steal the Neff's secret recipe—you or Cal?"

Desmond's smug expression disappeared. "I don't know who you're talking about."

Not taking his eyes off the other man, Rohan flipped open his laptop. Desmond's gaze flicked to the screen, took in the high-school picture of his sixteen-year-old self.

"Desmond Simmons. Younger brother to Cal Simmons. The man Troy Neff had fired and who later plastered their proprietary IP on the Internet, bankrupting the family." Rohan lowered his voice. "The hacker I tracked down and whose life I took apart, piece by piece."

"You fucking savage," Desmond hissed, taking a threatening step toward him. His seductive persona gone. "Do you have any idea what you did to my brother?"

Rohan stood from his relaxed lean against the counter. He had about twenty pounds on the man, all of it muscle. "Of course. I orchestrated every one of his bad days." He rubbed a thumb across his chin. *Time to test his hypothesis about the size of the Collective's membership.* "But what I can't work out is why you created the ruse of a hacktivist group. Why not retaliate as soon as you realized who'd ruined your brother?"

"Because I wanted to corrupt the incorruptible," Desmond snarled. "You thought yourself so noble going after Cal. Like a fucking knight in shining armor. I didn't want to just take away your money, your job, and your home, like you did my brother." A maniacal smile raked across the hacker's face. "I wanted to take your blackened soul."

If Rohan hadn't been so disgusted with himself for being taken in by this vengeful weasel, he would have been impressed by the guy's patience and dedication to his goal.

"Well, you didn't blacken my soul," Rohan said. "Guess what that makes you, Desmond? A big fucking loser."

Desmond lunged for him.

Prepared for the move, Rohan surged forward and rammed his fist into the man's solar plexus. The hacker bent over, struggling to draw breath through his constricted diaphragm. His face scrunched up as pain radiated through his torso. Finally, he crumpled and fell to his hands and knees.

Rohan crouched a safe distance away. "Despite my best efforts, Cal seems to have rebuilt his life—respectable job, loving wife, nice home, child on the way."

Desmond gave him an angry sidelong glance. "Leave him," he wheezed, "alone."

"My level of interest or disinterest in your little brother's current state of happiness depends solely on you."

The hacker eased back to sit on his heels. His right hand pressed against his chest. "What do you want?"

"Two things. First, you're going to give me your damn decryption key so I can unlock our files."

Desmond's lips firmed, then he nodded. "What else?"

"Who killed Killian Byrne?"

Fear crossed the other man's face and he dropped his gaze to the charcoal-tiled floor. "I—"

"Don't lie, Desmond." Rohan's phone buzzed in his front pocket. He ignored it. "My hacking skills have improved a hundredfold since my last skirmish with your brother."

"They'll kill me."

"Sheriff Kingston won't let that happen. She might even work a plea deal with you."

Desmond squeezed his eyes closed, then let out a defeated sigh. When he looked at Rohan again, he said, "I'll tell you everything, but I want a guarantee that you'll stay away from Cal."

Rohan stood. "My word is the only guarantee I have to give."

"I'll take it."

Surprised, Rohan added, "But only if you tell me everything."

Desmond nodded and climbed carefully to his feet. "It all started two decades ago."

71

LENA PACED IN FRONT OF THE LARGE MIRROR ABOVE A ROW OF stainless-steel sink bowls while fanning her flushed cheeks.

After recognizing her parents' murderers, she had panicked and used Maggie's Pass Go card to get buzzed into the inner sanctum of the station. Instead of doing the smart thing and running to Maggie's office, she'd followed her instincts and dashed into the nearest ladies' room.

Thank the mother of all gods that Maggie had preapproved her entry, or she'd be trapped in the waiting room right now with all the ingredients of her worst nightmare.

Lena considered tracking down Rohan. His brilliant mind could help her piece together what was going on in no time.

But she couldn't pull him away from his interrogation of Desmond. He'd already set aside his hunt for the Collective to help with her hastily organized sting operation. She couldn't—wouldn't—disrupt his opportunity to get answers from the hacker.

So she channeled Rohan and drilled through other

reasons why Scarface and Curly would be acting bodyguard to either Blaise or Gerard Palmer.

If she'd seen either of them separately, she wasn't positive the puzzle pieces would've slid together. But after all of these years, those two were still a team. They couldn't have been much older than she was now at the time they'd cold-bloodedly taken her parents' lives.

In front of their five-year-old daughter. That takes a certain kind of evil.

Her phone vibrated, startling her. She fingered it out of her back pocket and checked the ID.

Ash Blackwell.

Before he'd left for Hendersonville, they had exchanged numbers. He'd promised to notify her if he learned anything new from her grandparents.

Had that only been this morning?

She started to accept the call, then hesitated. Whatever he had to say, she desperately wanted to hear it. But her mind was jumbling back and forth between the present and past. Her heart raced and her emotions teetered on the edge of a full-blown panic attack.

Could she take another shock right now?

No, absolutely not.

Hitting Decline, she stuffed her phone back into her pocket. She would call him as soon as she could figure out her next move. Returning to the waiting room was out of the question. Lena knew her game face was for shit right now.

The restroom door flew open, and Lena braced herself for the worst.

Kayla entered and shut the door behind her. "Is everything okay? I saw you run in here."

"Did you see the Palmers and their bodyguards?"

"They're at the front desk, why?"

The pressure on Lena's chest increased to the point of pain. She couldn't reason herself through this. She didn't know why either Palmer would put out a kill order on her parents.

Only a few days ago, she'd been standing right next to Blaise Palmer. Had he known who she was? He'd asked her several questions about her family.

Had he been probing? Or making idle chitchat?

Then she recalled Desmond had posed similar inquiries when he'd been playing the part of Angler Dean.

No, not idle talk. Probing, assessing questions.

For what purpose? To verify her identity? To ascertain how much she remembered from that night?

She stared at the lobbyist, not wanting to get her new friend tangled up in her messy life any more than necessary. The outrageous woman had already more than paid back her favor. Lena had to keep her clear of whatever bomb was about to drop.

Producing a chuckle, she rubbed her forehead. "No reason. I'm . . . not myself right now. Izzy, my grandparents, the fire, Desmond—it's all a bit much."

"Agreed. You've been through more than anyone should have to face in a lifetime, let alone in twenty-four hours." Kayla crossed her arms and leaned her back against the door. "But I'm not leaving here until you tell me what has drained all the blood from your face."

"Kayla, I can't ask you to get any deeper into the muck of my life. It's too dangerous."

"You're not asking, and I'm not budging."

Lena's throat tightened. First, the Steele and Kingston ladies had offered their assistance, then Rohan and the Blackwells, and now Kayla Krowne. For someone who had, for many years, depended on her own wits to survive, she now had an abundance of people to lean on.

Grateful tears burned her eyes. She mentally iced them down while she gathered her thoughts. Later—she hoped—there would be time for gratitude and hugs and copious tears.

Now, she had one last puzzle piece to pop into place.

"The bodyguards who accompanied Blaise and his father to the station murdered my parents twenty years ago."

72

BACK IN UNIFORM, DEPUTY SULLIVAN SHOULDERED OPEN THE restroom door and gave Rohan a knowing look.

To Desmond, she said, "Hold out your wrists and put them together."

Once the hacker complied, she handcuffed him and led him back to the interrogation room.

"Did you get everything?" Rohan asked into his comms.

"Loud and clear," Cruz said. *"Man, I always knew you were a badass, but you're a fucking scary badass."*

"Only to those who are a threat to the ones I love."

"Another Blackwell taken down by the Friary's love spell. Oh, goody."

Rohan headed toward the waiting room. "You're next."

A short silence, then his brother quipped, *"No reason for me to bring a lady here, so I'm in the clear."*

Rohan recalled his brother's comment about having a dark-haired beauty in his sights and grinned. *Enjoy La-La-land while it lasts, bro.*

"I sent the recording to Maggie," Cruz said. "Minus the Rohan self-incriminating parts."

"Much appreciated. I'm on my way to find Lena."

"Want me to stick around?"

"No need. Thanks for your help today. I couldn't have done it without you."

"Yes, you could've, but you're welcome."

Rohan made his way toward the front of the station, passing Maggie's office. She clutched a corded handset between her shoulder and ear and palmed her cell phone, too. A white Bluetooth earbud hooked inside her other ear, as if she were listening to two conversations at once.

She looked up and motioned for him to come inside. Holding up a finger, he continued onward.

As he neared the front, the decibel level of a dozen voices talking above each other grew. Phones rang. Feet shuffled. Chairs squeaked.

The busy bullpen made Rohan think of the Annex's Theater, but on a much grander scale.

A movement to his right caught his eye. Kayla emerged from the ladies' restroom, a fierce expression molding her pretty features. In contrast, Lena's brown skin had a sallow cast to it, as if she'd tried livermush for the first time and the local delicacy had come up wanting.

He moved to intercept them, then noticed they were headed his way, so he paused. Raised voices from the direction of the reception area reached him, though he couldn't make out their words, nor could he see them through the wall of frosted glass and stone, separating the public area from the rest of the station.

"Rohan," Lena snaked her arms around his waist and buried her face in his chest. Her body trembled as she whispered, "They're here."

Holding her close, he hooked a finger beneath her chin and added pressure until her gaze met his. "Who's here?"

"Scarface and Curly. The people who killed my parents."

His head whipped up. "Where?"

Lena broke eye contact to glance around the station. When she said nothing, he sent Kayla a questioning look.

"They're bodyguards to either Blaise or Gerard Palmer. We're on our way to speak to Maggie." The lobbyist did her own scan of the room. "It would be best to get her somewhere less conspicuous."

Lena lifted her head to peer up at him. "How did your conversation go with Desmond?"

"Informative." He turned Lena toward Maggie's office, shielding her with his body as best he could. "Sounds like we all need to have a sit-down with the sheriff."

FEELING THE STRONG COMFORT OF ROHAN'S BODY AGAINST hers helped calm the tremors attacking Lena's muscles. She had experienced the sensation twice before in her life and hoped never to do so again.

"The sheriff will be with you any minute, Mr. Palmer," Shari said in an authoritative voice that rose over the cacophony of the busy station. Heads turned toward the partition, separating staff from the public, and the bullpen quieted. "Please return to the waiting room."

"Do you know who I am?" Gerard Palmer asked.

"Yes, sir."

"Then you know I don't wait. My son's fiancée is here on some absurd charges, and I demand to speak with Sheriff Kingston."

Rohan's body turned to granite beneath her touch, and Lena's last nerve frayed.

"The sheriff will be with you any minute," Shari repeated.

Gerard lowered his voice. Too low for Lena to hear his words.

"As a matter of fact, I do love my job," Shari said to his obvious threat.

"Stay here," Rohan ordered as he made to intervene.

"Wait." Lena pointed. "They've got it."

Two armed, broad-shouldered men, with badges clipped at their waists, pushed out of their chairs and headed toward the reception area.

Grasping her hand, Rohan said, "Come on." He guided them to Maggie's office and rapped a knuckle against her door.

Maggie sat upright at her desk, a cell phone at her ear and a frown etched in her brow. She murmured something to the person at the other end of the line, removed the bluetooth device from her ear, and tapped the screen before setting her phone down.

"Come in and shut the door, please," Maggie said, rising from her chair. "I'd ask y'all to have a seat, but shit's piling up on my doorstep faster than I can shovel it away. I have a fairly good idea of where all of this is headed, but I need y'all to fill in the blanks. I'll keep my part brief and succinct. You do the same."

Everyone nodded.

Rohan set his laptop on one of the guest chairs.

"Cruz sent me the recording of your conversation with Desmond Locke—or rather Desmond Simmons. Evidently, Palmer's chief of cybersecurity has been wearing many hats, not just black ones."

Lena glanced up at Rohan, at his set jaw, then returned her attention to the sheriff.

"By hacking into your car, Desmond overheard a conversation between you and Cruz, where you discussed needing a copyist to carry out a recovery."

Jaw set, Rohan nodded. "He and Izzy were already lovers and confidantes by then."

And they each had people they wanted to ruin.

"They spent the next two weeks devising an elaborate plan to ruin Lena and me."

Lena frowned. "Wouldn't part of their plan have depended on BARS hiring me?"

"They set up bogus commissions with your competition, ensuring they were booked for the next few months. Then they sabotaged the commission you had lined up after the Catawnee."

Lena recalled the unexpected opening in her schedule because of her client getting a divorce. "What did they do?"

"The wife received pictures of her husband with his mistress and a young boy."

"Good Lord."

Maggie's attention shifted to Rohan. "For reasons I'm not quite clear on, due to *issues* with the audio, Desmond seemed bent on—" She paused. "How'd he put it? 'Corrupting your soul,' yes?"

"His brother and I had a difference of opinion on what to do with a recipe," Rohan said. "I served up a better dish, and they both took it personally."

"I don't have time for Blackwell games, Rohan. Is there something here I need to know?"

Rohan shook his head. "Old news that a small mind has been stewing about for far too long. You won't get any blowback on this. For what it's worth, you have my word."

Piecing together some of what he'd shared with her at the motel, Lena read between the lines. The hacker who'd stolen the Neff family's secret recipe must have been

Desmond's brother. Although Rohan hadn't provided specific details, he'd made it clear that the thief had paid for his crimes.

Later, Lena would ply him with a bourbon or two and get the full story.

"Did Desmond say anything about Palmer?" Kayla asked, squeezing Lena's free hand.

The sheriff's green eyes zeroed in on the lobbyist. "As a matter of fact, he did, and that's where things get murky. Desmond set up surveillance equipment in Senator Palmer's office. About the same time he and Izzy were devising their plan, he overheard a conversation between Blaise and Gerard that piqued his interest." Maggie looked at Lena again. "About you."

Lena swallowed back her fear and nodded. "Earlier, after you left me in the waiting room, I saw the Palmers arrive."

Sensing her inner turmoil, Rohan shifted closer and the heat from his body helped penetrate the chill creeping beneath her skin.

"A man and woman accompanied them. Bodyguards, I think. They were there, in the car with Neil and I, the night my parents were murdered."

"You think these bodyguards killed them?" Maggie asked.

Lena nodded and told them everything she remembered, including her suspicion that the bodyguards had approached her on the street several days ago on her way home from the art supplies store.

"Time has altered their appearance some, but I'm certain it was them."

"You said they stood on opposite sides of you, so when you spoke to one your back was to the other?" Rohan asked.

"That's right. Why?"

"Now we know how they planted the GPS device in your purse."

Maggie's gaze shot to Lena's shoulder bag.

"Long gone," Rohan said.

Kayla asked, "Why now? Why all this interest in Lena two decades after the fact?"

Lena winced. "I might have accidentally hit the hornet's nest."

"What do you mean?" Maggie asked.

Needing to move, she pulled away from Rohan and Kayla and strode to the window. The entire town center spread out below. Anyone standing here earlier would have been able to watch the incident with Izzy play out.

"I can't explain why now. Maybe it had been the bad session that day or the three glasses of wine that followed." She closed her eyes. "Or realizing it was his birthday." She drew in a breath and squared her shoulders. "Whatever the reason, I got a maggot in my head to see what the Internet could tell me about Neil Jones." She turned back to them, arms folded around her middle. "For ten years, I had avoided any connections to my life with Neil. He told me to run, and I did. And I never looked back. Not once, until a few weeks ago."

Rohan strode up to her and cupped her face. "He was the only father you knew."

Lena thought of the photo she'd carried around for a decade and her throat hurt with the effort to hold back the tears. "I think he must have lost his family. His wife, his daughter. That's why he wouldn't let them kill me along with my parents. I reminded him of his little girl."

Warm lips pressed against her heated forehead, then her nose, then her mouth. A reassurance. A promise.

He didn't have to say the words. She heard them through his touch.

I love you. You'll never have to run again.

She believed him. Wanted to believe him. But if a powerful man like Senator Palmer was behind all of this, how could she stay?

73

ROHAN COULDN'T THINK OF A DAMN THING TO DO EXCEPT PULL Lena in his arms and hold her close. The pain marring her beautiful face was almost his undoing.

She'd known so much loss, so much heartache. Yet she'd survived somehow. Thrived even.

But now, it was all crumbling beneath her again. With the light of a single match, Desmond and Izzy had stolen her home, her livelihood, her safety. They had stripped her down to her most vulnerable element and laughed about it.

Fury erupted inside in him unlike anything he'd ever experienced before. If the law didn't punish them both for their crimes, he would.

With great pleasure.

A knock shattered the black cloud hovering inside the room.

Maggie nodded at her assistant through the glass door. Shari opened it enough for her upper body to squeeze inside. "Apologies, Sheriff, but Gerard Palmer's attorney has arrived, and he's demanding to see his client."

"Client as in singular?"

Shari nodded.

"Which one?"

"Isabella DeCarlo."

"Give me five more minutes, then bring them back."

"The senator's daddy won't be happy about the delay."

"*Daddy* can go sit on a popsicle for all I care. Five minutes. Not a second earlier."

"Yes, ma'am."

When the door closed again, Maggie pinched the bridge of her nose. "I'm going to owe her the biggest coconut cream pie Jeanine's ovens can hold." She dropped her hand. "Cameron, you're up."

Cameron?

"Ash?" Rohan said, drawing Lena back toward the desk.

"Glad somebody answered their damn phone," Ash groused through the cell phone lying on Maggie's desk.

She hadn't disconnected from the call when they'd entered. She'd switched it to speaker. His brother had been listening the whole time.

"I spoke with Mr. and Mrs. Kumar," Ash said. "Lena, they're good people. They hope to meet you soon."

Lena pressed her fist against her mouth, then said, "Thank you, Ash."

His brother went on to explain that Lena's dad had been an artist, a painter, like her, and her mom had worked for the *Asheville Times* as an investigative reporter.

"Mrs. Kumar told us that her daughter-in-law Morgan had been working on a big story, involving a politician misusing his campaign funds. Evidently, someone on the senator's staff had sought her out and was feeding her information, until . . ."

"That night," Lena finished.

"Did anyone from the *Times* corroborate Mrs. Kumar's recollection?" Maggie asked.

"Not yet, but we have calls in to some old-timers we've worked with in the past." Paper shuffled. "But we don't really need them."

"Why not?" Kayla asked.

"Because, Miss Krowne," Ash said with a new edge to his voice, "we have something better."

"Like what, Mr. Blackwell?"

"Morgan's research and the article she never had a chance to publish."

Lena sucked in a sharp breath.

Rohan asked. "The Kumars had it?"

"No, Morgan's sister Renee."

"Sister?" Lena said, awed by the thought of having another living relative.

"I'll get into how we found her later," Ash said. "Renee told us the day before Morgan was killed, she stopped by and asked if she could hide some birthday gifts for Jahan in her basement. A few months after the funerals, Renee opened the boxes, thinking she should donate the gifts, but found folders and clippings and handwritten notes, none of which made any sense to her. She closed the boxes, and they've been collecting dust in her basement ever since."

"You mentioned an article," Lena said. "Wouldn't it have explained to my aunt what was in the boxes?"

"She never saw the thumb drive. It was at the bottom of a box, in the corner. I suspect it slid down there during transit."

"I take it Blaise Palmer was the subject of Morgan's investigative report?"

"You'd be right."

"So, what?" Kayla said. "The new senator found out Morgan was about to publish the report and had her killed? That seems like a pretty extreme reaction to a misuse of campaign funds accusation. Especially since most politicians would simply blame it on staff error or call it a misunderstanding of the rules or outright deny any wrongdoing and continue serving without repercussion."

"That's how things work today," Maggie said, "but not twenty years ago. Financial fraud was a pretty big deal back then."

"I agree with Kayla," Rohan said. "Why not produce a smear campaign against Morgan Kumar or harass her in some other way? Putting out a kill order on an entire family reeks of something bigger."

"Morgan noted she had observed the senator with a particular young man, one of his staffers, on several occasions. From their body language and furtive touches, she had deduced they were lovers. Late one night, she witnessed an argument between the two. Palmer seemed to be the one doing the mollifying. The disagreement soon fizzled and the two engaged in a passionate kiss."

"Newsworthy, I suppose," Rohan said, "from the perspective that the senator had kept—is still keeping—his sexual orientation private."

"Which is his right," Lena said.

"Agreed, but that's not how it works when you choose a career in politics or Hollywood. Every facet of your life is picked apart for public consumption and judgment."

"The truly newsworthy part," Ash said, "was the black Mercedes that pulled up next to the kissing couple and, after a heated exchange with the occupant in the vehicle,

Blaise climbed inside, leaving his lover behind. A few days later, a tourist found the staffer at the bottom of an overlook along the Blue Ridge Parkway. His death was deemed an accident."

"Just like my parents' car crash," Lena whispered.

74

LENA HAD KNOWN FOR DAYS, MAYBE EVEN YEARS ON A subconscious level, that her parents' deaths weren't an accident. Now, hearing about another innocent young man getting caught up in the same political intrigue caused an ache in her heart.

Maggie looked at her phone. "Time's almost up. Shari will be here with the Palmers any moment. Anything else, Cam?"

"Just one more thing. We got a hit on the photo of Neil Jones that Rohan sent to me."

Lena held her breath, and she gripped Rohan's hand harder as she waited to find out the true identity of the man who had kidnapped her and raised her as his own.

"His real name is Neil Pelakova. He got into some trouble as a teenager. Nothing major—petty theft, fights. He met Kennedy Williams in college. Fell in love, got pregnant. I'm guessing no insurance and the bills started rolling in. Picked up a second job as a security guard. Was good at it and, within a year, became part of Gerard Palmer's personal security."

"Gerard Palmer?" Lena whispered.

Which meant Curls and Scarface worked for him, too.

"Gerard killed Lena's parents to protect his investment," Rohan said.

"His son's political career," Lena said.

A short silence followed while everyone digested this new revelation.

Maggie cursed, then yelled, "Sullivan!"

The deputy all but slid inside the office. "Yes, Sheriff?"

"Two bodyguards accompanied the Palmers. Throw them into a holding cell."

"What reason should I give them?"

"They're wanted for the murders of Jahan and Morgan Kumar."

"Anything else?"

"Free up the interrogation rooms and make sure none of the prisoners talk to each other."

When the deputy left, Maggie rotated her shoulders as if to release the tension gathered there. "Thanks, Cameron. I'll be in touch." She tapped her screen and looked at each of them in turn. "It's best if you leave this next act to me. I'll fill y'all in once the dust settles."

"I'm staying," Lena said.

"That's not a good idea—"

"I'm staying. I've been running my whole life because of these people. Never again."

"Let us observe the interviews from behind the one-way mirror," Rohan said. "They'll never know we're there."

A muscle twitched in Maggie's jaw. "Don't make me regret this. One wrong move, and Palmer's attorney will exploit it until the case blows up. Understand?"

They nodded.

"Okay, get out of here."

Kayla reached for Lena. "This is where we part ways, my friend." She glanced at Rohan. "You're in excellent hands."

Lena hugged her hard. "Thank you."

"Okay, okay," Maggie grumbled. "Get out of here, all of you."

Rohan picked up his laptop and stretched his hand out toward Maggie. When she clasped it, he said, "I won't ever forget what you did for us today. If you need anything, ever, call me."

Maggie smiled and jerked her chin toward the door. Her warrior's mind already preparing for the next battle.

Lena turned toward the bullpen, and Rohan halted. "The interrogation rooms are this way." He pointed in the opposite direction.

"I know, but I want to see."

He seemed to understand and gave no more resistance when she led him to the far side of the bullpen. She held his hand as Shari guided Gerard, Blaise, and a pencil-thin attorney into Maggie's office.

Rohan whispered near her ear, "I'm sorry about the Frida."

She glanced up at him, unable to suppress the twinkle in her eye.

"What is that look for?"

"*Self-Portrait with Braided Hair* is safely tucked away in Kayla's trunk."

"Her *trunk*?"

Lena returned her attention to the sheriff's office. Witnessed the Palmers' outrage turn to confusion, then to stony silence.

"When Kayla took me home to change, I asked her to add it to her collection until I could figure out what to do with it. We didn't have enough time to stop by her house. So the portrait is in her trunk."

"Small mercies. Although not ideal to have a multimil-lion-dollar painting in a trunk," he said, humor lacing his words, "but better than in a burned-out building."

She gave him a sideways glance. "Has anyone ever hired BARS to replace a forged museum piece with the original?"

His eyes flared as understanding dawned, then he looked at her in the same way he had stared at the Caravaggio days ago. With wonder.

"I think we could fit Frida into our schedule, with the team's agreement."

She smiled and turned back to the live drama playing out. "Of course."

Uniformed deputies cuffed the senator and his dad before marching them away. The elder's normally ramrod straight spine was now curled at the shoulders. His son's face was pale and glistening with sweat.

"According to Desmond," Rohan said, "Palmer's body-guards killed Xander when he walked in on them at the studio."

"They were there for me?"

"Your presence at the studio confused them, so they were in the process of setting up surveillance equipment when Xander surprised them."

"They covered it up by making it look like a suicide."

A warm hand rested on her lower back. "Was I wrong to tell you?"

She shook her head. "I prefer to know the truth, even if it hurts."

He moved to stand behind her, bringing her back to rest against his chest, his arms crossing at her middle. "You're not doing something illogical like laying the blame for his death at your door, are you?"

Four uniformed deputies led Scarface and Curls past them, toward the interrogation rooms. Unlike the Palmers, who let others worry about the dangers around them, the bodyguards scanned and assessed their surroundings.

Lena layered her hands over his. "I know who's to blame."

Scarface felt her malevolence first, then Curls. Their gazes met, held. Lena waited for understanding to dawn, to bloom into fear.

Then she smiled.

For maa *and* pita.

And me.

75

Rohan drove to Lena's cabin, feeling a rush of excitement about seeing her again and about the evening ahead.

The past week had been a whirlwind of activity, and he was looking forward to spending the next several hours doing nothing but ensuring Lena's happiness.

As he'd expected, Izzy, Desmond, Curls, and Scarface had all struck deals with the state's attorney, agreeing to testify against Gerard and Blaise Palmer for shorter prison sentences.

Faced with extraordinary pressure from his party, Blaise had resigned from his senate seat, and Kayla was now working her lobbyist magic toward persuading the governor to appoint a well-respected female county commissioner to the position.

With Desmond's decryption key, BARS's network was up and running again. It had taken a few days to get everything back online and performing correctly. But thankfully, they hadn't lost any information from the attack and subsequent recovery.

Even though they had avoided financial disaster, Lena had insisted on still investing in the company. She wanted a way to make amends for all the fraudulent works of art she'd had a hand in distributing throughout the world.

But the family had encouraged her to put her money toward expanding her business. Set up an educational arm to teach teenagers about art and offer lessons in drawing and painting.

Excited by the idea, Lena immediately started the hunt for another abandoned building. One big enough to include five bedrooms—one for her and the other four to provide sanctuary for the older kids Rohan had found in Xander's penthouse.

Rohan planned on making sure she didn't need to occupy the fifth bedroom.

The younger three kids were making their way through the adoption process with good families. Lena had met with the teenagers, told them about her life with Simon, and asked if they would like for her to become their legal guardian.

They had eagerly agreed.

Her decision hadn't surprised him. Lena's heart was as big as her talent. What had surprised him was her discussing the guardianship with him first. Her concern about his opinion filled Rohan with hope about their future.

And just last night, Maggie had stopped by on her way to Jay's football game to tell Lena that a judge had rescinded the court order for her arrest. Copious hugs and tears had ensued.

"Uncle Rohan!" Sadie's muffled yell penetrated his car window as he rolled to a stop outside Lena's cabin.

He glanced over to see her tearing across the meadow, wearing the white smock Lena had gifted her and a huge smile. Once pristine, the protective layer was now splattered with every hue of the rainbow.

"What's up?" he asked, exiting his vehicle.

"Operation Paint It," she panted, pointing a paintbrush in the direction she'd just come from. "Success!"

"Lena's painting on the blank canvas?"

"Yes, yes! Go see, go see!"

"Will you do me a favor?"

She nodded and bounced up on the balls of her feet.

"There are two packages on the passenger seat. Will you take them inside and put them on Lena's bed?"

"Are they for tonight?"

He waggled his eyebrows, making her giggle. "You'd better run home afterward, so you won't be late."

"My art station—"

"I'll make sure it gets back to the cabin safely."

Before she could run around the car, he plucked the wet paintbrush from her hand. She laughed and wiped her hands on a towel hooked over the tie wound around her narrow waist.

Rohan had considered trading in the Verge for a pre-technology classic vehicle. But he loved that damn car. Instead, he'd contacted the manufacturer and alerted them to the vulnerabilities of their system. He might have even given them a few suggestions on how to fix the issues.

He found Lena standing before the infamous blank canvas in the shade of a giant tulip tree. She wore a larger version of Sadie's paint-covered smock over leggings and long-sleeved tee. All that glorious hair secured at the back of her head by a large clip.

"Hello, gorgeous."

At the sound of his voice, she turned and grinned.

Rohan's step faltered at the sight of her. She had paint . . .

everywhere. Her hair, her face, her neck, her hands. In all the times he'd watched her paint, he'd only ever seen her get paint on her fingers.

She looked adorable.

And happy.

"I did it," she said, moving to the side so he could see.

It was a landscape, but unlike anything he'd ever seen. She'd hand-sketched the scene and was now applying strategic splashes of color.

Puffy clouds raced across an azure sky. A tall, ominous cloud shimmering with lightning gathered behind them. Something about the little clouds beckoned him forward. Yet as he drew closer, the illusion changed, solidified into an unremarkable splash of white.

He backed away a few feet and one of the clouds transformed into a child's face. Others did, too, and their tears rained down on a mountain meadow teeming with wildflowers of every shape, size, and color.

Some of the flowers leaned into the rain and some hunched together petiole-in-petiole. Others sagged to the ground against the weight of the child-cloud's anguish.

One courageous sunflower, whose brown center took on the characteristics of an older version of Lena, ran toward a small cloud that was being swept into the forbidding thundercloud.

A tangle of emotions caught in the center of his chest as he stared at the dual scenes.

Lena moved to hover at his elbow.

He traced a finger a few centimeters above the pencil sketch of the orphaned teen clouds and their families before moving on to the painted sunflower who was leaving a trail of wilting petals in her wake.

"Your mom?"

He heard the audible click of her swallow. "Yes," she whispered.

He pointed at the fat-cheeked cloud being sucked into the storm.

"You?"

She nodded.

"It's beautiful, Lena."

"I have so much more to do—"

"It's beautiful," he repeated, wanting her to believe it. "Emotional." He placed a hand on his chest. "I can feel their sadness, their fear."

"Their hope?" A paint-covered finger pointed at the sun's first rays pushing through the roiling clouds.

"Their hope," he agreed. "I would kiss you, but I can't seem to find a paint-free spot."

"A little paint never hurt anyone."

"True, but I see a clean spot right here." He kissed the area behind her ear and loved how she angled her head away to give him better access.

He accepted her invitation and trailed a path down her neck, along her jawline until he reached her lips. He let her know how much he missed her, even though it had barely been ten hours since she'd slipped out of his bed and returned to the cabin.

Though all of her possessions remained here, she spent her nights with him at the Friary. Tomorrow, he would ask her to move in with him permanently and use the cabin only as her studio. He didn't think she needed more time, but he'd give her as much as necessary.

Pulling back, he said, "As much as I would enjoy a tryst in this meadow, you might need the time to, um, wash away today's exertions."

"Ohmygod, what time is it?" She pulled her phone out of

a pocket in her leggings and checked. "Crap!" She started flinging her extra brushes into a carrying case he'd found for her.

He grasped her shoulders and turned her toward the cabin. "Go take care of you. I'll handle this."

"Are you sure?"

"What else am I going to do for the next hour?"

She made a face, then lifted up on her toes and kissed him. "Thank you."

"My pleasure. Open the two packages on your bed first."

Her eyes widened. "Presents?"

"Yes, now go or we'll be late for dinner."

As she ran toward the cabin, she yelled, "I knew there was a reason I loved you, Rohan Blackwell."

Rohan smiled.

I love you too, Anjali Kumar.

LENA'S FINGERTIPS TOUCHED THE PENDANT, HANGING FROM A delicate gold chain around her neck.

The last time she'd seen the gold pendant was when she'd placed it in Ash's hand, asking him to give it to her grandparents as proof of life.

The heirloom had come back to her in a box. Inside, she found a note.

The symbol on the back represents the Kumar family's motto. Devotion. I gifted it to you on the night of your fifth birthday. Welcome home, Anjali.

Love, Dadi

Just thinking about it again made Lena's throat tighten. Why had Ash given it to Rohan instead of her?

She had *questions*.

They would've been answered by now if her life hadn't

blown up. First the arrests and the endless statements, then filing insurance paperwork and searching for a new home studio, despite Rohan's assurance that she could use the cabin for as long as she wanted. If that weren't enough, she was going through the legal process to become a guardian to *four teenagers* while finishing the Caravaggio for the Blackwells.

She still couldn't believe she would be responsible for four precious lives. The thought terrified and excited her, in equal parts. But she, more than anyone perhaps, was uniquely qualified to help them transition into a stable and loving life.

She knew her decision had taken Rohan by surprise. Although they were spending more and more time together, they hadn't made any promises to each other. Becoming a guardian to those kids had become as important to her as Rohan's family was to him. She hoped—no, she knew in her bones—that he understood.

The series of delays had nothing to do with Lena's fear of not measuring up to her grandparents' expectations. Absolutely nothing.

Honestly, how many families could—or wanted to—say they had a genuine art forger in their ranks?

When Sadie had shown up on her porch this afternoon, asking to paint outside again, Lena had nearly balked. But she hadn't had the heart to disappoint the girl, so she'd grabbed her easel and set up under the tulip tree.

It wasn't until she'd gone back inside to get her canvas that she realized she was commission-free. She had nothing to copy.

An unexpected panic had swept through her until Sadie had skipped into the cabin, snatched up the blank canvas, and skipped back out.

Lena had counted to ten, squared her shoulders, and followed her student. As she walked through the meadow, she'd noticed a small cloud in an otherwise cloudless sky. An unaccountable sadness had gripped her.

Her mind started making connections to the events over the past two weeks and, before she knew it, her hand was racing over the canvas, sketching out the scene as if it were a storyboard.

When she finished, she and Sadie had stared at the canvas, a little awed at the transformation. Then Sadie threw her arms around Lena's waist and exclaimed, "I knew you could do it."

Lena had vowed then and there to contact her *dadi* and schedule a visit. It was time.

She backed away from the full-length mirror attached to her bedroom door, swinging her hips left and right. The green teal dress hugged her arms and torso, then fanned out into a voluminous skirt.

Intricate gold embroidery adorned the bottom third of the skirt and scalloped neckline. The skirt's split front revealed legging-style silken pants beneath.

Lena grasped the edges of the split skirt and twirled in place, loving how the material rippled outward.

A double-knock preceded Rohan's dark head peeking around the door. "Time to go, Buttercup."

Lena jolted to a stop. Her skirts swished against her legs.

Rohan's smiling face transformed into one of male admiration. He prowled toward her, and Lena couldn't help but feel beautiful under his intense regard.

She drank him in, too. Since she'd left him in the meadow, he'd added a dark blue, thigh-length dress coat over his black, long-sleeve, V-neck tee and slacks.

He looked absolutely delicious.

Thunder rumbled in the distance.

"Sounds like you finished cleaning up my mess just in time," she said.

Rohan cupped her face with both hands and bent to kiss her. The gentle, almost reverent, slide of his tongue against hers made her eyes burn.

"Do you like your gifts?" he asked.

"I love them. Where did the dress come from?"

"Same loving person as the pendant. A traditional Indian *kameez* with *zari* embroidery. The *shantoons*," his fingers trailed up her leg, "were my suggestion."

"It all feels . . . right. Do you think they'd mind if I wore this to dinner tonight?"

He smiled. "I'm sure they'd be delighted. Ready?"

"I would rather see you in this coat," she plucked at his black tee, "without this."

"Later," he promised. "Tonight, I must share you with the family." He glanced down at her bare feet and frowned. "I didn't think—"

"No worries." She pulled away to rummage in her closet and held up a pair of gold stilettos. "Shoes are my superpower."

Ten minutes later, they dashed into the Friary, laughing and wiping droplets of rain off their faces and shoulders.

"How pretty," she said, noticing the candles and multi-hued flowers on the entryway tables.

Then her nose picked up on a familiar scent. She closed her eyes and inhaled the rich aromas of cumin, ginger, turmeric, and other spices she couldn't name.

"Did your mom make an Indian dish for me?"

"You'll have to wait and see." He grinned. "We're gathering in the Great Hall before we eat."

Weaving his fingers with hers, Rohan led the way to the

large rectangular room that boasted an enormous fireplace at each end.

The scene that opened up before her took her breath away. More candles and flowers decorated every available surface, and illuminated stars hung from the giant timbers above. Lanterns lined both sets of stairs leading to the second level and strings of flowers curled around the banisters.

She was aware of the entire Blackwell clan, Sadie and her family, and even Kayla watching her reaction.

But what drew Lena's attention was the silver-haired couple standing with their hands clasped together in the middle of the room.

They both wore what Lena considered traditional Indian-style dress, but she was embarrassed to admit she didn't yet know the names of the garments.

Rohan whispered in her ear. "Happy Diwali, Anjali Kumar. My love, my life." He kissed her temple. "Go say hello to your grandparents."

He released her hand and stepped back.

She moved forward, then paused to peer over her shoulder at Rohan. Saw tears brimming in his eyes.

"Thank you," she whispered.

Smiling, he gave her a watery wink. "Team effort."

She took in the crowd around her. Looked into each of the eyes, and let her gratitude and love rise to the surface for all of them to see, to feel with their hearts.

Lena rushed forward, into her *dadi*'s and *dada*'s open arms. The three of them laughed and cried and laughed some more.

Festive Indian music began to play.

Dadi finally set her away. "Let me look at my baby girl."

Her grandmother's voice held a slight accent. Lyrical and beloved to Lena's ear.

She hugged Lena again and whispered, "I have so much to tell you about your *maa* and *pita*." Then she straightened. Placed a warm hand on Lena's cheek. A twinkle in her dark eyes.

"But first, *samosas*."

ACKNOWLEDGMENTS

Enormous gratitude to my husband, Tim, for his patience and unwavering support, as I navigated—sometimes successfully, sometimes unsuccessfully—the personal and professional twists and turns that 2022 threw at me. It was a challenging year, but your strength and love helped me cross the finish line.

Adrienne Giordano, you know.

As always, I'm indebted to my editor, Kristen Weber, and copy editor, Martha Trachtenberg, for their keen eye and invaluable insight.

Huge thanks to Stuart Bache for creating the perfect cover for *Cross Roads*.

Much love and appreciation to our powerhouse behind-the-scenes team—Donna Duffee, Heather Machel, Leiha Mann, and Sandy Modesitt. And a special thanks to Maureen Downey for keeping me in her thoughts.

Liz Semkiu and Sandy Modesitt, thank you for spending your precious time hanging out in our world.

To the wonderful readers on my review crew—mega thanks. Y'all rock!

And lastly, I want to send my heartfelt thanks to every reader, bookseller, librarian, reviewer, and blogger for supporting my books and helping me get the word out about them. Big, big hugs!

ABOUT TRACEY DEVLYN

 Tracey Devlyn is a *USA Today* best-selling author of historical and contemporary suspense, which often contains elements of mystery, romance, and environmental crime. Despite the thrilling, emotional ride she crafts for her readers, Tracey enjoys an annoyingly normal lifestyle with her husband and rescue dogs at her home in the mountains of North Carolina.

For access to exclusive content, new release notifications, special promotions, and behind-the-scenes peeks, join Tracey's VIP Reader List at https://TraceyDevlyn.com/ Contact.

Made in United States
North Haven, CT
12 April 2023

35338942R00254